COUNTDOWN
TO
OSAKA

COUNTDOWN TO OSAKA

Joe Hefferon

NEW PULP PRESS

Published by New Pulp Press, LLC, 926 Truman Avenue, Key West, Florida 33040, USA.

Countdown to Osaka copyright © 2018 by Joe Hefferon. Electronic compilation/ paperback edition copyright © 2018 by New Pulp Press, LLC.

For information contact:
Publisher@NewPulpPress.com
ISBN-13: 978-1945734243 (New Pulp Press)
ISBN-10: 1945734248
Printed in the United States of America
Visit us on the web at www.newpulppress.com

COUNTDOWN
TO
OSAKA

Acknowledgements

I'd first like to thank Jeroen ten Berge for designing yet another fantastic cover. He has that knack for knowing what I want before I do and capturing the essence of the story. He has worked hard to take his remarkable gift to the top of his profession.

A special arigato to two women, both wonderfully creative in their own vocations, who helped me with the Japanese translations and culture:

Yuu Asakura (Osaka) gave me great insight to the unique ethos and patois of the Osaka Prefecture and dialect, which aided in creating the back story of my hero. She is a true professional.

Aiko Tanaka (Tokyo) was invaluable in helping me understand the beauty of the Japanese language. I could not have written the poems and clues without her patient guidance. She is also really funny, so working with her was too easy.

My proofreader, Julia Gibbs, is like having a grammar professor, stylist, mentor, and confidant, wrapped into one very polite British lady, who happens to speak French, which certainly helped with this book.

It's fun to collaborate with people who love their work, and these folks certainly embody that sentiment.

It seems obvious to thank the publisher, but I enjoyed working with the simple, direct style of the publishing team at New Pulp Press.

And although he won't read this, I thank Elmore Leonard for inspiring me to write a story of this kind. I wish I'd had the opportunity to meet the man.

Joe Hefferon

For Kaitlin

Chapter One

Osaka, Japan

THE FIRST TIME she saw Johnny Kubo, Koi knew she would kill him.

He'd stumbled out of the Bar Onsen on the Sakaemachi and knocked her mother into a street sign. He blamed her for being in his way, called her a whore.

Koi knew in that moment, she just didn't know how or when.

Last night she followed him for three hours while he shopped for electronics in Denden Town. She wanted to move on him in the noisy crowds but he had too many people around him, other clan members and flirty off-duty hostesses from his boss's clubs, a flaunting entourage of reputed libertines who demanded discounts at every store in the district.

This morning she watched him from the Mister Donut across the street as he stood in front of Juso Station, his back against a lamppost. He wore a black suit with a starched white collared shirt and dark glasses, looking at a betting form for the Sumo—morning coffee in a paper cup. Koi thought about that night on the Sakaemachi, under the red lanterns. She had stopped on her way to school to bring her mother tea after her shift. Her mother looked tired in the early morning against the backdrop of concrete alleys and the neon clinging to the walls like an invasive species. The door swung open behind her mother and

Johnny swung with it, stopping his fall with her mother's back.

Ten years had passed since that night. Memories could wait. She had a job to do.

Koi wore a common sweater and a black beret pulled low to her sunglasses resting over a polka-dot surgical mask—Osaka normal. She could feel the weight of her tanto knife in the messenger bag, slit on the side for easy access. She would stick him between the fourth and fifth ribs, perforating his lung and heart. Kubo carried his cell on the left side; she'd come at him from the right.

Johnny Kubo was a member of a rival yakuza clan and a reckless boozer. His clan had a penchant for western handles. Johnny had soft eyes so his crew gave him as American a nickname as they could muster. She never knew his real first name. It didn't matter. He'd become a problem for her bosses, and she had orders. If she didn't kill him by sunset she'd have to apologize, meaning she'd lose a knuckle off her left pinky, not a pretty look.

Being so absorbed in his Sumo, he'd let his guard down. He paid little mind to the people around him, partly out of arrogance. He thought well of himself, thought he was untouchable. No one would dare cross him, let alone attack him. He drank his coffee and planned which matches would be fixed and where he would lay his biggest bets.

She crossed the intersection with a score of people looking at their phones.

The morning sun had the numbers in shadow so Kubo brought the paper closer to his face. He never saw her coming—in and out like a sewing needle. Koi wiped the blade across his back as she slipped into the crowded mall under the glass canopy of Juso Station toward the subway, head down and weaving among the shoppers and salarymen. She passed a young couple laughing and bouncing their toddler up the stairs, counting along for him as they rose, *"Go, Roku, Shichi..."*

She stopped to watch them, all three smiling.

Chapter Two

JUST SHORT OF MIDNIGHT in her boss's office above the Club Spiral hostess bar in the Tobita Shinchi district, Koi bowed to her *Oyabun* an aging jackal named Hayato. She wanted to ask him a question, afraid she already knew the answer.

He returned the bow, though it didn't amount to more than a dip of his head, then told his bodyguards to wait in the outer office.

She walked to the far end of a conference table and turned to face him, holding her motorcycle helmet in front of her. "I want to leave yakuza," she said. "Promised my mother. Can't let her die knowing I am still doing these things. I want...other things. How can I get out?"

"Get out?"

"Yes. Want to have an outside life. I no longer wish to be a member of this or any clan. Have survived for years without doing prison time or getting seriously hurt. Before all that changes, now is time for me to leave forever."

"Koi, there is only one way. You know this. You are yakuza for life—your life. You can be banished but you don't just shed your tattoos and walk away."

"With respect, Oyabun, there must be another solution. I have broken a lot of bones, taken lives for this clan. I have been loyal, but this is no life for me." She stood taller. "I want out."

"Sit and keep your voice down. I ignore your

impertinence and the flippant way you address people because you are so skilled. But we have rules."

"I'm aware of the rules, Hayato." Koi slumped into a chair, oblivious to the point of his reprimand.

"There could be an order for *hamonjo*. It is reversible if you change your mind. A *zetsuenjo* cannot be reversed."

She sat up. "I don't want to be excommunicated, reversible or not. I have earned respect and I want to leave with honor. I deserve that."

"Deserve is a term rarely applied to others. It is mainly for the self."

"I want out and I want my honor intact. My mother deserves that much. So you see, the term is not always so self-serving. She needs to die in peace and with dignity. She has suffered enough because of rules. I need to have a, how to say, a normal life. *Shiran kedo.*"

"Normal. What is normal in this life? This is what is normal for both of us, for all of us. It is our life, no other." He studied his interlaced fingers as though he'd never noticed them set that way before.

Koi wondered what he might be contemplating.

He rose and walked toward a hidden closet. "Wait here." He stepped inside.

Koi feared no man. She never shied from danger or confrontation. But at this moment, in the presence of her sponsor, looking outward at the possibility of facing an unknown life without yakuza, her heart thumped.

Hayato returned, whispering into his cell, carrying an ornate, polished wooden box. Silvery threads in the chalk lines of his suit glinted off the amber light of the table lamp.

She felt the sweat run from her armpits like spittle. *Jigai? Īe.* "Hayato san, I—"

He pocketed his cell and set the box before her. "I, I what, Koi? You have changed your mind?"

"I only wanted to have a conversation with you, to discuss options. I thought you would act more as an adviser."

"I am yakuza first," he said. "You know I sponsored a woman at great risk to my personal reputation."

"I know. Unfortunately, I know, all of it. I only wished..."

He held up a silencing hand. "Koi, it saddens me to present this to you. Many years have passed since I sponsored you. I believed one day you would have a leadership role despite your being a woman, but I may have underestimated your impetuousness. You have some problems so you make a rash decision. In matters of business you have been practical, in matters of emotion, not as thoughtful. You shall have your wish. However, the only way out with honor is this. We will, because you are my *kobun* and out of respect for your accomplishments, give you three days to act."

"Act? Three days to think, maybe. I can come and speak to you again, no?"

"By coming to me tonight, you have already decided. Your fate is out of your hands, only the means remains for you to choose. To show your bravery and loyalty to the end, you can take this ceremonial blade with you, clean your home, dress in respectable *yukata*, tie your knees together, drink again the *saki* as in *sakazukigoto* and leave yakuza as the blood leaves your neck. In this way, you leave while showing respect for tradition and order. We will save a burial space beside you for your mother. You will have a nice funeral. Her honor will be restored by your gift."

Gift. Thoughts of a new life atomized in her eyes. She had no choice but to accept her fate, revealed in his implicit threat. She knew too much. Either she ended her life or they would—just like that. "Yes, Hayato san."

"Go then." He turned away and looked out toward the window at the horny clamor below.

Koi took the box. Its weight felt only in her heart. She reached for the door as his cell buzzed. "Wait," he said. He spoke into his phone as though he were in a confessional. For a full five minutes he talked, listened and grunted. He finished and pointed for her to return to her seat.

"Yes?" she asked.

He hung up. "There may be another way, a final mission. You can earn your way out, but it will take all the cunning and bravery for which you earned your name."

"I'll do it, whatever it is. Just tell me."

He said, "This is the way it will be. Your assignment is very important to the clan. Failure is not something you wish to consider. Now listen." He poured some scotch over ice. "It has been discovered that a French arms dealer, a very dangerous man known only as Le Sauvage, holds a clue to the location of a very large cache of gold."

"The gold is in France?"

"No, Japan, or somewhere in Southeast Asia."

"Is this Yamashita's gold? I've heard that was in the Philippines. Marcos already plundered it."

"Again, no. Patience, Koi."

She nodded.

He continued. "In 1868, the Osaka Castle of the Tokugawa Shōgunate fell to the Imperial forces. In short, some one hundred eighty thousand *Ryō* gold coins, were recovered and turned over to the Imperial commanders by French military personnel who were loyal to the Shōgun. A final gesture of surrender. However, the remaining war funds of the Shōgun were never recovered. The exact amount is unverified in the few official accounts of the matter, but people we have commissioned to study this treasure place the value at nearly twenty billion Yen."

"*Uwa, kyodai na,*" she said.

"Yes, an enormous sum. French soldiers fought alongside the Shōgun. One of the colonialists, a cavalry instructor, Corporal Andre Cazeneuve, returned the *Ryō* after recovering from his battle wounds. It was a gesture only, a token portion of the gold. One would think he would have been imprisoned or executed, having been a defender of the Shōgun, but after rehabilitating in France, he was hired by the Imperial army to train their Arabian horses. Curious but irrelevant. He died here in Japan in 1874."

Koi jumped in. "So, he was at the battle when Osaka Castle fell. He may have known where the gold was hidden or helped to hide it himself."

"Precisely, except he never told anyone, we surmise, while in Japan. What we have learned is that he may have passed the information to a descendant through a diary, found among Cazeneuve's possessions. The diary was stolen from the Yūshūkan War Museum in Tokyo, almost thirty years ago. That colonel's descendant, we believe, is

9

Le Sauvage. We think he will try and acquire this gold. We cannot, especially as yakuza, we *cannot* have a man with his reputation and ambition in possession of so much wealth. This is a treasure that belongs to Japan."

Koi kept her emotions in check before her boss. "I understand. My mission is to find him and get the secret before he steals the gold."

"Yes. Then kill him and return here. You will then be permitted to leave yakuza with honor."

She stood. "Do we know where this man is or where he is going?"

"He is a merchant of illegal arms and thus moves frequently and discreetly, under heavy guard of former French Foreign Legionnaires and ex-special ops soldiers, all European of some sort."

"What is his real name?"

"That is not known, not even to Interpol."

"Then how does anyone know who his ancestors are?"

"We may have done business with him in the past, during the last turf war, but even then, only through intermediaries. Everything is pieces of a puzzle. We only know he is rumored to be a descendant of Cazeneuve and that he may live near Nice, but he lately goes to Vietnam to transact business with Philippine terrorists, Abu Sayyaf. Start there. Find out what you can. Your excellent English will help you along the way. He will be well protected in Vietnam but may let his guard relax in Nice if he thinks he is safe. If you can flush him in Saigon perhaps you can track him to France.

"Our connections in the police will provide you with as much background as they know. They will do what they can to get intelligence from Interpol but the flow of information will be monitored. Interpol will want to know who is asking about Le Sauvage and why, so we must use extreme caution and go on limited intelligence. You will be traveling on your own, with access to accounts for cash and contacts for weapons, which you will first obtain in Marseille. We will set that up depending on what happens in Vietnam. No one is to know of this. No one. Only two of us here know the purpose of your mission."

"I'll make you proud, Oyabun."

"You have no choice. You already know more than you should. If you complete the mission, you will earn your right to leave. If you fail, you will die."

She knew he would kill her if she failed, despite their association. It was the code. She hadn't been a member long enough to retire and yakuza always feared women would be weak and go to the police. Koi also knew she might die trying to stop Le Sauvage. *No matter*, she thought. *I'm dead either way, better to die fighting.*

"One more thing."

"Yes, Hyato san."

"You haven't much time. Le Sauvage will act soon. He is wanted by Interpol. He has never been arrested but they may be closing in on identifying him. If he is arrested before you reach him..."

"Understand. How much time do I have?"

"No more than three weeks. By then, the investigators at the Tokubetsu Sousakan, working with Interpol, will have the authorization from all fifty District Courts for surveillance, and a major dragnet. He won't be able to make a move on the gold. He can't take the chance of getting caught. The secret will get passed to an unknown actor or die with him."

I have twenty-one days to live. "Twenty-one days." She repeated it aloud to anchor it.

Hayato nodded and pointed her toward the door of his office.

She bowed and left.

The music pulsed louder as she descended the stairs. Koi stopped at the bar on the way out and snapped her fingers for a regular cocktail. On the bar in front of her, a pole dancer crouched on her knees, taking fake dollar bills from a bare-chested yakuza soldier's pants with her teeth. Koi dropped the olives on the bar, drank a dirty vodka Sachai in two gulps, kissed a hostess on the mouth and left.

Earlier that morning, in Vietnam...

Chapter Three

DOWNTOWN SAIGON never gets comfortable. Even in January, the humidity hangs like hot laundry around your neck. The streets smell of fish oil and duck; charcoal and incense. You can't take twenty steps without someone trying to sell you a knockoff watch or a Zippo guaranteed to be used in the war by American GIs, engraved with misspelled military slogans like, Sempor Fiddles.

The gentrified wouldn't call it a walkable city, but that's how you get around unless you own a motorbike. Every guy who isn't shoeless looks like a government official or a party member—someone who could ruin your week. Scooters loaded down with live poultry juke skeletal men on bicycles pulling mini trailers of construction debris. Women sell sparrows from crowded wooden cages to release at the temples, a beggar in work gloves drags her legless body through the streets, her stumps tied to a leather pad. Jobless men sit on their heels on the sidewalks and play *xiangqi*. It's tropic indolence in a faraway land of promise, unless you live there.

But the food is delicious. A tacit embrace of, or perhaps a reluctant handshake with capitalism has improved the economy. The new digital hope blends with vague cultural effigies. The black-haired schoolgirls in white *ao dais* float over the dusty streets, always in flocks of four or five like giggling egrets, in every way more beautiful than whatever the communists brought down from the north. The men of Ho Chi Minh are disinterested. The women of Vietnam, entrancing. You move the country twenty degrees off the equator and it'd be paradise. If you were sitting on a beach in Nha Trang, two cocktails in, you might believe it already is.

The men in the rented cars, however, weren't there for leisure.

Only a few of the most loyal knew Le Sauvage's real name. He was a phantom to international law enforcement and a specter among the criminal element who referred to him only by his moniker—earned by deed, billowed by legend. When those he dealt with met him, they wished they hadn't, because once he knew them, he never forgot. He'd look at them with eyes that said he could find them anywhere and kill their families en route. His crew referred to him as boss when they worked, as other names when they met in public places, sometimes Jacob, sometimes another name, depending on which part of the world they were in. It rarely came up—they wouldn't put themselves together in social situations unless it could lead to work or they were surveilling a potential client. The rumors persisted that he sold French-made armaments to the most unsavory characters, the ones the public entities couldn't entertain.

An hour north of the city, the first car had stopped at the designated spot on the bank of the Mekong. The driver stood outside his door. Tiago Chastain dreaded leaving the air-conditioned rental van, but there was Spanky, right on time, waving and smiling that tour-guide smile of his. With his graveyard teeth and an independent left eye, there was something likable about the little cherub, but it wasn't his body odor.

Hubert got out first and cringed at the heat. He put a hand in his waistband and opened the sliding door for his boss and Bouchet the money man. A chase car pulled up after Hubert signaled. Two men exited the car; both were Gulf veterans and wearing the sort of permanent ruddiness that comes from surviving desert warfare.

Spanky called out from the approaching boat. "Hello, Mister Boss. *Bon après-midi, Monsieur*. See I'm learning Fr—." The boat collided with the bulkhead.

"Just drive the boat, Spanky. Learn French later." Chastain couldn't place Spanky's age, thirties maybe, a rough thirty-five. He had the look of a man who was sickly as a child, never quite developed, more bloated than pudgy. He'd been kicked out of the *Tam Binh* orphanage at fifteen and worked the streets of Saigon, learning whatever bits of tourist language he could to entertain them and survive.

He reminded Chastain of the boy in the black-and-white American reels with French subtitles he watched as a kid. He'd long forgotten his Vietnamese name, if he ever knew it.

The men joined Spanky and a small barefoot boy of twelve or so who ran the rope lines and walked along the outside edge of the boat without ever looking down. He never spoke. The crew's pilot, Fournier, stayed with the vehicles. He sat in the air conditioning and smoked his *Gauloises*.

Fournier had easy access to *St. Étienne* M12SD submachine gun, Tanguy carried one as well. All the men carried .40 caliber semi-auto handguns except the boss,

15

who rarely armed himself. Together they had killed more people than the Donner party. Ordinary men can smell it on them or see death in their eyes or both, but step aside nonetheless. A certain kind of woman can't stay away from them, the kind who thinks she can hump her way to the other side of the brooding façade, get inside and find her dad or some other guy who held sway over her heart. She always left disappointed or drank herself stupid.

The men looked out toward the horizon, not much for talking. In taverns after or between jobs when they'd have time to drink together, the ball-breaking would commence, a little arguing maybe if Tanguy got pissy about religion or something else that chewed at him, but not now, not when they worked.

Spanky steered the family boat back up river, the air more tolerable now in the northern wind. He turned at an unseen marker into the jungle and up a muddy Mekong tributary no more than eight feet wide. Here the crew put their hands on their weapons. The sounds of the river receded as they moved deeper into the verdure. The motor spat blue smoke but gurgled rhythmically through a tunnel of wide-leafed vegetation around a bend to a small clearing in the bush where the children waited with rice wine and sapodilla fruit.

Another boat sat waiting by the muddy edge, held in place by a teenager, neck deep in the brown water, feeling the bottom for crabs while he waited like a human piling.

Hubert and a gun named Marin stayed with Chastain and Bouchet while Tanguy walked beyond the kids and into the thickening smell of coconut oil boiling in a large steel wok over a propane stove near the family hut.

The Filipinos waited, five anxious terrorists as comfortable in their surroundings as they could fake. Tanguy sized them up and returned to the boss. "There's five, three armed, no extra ammo. They want to kill something but it won't be us, not today."

Chastain had been talking to the children and hefted a piece of the root-beer-tasting sapodilla, grateful to the kids. He passed on the rice wine but his men all took a hit, gave the kids some coin. "Come, children," Chastain said. "Let's go find Poppa."

Spanky barked at the boy to stay with the boat and followed behind the others at a five-meter gap. They walked roughly thirty meters around random mixed-breed chickens and broken furniture to the main structure, not a home in any western sense but the family's only option, dry now, some weeks beyond the rainy season.

Chastain ignored the terrorists and walked to the man of the house. He shook his hand with a pleasant smile and fifty US dollars for the use of his property. Ngo's family would eat for six months on that money.

Chastain took a sideways seat at the short bamboo table and waved for the terrorists to sit, Bouchet the money man across from Chastain. The Filipinos grabbed buckets and mismatched plastic stools and formed a semi-circle in front of him. Hubert sat behind his boss, flanked by standing mercenaries.

Chastain spoke in French, only the mutt's leader understood. "First, before we talk specifics, where is my deposit?"

The leader, the only one with a working brain and actual balls, pulled a fat envelope from under his khaki shirt. "One hundred fifty thousand US, changed this morning to new Dong at VP Bank on Nguyen Chi Than, as instructed." He leaned forward and placed the money on the table.

Without shifting his eyes off the terrorist, Chastain pushed the envelope to Bouchet who flipped through it while everyone watched. He nodded and pocketed the cash. Ngo's children, a younger boy and girl no older than ten, weaved among the men offering them homemade rice wine and fruits, singing local songs and looking for tips. Ngo shushed them.

As he did, two of the Abu Sayyaf crew, one with a scruffy mustache and one with wire-rimmed glasses and long hair, leaned in to one another and spoke in Tausug dialect. Tanguy and Marin noticed but didn't move, already prepared to shoot first. The long-haired one curled his lip as he eyed Ngo's daughter from her neck to her ankles. He laughed and slapped her on the ass. She ran to her father who pushed her inside.

Chastain reached back to Hubert who placed his Sig Sauer .40 caliber in the boss's hand. Chastain shot long-hair in the face and sent him reeling off his stool. He kicked the man's teeth in before he died. Chastain growled in French. "Any more pedophiles among you? Huh? Take your death like a good soldier of your god now."

The terrorists didn't understand the words but got the sentiment. They all froze except for their eyes—scanning, looking for a sign from their leader or a tick in the tendons of the special forces, the next shot. None came. No one spoke or moved an eyelid. Spanky shit his pants.

Chastain informed his conferee that the price just

went up ten percent. The man didn't balk. Chastain laid it out for him. "One hundred fifty FAMAS G2's, fifteen thousand rounds of 5.56 NATO. Three cases Russian F1 grenades, seventy-five pounds of C4, two dozen detonators. No instructions, figure it out. Sixty Tokarev nine millimeters, three hundred rounds each. That's it. One hundred eighty thousand upon delivery. We will contact you with details. Now get off this man's property before we bury all of you here. Take that child rapist with you."

The leader hustled his crew who complied and dragged the dead one to the boat.

Chastain told Bouchet to give Ngo the equivalent of two hundred US in Dong from the envelope for his trouble. The man cried with appreciation and hugged his children. Sauvage and his crew walked away.

Spanky cleaned his ass in the water and turned the boat back out toward the Mekong, a dirty tablecloth wrapped around his waist. The boy held his nose and laughed at him. Everyone smoked as they pulled off, including the boy, a fresh pack from Tanguy. The boy dangled his shoeless feet from the prow. He yanked a foot in when it brushed across the dead terrorist in the riverside churn.

"There are cleaner ways to make money," Chastain said, looking down at the bobbing corpse.

Bouchet agreed. "But this is what you are good at."

"And all we know," Hubert said.

"In due time, Hubert. *En temps voulu.* Stay ready."

***

On the flight back to France, Hubert sat in coach,

19

three rows behind the boss's first-class seat. He read Flaubert, though he didn't quite understand him; he thought it would make him smart. The rest of the crew took separate flights.

Chastain drank bourbon over ice. *Je suis malade*, he thought, *sick of it all*. He thought about what he needed to do next, not wanted but needed to. *A necessity overdue.* He'd waited long enough, become too quick to kill. It had become an addiction. Twenty years ago, he'd have beaten the kidneys out of that pedophile and left him to think about his actions. He would have thought he was teaching him a lesson. *They never learn*, he thought. He thought more often after he acted these days. *Pourquoi s'embêter? No one cares.*

He looked over his shoulder at Hubert, immersed in his book. Chastain took a letter from his pocket and read it again. He touched the words as if he were touching someone he cared about. He folded it back into his shirt, finished his bourbon and closed his eyes.

Chapter Four

KOI SWEAT THROUGH a double *tabata* routine after a circuit of weights, then finished off with inhuman stretching. A forty-minute workout that began at 05:30, then a two-kilometer flat-out run back home. Udon noodles with beef and a raw egg for breakfast. She checked her list: pack, send a package, check-in online, print boarding pass, say goodbye to mother.

Twenty days left.

Koi wore a long-sleeved black turtleneck to cover her tattoos and to avoid becoming irritated by the stares of the hospital staff. She leaned over her mother's bed and made promises she didn't know she could keep. "I'll be back soon. It's not so bad, just a setback. We'll go to the lake up north in Takashima. Yes, Lake Biwa, your favorite. Yes, it is peaceful."

A young nurse with her hair colored an unnatural red came in wearing those loose-fitting hospital clogs that slip when they walk so the heels tap the floor. They all wore them in the cancer ward. In the quiet hours, you could focus in on the sound if you wanted to figure out which nurse was coming by or just to agitate yourself.

Koi wondered why they seemed a size too big, as if there might ever be a reason to make a quick exit from your shoes. From the chair in the hall where she often sat, she would watch them clip-slide back and forth to attend to dying patients, or when they went in to change her mother's diaper or some other undignified act she couldn't bear to watch. The noise from the clogs grated on her.

The cranberry-haired nurse looked at the monitor and logged her mother's temperature, pressure, heart rate and blood gas, then left with a nod and the slightest counterfeit smile.

Koi stared her out then turned to her mother. "Don't worry so much, Okaasan. I am strong and we are stronger together. It will be well in the end." Koi kissed her on the forehead, held it long enough to smell her hair. She checked the tubes in her mother's arms; nothing kinked, no loose wires to sound alarms and bring the nurses and their annoying shoes.

Time to fly.

France would likely be on the agenda, but not yet. The last information the police moles gave yakuza put Le Sauvage in Vietnam. Within hours she'd land in Ho Chi Minh Airport, with a new day swelling across the Philippines, the sun pushing over a hundred islands in a laid-back Pacific, silhouetting the fishing trawlers of Phan Thiet to her left. She looked at her passport, hadn't seen her full name in print in many years. She couldn't remember smiling for the picture yet there she was, a happy traveler, parts unknown.

She picked up her duffel from the carousel. No one without a ticket walked the interior of the airport. It looked to be on perpetual holiday. Once outside, she scanned the herd of drivers with their hand-printed placards hailing their charges, the heat of the day already melting their foreheads. She found hers as arranged, in

Vietnamese and Japanese characters, Hiroki, no need for the driver to know her real name. She walked up before him, bowed and tapped the paper then pointed at herself. He said, "Da da," and took her bags to the Chinese-made Geely sedan, a lousy knock-off design of western flair, about as safe as a cardboard flame thrower.

She'd booked a two-bedroom suite in the Somerset in District One because a foreigner on business would go unnoticed in the hotel compound. It was within easy walking distance of downtown and the areas near the Saigon River where she might find the type of character who knew someone who could help a bitter woman find a guy who'd pissed her off beyond reason. That was her story, and she'd pay for information.

First evening down, just getting the lay of the city. She sat under the open rafters of the Somerset's poolside café eating fried rice and *ga kho* chicken that her tired muscles appreciated. She asked her waitress to unroll the rattan curtain next to her table, not because she didn't want to see the pool but to give anyone who might require them, one fewer sight-line.

Only Hayato and the *kumichō* knew of her mission, so he had implied, along with everyone else who'd probably heard, she'd left the country. The bodyguards acted like voiceless Akitas but they weren't deaf and talked amongst themselves in the baths. They wouldn't know much but they'd all know something. She could trust no one and because she had asked out, was no longer trusted herself. They could get to her mother, however, reason enough to see it through. She guessed the yakuza bosses figured that as well. The idea that her bosses knew she would push herself as far as possible eased her mind enough to finish her rice and the Austrian Riesling sweating the glass on the bamboo mat.

The muted café lighting and the pool's blue glow relaxed her so she could rest before heading downtown. After an hour nap she headed to the Saigon shadows, armed with only her tanto sword in the messenger bag, left in an overnight air-freight package at the guest services desk.

First stop by the river, an open-front local bar, with pink fluorescent bulbs and scratchy techno-music. Three greasy cargo handlers sat smoking in a corner and drinking warm Tiger beer. A bartender named Ha by nametag who looked as though she'd put her makeup on with a butter knife, offered nothing resembling a smile. She gave Koi her drink, overcharged her then turned back to two flirting Chinese businessmen, drunk enough from a client dinner to wander in the place and be relieved of some *dong*. They waved her over and ordered more shots of diluted Johnny Walker, reached for her hands and told her she was sexy. One traced the curve of her hips in the air. Whatever they thought Ha might do for them existed only in their scotch-hazed aspirations.

Nothing happening; move on, to the next joint and the next, and two more after those. Everyone either ignored her or claimed to know nothing until she stopped for a bowl of *pho* at a walk-up eatery.

He found her.

"Who you look for, lady?" He spoke in Vietnamese. She looked away so he tried his English. He asked again who she was looking for.

"Not you," she said, and continued to eat her noodles.

"You looking for cocaine? No cocaine around here, maybe heroin. I know someone, not me but someone."

"I'm not looking for drugs. I'm also not looking to get angry, which is what you're making me. Screw off, *baka chaun*."

"You police from someplace? CIA? I see you go to many places and look around. Who you looking for?"

"I said I wasn't looking for you, so why would I answer your questions?"

"You want to know about Abu Sayyaf, right? Dead one found here. Everybody talking about it and then you come here, stranger. I know the people. You pay me ten dollar US. I show you them."

"I'm not interested in your dead Arab."

"He is no Arab. Abu Sayyaf, Filipino. Muslim, Muslim you know? You have money or what?"

"Listen, troll. I'm not paying you for information I didn't ask for, now get out of my way or I'll disembowel you."

He looked down at the short sword slicing a button off his shirt. He swallowed and stepped aside. He watched her leave the yellow overhead light of the food stand and go into the night. His hands shook as he dialed the number.

Koi walked down to the Saigon River to think. Skinny men in broken sandals offloaded bags of coffee and rice from a barge resting under bare bulbs strung across a jury-rigged extension. She didn't notice the skyline, the tinsel city-scape, the way the city had grown cosmopolitan in the last decade. The government welcomed the foreign cash; the people worried about history. Koi concerned herself with neither. She only looked to the water for answers.

It's got to be him. Who else would leave a dead terrorist at a meet? He was here and I missed him. There's no way he would stay in the country long if a deal went bad. She slammed her fist against a rail overlooking the river. *"Kuso!"*

She had to move tonight to track him, perhaps find him in transit where he might be prone to a mistake. Get the next flight to Marseille? Maybe. Where had he done business before? Would he stop over or just go to home base and regroup?

Get back to the hotel, wash it off, sleep, plan.

She took the quickest way back to the Somerset, cut through an alley toward Nguyen Binh Khiem—her first mistake, too deep in thought, worried about the timetable and not her surroundings.

The troll from the pho joint spoke into his cell, identified her for them from across the street. One started toward her. Tall by Vietnamese standards, the wannabe gangster walked past her and bumped her shoulder. She turned to curse him when the other two came out of doorways and at her back, a classic mugging move.

This loosely united team wasn't in the direct employ of the man they knew as Le Sauvage, but looked after his interests in the city, meaning he sometimes hired members of their crew through a third party when he transacted in Saigon. He paid better than most. Surely, he would be grateful if they took out some nosy woman asking about his business.

She felt them close. Her training kicked in. Koi cartwheeled shoulder-over-shoulder with the skinniest one.

She drew her tanto as she spun. She landed and stayed low, thrust her blade north through his pants and with a flick, opened his nutsack. He didn't react to the pain at first, still trying to figure out how she moved so quickly when he'd had the drop on her. Blood ran down his legs. He felt his crotch and discovered he had just been dispatched by a roadside vasectomy. He could have grabbed the Ho-era .32 in his rear waistband but he held on to his marbles with both hands to keep them in the family. He fell to his knees and prayed to Buddha.

Number two and tall guy came at her together, number two with a cleaver. Koi whirled and caught him at the wrist; the cleaver and his hand flew into a bin. He screamed at his stump. Tall guy swung his chain but she sidestepped it, bringing the blade up across his face and slicing off most of his lips and the tip of his nose. He whipped the chain overhead, his final mistake. She cut his carotid lengthwise and was a half-dozen steps gone before he fell into the spray of his blood.

Some residents came to the upper alley windows when they heard number two yell but soon ducked back inside. They didn't see anything, never do down by the river. Koi didn't look back; these inept goons weren't the types to run to the police with their problems. She hit Nguyen Binh Khiem in full stride and waved cash at a young woman on a scooter who rode Koi past her hotel. Koi scoped it out as she buzzed by, then tapped the woman on the shoulder. She let Koi off by the Gem Center at the end of the block.

Koi walked back to the Somerset when the woman was out of sight. She worked the exterior of the hotel complex before going inside. It seemed normal enough, no one waiting. She locked her door, took a bottle of Polish vodka from the freezer and swigged a couple of swallows on the way to the shower. She stood naked before the mirror as the room steamed, a bottle in her hand. She used to love her tattoos, now she hated that they covered so much of her—the sleeves on both arms, her thighs, across her entire back and butt, around her ribs and down to her tender parts. In Osaka, she wouldn't be permitted entrance to public pools because her artwork would scare the kids, and probably their parents. Yakuza always made her feel strong, proud of the way she endured the prolonged pain of the Irezumi tattoo method; her favorite had been the koi fish that ran the length of her right calf, surrounded by water splashed with tiny skulls. Now despite her taut body and cover-girl face, her tattoos made her feel like a leper.

She took a slug of chilled vodka, then another, overturned the bottle in the sink and stepped into the fog of the shower stall. She sat on the tiled floor, waiting under the water till the buzz kicked in, then dried herself and fell onto bed with her hair still damp. She let the vodka take her away. She woke a few hours later, chilled by the air conditioning, rolled her naked body into the blankets and slept till dawn.

In the morning, she worked on changing her flights. She found one leaving within two hours that had a short layover in Dubai. She ditched her loaded messenger bag in the dumpster and hired a driver. Ten hours later she waited in Jack's Bar & Grill in the Dubai Airport for her transfer flight to Marseille. At another time, she might have been captivated by the sheer breadth of the place or the billions in commerce it represented. Were she better educated she might have thought metaphorically about the teeming internationalism, the unknown intentions of thousands of strangers moving around her, about how it represented the way her life might end, lost and forgotten in the blur of it all.

No.

She'd only slept a rough four hours on the flight but, *it's too early in this thing to complain about being tired.*

The clock wouldn't wait.

Chapter Five

CHASTAIN DISEMBARKED in Nice with Hubert, each man with train tickets in their jackets, Chastain's to Nimes and Hubert's to Avignon, in case they were questioned at the airport. Hubert called his man who arrived with Hubert's car at the international departure lane, followed by the driver's cousin in an '87 Renault with no back seat.

The man helped Hubert load his bags and gave him the keys to the Audi. Without talking, he left with his cousin in the teen's Renault, a grungy, avocado-colored wreck that dragged its muffler. Hubert watched it go, wondering if the car could make it another thousand meters. Chastain came outside after they left. He threw his bag in the back seat and stepped into the soft leather seats.

"That Renault," Chastain said.

"I know, embarrassing." Hubert turned west, where the signs pointed to the access road to *La Provençal*.

"Just take me to the Hotel Ibis on the Airport Promenade. I'm not going home just now."

"What? Sure, whatever you say, boss, but that's a shit hotel. Let me take you to t—"

"The Ibis. Let's move."

"You have a woman waiting for you, boss?"

"No. No questions, just listen. I'll be gone for a few days, maybe three or four. I'll explain everything when I get back. Use my private line but only in an emergency. I don't want to be disturbed."

"Received."

"Stay alert while I'm gone, no benders."

"Alert for what?"

"Nothing, just keep a close eye on everything till I get back. Here is it, pull over here. I'll walk the rest of the way."

"I'll leave my cell on, boss. Hey, the money?"

"They won't make transfer of the money from Vietnam until I call them. Have Bouchet pay the men for the trip from the Dutch funds and check the international news. Find out if anyone is chattering about our friend in the Mekong. *Bonne nuit.*"

What's he up to? Hubert didn't like that the boss changed plans last minute. They usually did these things to throw off tails, but Hubert was an inside man, privy to all of the boss's ways if not all his secrets. And, *that hotel,* low class, for student travelers and people who missed flights and needed a cheap bed for the night. No amenities. Chastain usually treated himself better than that.

Uneasy, Hubert drove off but stayed in the area and swung the Audi back into the lot to see if the boss left the Ibis.

He did. Chastain got in a taxi that Hubert followed to the Radisson Blu Hôtel on the *Promenade des Anglais,* closer to the water and more suitable for Chastain's means.

Hubert laughed and drove off. "Hah, so he is getting laid."

***

Chastain checked in. The first thing he did after

dropping his bags and jacket was take off his shoes and fill the bucket with ice from the machine in the hall. He'd bought a bottle of Basil Hayden bourbon at the duty-free and planned on marinating those cubes. He poured it over the ice in a water glass and sat on the bed, pulled the letter from his pocket and drank. After a few long swigs, he refilled and took up his cell. *Make the call*, it still being morning in Japan. He almost hung up after five rings.

"Tiago?" She tried to sound hearty.

Her voice choked him. "Hello, Mikie."

"No one has called me that in a very long time."

"What have you been up to?" An awkward question but it started things off.

"I work for people who keep me busy," she said. "I don't make much money but I work. Are you making money? I won't ask about your work just now."

"It's all right."

"Listen," she said. "I want to apologize but saying I'm sorry would never be enough. You have many reasons to be angry with me, and maybe hate me."

"But one reason to forgive you, and that is all that matters now."

"You obviously read my letter."

"I was happy to see it. Glad you remembered how to reach me, but I gave up believing you ever would."

"Time changes many things, I suppose, or else perspective. You know I, Tiago...I should have told you I had gotten pregnant, I am so sorry."

"Yes, you should have."

"I knew you would stay if I told you, but you were in

too much danger. My father always blamed you for seducing me and would have had you killed if you stayed. I had to cut off all ties to you or they might use a connection to find you. Please understand."

"I do. I have come to understand a lot of things. So, what of our daughter? Why is she in so much trouble?'

"Emiko is her name because she smiled when she was born."

Chastain sipped whiskey, knowing he should have asked her name.

She said, "But I always called her Emi because I knew that is how you would have said it to make it French. She is a beautiful woman but troubled. She cannot fight these forces alone."

"I want to help but you need to tell me more."

"Emi would accept your help if you could get to her but Koi is out to kill you I'm afraid. Emi has a soft heart, but Koi is a warrior."

"Who is Koi?"

"I told you. She is Emi's protector and very deadly."

"I am deadly." He looked down at his socks. "If it will help me get to Emi then I will kill Koi."

"You're not making any sense. You cannot do that, silly man. Without Koi there is no Emi, but you must get to her. It is the most vital thing in my life. She is my only child."

"Mine too." Though he couldn't be quite sure. "You think yakuza is after her? Why?"

"It's been said she knows things, that she may go to the police."

"Why can't she?"

"It is not safe. They will get to her. They have people in the police force."

"Then I know my mission. I will find Emi and take you both to Nice."

She started to speak but thinking she was about to protest, he cut her off. "Now what about this hidden gold you wrote me about? It would be a great start to her new life if she were rich and I'd love to steal it from under the noses of yakuza."

She smiled. "Tiago, breathe in, there is more you must know about Emi."

He let her say it into the quiet phone.

"She is an older sister, an *ane-san*. It's a term usually given to the wives of the family heads."

"Wait, she—""

"Yes, Tiago, she is yakuza."

He slumped back against the pillows.

"She is trying to get out. She holds the secret code to the location of the gold, but she doesn't know it."

"So that's why she is in danger. They are afraid she will become an informant. Wait, why didn't you tell her about the secret code?"

"Because she would try to find it on her own. She is stubborn but can't do it alone. It's one of the reasons I contacted you."

"When you wrote about your great grandfather and the siege at Osaka Castle I started my own investigation, beginning with family archives, such as they are. The diary is nonsense. There are entries about the gold, but nothing to act on, no direct information. It's legend more than fact."

"It's not, Tiago. There was a second to the Shōgun Tokugawa, a sort of adviser and priest named Tsugumichi who swore allegiance to restoring the Shōgunate which, of course, never occurred. He was wounded in the siege, but on his death bed, he gave a coded message to his son and told him to await a signal from the French loyalists, to wait until the Shōgun needed the gold to fund his dynasty once he was back in power."

"Which he never did."

"Yes. That man died but his first-born son knew the codes. They were to be used along with the interpretation of poems written on a map of the perimeter of Osaka Castle, more of a work of art really. It's not a map. What are the words? A painting, yes? It's like a large architectural drawing, beautiful and simple. I believe the only colors on the linen are those of the cherry blossoms, otherwise it is just black on parchment. The work is some three meters high and twice as wide."

Chastain, intrigued, asked the obvious question, "Where is this artwork now?"

"It is hanging on a wall in the National Museum of Art in Osaka. The painting itself is of some historical value but not a priceless national treasure. The poems are written in Japanese characters with old-style brush, on the map beside a fallen cherry blossom tree. But it is useless without a way to decipher it. No one has ever attempted it because nobody knows its real purpose. It hangs there in the open and visitors just read a beautiful but rather confusing old poem."

"And Emi has this key to the encrypted poems?"

She smiled. "Why do you sound so incredulous? There

is a lot of history you missed while you've been out doing your business."

"I provide the means, not the motivation. Don't be disenchanted. So tell me how."

"I am not disenchanted. The *irezumi* tattoos on her back hold the clue, a part of the coded message from the French. The tattoo artist was a descendant of Tsugumichi. He was a man loyal to our family and the heritage of Osaka but not fond of yakuza ways. Despite the amount of business they gave him, it bothered him that his art was on the bodies of criminals."

"Was? He is dead?"

"Yes, sad to say. Taken by heart disease. But in his remaining days, in the last tattoos he did on Emi's back, he gave her the clues without her knowledge."

"How baroque."

She laughed. "Yes, I suppose."

"How did you find this out?"

"A letter left to me, found in his possessions when the city foreclosed on his shop and home. He had no living relatives. They didn't open it out of politeness and handed it over to me, unbeknownst to them, a national treasure. Now, say it."

"How Japanese."

"Yes. But now she is missing and they say the yakuza is after something big, perhaps the gold. I'm afraid they know about Emi. Can you please help her? They will kill her."

"Please? You don't even have to ask, I will find her, I promise you that and once she is safe, we will have another conversation, a golden one."

"Don't let Koi stop you. Don't be fooled. Find Emi."

"I'm on my way to Japan, leaving in the morning. Goodnight, Mikie."

"Goodnight."

"Oh, one more thing..." She had hung up.

Chastain finished his drink. He confirmed the reservations he'd made before he and his crew left Vietnam. He'd booked a multi-connection flight that left the next afternoon, stopping in Charles de Gaulle and then a Japan Airlines flight on to Honshu. He'd sleep the best he could between Paris and Tokyo.

The man who had stared down armed terrorists, mercenaries, self-appointed junta generales and rogue bandits in dozens of shitholes and warzones around the world, was nervous about seeing a young woman who had information that would change his life and those within his circle. Two of his most challenging jobs lay before him; each one had to go perfectly or both would fail.

Nineteen days left.

Chapter Six

Marseilles.

KOI PAID CASH for a private room in a terracotta hostel owned by a Greek couple.

He rarely looked up from his newspaper. Her parents had named her Anthoula and she made a fuss over Koi's silken hair. "So straight until the very end where it flips, like a movie star, like in the old movies, just a little flip, yes? So beautiful."

"It's not a flip, it just bends a little," her husband said. He waved his hand, accustomed to correcting her. "It's the humidity."

"Oh, so now you know about what humidity does to Chinese hair? When did you become such an expert?"

"I've heard you complain about it enough."

"I'm sorry, beautiful girl. How long are you staying?"

"I'm not Chinese. I'm Japanese. I'll be here for two nights, can I have the room key, please?"

"You see, Anthoula?" He waved again. "She's not even Chinese, so maybe I am right."

"That doesn't change how she looks, only where she comes from. Leave a woman's hair to me and maybe you should stop staring at her."

"You mentioned her beauty firs—"

"The key. I need the key."

"Of course, *koukla mou*, here it is. Such beautiful straight hair. Like a movie star."

Countdown to Osaka

Koi hoisted her bags and turned into the winding stucco staircase, narrow and painted a pinkish-yellow, so many coats over the decades it crackled in chunks that scraped your arms if you listed one way or the other on the way up.

Koi set her bags down on what could have been a monk's bed and pushed the velvet curtain away from the small window sunk high in the wall. She stepped up on a stool and looked out at the port to the left in the space between the buildings. The fishing boats moored for the afternoon; the men smoked and ate sardines and drank Provence rosé except for the old Greeks who still preferred the ouzo or cassis. Sometimes the French would offer them the superior rosé which they would accept of course, but only to be neighborly.

She unpacked a few things and changed into boots, yoga pants and a purple t-shirt she favored with the sleeves cut back and a ragged V in the neck. No hiding the tattoos in Marseille. She had no weapons for the moment but felt as comfortable without them. She practiced a style of Shitō-ryū Karate originally brought to Osaka from Okinawa. She could snap your knee and knock out a couple of teeth before you could finish checking her out.

The Old Port didn't renovate every time a new ethnic group or diaspora settled in; the new residents just changed the restaurant signs and menus. Some stayed, some left. Most just blended in and picked up bits of new language or another ingenious way to broil fish.

The Al Qemib had a six-stool bar and a dozen tables inside, three or four outside depending on the rain. They served flatbread and Moroccan *tagine*, Palestinian *makluba* with lamb and sometimes when the cook felt energetic, a better *bouillabaisse* than the temperamental French. It sat uphill off La Canebière to the north and west on the Rue Saint-Bazile, turning right into an alley that didn't appear on internet search grids. She didn't have to introduce herself to Mahmoud, a Palestinian loyalist with hands like pig iron. No one who looked like Koi could be expected to pop into his café at random. He liked the yakuza because they didn't interfere in the affairs of Palestine and they paid on time.

He pointed for her to go into a back room then smirked at the few patrons as though his date had arrived. Inside he gave her a worn gym bag and told her in Arabic to look it over. She would anyway, despite not knowing what the hell he'd just mumbled.

She unzipped it and grabbed the tanto sword, wrapped in chamois, Korean-made, not to her standards but deadly in her hands, sharpened well enough. Two boxes of American-made .380 hollow points and ten of 9mm lugers, 115gr hollow points. *Why?* The Beretta Cheetah 84FS that she seemed satisfied with would take the .380 rounds, thirteen each in double-stacked magazines, another one in the chamber. But the 9mm ammunition surprised her, and so did the next item in the bag, a Hechler & Koch SP5K submachine gun with fifteen and thirty-round mags. *What the hell am I getting into?*

Mahmoud tapped the Beretta and said, "good for woman, small," in his mangled English.

Koi flipped a look at his crotch, spun the gun and said, "Yeah but it's well-crafted and reliable and in case you're interested, I can castrate you at thirty meters with it." She smiled, sort of.

Mahmoud smiled wider, not really knowing what she'd said but happy his dick might be involved. Which reminded him; he slid a butcher-block table around and knocked a metal bowl to the floor while grunting, just to be sure no one outside would interrupt him getting his *qadib* wet. Koi rolled her eyes.

While he worked his *kabuki* routine she belted the tanto under her t-shirt and then picked out the final item, a small brown envelope, inside an ATM card with a PIN and '25k, US', on a sticky yellow paper and five-thousand Euro in odd bills. *Generous*, she thought, but thought again about the timetable and how her bosses likely figured she'd never have the time to spend it. It had weighed on her while walking up the roads to this exchange. Did they really think she'd be able to break Le Sauvage? Maybe they already knew the clue to the gold and just wanted him dead to eliminate the competition.

With Sauvage dead she was of no value to yakuza.

The idea that this might be a *hissatsu* job angered her, because she didn't know if she was certain to kill Le Sauvage or she was certain to die. They might disavow her, or they would send someone for her. Maybe Tanaka the Bull, but he was afraid of flying, or Ino the Snow Leopard, *sneaky Ino*. Both ruthless and neither liked that a woman had been held in such high esteem as to be an enforcer and their equal in the clan. *In name only*, they might think; they never saw her as such. They might even bid against one another for the job that would take her out.

Meantime, Mahmoud was warming to the idea of enjoying a little Japanese dish and gave her his best wink and a pump of his fist at the waist. She told him to find a goat and left through a window.

***

She got back to the hostel without facing any immediate peril and went to work. She loaded the magazines and the weapons, left the chamber open on the H&K but racked a round into the Beretta, then replaced the thirteenth round in the mag. She memorized the PIN and hid the bank card in her backpack, took some Euros and stashed the remaining bills. She stuffed the gym bag in the trash in the common bathroom and managed a quick shower while she threw off the idea that Mahmoud may have had her followed. He'd delivered what she was there for, he just didn't get his bonus. The shower didn't get hot but the cold water helped to clear her head.

The night had cooled. She changed into jeans and a leather jacket to cover the butt of the Beretta in her pants. The other weapons she jammed under the thin mattress. Koi looked the room over before going out and hoped the owners were too interested in bickering to explore her stuff.

She lingered wharf-side among the sailboats lined up like bullets in a belt, checked out the scooters, the hipsters who wanted an authentic French vacation away from Paris, who cooed at the limestone façades and took photos by a long-legged elephant sculpture. She walked along with them, just close enough that someone might assume they were together. She wandered farther from the pleasure craft, closer to the merchant ships with foreign flags. She watched for the unshaven, the ones with wary eyes who didn't look at the police and didn't take a picture

43

by the elephant. She followed them to their bars off the tourist tracks to places where someone might speak of Le Sauvage.

Koi sat on a corner stool in the Bar Tabac and ordered a vodka shaken with ice and poured into a short tumbler with an olive. She ate a pork rillete from a stoneware crock with a piece of baguette and thought about her mother, how she would tell Koi to make a run for it while she had the cash. Maybe she could make it to Canada or someplace warm like California where she could teach karate and marry a surfer, a place where people could marvel at her tattoos and she could lie about their origin, lie about everything in her past except to say her mother was one helluva knockout, something that sounded American so she could fit in.

She spotted him across the bar, trying to charm a waitress who had all of her cleavage and most of her teeth. He was different from the rest, still a little nervous in his role as a journeyman rogue, cautious among the genuine articles in the pack around him. He'd run away from his home in Belgium where it had sedated him to talk to his parents.

He's the one. He will want to show off to get in my pants. Maybe I'll let him if he can hold his liquor, cute for a gaijin. Koi told the bartender to send him a drink, the same as hers and to hell with him if he didn't like vodka.

His inclination was to decline the drink until his head swiveled enough to see Koi. Those black eyes, lips wet from her drink. He took his gratis cocktail without looking at the bartender and swaggered over for a sniff. "*Bonsoir, fille sexy.*"

Yes, he's an idiot. He'll do. "Bonsoir, homme robuste," she said.

His chest swelled. He asked, "D'*ou t'es-tu envolée, mon ange?*"

"My French is less than my English." She said it trying to sound sheepish then pushed her chest closer to him and pushed her drink against his. "*Parlez-vous anglais?*"

"I do. I also speak the language of amour."

This kid's a walking cliché. They chatted a while and drank chilled shots of *Café Patrón.* He said he'd never seen so many tattoos on a woman. She must be brave. She told him she liked the pain. She pretended to be quite interested in his exploits, his love of the Marseille nightlife and his many friends in the port.

Finally, she said, "Enough bullshit, tell me more about this language of love you speak."

"I would prefer to show you. I live close by."

"Let's drink first. I feel a need for a party. Let's have more vodka."

"Let me buy this round."

"You have money and handsome looks? Lucky me." She worked him like a pizza dough.

"I have some influential friends around here. I don't like to brag but I know people. We make money."

"I'd like to meet your friends."

He didn't want anyone cock-blocking him. "Later for sure. They are busy right now."

"Busy with what? What kind of business do you do?"

"We do whatever certain people need us to do," he said, getting cocky with her leg pressed against his. He wanted to show off by ordering another shot of vodka. It put him past his limit.

She could see his eyes trying to stay focused. She had him. "Let's go to your apartment. I bet it's really a macho place." She threw some Euros on the bar and he waved her ahead of him. She walked out like a ring-card girl. He watched her hips. Round two was about to begin.

He lived in a dump, as she expected. She took off her jacket.

"Guillaume." He dared to touch her t-shirt, close to her breast. "My name is Guillaume, did I tell you that?"

"You did. A handsome name." She pushed his hair around and kissed the air just short of his lips. He had a kind of youthful charm, still trying on his masculinity but not quite sure how to wear it. He seemed fit, probably worked out when he wasn't pushing through a hangover or smoking the hash he bought from the North Africans. His young muscles bounced back after relapses without much effort. He had a flat stomach.

"Take your shirt off," she said.

"You first."

"That's not how it works. You were in charge of the drinks but I run the sex. Take it off."

He laughed at her dominance, kicked off his sneakers and pulled his shirt over his head. She pushed him back on the couch, leaned into him and toyed with his tongue, sucked on his lower lip and ran her nails along his ribs. He reached for her ass but she grabbed his wrists and pushed them to the couch, the Beretta in the small of her back. She grew warmer, the vodka and the tension of the last few days had her needing a release. She pressed her crotch against his thigh and slid it up and down, swelling a little in her underwear.

He said he'd never been with an Asian girl.

"You'll never be able to say that again."

"You're funny," he said, "but sexier than that. I hope you don't mind if I tell my friends about you."

"Tell them what you want, handsome man. Maybe I'll do your friends too."

"Hey, one at a time."

"Your friends might want to watch me suck you off."

"Oh shit," he said, turned on by how blunt she was.

She sat up and straddled him, lifted her shirt. "Tell me about your friends, mysterious man. Are they dangerous like you?"

He relished the compliment. "Some are."

"Did you ever hear of a man they call Le Sauvage?"

"Everyone has, but why are you asking me now?"

"It would turn me on if you knew him."

"I'm turned on right now."

"I know I can feel it getting harder. I want it." She rubbed hard on his crotch.

He breathed ever harder, her face moving in and out of his focus.

She showed him her chest. "So, do you know him?" She let him touch her nipples.

"I've never met him, but I had drinks with a friend of one of his men, a special ops guy named Tanguy, I think. My friend has had drinks with him on his boat. He sent me a picture. It's in my phone, I'll show you later. The guy is a killer, they say. He once got very drunk and told my friend that Le Sauvage lives in Nice, 'everyone but the cops knows it', he said."

She moaned. She had enough information and a name but not the release she needed.

He reached to open her jeans. He said, "C'mon beautiful, enough talking, let's have this pussy."

"Yes, let's." She opened his button fly and reached inside his shorts. He lost it in her hand.

"Ahh, *kuso*, I knew you couldn't be a man."

He started to apologize when she snatched the Beretta and slapped him across the jaw. The steel rail of the pistol nailed the nerve along his mandible and knocked him out. She wiped her hand on his shirt and threw it on his face. He wouldn't know what happened when he woke, only that he might have gotten laid and his jaw might be broken.

As she put her jacket on she wondered if she should kill him. She decided he would be too embarrassed that a woman had broken his face to talk about her questions and he probably wouldn't remember anyway, the benefits of a vodka-shooters memory-wipe.

Koi endured a restless, sweaty, alcohol-degraded sleep, waking often to drink water and find a cool spot on the pillow.

Time to move. To Nice in the morning. Another night down.

***

Koi left at dawn with eighteen days left.

Anthoula came around the corner from the kitchen wiping her hands on her apron. "Where are you going, my Chinese movie star? You are leaving a day early, why?"

Koi head-butted her. Anthoula fell behind the makeshift reception desk her husband had built from old pallets. "Do you want to know why I'm leaving? I'm fucking Japanese, that's why."

Koi walked to the Quai de Rive Neuve and found a taxi to the Gare de Marseille where she could buy a train ticket to Nice.

She arrived at 11:30 at the Gare de Nice-Ville. She called her mother's bedside but no one answered. She checked her watch; it would be 3:30am in Osaka. Through the opaque textile arches over the tracks she felt the sun on her skin but not the Riviera, only pressure. She had two pieces of information, the name Tanguy, possibly a soldier of Le Sauvage and a picture of him standing with another man on a boat which the premature ejaculator had said was taken in Marseille but could have been anywhere. There weren't any landmarks in the background of the picture, only blue sky and a partial name of the catamaran, cut off, *-re dans la Morte*, something in death. If it were docked there, she'd find it. In such a pleasurable place, few catamarans would have death in the name.

Chapter Seven

WHEN HE PLAYED *'Recuerdos de la Alhambra'* it sounded as though three guitars were playing at once. Sacha Allain Trudeau watched him from the balcony, where he could cry without disturbing the rehearsal.

Sacha would sneak in from next door at the Stade Charles-Erhmann, the outdoor venue where he worked as a bartender. He would set up his station hours before his shift and race through an electrician's gangway for the overhead lighting to sneak down into the upper tier.

Emmanuel Gallén had never appeared at the Palais Nikaia or anywhere else in Nice. If he were to appear in Nice, there wasn't any other place he would perform. He'd put it off because the acoustics didn't suit his intimate style, or so he'd been told. It was actually the money; it always is. When his agent got his price, the acoustics became just right.

Trudeau sat on his heels and gripped the rail, focused on Gallén like an imperial eagle. The 'Serenata del Mar' was his favorite, until today, or maybe not. He couldn't decide. He knew nothing about classical or Spanish guitar. Before he saw Gallén, a classic was a Taylor Dayne dance hit, badly remixed for the beach clubs. He only knew that when Gallén played, he fell in love, over and over again. Each time his fantasies grew more intense. A drink at a chalet became sex on the mountain. A walk on the beach, a sunset marriage—a perpetually turgid rhumba of

51

champagne, torn t-shirts, deep-throated kisses and sleepy-eyed disbelief.

He first noticed the guitarist at the Café Raison where he'd stopped to apply again for a job that never seemed available to him. Trudeau smiled at him but Gallén was thinking about Shubert, his eyelids closed and his fingers playing the notes in the air. His intensity melted Trudeau.

"Who is he?" Sacha had asked the barista.

"He is Emmanuel Gallén, the classical guitarist. He is rehearsing a concert at Palais Nikaia. Don't you read the papers? Wait, you work next door, don't you?"

Sacha checked his watch, 2:10. *Shit. Run.* The 2:15 tram to Place Masséna station and then the walk to the cafe. He'd make it.

He wouldn't.

***

The taxi dropped Koi at Hotel La Villa in Nice, a short walk to the Promenade des Anglais where she could start her search for Tanguy after stashing her equipment in her room. Despite being surrounded by tank tops and bikinis, she had to cover her weapons. She dressed in athletic wear: jogging pants, a thin white track jacket and sneakers, her hair tied back. Underneath the fitness-model exterior, she was strapped for a violent confrontation, including the tanto taped to her thigh.

Koi walked the marina. So much wealth, so much leisure in one place—everything and everyone in a constant state of being polished, buffed, pampered and on display. She found Tanguy's catamaran within a half hour, *Victoire dans la Mort*, Victory in Death. She winced at the irony of her mission then devised a quick plan. She ran to the marina manager with a frantic plea to reach Monsieur Tanguy to deliver an urgent message, an emergency in the family. The manager pleaded ignorance but suggested she call his cell. She grabbed his shirt and advised him she wasn't a fool and would have if she had the number, "so please, before the police are involved, direct me to him."

The manager had been around long enough to know Tanguy didn't have much of a family and sent her on a false objective while he called Tanguy, but not too far in case she was legitimate. Tanguy thanked him and called Hubert.

"Did she look pregnant?" Hubert asked.

"That's not it, I'm sure. Funny joke but not what concerns me."

"Let's hear it."

"This morning I received a call from a friend in Marseille who told me a punk kid from Belgium got his ass kicked by an Asian chick last night."

"So?"

"So, she had been asking about the boss. This kid is saying they were drinking and he fucked her. He says he may have mentioned my name to her. Now there's a mysterious Asian woman in Nice who claims to have a message for me? I don't believe in coincidences."

"What do you mean, Asian? Is she Filipina? Where is she now?" asked Hubert. He wondered if an Abu Sayyaf black widow had come for revenge. Not likely, it being too soon, but something wasn't right, especially after the way the boss switched up hotels on him.

"The marina manager is an old sailor with street

53

smarts," said Tanguy. "He sent her to the new condo complex by the Place Masséna station to inquire. She should be easy enough to find."

"Take Marin and Mayko with you. I'll call the boss and tell him to lay low."

"Maybe you shouldn't tell him until we find her."

"Maybe you should do what the fuck you are told, eh? And, Tanguy..."

"Yes."

"Get someone in Marseille to break that Belgian kid's ass again. Tell him to sober up and go home to his mommy."

"*Oui, c'est comme si c'était fait.*"

"*Bien.*"

Hubert called Chastain but got no answer. *That must be some piece of ass.*

***

The taxi let Koi out in front of the condo complex. "Kuso," she screamed as she spun in place. It was still under construction. She'd been duped. She called after the taxi but after the driver turned up the volume, and the reggae overrode her call. She asked a woman carrying a carpet remnant under her arm where she could find a taxi stand or tram to take her back to the marina. The woman cursed in French and pointed at the carpet with her face and shrugged as though its existence had deafened her.

Koi spat and walked toward the café to compose herself. *Think, plan, act.*

A silver Citroën C5, three-deep with armed beef, circled the blocks around the construction site. Marin spotted her first. The others looked around to see if she worked alone. They saw nothing that indicated she had help. This would be easy, or so they thought. Grab her, drag her in the vehicle and find out what the hell she wanted with the boss.

Koi breathed in, held it and let it out on a count of twenty. One time did the job; her senses were regained, emotions in check. She saw the Citroën in the reflection of the glass, three men looking her way, one pulling up his hood, none of them smiling. The tram stopped between her and the sedan which gave her cover to move.

Sacha Trudeau stepped off the tram and gathered himself before making his approach to the café. Today he would introduce himself to Gallén.

Not today.

As the tram pulled off, Koi ran with it, stopped to let it clear and popped two rounds off from the Beretta, striking the side mirror with one and the shoulder of the wheel-man with the other. Mayko yelled that he was hit but put the car in reverse and used the tram for cover.

Trudeau began shrieking once the shots rang out and continued as he ran into his apartment building.

Tanguy yanked himself half out of the passenger window and sprayed her with a three-shot burst of 5.56 rounds that chipped the concrete at her feet but missed flesh. She charged harder. Koi ran across the tops of parked cars and emptied the Beretta's magazine while pulling out the SP5K. Mayko slammed the emergency brake on the Citroën, spun it 180 degrees and drove off. She shot fifteen rounds, reloaded and stopped running. Within seconds Mayko pulled the same 180 maneuver and headed back at her, this time with Marin on foot barreling down the sidewalk at her and Tanguy popping off more short bursts of fire.

She flipped off a Peugeot, rolled on her back and spun to one side then shot Marin in the feet. He hit the deck in a bloody tumble. His weapon slid to the curb. Koi ran away from the shooters as low as she could, using the parked vehicles for cover, but the tactic slowed her pace. The Citroën caught up. As she rose to fire, a baker's van with a preoccupied driver clipped the sedan just enough to knock Mayko off his game. Tanguy climbed over the hood next to the van as Koi fired. Her 9mm rounds hit him in the collarbone and throat, the second shot ripped through his neck and into his brain stem—instant death. She sprayed Mayko but he ducked in time. Two down. Reload on the run. She drew Mayko to an alley but the magazine stuck in the H&K and he was closing in on her, blasting away with a 7.62 automatic rifle with his off hand. The missed shots made holes in the dumpster ahead of her. She wouldn't have time to dance around with an empty Beretta and a jammed machine gun. Her tanto didn't deflect rifle slugs.

She made a jump at the dumpster, bounced across the alley to the top of a delivery van and back across the alley again *parkour* style to a fire escape as projectiles blew off chunks of brick and mortar around her. Mayko fired till he was empty, missing her as she defied gravity and climbed the side of the building like a spider monkey.

By then Marin had dragged himself to the mouth of the alley where he tried to call in reinforcements from his cell phone. He watched the front and alley side while Mayko ran to the back of the building. Mayko tossed the strapped rifle to his back and drew his .40 caliber Sig. He eased in the rear door, then performed a stair ascension in quick step, no sirens yet outside. Marin would be arrested; he'd worry about him later. First the girl.

While Mayko breached the building she had climbed, Koi took a run and jumped to the rooftop across the alley. Marin didn't see it. She pried open a hatch and climbed inside with her tanto drawn and braced under her forearm. The apartments were quiet except for music coming from the one at the top of the stairs on the next level down. She could use the loud music for cover.

Sacha Trudeau played Neil Diamond music to soothe him when his nerves frayed. A gunfight on his quiet street had put him in a panic. Koi listened from outside his door, tried the knob. Trudeau had forgotten to lock it. She turned the knob and shouldered it in as Trudeau sang 'Holly Holy Night' with all his frightened might. When she rushed in he fell over the hassock and lay on his back. She parted his lips with her sword and shushed him with a finger to her lips. A trickle of blood ran off his mouth. The music agitated her. She spun the tanto in her hands and smashed his record player with the back of her sword. He pursed his lips in annoyance, then opened his mouth for her to replace the sword.

"Are you going to kill me?"

She couldn't understand him with the steel in his mouth. "What?"

He pointed at the sword with his eyes. She pulled it out and rested the point on his chin. "Speak."

"I asked, are you going to kill me?"

"Not yet, well yes, actually, unless you do precisely what I say."

57

He nodded that he agreed.

"Who is here with you?" she asked.

"No one."

"When will your wife be home?"

"I'm gay."

"Aagh, what? When will your faggot lover be home?"

"I don't have a lover, or a faggot."

"Don't lie to me."

"I'm not, I swear, please don't kill me."

"You live alone?"

"Yes."

"Are you lying?"

"No, I am sorry to say."

"Get up and lock the door. Don't try to run or I'll slice your hamstrings."

"That's very specific."

"Do it now."

Koi peeked past the curtains at the police activity below. She watched as Marin tried to run from the police on his knees. They kicked him onto his face and cuffed him. The responding gendarmerie were pummeled with witnesses; "There are more shooters, one ran down the alley, they were trying to kill a woman, she has a gun as well, there is a dead man over there, she flew up the side of this building like a succubus, a devil woman, I think. They must be terrorists, no? Why weren't you here to stop them?"

Inside.

"Are you running from the police?" asked Trudeau.

"I don't run from anyone, but they are not who is

chasing me. Be quiet until I ask you to speak."

"I'm sorr—"

"And sit down, on the floor. Stay put or I'll knock you out."

Two police cars grew to five, three more on motorcycles. They fanned out, surrounded the building where Mayko, the Ukrainian wheel-man, searched for her, bleeding from his shoulder, his eyes burning from the sweat running off his blonde hairline. The police set up a perimeter and called for a special-weapons team. The flustered pedestrians were herded into a makeshift corral behind a police van.

Mayko heard nothing, no signs she was still on the move. It would be impossible to search the entire building alone and his mates couldn't help with so many police about. He needed a way out. He found it. He dropped his rifle in an apartment under renovation and slid down a construction chute to the dumpster, rolled into a basement entry in the adjacent building, two over from Koi, and escaped. He wore tactical gloves so no prints were left on the weapon. He called Hubert.

"Tanguy is dead. Marin is in custody. Who the fuck is this girl?"

"*Putain.* Get back here. Meet me at the park behind the armory. You better have a good explanation."

"You'd better watch your tone. My friend is dead and I don't know what the fuck is going on. I'll be there in twenty minutes."

"I don't know either, asshole. Just get over here. *Putain.*" He kicked over a chair.

***

Koi looked back at Trudeau, who just sat there quivering. "What is your name?"

"Who, me?"

"From now on each time you play dumb you will bleed, understood?"

"My name is Sacha Allain."

"Okay, Sacha Allain. Just do what I tell you when I tell you and nothing more. Are you expecting anyone today, any visitors?"

"None that I want, but no, no one should be coming here."

"Very good. Now sit still."

She was stuck, another day would be wasted. Sixteen left. There was no way out with such a strong police presence and so many locals with cell-phone cameras just waiting to catch the action. She had to wait them out. But, how long? *How did those assholes know I would be there? The marina manager knew but why would he send this crew? I should have killed that no-fuck pretty boy in Marseille. He must have said something.*

One thing struck her. If they came for her so quickly and so heavily, she must be close to where Le Sauvage slept.

She could stay here the night, rest and have Sacha make her food.

Chapter Eight

CHASTAIN TRAVELED under his Luxembourg passport. He sat on his hotel bed, drinking a glass of bourbon over ice, his head down and stroking his eyebrows with his thumb and middle fingers as if he were trying to spread them out—habit. He held the address of the hospital in one hand and liquid circumspection in the other.

He'd landed in Kansai International on a private jet from Tokyo then took the bullet train down to Osaka. So many changes in travel patterns, always evading detection, living on the backlit edge of the netherworld.

He called Osaka City General Hospital and with a mix of languages, confirmed she was still a patient. He hired a car and had the driver stop so he could buy flowers from a roadside market. He didn't like flowers and couldn't remember if she did, but *it's what you do*, he thought, *it's what you do*.

The smells and sounds of Osaka brought him swirling back twenty-nine years, to the pretty woman in the navy-blue dress who covered her mouth when she laughed and didn't seem to mind that the merchant seaman had dirty hands. She helped him pick out a gift for his mother and a day later, when he stopped by her shop again, he brought her soba noodles and shrimp in a carton and with it a note he'd written in Japanese *kanji* characters with the help of a shipmate. It read, 'You smell like cherry trees and you are cute like a dog', but she knew what he meant and he got embarrassed when she laughed so hard. She took his hand and he knew it would be all right.

He stepped off into the sterile quiet of her floor, the ping from the elevator adding a final knot to his stomach. The nurse at the station nodded and smiled in that way they do and he showed her a note with the room number and her name. She took him by the elbow and brought him to her door, whispered, "*sayonara ima no tokoro,*" and turned away.

He hadn't cried since he was a teenager but when he walked in, heard the beeping of critical monitors, saw her sallow skin, her boney arms, the distance in her eyes and the soft white hat to keep her head warm, he only saw the woman he still loved.

He set the flowers at her side and fell to his knees, kissed the back of her hand, afraid to touch her face. He wrapped his fingers around hers.

She said, "Please come closer, Tiago, I can't see you down there."

It hurt him to hear her voice so thin, but he could hear her humor still. It made him smile. He wiped his eyes and stood, leaned over to her and said hello, using the nickname no one had called her in almost three decades.

"It's good to see you again, Tiago."

"I am happy you remembered how to find me," he said.

"Why would I forget? I'm glad the book store still delivered your messages."

"A letter from Mikie? How could I resist?"

"Happy to know I am still irresistible. You look very

handsome, a little gray but only where the sunlight finds you."

"It doesn't find me so often these days, so I must look pretty good, eh?"

"Always, Tiago. Thank you for coming."

"I am sorry it took so long. I came as soon as I could arrange it. How are you getting on these days?"

She coughed. The strain of a single cough seemed to wrack her frame. "I am what they say I am and one has to accept it. But I can't accept my daughter being in such danger. I won't."

She cried dry tears.

Chastain said, "You sounded stronger on the phone. I didn't expect..."

"It's all right. I put on quite a show, no?"

He couldn't answer her; his throat had almost closed. He fought back more tears, twenty-nine years' worth. Lost love, missed opportunities, guns and treachery and violence and wanting to do something to make amends, to see Emi. His face contorted. He said he still loved her.

"Then help us. I have this for you. It's a bit bad, my handwriting, but it's everything I could think of about who Emiko's friends might be, who she can't trust, where she goes, eats and trains. It's everything I know but I'm sure she's kept much from me. I don't care what she's done. I don't care about the gold. I just want her out. I want her to have a chance to breathe air not owned by yakuza."

"I promise, Mikie. I will find her." He leaned in to kiss her. Her lips were dry. She said, "*Watashi wa kowaidesu,*" and began to cough, and the monitor sounded and a nurse came in as though she'd been there all along.

He asked, "What's happing? What's going on?"

The nurse calmed him with gestures that said it was under control.

An older nurse who spoke English told him she needed to rest. He should go. He touched her arm and said goodbye, not knowing if he'd never see her again. He'd left his skullcap inside her room and turned for it but another nurse went in ahead of him and he decided to leave.

Chastain called for the car service. While he waited, he turned on his emergency line and found three messages from Hubert. He called.

"Boss, where've you been? I looked for you at the Radisson but I found no trace. Where are you? I must come get you now. You may be in danger."

"I'm not in France. I'm in Japan and I'm always in danger. Now, what's going on?"

"Japan? Oh, *baiser un chien*, I can't protect you when you're ten thousand miles away."

"What is going on, Hubert?"

"Tanguy is dead. Marin has been shot and is under arrest."

"How the fuck did all this happen, and in Nice?"

"Yes, some Asian woman covered in tattoos was asking about you in Marseille and tracked Tanguy here. They went to snatch her up and got in a firefight on the street."

"Koi. *Putain*."

"Koi? What does that mean?"

"Her name is Koi."

"You know her?"

"I know who she is. I can't believe she is already in

Nice." He clenched a fist at nothing. "Over twenty-five years I've evaded the police and this fucking bitch finds me in a few days? Unbelievable. I need you to find her and hold her for me."

"She killed one of my men and she's dangerous. If I get a shot I'll—"

"You'll do as I say. Do not kill her. I need her alive. Alive, breathing, talking. Is that clear?"

"*Oui, patron. Je comprends.*"

"*Bien. Je suis sur mon chemin de retour. Twenty-four heures.*"

Before Chastain left for the airport he went to The National Museum of Art. He paid no attention to the skeletal architecture that greeted visitors but breathed better, for a time, within its expansive floor space. He found the painting of the castle after some trouble. It seemed to be an afterthought, more a decoration for the exhibit than a part of it.

He stared at it, making no immediate sense of it but wondering if the characters he photographed really held a secret to his new life.

Chapter Nine

SACHA'S APARTMENT wasn't so much decorated as splashed with posters, photos, playbills and other residue from his affection for live performers. It smelled of bergamot. The landlady, a numinously carnal woman named Candide who looked older than she believed, leaned against the wall outside his door and tried to listen. She heard conversation but couldn't make anything out. The police had been by twice to ask if anyone had come in that she didn't recognize. She could only claim ignorance. "Today is a baking day. Today a cranberry and pecan *flaugnarde*, if the officer would like some."

"No." Then he asked, "Did you not hear the shooting, all the yelling?"

"I heard some noise but my kitchen is in the rear and I like the opera, Puccini."

"Good day, *Madame*."

"*Mademoiselle, s'il vous plaît.*"

"*Bien entendu.*"

The officer had irritated her. She knew her tenants better than they realized. She cocked her ear toward Sacha's door again, then tapped. "*Excusez-moi, Monsieur*, is everything all right? I heard noises."

Koi glared at him. He got the message.

"Everything is fine, Candide. Just fine."

"Well done, girl. Tell me again your name."

"Well it's not, girl. It's Allain."

"Is that your first or last name?"

"Last, Allain."

"Do you have a job?"

"Well it's temporary."

"I don't care, Ellen. I asked if you had a job."

"Allain. My first name is Sacha and yes, I tend bar at the Stade Charles-Erhmann. It's a short tram ride from here. It's a venue."

"A venue? For what?"

"Concerts, shows and other things. I'm going back to school in—"

"Shut up. Do you work tonight?"

"Yes, I'm supposed to be there by seven."

"Call out."

"I can't do that, I'll lose money. This is a big night for me."

She nodded as though she agreed then walked over to him and slapped him across the face. He moaned and she grabbed his hair, shoved the Beretta between his teeth. He reconsidered.

"What should I tell them? I've never done this before."

"Tell them you are sick, Elaine, just tell them something and do it now. You're staying with me tonight."

"You hurt my face. Can I get up to use the phone, please?"

"Go do it, then sit back down here where I can see you."

She needed time to think but didn't want to be trapped to do it. She fixed her weapons while he was on the phone. He watched her reload each weapon with the one

68

remaining magazine for each and fixed the magazine release on the SP5K. He had hung up, just stared at her now, scared and fascinated with her dexterity and obvious knowledge of the guns.

The search of the building across the alley proved negative for suspects. No one else was brought out in handcuffs. *The prick got out*, she thought. The crime scene work, area canvass and interviews by the detectives were in full swing. Media trucks arrived. She'd sneak out in the morning with her hair tucked in one of Sacha's hats and maybe a sweater, to look like a homebody who just needed to pick up coffee. *Coffee.*

"Hey, do you have coffee?"

"Yes, I can make espresso."

"You can't just make a cup of coffee for me?"

"I can, I was offering—I thought. I'll make a pot of coffee."

He moved to the kitchen and she took in the place. "What is all these papers you have all over the walls."

"It's from the Stade."

"It looks like a dressing room at a cabaret."

"It's not a look for everyone. Memories mostly. Shows I've seen."

She watched him. He knew his way around the kitchen, not like he'd lived there a long while but rather that he enjoyed it, liked having company and serving them. Koi thought she might have to kill him. She might not. He wouldn't know who she really was or where she would be going. She'd tell him nothing. *What could he say, I was here?* Under duress, not his fault. He couldn't be expected to overpower her. The last person she decided not to kill got her in this shit. This situation was different. He was a hostage now. Her fingerprints would be here but not on file in France. They'd have to search Interpol's database. She'd be dead before they identified and hunted her, dead or so far gone they'd lose track of how to get home.

"How do you take it?"

"Black."

"Sugar?"

"No."

"Figures."

"What?"

"Nothing. Here you are," he said. "Can I ask your name?"

"Why would I tell you anything about me, especially my name?"

"So we can communicate? Maybe?"

"I'm the only one here. If you're speaking I'll know it's to me. Thank you for the coffee, it's good. Sit. Listen, the police may come here, maybe later, maybe in the morning or maybe not at all. They think all players are gone now. They'll be looking for witnesses."

"I didn't see anything. Well I saw you but then the shooting started and I just ran."

"Stop. You didn't see anything. Get it? If they knock here, you answer and say what you want about getting off the tram, but you heard shots. You ran. You didn't see anything. I'll be over there behind that wall. If you tell them, I'll shoot you. If you tell them, they'll arrest me and then I'll be killed in jail. The police can't protect me, not here. So, if I'm going to die because of you, I'm taking you with me."

"I understand." He looked as though he believed her. "Did you kill anyone on the street?"

"Self-defense."

"You shot first, between you and me, small talk."

"They were there to kill me, so it's self-defense, it doesn't matter who gets off the first shot. I'm justified."

"Then why don't you go to the police?"

"I just said I can't and if you ask me any more questions I'll drown you in the toilet."

She drank the coffee and another cup. He made nervous talk. She took him to the bathroom so he could pee. He couldn't fit out the window but she didn't want him locking the door. The night fell. They sat in the darkness except for the television. She didn't want silhouettes in case Sauvage had sent more men back to the area. He'd have more men, men in every city in which he operated. Most he couldn't trust with access but he could give them an assignment and they'd carry it out.

The local news reported the shooting. "One dead at the scene, one wounded in police custody, two at large, unclear if terror is involved, no indicators at this time. The man in custody has not been identified. There are rumors the police know but are not divulging it yet. The dead man as well, pending notification of family."

Nothing on the news surprised her. "An Asian woman appeared to be the target of a kidnapping, one witness said, another said she was a shooter, but the police would not confirm."

The night dragged on with her thoughts. What options

were left? Few, if any. She had no other clothes, no more ammunition. Most of the cash was at her hotel but she had the bank card. It meant exposing herself unless she went out early in the morning before the detectives returned. She could see Sacha was growing tired. They both needed rest or they might make a stupid decision; one by him could get them both killed.

She told him to sit up on the floor in front of the couch and she sat behind him, back to back. "Lean against me and rest. If you try to leave I'll feel you. I'm a light sleeper, don't test me."

In the early morning, the news surprised her. The dead man had been identified as Maurice Tanguy, a former special operations soldier who worked as a technical adviser to an international construction firm. He left behind a wife and two teenaged boys in Grenoble. *Surprise. He lied to his wife and family. Family. Kare no ayamachi, he would have killed me. He put himself at risk.*

Seventeen days left, fewer when you counted a day lost going back to Japan. Sacha had finally fallen asleep. Koi pushed off him to stand. She had to pee. He was still groggy so she propped a chair by the door and went. She came out to find him on the couch. He wouldn't have run, he said. She'd probably catch him anyway.

"I'm hungry," he said.

"So eat. What do you have?"

"I guess toast and some ham. I'll make coffee."

"Cook for two. Make the coffee like yesterday."

They ate mostly in silence. She could see he had questions piling up. His fear seemed to be replaced by a resolve. Either she would kill him or be out of his life, nothing in between. He hoped for the latter, refused to acknowledge the former.

"We have to go out. I need clothes and you need food. I'd send you alone but you wouldn't come back. I wouldn't be able to hang around long enough to determine if you disappeared on me or just got delayed. I'm not going to do that. We'll go together. When I come back I'm going to make a final plan to leave. How you act when we are outside will determine if I leave you watching television or watching yourself bleed out in your own bed."

She pushed a side table from the wall and unplugged an extension cord. "Put the dishes in the sink and put your hands behind your back. I need a shower." Koi put him face down on the floor away from the windows. She put her weapons on the sink and ran the water. She hadn't taken a hot shower in three days. He watched her through the crack in the door, marveled at her tattoos. He'd never seen so many on one person but he didn't think she'd care what he thought about them.

In the shower, it struck her that she hadn't checked in with her *oyabun* since before she left Vietnam. She'd buy a prepaid phone. Hayato would say something that stayed with her, but not register right away. It would come back to her when she replayed the conversation in her mind later that night.

Sacha gave Koi a Lady Gaga sweatshirt to wear and a ball cap with sequins on the brim, and white-rimmed sunglasses. He commented that at least one aspect of his life served her. She ignored him and pulled her ponytail through the back of the cap. They took the tram to another neighborhood so he wouldn't be asked to introduce his friend if they ran into someone he knew. They bought bread and meat, jeans and t-shirts, a backpack for her stuff. They bought wine for him, either to celebrate his liberty or toast his death.

In another life, she might have enjoyed shopping in Nice with her gay friend, a thought that would have never formed in her head in Osaka or Tokyo or any other place in Japan within her yakuza cosmos, one never conjured in the minds of the *yaku-dansei* subculture in which she traveled and if it ever did come up, would be assailed by reactionary machismo, laughed at or otherwise banished from the company such men kept.

But she didn't have another life except in her poetry or in the fly-by glances at children and their parents. It grew more possible with each passing hour that the life she had could end at any moment. At every turn, every new face that looked her way could be one of Le Sauvage's guns. A sniper's laser could be on her back as she looked in the market windows at her lunch. She'd have just enough time to watch her heart burst through her chest before she died.

She and her temporary friend had to get back to Sacha's apartment and plan her moonlit run.

As they were walking up the stairs they heard Candide's footsteps skitter down the hall and up the next flight. *Had she been inside?* The question crossed both their minds. Koi hadn't left anything identifying but there were two coffee cups in the dish drain, two plates. If she killed Candide now, Koi couldn't know if the landlady had already called the police.

Chapter Ten

KOI CALLED HAYATO from the bathroom, watching Sacha through the crack in the door.

He looked with his head tilted at some of his show posters, trying to measure them with his eyes to see if they'd fit better on the other wall. He wasn't, for the moment, thinking about being killed. What he thought about was making his place look less like, *what did she say*?

"Koi," Hayato began. "I would have liked an update sooner. You are still at it?" He meant he was surprised she hadn't been killed.

"I am close to him. If you saw the international news you might have heard about an incident."

"In Nice? Yes, I saw that. When they said an Asian woman was unidentified and at large..."

"The home base of Le Sauvage, for certain, but don't yet know his name. The mention of him in certain circles brings fear to people's eyes. No one will dare to cross him. I must find a way to cull him from his pack. I have a plan." She lied. The next bit of news rocked her back against the sink.

"We have someone watching your mother, Koi. For her protection, of course."

Her back muscles clenched. Her throat went dry. "What do you mean, protection?"

"We look out for our own. You should know a man came to visit her, a French-speaking man, middle-aged. He brought flowers but did not stay long. We lost him after that."

Watching her. "Do you think it's him? Le Sauvage? Why would he be there?"

"I told you he has international connections. He may have identified you already. Perhaps he posed as a friend and asked your mother where you were? We can't be sure of course but he is a careful man. It is unlikely he would leave himself out in the open like that. More likely the man was a representative or maybe nothing at all. Is your mother so close to a gaijin that he would visit her?"

"No. I'm coming back as soon as I can. They are looking for me here. I will find a way."

"Things are moving quickly," he said.

He means my time is running out. "Oyabun."

"Yes, Koi."

"Why were you watching my mother?" Her anger showed.

"You are on an important mission for us. We know how much your mother means to you. We just want to keep her safe until you return."

"I see. Well count on it, Hayato san. Count on it." She hung up. She yelled and smashed the bathroom door with an elbow. They weren't protecting her, *the lying snakes.* The threat was not lost on her. "You fail, mother fails."

She repeated the questions to herself. *How did he know? Who is this man? If he hurts my mother I will kill him slowly and then everyone he has ever loved.*

Koi had worked hard in her life to control her

emotions, prided herself on it and swore it was what kept her alive. But the rage was boiling up. Her mother was in danger and she was stuck in Nice. All she did for yakuza and now they held her dying mother as leverage. The man she hunted was closer to her mother than she was to him. She lashed out, grabbed Sacha by the neck and asked him why she shouldn't kill him right now. "How do I know you won't tell the police about me, huh? Answer me." He couldn't speak, she was choking him out. She let go, breathing in slowly, counting.

Sacha snapped, called her a murderous bitch. "You have all the charm of a sandpaper dildo but for some ungodly reason I like you, not romantically, not in the way that makes me want to, you know..."

"Fuck me?"

"Yes, and while we're at it, fuck you. No, I don't want to have sex with you but I fucking like you but I don't know why, you insane, sociopathic, psychotic fucking murderer. I'm sorry, that's harsh. I liked shopping with you, if that matters. Never bought baguettes with a killer before."

***

Candide thought she might offer Monsieur Trudeau some flaugnarde. Perhaps if he had a guest, he would invite her in. The muffled arguing stopped her at his door, then leaning in, waiting, she knocked and said, "Monsieur Trudeau? Monsieur Trudeau, are you okay in there?"

"We're fine," he yelled. Turning to Koi, he said, "God, I hate that nosy cunt."

"Tell her."

"I hate you, you nosy cunt."

Koi punched him in the stomach. "Louder."

"I can't breathe."

"Stand up and say it louder." Still angry at Hayato.

"I hate you, you fucking nosy cunt."

Candide scurried back down the stairs. He seized on a moment of inner strength, grabbed a vase and whirled to hit Koi. Before he turned a full 180 degrees she'd thrust her tanto knife through his belt and nicked his stomach. The excitement relaxed her.

He tried to yell but stopped himself. "Ow. How do you know what's going to happen before it does? You could have killed me. Wait, why did you stop?"

"Shh." She put a hand to his mouth. "What is that my blade nicked in your gut?"

"Nothing."

"Do you have a belly-button ring?"

"It's small."

"Take it out, Brittany, before I cut it out."

He lifted his shirt. "I'm bleeding. I need antiseptic."

"Now."

"It's hard to grasp, it's slippery."

"*Doke, bakayaro,*" she cursed. He yelped as she ripped it off and threw it in the sink. "Now you have something to cry about."

"What is wrong with you?"

"Me? You lied. You told me your name was Allain. What is your real name?" The knife at his throat.

"It is my real name, I swear." Blood drawn. "Stop, please, please stop hurting me. My full name is Sacha Allain Trudeau. I use Allain as a stage name."

She pulled the knife back, pressed her nose against

his. "A what? Why?"

"I dance in the gay clubs sometimes. The tips are good."

"I can taste the vomit in my mouth."

"Don't judge."

"Ach, go clean yourself, Trudy."

"Trudeau."

Sacha stood by the sink, less convinced he'd ever get to redecorate his apartment. She sat on the radiator cover, looking out the window, looking different than Trudeau had seen her until this moment; defeated, he thought, or near it. It scared him. She might do something rash and involve him. She looked like she wanted to cry. He said he'd make coffee and he had some Pernod hidden away.

He asked her to drink some, working to save his own life now. *Identify with her.*

"Thank you," she said. "Did you put a little bandage on it?" She had the wound-care skills of a prize fighter's cut man.

"I was going to remove it soon anyway, for the winter."

"Winter comes for us all."

"Listen, since we're stuck together, why don't you tell me about yourself? You already know about me and my passion."

"Obsession."

"Whatever."

Koi was reluctant at first, never trusted anyone enough in Tokyo or Osaka besides her mother to open up to. Sacha looked to be about her age. "My father left when I was small," she said, "well actually, before I was born. My mother worked as a hostess and then bartender in the red-

79

light district in Osaka. It's called Juso, by the brothel section called Tobita Shinchi. It's not a highly respected way to earn a living, but the best a single mother could get and it paid the rent. Used to come home from working all night and feed me before school. When I got older I would go to where she worked and bring her tea. I would wait for her outside the bars. I got to know the children of the night, yakuza kids and the other lower class like me. My mother was very sad when I told her I wanted to be yakuza. She said, 'you will be protected from outsiders, but who will protect you from the inside?' I only know now what she meant."

"You can change."

She made a face.

"Don't laugh," he said.

"You know nothing, singer, nothing of the dead souls." She walked off to the kitchen.

"Why don't you try being less sinister?" he asked.

"Why don't you blow me?"

"You don't have a cock."

She returned with more Pernod, checked out the window. "How do you know what I've got?"

"I saw you getting out of the shower."

"There's hope for you yet."

"Hope? So, you've decided not to kill me?"

"Only decide who to kill, not who to spare."

"How Spartan."

"I like the Spartans. Come back a winner or don't come back."

"That's a loose translation. You should read more."

She grabbed the butt of her Beretta.

He put his hands up. "I'm sorry, I get pedantic when I'm nervous."

"Watch your tiny mouth. I survived twenty-eight years without you. I'll get through this too."

He touched his lips, then took a chance with his next question. "Why don't you look as Japanese as other Japanese?"

"I look plenty Japanese."

"There's something, *je ne sais quoi*, something about your features."

"My father was French."

He shrieked.

"Keep your voice down. It's not so special news. Two grandparents Japanese and my mother." She pointed at her chest. "Born in Osaka. That makes me Japanese. I'm nothing else, certainly not French. I don't surrender."

"Ancient history." He sang it softly as he turned to the window. "Were you close with him?"

"You ask too many questions. Why you keep looking out the window? You think your imaginary lover going to blow you kisses?"

"That would be fabulous. So, were you close with him?"

"You don't listen. Ran away before I was born. Not close. Don't know if he is alive and don't care. Heard he was killed by a train in Algiers."

"Yet here you are in France. Are you looking for him?"

"Told you, I'm on a mission. What are you looking out there for?"

"It's 2:30."

"I don't ask you the time."

"Every day at 2:15 he leaves the rehearsal hall for the tram to this stop, then walks to the Café Raison and orders a latte and a *dariole*. I planned to introduce myself to him but now I'm your hostage. The concert will be over and he'll be back in Spain. I may never get another opportunity."

"Toughen up. I'm saving you from heartache."

"How can you be so sure?"

"Let me see him. Step aside. Which one is he?"

"Off to the right in the jeans and boots. He wears a scarf and glasses so he isn't recognized."

"He's pretentious and he has a big nose."

"He's a genius and I'm infatuated with him."

"Forget it. Even if he is a *nanshoku* he'll just leave you for another boy in the band. Your type is too whimsical for love."

"That hurts."

"Anyway, how do you know he doesn't like girls?"

"I know."

She walked away. "*Yume bakka ri mite.*"

"What does that mean?"

"It means you are a dreamer."

He turned back to the window, downed his drink.

***

Hubert stepped from his car. The police had cleared the scene. The media, gone. The story soon to be relegated to speculation until the police updated them. A robbery, a drug deal, terrorism—marauders from the Alps? Anyone's guess.

Hubert looked down at the crime-scene markings of his younger comrade's body. He thought about where they grew up, in the Aix-en-Provence north of Marseille, where the sidewalks are wider than the streets, under the tall sycamores, in the courtyards and the warm yellow walls of the Cathédrale Saint-Sauveur where Tanguy married and where he told his first lie to his bride. They never met in their youth, but Tanguy served under Hubert in the Brigade des Forces Spéciales Terre. There trying to quash intractable violence, peacekeeping missions in the remote villages of Côte D'Ivoire staving off the slaughter of civilians, supporters of the outgoing regime, or was it the incoming one? He couldn't remember. He remembered the dead mothers, clinging to the dead bodies of their children, piled in the village center and burned with a petrol accelerant. They were too late to save anyone that morning but Tanguy went into the brush on his own and killed every man he saw who held a gun or machete.

Hubert walked the alley where Mayko had chased Koi, looking around in case she had dropped something the police missed.

"Are you looking for the spider woman?"

"Who are you?" asked Hubert.

The boy looked eight or nine, young enough to still be naive. "I am Rudi. My papa owns the print shop around the corner. I saw the Asian lady climb right up the side of the building."

"Is that right? Which building, Rudi?"

"This one, right here. She jumped from the trash to the truck and whoosh, over to the other side and then up, up, up."

"Did she come down, down, down?"

Rudi's father called to him from the corner.

"I have to go, Monsieur. She did not come down."
Rudi ran to his father and pointed over his shoulder. "She
flew in the air to the other building."

Hubert looked skyward and wondered. *Fleeing or
hiding out? One way to know.* She hadn't been seen by
witnesses on the street. Maybe she hid in a vacant
apartment for the night; she could have left a clue.

He went into the vestibule, the creak of the iron door
echoed off the marble walls. He checked the names on the
mailboxes and door buzzers, nothing that seemed Asian,
no matter. *Ahh, the manager.* He rang the bell. Nothing.
He peered into the common hallway through the beveled
glass of the inner door. Rang again. The door buzzed and
clicked. Hubert turned the brass doorknob, stepped inside
and listened. The apartment building was midday quiet,
four floors, six doors per floor, no elevator. He heard a
door open at the far end of the hallway. No one called out.
"*Bonjour*?" he said.

"*Oui, bonjour. Qu'est-ce?*" A voice from the door.

"Are you the proprietor or building manager? I just
have a question."

"We have no vacancies at the moment." She took a
step into the hall wearing a widow's dress and what his
mother would have called a day hat, as if she were on her
way to a support group for reclusive starlets.

Hubert walked toward her, smiling like an insurance
salesman. He offered his hand. "I am Ricard with the *Nice-
Matin*, would you mind answering a few questions?"

"About what?"

"The shooting."

"Which shooting?"

84

"The one on the street, yesterday. Were you out of town?"

"I don't go out of town."

"Did you see the shooting?"

"I already spoke to the police."

"I am not the police. I just want to know if anyone here saw anything. We're doing a story, you understand, possibly involving terrorism. Interviews with witnesses would help."

"There are no terrorists here."

"I didn't mean to suggest that. The story is about terrorism."

"The police were here. They put up a flyer in the lobby with a contact number. Perhaps you saw it."

"I did."

"Did you call them? Maybe they can save you some trouble."

He smiled. Insurance salesman. "Some people are reluctant to speak to the police."

"I am one of those people."

"Are you reluctant to speak with me?"

"No."

"Well, did you see anything?"

"No."

"Did you speak to anyone who did?"

"No."

"Did they see anyone run in here?"

"Why would anyone run in here?"

"People run from such things."

"No one runs here. This is a nice building. I made a flaugnarde."

"*Quoi?*"

"Flaugnarde—pastry. I was baking when the police said the shooting occurred. Someone was killed, no?"

"Someone was, yes. A tragedy. Perhaps we can help to find the killer, if we all cooperate."

"This is a quiet building."

"Which is why a tenant or landlady would take notice if someone ran in here, after a shooting."

"You raise a good point, but no."

"No, what?"

"No one saw anything. No one ran here."

"Are you certain? What about from the roof?"

"The roof?" She looked up.

"Yes, the police said someone ran down the alley and climbed to the roof."

"How could they do that?"

"It's a mystery. Was anyone on your roof?"

"You mean a witness?"

"No, I mean, did anyone involved in the shooting climb on your roof, or jump there from the next building?"

"I don't see how that's possible."

"So you know nothing, nor do your tenants. Are you certain?"

"*Mais oui.*"

"*Au revoir, Madame.*"

She closed her door. "*Mademoiselle.*"

She's lying.

He's no reporter.

Chapter Eleven

THE PERNOD GOT TO HIM. Sacha fell asleep on the couch. Koi called her mother, who said only that the man who visited her was there to help. Before she could ask her more, an unexpected visitor caused Koi to cut the call short. She promised she'd call back as soon as possible.

Candide presumed Sacha might want to know about the ominous man disguised as a reporter who had been asking questions about surprise guests. But Sacha's 'naughty rebuke' as she called it, of her last inquiry had her reconsidering her desire to change him back to his heterosexual origin, a desire instigated by her belief, based upon her Tarot reading of him, that he had trapped within him her vision of a virile man, one who, once free of his deviant shackles, would be sexually grateful, a man she hoped to unleash in a lustful intervention over French 75s and dark chocolate, if he would just give her the chance. She switched from boots to pumps, opened the top buttons of her dress, pulled her breasts to the center of her bra, added another layer of lipstick and removed, then re-donned her hat—before removing it again, to avoid giving him the misperception that she had appointments and would be unable to stay for tea.

Her thigh-highs itched a little when she walked, doing her best Rita Hayworth as she worked the hall to his door. A long, slow breath in, a gentle rapping.

"Monsieur Trudeau? Monsieur Trudeau, may I have a

word?"

Koi poked him. "Hey, Trudy, wake up. That nosy landlady is knocking. We can't keep ducking her, she'll get suspicious."

"She's crazy. She wants to free me from my gayness."

"I may let you live after all."

"Bitch. Go in the bathroom, please. I'll shoo her."

Sacha opened the door a crack to where his foot stopped her from pushing in. Only her Roman nose and cleavage were visible in the biased afternoon light.

"*Bonjour*, Monsieur Trudeau. Your door seems to be stuck."

"It's not stuck, I'm blocking it. I'm sick." He turned and coughed. "You know you can call me Sacha?"

"Sacha." She repeated, adding extra breath on the end.

He wrinkled his nose.

Koi put her hand over her eyes.

"Sacha," she said, enjoying the familiarity. "I need to speak to you about a most urgent matter. May I come in?"

"I'm," coughing again, more exaggerated, "really sick. I called out and everything."

"I can fix that. But first..." She pushed her lips into the opening.

He leaned back.

"I believe you may be in danger. Someone was here."

He wondered if he closed the door on her lips would she keep talking. "That was just a friend from work. She brought me uh, scones and, well she's gone now."

"Not her, him."

"Who, him?" He opened the door another half swing.

She arched her back.

He noticed a bobby pin dangling from the side of her head. "Why would I be in danger, Candide? Great shoes."

"Oh, *merci*. I bought them in Paris for—"

"Danger?"

"*Oui*. A man was here briefly and just a while ago. He asked questions about the shooting and who may have..." she'd sidled her way in now, "rushed into my building during that horrible event in the street. He said he was a reporter but I think he is..." She paused, looked behind her. "Le Milieu."

"The setting?"

She laughed and recomposed. Standing full into his apartment now, taking it in, moving toward him. "No, *bel homme*, Le Milieu is the mafia of Marseille."

"Mafia? How do you know?"

"He had the look."

"You mean like, his outfit or...?"

"The man who was here is not who he pretends." She put her hand on his chest and lowered her voice. "He has death in his eyes. He has killed men. I have seen these men before I... I am not as young as I look." She ran her fingers through her hair, caught the bobby pin.

Koi listened from the bathroom, biting her lip at Sacha's incompetence, while knowing Candide was almost right. Death was in the cards, but brought by Le Sauvage, not Milieu. He'd sent the man to probe. They'd be back. It's time to go. *Get rid of her already.*

Sacha eased toward her.

She thought he might kiss her, that he might be grateful for the warning, but he was pushing her out.

"I really appreciate your telling me this but now I am a

little frightened and I think I should call the police."
Backing her out.

She grabbed the door and frame to hold her ground. "I
can protect you. I have a pistol."

"Oh my."

She locked his eyes, he could smell her *parfum*—
Thierry Mugler, Angel? Momma? Sacha decided to tease
against her desires, give her a little hope for a rendezvous
later. He stepped between her legs, letting her feel his
thigh between hers.

She looked down, then up. Down. Up again.

"Allow me time to take something for this cold and
rest, perhaps a shower. I'll come to your place later." He
said it with two unenthusiastic fingers on her chest, just
atop her bosom, gently pushing.

She squeezed her breasts against his fingers. "I'll oil
the pistol. We'll make a plan."

"A plan, yes, good plan." He pulled his fingers out. "I'll
see you soon, Candide."

She pursed her lips and turned into the hallway.
Sacha.

Sacha locked the door and imitated her breathy voice.
"I have a pistol."

Koi ran to the window, double-checked the magazine
in the Beretta and pulled on her running shoes. She
grabbed her backpack and organized her supplies. "Have
to go now. They find me here, I can't defend myself. Have
to get them on the move." She looked toward the door,
then the window. Checked her watch against the digital
clock on his cable box.

Trudeau asked, "What are you doing? Why are you leaving now, maybe we should call the police? Candide is crazy, this could be nothing."

She cut him off. "You don't get it. These men are professionals. She knows I am here, or was. If they asked her, she lied and they'll know it. They will be back to interrogate her and search this building. I killed one of theirs. I am after their boss. I can't explain all that now. I'm leaving."

"What about me?"

Almost finished. Strapping on her tanto and the SP5K. "If they think you know where I am they will cut you into pieces to find out."

Trudeau put his hand over his mouth.

"I'll tell you nothing, so you'll know nothing. You were my hostage. I talked on the phone but only in Japanese. You didn't understand. You are glad to get rid of me. Got it?"

"No."

"What is so hard to understand?"

"What if they torture me until they are convinced I know nothing? I can't handle that. I'm going with you." He moved to his closet and took down a valise. "I can pack in a minute. I don't need much."

"You can't come with me. You will slow me down. I have to work alone. The mission is everything. I have to move quickly or we'll both die."

He began to panic, near hyperventilating. He yelled, "Fuck your mission. You can't leave me here with these men."

She slapped him, grabbed him by the throat and

shoved him onto the couch. "How about I just kill you now and spare everyone the trouble? Listen to me, carefully. When Le Sauvage's men come, and they will come, you tell them I once let it slip that I was going to Vietnam to find terrorists. You don't know why or how but that's where I am going. Tell them I am a horrible person and you are grateful I am gone. It's true so, they will believe you. I can't tell you anything more."

"What the hell are you talking about? Who is Le Sauvage?"

With no time to waste, Koi relented. She told him about her dying mother, about yakuza, the undiscovered gold, and about how killing Sauvage was the one impossible chance she had of earning her freedom and honor for her family. In minutes she raced through her life story while she secured her weapons and backpack. She told him about being raised by a single mom and how her mother suffered indignities from traditional people. She wanted her mother to die proud, with peace in her heart. It was all that mattered to her in the few remaining days of her mother's life and possibly her own. Yakuza could be setting her up for a fall. She wouldn't let that happen. The gold meant nothing to her, but she had to leave, no more talk.

Candide's scream was heard throughout the building. "My flaugnarde!"

Chapter Twelve

WHEN CANDIDE TOLD HUBERT to fuck his mother, Mayko rushed her, knocking her, the kitchen table and her flaugnarde to the floor. Hubert told him to cover her mouth. She kicked at Hubert, who stood out of range. She scratched at Mayko but couldn't get past his cannonball shoulders. He pinned her arms.

"You see, *Madame*." Hubert held up a finger to interrupt himself. "*Mademoiselle*, you say, uh? Such a waste of abundant breasts. The thing is, the man who is holding you is impatient. He is an enforcer by trade and a brute by birth. He is also, like myself, intolerant of liars. He wants to kill you and he may. He also wants to rape you but I don't really have the time to waste while he ravages you with his extraordinarily large Ukrainian prick. I will ask you once and if you don't give me a satisfactory answer, I and my Ukrainian soldier will lose our tempers, *n'est-ce pas*?" She nodded.

"A woman came into your building, yes?"

Candide shook her head, no. Mayko punched her in the ribs. She grunted and began to cry.

Hubert said, "The way I see it, if she had merely come through the hatch on the roof and fled out a window you would have told me earlier. This leads me to believe she is still here and you know where."

She shook her head again. Mayko pressed his knee into her stomach. She could barely take in air through her

93

dripping nose.

"So tell me, *Mademoiselle*, which apartment is she in? My friend will remove his hand so you can answer, quietly, please."

Candide sucked in air and spat at Mayko. She turned to Hubert. "I will never betray my Sacha. Go to hell, Milieu."

Mayko looked up at Hubert who nodded. Mayko produced a blade and rammed it through her sternum. She slumped. Her head fell to the side, half-open eyes taking in the crumbled pastry.

Sacha asked Koi what Candide could be yelling about. Koi knew they had returned. She peeked out the window. The Audi and a Peugeot sedan out front, one man covering the front door. She ran to Sacha's bedroom and looked down the fire escape. Another gun covered the rear. *Best route, alley across the street.* "I have to go now," she said.

"What about me?"

She cinched her knapsack. "Go into the hall and look into the stairwell. They'll be looking for a woman. Come right back in and tell me if you see anything. Go now, you'll be okay."

Hubert had checked the mailboxes and tapped Sacha Trudeau's name. "Third floor, E. Get on the handheld and tell Beatto and Chuinard to be alert. Let's go."

Trudeau ran back in and locked the door. "There are two men coming up the stairwell. This is it. I'm so scared. Why did you do this to me? How can you leave me to fend off these men?"

"You'll be fine. I promise. They will know you are a hostage. I'm sorry. I have to go. Goodbye, Sacha." She began to ease the window open.

Sacha said, "Please don't leave me here. They'll kill me. I'm a fucking witness, you know. I will know them. Did you think about that?"

Koi knew he was right, she just couldn't tell him before. She had seconds left before they'd be at the door. She ran across the apartment and jammed a chair under the doorknob. "Can you run?"

"I play tennis, mostly to meet people, I..."

She pulled him by the shirt back to the bedroom window, closed the door behind them. "I'll get you out of town, after that you'll be on your own. I'll make them chase me. You'll be safe to return in a day. Follow me closely and do exactly as I say or I'll leave you to them like a wounded impala."

"Okay, okay. I'll stay right on your ass."

"And no talking, let's go."

The handheld radios crackled. Hubert whispered, "We're at the door, stay alert."

Chuinard looked back down the alley toward the street. Koi climbed through the window, leaned over the rail and shot Chuinard through the skull. "Run now, Sacha."

Beatto heard the shot and ran inside through the front. Hubert and Mayko hit each other as they tried to shoulder the door. They took a step back and Mayko tried to kick it open. The chair held. He bounced back then bulled his way through, smashing the chair. The men scanned the apartment, Beatto running upstairs. They checked the bathroom and kitchen, the living room closet and behind the couch. Koi and Sacha had made it down two levels, one more to go. Hubert signaled Mayko to breach the bedroom door. He kicked it in and Hubert covered his back. The cool air was pulling the curtains out the window. Hubert ran to climb out, calling to Chuinard. Mayko reached Beatto on the handheld and said they'd gone out the rear.

Beatto grunted and ran back down the stairs.

Koi and Sacha jumped from the ground-floor ladder and hit the pavement running. Hubert spotted Chuinard on the deck in a small pool of blood. Dead. The alley was to his blind side. Mayko followed him out, Beatto huffed back down the stairs and to the vestibule where he ran into Monsieur Safranak on his way in from the market and both tumbled to the marble floor.

"Oaf."

Koi and Sacha had a twenty-five-meter head start. Hubert spotted them on the turn for the second landing. "The alley, the alley. West. They are running west."

Beatto limped down the alley, saw Chuinard and turned left, meeting Hubert and Mayko as they jumped off the fire escape. Hubert told Beatto to get the car and head her off. He and Mayko gave chase.

Beatto was in good shape for forty-two, but his body armor, the stairs and the sprinting had started to slow him down. He got to his Peugeot and peeled off into traffic.

Mayko dropped to a knee and took aim at Koi. "No," Hubert yelled. "Alive, we need her alive, you fool. Run, let's go."

Koi and Sacha started left to the boulevard, spotted

the Peugeot. "*Merde*," Sacha said.

"No, keep running this way, he's trying to cut us off, we'll get behind him. Run faster." While she ran, Koi wondered if Sauvage was among the men in this crew. *Not likely. Too dangerous to be exposed. He's sent his pocket army.*

As they made it to the end of the alley, Koi saw the Peugeot turn right at the next corner, against traffic.

Sacha pointed to the boulevard. "The tram, the tram."

She yanked him and took off; they caught it as the doors closed. Hubert and Mayko ran down the alley, called for Beatto to circle back. When they got to the boulevard they split up, and Mayko ran left back toward the apartment. Hubert took a few steps then spotted the tram ahead. "The tram, they are on the tram." He radioed Beatto who paralleled the tram then turned and cut it off three blocks down, Hubert and Mayko running.

Beatto blocked the tram with the Peugeot, jumped out with his weapon drawn. The tram operator froze. Koi sprayed Beatto with the SP5K through the front windshield of the tram. "Let's go."

Sacha hadn't blinked. He followed robotically, blocking out what he saw, trusting Koi to save his life.

"Get in and slide over." She pushed him.

Sacha jumped in the open driver's door of the Peugeot and scrambled across. Koi shifted into gear and nailed the gas pedal as Mayko checked the tram through the rear window and Hubert ran to the front. He fired two short bursts at the Peugeot, trying to take out the tires. She cut across traffic as the sound of sirens wailed toward the boulevard. Hubert's men—defeated, again.

Countdown to Osaka

Mayko looked down at Beatto then glared at Hubert. "Why does this *koorva* have to be taken alive? How many men must we lose?"

"Orders. Move."

Chapter Thirteen

LARGE MEN IN TAILORED BLACK SUITS stood silently with their hands folded in front of them. They dipped their heads and stepped back as he passed by.

Hayato slipped off his shoes and entered the residence of his oyabun, the kumichō. *"Ojyama shimasu."*

"Moukatte makka?" asked Nakane.

"Bochi bochi. Kyouwa omaneki arigatou gozaimasu."

"Ii, yoi."

Hayato thanked his host for inviting him in. Although Hayato had been in his home numerous times he still deferred to tradition, the requisite pitter-patter before moving on to business conversation. Hayato told the clan's leader that Koi would be returning to Osaka.

As they spoke, two more fit and suited guards stepped away from the leaders and into an adjoining room.

The kumichō expressed mild admiration that she had accomplished so much in just a few days but had not changed his mind on her eventual demise. Her mother was dying anyway. She had no other family. "Her father abandoned her mother, and her," he said.

Toru Nakane was old school yakuza, so his cavalier attitude toward this obligation to Koi surprised Hayato. Perhaps it shouldn't have. Nakane's reverence for the codes of honor had, at least in Koi's case, been superseded by his disdain for having a female assassin in his outfit as well as his sense of hierarchy. Women did not belong, but out of respect for Hayato, he authorized her induction. Though he privately recognized her talent and loyalty, he had determined years earlier that he would exploit her until she outran her usefulness. Once Hayato told him of her desire to leave the organization, he'd made up his mind. The Takumi-Gumi clan must always be a priority over Hayato's relationship with Koi. Though Hayato was fifteen years her senior, Nakane had begun to believe Hayato's affection for her ran interference for his clan loyalty. Nakane once asked if Koi's beauty had perhaps clouded his judgment.

Hayato dismissed the idea. "I am her sponsor," he had said, insulted by the implication, "and nothing more."

They reviewed the operation and the time lines. Nakane said his contacts in the police told him the procedures for the warrants to conduct the investigation and wiretaps were underway. Things were falling into place for Nakane and he grew more resolute. "Koi cannot be included in the final push for the gold. This amount of money will give us power beyond what we ever hoped for. I won't have someone who is no longer committed to the clan be a part of it," said Nakane.

"What about the code of *giri*?" asked Hayato. "I should honor my promise to her if she succeeds."

"I made no such promise to her. I merely suggested it to you as incentive for her to achieve the objective."

"But, kumichō san, I did promise. I gave her my word that she would be rewarded with her freedom if she succeeded. She's on a good path at this moment."

"I will consider a *zetsuenjo* if she kills Le Sauvage but we don't recover the gold."

"With respect, an excommunication of that level is dishonorable. If she succeeds but the gold is not recoverable, that is not her fault. Would you at least consider a *hamonjo*? A *zetsuenjo* is irreversible and she has served us well."

Once a clan member has been marked in this way, even someone who associates with that person could be met with violence and certainly disgrace for a man of Hayato's status. On the other hand, the *hamanjo* is like a dishonorable discharge from the military. It's an ugly blemish on your record but you can still have friends and redeem yourself professionally.

"I will reflect on your argument, Hayato." Nakane said the words but didn't intend to follow through. He'd made up his mind and his impatience showed on his face, a face that Hayato saw as a hoary macaque, preening himself on a hot-spring rock in a snowy Yamanouchi valley.

Hayato had offered Koi an honorable way out that would have satisfied Nakane had this business of the gold not come up.

Nakane never intended to have Koi succeed in finding out what Le Sauvage knew about the location of the gold. He knew it was an impossible task. His only desire was to expose Le Sauvage, and identify him or enough members of his crew so yakuza soldiers could track him to the gold and kill him. He would have a *kuromaku* clean up the bodies. Without telling Hayato, Nakane had already dispatched Ino to France to shadow her.

"*Arigatou gozaimasu,*" said Hayato.

"*Hona sainara.*"

Countdown to Osaka

Hayato said his goodbye and left Nakane in his home, a five-thousand square foot concrete ranch with a red-tile roof, overlooking multi-level gardens and ponds, a putting green, a view of the Mount Miyama from the pool and an interior that rivaled the National Art Center in Tokyo, all in a trippy blend of traditional Japanese aesthetics and gangster gaudiness.

Hayato's driver opened the door and waited. Two more of his men waited in a lead Mercedes, polished to a deep gloss. Hayato looked out at the quiet order of the gardens. He thought about Koi, about how the murders she'd committed for them would never be enough to allow her to take pleasure in the luxuries the kumichō experienced. Would he tell her, tell her to cut, run and never look back, forget about her mother and find a faraway country in which to live, where they wouldn't bother to chase her? He could get her money to start a new life; not to be rich, but enough to start.

The driver tossed his *manga* into the car and turned to his boss. "*Kirei*. Such a beautiful place," the driver said. "He must have two hundred koi in those ponds."

Hayato ignored him. *I am yakuza first. This is the family we commit to.* He sat in his Mercedes and poured Yamazaki 12-year-old scotch into a tumbler.

Chapter Fourteen

KOI SLOWED DOWN after she was sure Hubert and his men had not followed. Two marked police units passed her in the opposite direction, bumper on bumper, sirens and overhead lights blazing, as yet unaware they'd soon be looking for that very Peugeot. A quiet neighborhood had now been the scene of two shootings—one strange murder had become a spree. Three more bodies brought back the news media and this time the international crews came with them.

"Was it terrorism?" Reporters stoked fear across the airwaves in twenty-nine languages.

The Peugeot was too hot to hang on to; the police or Le Sauvage's tentacles would reach out into the city and snatch it up. They had to ditch it but not leave themselves stranded. If Le Sauvage was not among those who came for her, killing two of his men would draw him out. Now she had to find a way to trap him, unless he was already in Osaka. *Chikushō.* Koi pounded the dash. *Why would he be there without his men? He must have people everywhere.* She needed a quiet place to think.

Sacha had finally stopped crying. He'd become convinced he would either die within a day or be arrested as an accomplice and imprisoned until he'd aged beyond recognition. "I should have just let you kill me. I'm going to die anyway, I could have died at home with my things. All I wanted to do was meet a musician but instead I met a killer and her fucking criminal friends. Why couldn't I have missed the fucking tram?"

"You're alive now," she said. "If you are breathing there is hope. Stop whining and help yourself. I need a place to stash or dump this car and rest so we can think. Think, okay? What do you know around here?"

He sucked in air like a vacuum lock. "Okay, turn left here and go up the hill for about two kilometers. There's a villa around the next bend. My loopy aunt lives there. We can pull around back and put the car in her garage. She doesn't drive, she just complains and frets about her horoscope. It's quiet there except for her."

"Good."

He spotted the house through the leaves. "My gosh, there are a million trees here. We can *stash* the car before anyone sees it, okay? Do I sound cool now? I found us a safe house."

"Shut up."

"Right here, the garage, turn here by the brick wall. Stop, I'll open the doors."

They walked toward the house. Aunt Lara met them at the screen door with a 16-gauge bird gun, double barrel, neither loaded. Sacha yelled, "It's just me, Tante Lara, don't be alarmed. Put the gun away please, I have a friend with me. We want to make a good impression, no?"

"Is she Chinese?"

"Japanese," Koi said. "Japa—"

Sacha shushed her with a hand, sensing the anger in her voice. "So? Where's my kiss, Auntie? Come on, hugs."

"Who is she?" Aunt Lara had a way of croaking out her words in short, toadish bursts.

"Emiko," Koi said. "My name is Emiko."

Sacha looked at her with his mouth open.

She looked back at him, then at the black and white tile floor of the mud room. "You can call me Koi, it's kind of a nickname. Just call me Koi." She directed it at Sacha.

"Koi?"

"Koi, yes, Aunt Lara, we'll call her Koi. It'll be fun."

"Koi's a fish," Lara said.

"Yes, Auntie."

"You a Pisces?"

"I don't know," said Koi. "I would love some tea. Do you have tea?"

"Don't know?"

"She doesn't know, Aunt Lara. Let's have tea. Can you put down the rifle please?"

"It's a shotgun." Koi and Aunt Lara said it together. Sacha made a face and waved his hand.

"When's your birthday?" She put the shotgun on the server and ran water into the kettle.

"The beginning of March," Koi said. "March the fifth."

"Damn close."

"Can we put our bags down in the sunroom, Auntie? We don't want to impose."

"Staying over?"

"I don't think so, but we'll stay a while and visit, okay? I'm famished. I know you have too much food here for one woman. Would you be a dear?"

"I'll make something. Go on."

Koi followed Sacha to the sunroom, overgrown on the exterior by vines, rather negating the concept. Koi checked her bag, checked her jacket, her pockets and the bag again.

"The phone," she said. "I must have dropped it. I'll try the car."

She slipped by the aunt without further conversation, out across the slate path and into the side garage door. In the gray space, rusted and web-covered chains, gardening tools, saw blades and a pick with a broken handle, hung like remnants of an inquisition supply post. Dust floated in the near silence, ticks from the cooling engine. A cat groused at the disturbance from a shelf in shadow, startling Koi. She listened for the sounds of cars outside, none came. In the Peugeot, no phone. She could get another soon, *maybe use Aunt Loopy's meantime,* no one would trace it. She hoped it had fallen unnoticed somewhere and not been picked up by the police or Sauvage's men.

***

The police.

A detective found the phone in the blood and glass in front of the tram. The crime-scene techs secured it for fingerprints and a search of the phone's history. The detectives followed the parade of witnesses from the dead Beatto back to the same alley, the dead Chuinard, the apartment building, the dead Candide, Sacha's apartment; searched it for suspects, then secured it and had it combed over by the forensics team.

They found Trudeau's pay stubs and called the Stade Charles-Erhmann, asked for Monsieur Trudeau. "I am sorry, he has called out sick. Unusual for him, but he had the time coming to him. Is he in trouble?"

"We just need to speak with him. Please let us know if you hear from him. *Merci.*"

Sacha's apartment and personal history turned up nothing linking him to the shootings or the dubious dead men, nothing suggesting he had a relationship with an unidentified Asian woman. They found bloody napkins in the trash. DNA would be obtained from them and the glasses left on the counter along with the toothbrushes. The common surfaces were dusted for prints. Later the police would locate an elimination set from when Sacha had registered as a bartender, helping to rule out his prints from others found at the apartment.

The detectives discussed the probability he was a hostage, but his running with her presented doubts, doubts complicated by the idea he may have been running for his life from the hit crew, but why? What did he know that they may have wanted kept quiet?

Identifying the dead men would help. Finding Sacha Allain Trudeau alive, would help a whole lot more. The key to the grand mystery seemed to be the Asian woman. The detectives began the search for friends and relatives of Trudeau, given that suspects and people in fear usually go first to someplace familiar.

***

Ino had used the information from the kumichō to deliver himself to Nice, and the information from the evening news, to locate the right neighborhood. The problem for Ino; this neighborhood did not lend itself to anonymity. An Asian could be explained—an Asian in an expensive suit with his shirt half open exposing multiple tattoos lurking around a crime scene that had previously been occupied by a similarly featured missing suspect, could not.

While Hubert picked the boss up at the airport, Bouchet the money man, dressed in a jaunty cap with a Bichon Frise on his arm, could watch the unfolding drama unnoticed by the French troupe of onlookers. He spotted the Japanese gangster, a man obvious to Bouchet who'd spent the better part of his third decade as an investment banker in Hong Kong; he'd learned to differentiate among Asian ethnicities. He'd also made frequent trips for both business and pleasure to Tokyo and Kyoto where he laundered money for a few select clients. Yakuza always got a piece. He moved behind Ino, watched him trying to glean information about who had been involved from civilians and peripheral *gendarmerie*. Ino's English was spotty—his French, worse.

Bouchet telephoned Mayko, who had sent a young wheel-man who'd grown up in the slums of Stuttgart to wait for him and a guest one block south. Mayko dispatched young Potente to the meet in a nondescript tan Citroën. Bouchet smiled as he approached Ino from behind.

"*Monsieur*, I have a well-maintained Walther PPK, German manufactured for the record, pointed at your upper spine. I'll not hesitate to cripple you unless you slowly move to your right and walk to the next corner where we have a car waiting. There you go, good man. No need to alert the police. I could kill you before it mattered."

The fearless Ino asked where they were going, relieved that he had been found by the people Koi was probably brawling with, saving him legwork. Perhaps they shared a common interest he could negotiate. Bouchet told him to get in the car, front seat. The young Potente, light-heavyweight boxing champ of his former command in the Bundeswehr Heer, nodded a polite *bonjour* then promptly knocked Ino out with a jab. Bouchet's dog protested.

By the time Ino stirred, Potente's skills with a five-speed had them five kilometers out of the city proper. Ino's hands were bound with plastic zip cuffs, his head in a blackout hood. At a culvert near an abandoned barley mill, Potente transferred Ino into another vehicle, a Volkswagen pick-up with off-road tires and a Corsican driver named Orsu who'd long ago lost all contact with his personality but not his expertise with a switchblade. An over-under Franchi 20-gauge waited on the front seat.

In the gathering hillside mist, Bouchet spoke to the Corsican who hoisted Ino into the truck bed and covered him with a dirty canvas tarp, after emptying his pockets and tying his feet to a ring welded into the bed. Ino grumbled about the seating arrangements. Orsu just smoked and drove away. Bouchet and his dog returned to Nice with Potente. Bouchet spoke with Hubert and acknowledged the prearranged meeting spot.

The police had lifted prints off the phone and, finding no matches in local databases, sent them to Interpol. They traced the only two numbers dialed to Osaka and had sent emergency requests for their listings to the local police. The DNA would take more time.

***

With their stomachs full of *hachis parmentier*, home-baked crusty bread and a glass of local pinot noir, Koi's mind eased just enough to afford her a clearer vision of their immediate future. She'd never tasted anything as savory as this old-world collusion of ground beef and mashed potatoes but it only served to highlight their dilemma. They couldn't rest, not even for one night. A witness would have taken down the registration of the Peugeot, Sacha's phone records and family would be traced. It was only perhaps a few more hours at best before they determined Aunt Lara's place would make a convenient hideaway. She'd had no time to wipe down Sacha's place. Her fingerprints would be sent to Interpol. She held out hope her local arrests for minor offenses did not necessitate sending her records to the Interpol database, although with yakuza connections, they just might.

Koi had enough time before alerts would be sent to train stations and airports. She could get out of the country and back to Japan but she had to move now. The dinner conversation did not placate her growing anxiety.

"Koi, uh?" said the aunt. "Why do they call you that?"

"Auntie, it's just a name." said Sacha.

"No, it's okay," said Koi. "Been called that since about nineteen years old. In Japan, a koi is revered for mental toughness and stoicism. I won many *shogi* tournaments because my opponents could not fluster me."

"What's a shogi?" she asked.

"It's a game of strategy, played with tiles, something like chess pieces. Very challenging."

"Never heard of it."

"I've heard of it," Sacha said. He tried to be supportive in front of the lumpy aunt. "I saw it on the education channel." He refilled his wine glass, Koi turned him down.

"Getting dark," the aunt said. "Roads are slippery in this rain."

"It would be a rough drive," Sacha said. "Maybe we need some rest."

Koi gave him a look Aunt Lara didn't see while she cleared the dinner plates and fired a Gitanes Brunes, non-filter, with a stick match. She didn't offer a cigarette to her guests.

Koi would not be staying. After a long silence, she asked Lara a question that surprised Sacha but not Lara. "So, Aunt Lara," Koi said. "Do you by any chance have another set of car registration plates in that garage of yours?"

Sacha gulped some wine. Aunt Lara sucked on her cigarette then let out a long, phlegmy laugh, pointing at Koi with a crooked finger. "I knew it. I knew it. My Scorpio heart knew the moment I saw you that we would be a good match."

"Auntie, what are you talking about?" He made a face at Koi to remind her the aunt was loopy.

"You are a Pisces, pretty girl and as a Scorpio, we are best suited to help one another." She sat down next to Koi, lit another Gitanes and gestured to Sacha to fill her glass. "I know you are on the run from someone. I sensed it about you." Koi pulled back. "Don't deny, it's all right. In this feeling I am reminded of my youth at Lyon in 1968, May. We were striking the capitalists and that dick-nosed whore, de Gaulle. Some of us planted a bomb."

"Auntie Lara. Are you making this up? Maybe you've had enough wine."

"Shush, Sacha, I'm talking to Koi."

"Well, the bomb went off as planned, but what we didn't plan on was the protest that had been gathering outside the city offices. The hour was late. It was only meant to break windows and make people scared." She took a drag and a swallow of pinot. "A few people got hurt. We had to disappear for a while. We hid out on a farm near Chassieu for three weeks until the protests died down and the socialists made deals. I know how to evade capture. Come."

She led Koi down to her museum of dank, pulled a chain to light a bare bulb and headed toward the oil furnace where she poked around under framed movie and protest posters and then pulled off a woolen blanket, revealing a wooden crate. "Ahh, *c'est ici.* My little box of Lyon. So many years gone." She almost cried but stood up straight with her hands on her hips. "Open it."

Koi pried off the lid. Inside were four vehicle plates, two German, one Italian and one French. Assorted hats, scarves, expired passports, a trench knife, one moth-riddled sweater and several sets of eyeglasses.

Lara put on the red beret and said, "Carry it upstairs for me, Pisces, let's have a closer look."

Koi lugged it upstairs. It felt heavier than it looked. She set it on the table and this time accepted more wine, the threesome on their second bottle.

Aunt Lara began to empty the box, moving with a zeal Sacha hadn't seen in many years. Under the sweater, she found a box of shells for the bird gun and a .38 caliber revolver with no trigger, explaining the extra weight. "Move those things, Sacha, yes, here, take these to the counter. So, Pisces, are you hiding or running?"

Sacha looked at her and Koi said, "Running. Alone." She looked at Sacha, who appeared torn between relief and fear. "The airport. I can't take the main thoroughfares, the police will be on alert, maybe roadblocks. There is no time. I have to go now."

"Sacha will drive you. You sit in the back seat wearing a scarf and hat, with these glasses, yes. Read a newspaper, I have them in the mud room. Put the German plates on the car. The police won't notice right away and they are still scared of the Germans."

"Auntie."

"Ahh. True. Whatever, old feelings. I will tell you the best way, through the farm roads. Sacha, write this down. When you get close, take a taxi the rest of the way in. Take the next possible flight to another country and make plans from there."

Within fifteen minutes, she had prepared Koi a thermos of coffee, and given her sweet biscuits and some Euros to tip the taxi driver along with a small suitcase filled with just a blanket and sweater to give it heft. "Look natural," Lara said.

Sacha struggled with a flashlight under his arm and a bent screwdriver but changed the vehicle plates.

"Be polite in the airport. Think normal thoughts. Keep your tattoos covered and don't ask for much on the flight. Don't be noticed. Look people in the eye, avoiding eye contact is a tell, eh?"

Koi listened, made sense of it and opened the back door. She wanted to kiss the cranky aunt but remained reserved.

Lara spoke to her nephew. "Sacha, my dear boy, the

only one who visits me and eats all my food. When you drop off Koi, just drive away. You are a hired driver, not a friend, *n'est-ce pas?*"

"*Oui*, Auntie Lara, *merci.*"

"Don't thank me yet. You must put on the best performance of your gay life. Drive straight to the police and tell them all about the woman who kidnapped you and forced you to drive her to the train station. Tell the police she said no one would keep her from getting to Canada. Do you understand?"

"Yes, even gay people can understand such things."

Lara kissed him on both cheeks, said god-speed and saluted Koi, her *camarade contre les porcs. "Vive la socialisme."*

Koi didn't quite understand but, grateful for the assistance, returned the salute. She got in the back seat. "That's an interesting aunt you have there."

Sacha backed out into the teeming rain and drove away without responding.

Koi thought about offering an apology, a goodbye that might say she understood what she'd put him through, but he wasn't in a conversational mood and she didn't know how to change that.

Fifteen days left.

Chapter Fifteen

THE CENTRAL DIRECTORATE had taken over the case. Investigators received word from Interpol at the Nice office of the Police Judiciaire that the fingerprints did not match any subject in Interpol's files. However, facial recognition software determined, after thirty-six hours of cross-referencing CCTV footage from the neighborhood of the shooting and the beach area, that the woman spotted at the scenes of both shootouts was likely of Japanese descent and given her extensive tattoos, possibly a yakuza organized crime member. A prepaid phone had been found with calls made to Japan. What yakuza may have been involved with in Nice, if anything, could only be speculated, but an arms deal seemed the default suspicion.

Some people who watched the news came forward, most offered nothing useful. They just wanted to be part of the story. A local Nice broadcaster said, "Authorities interviewed a taxi driver who claims to have picked up a woman several days earlier near the marina and brought her to the construction site of a new condominium complex in the normally quiet, suburban Nice neighborhood. She paid in cash, Euros."

The police later identified Guion Chuinard as having an extensive criminal background, with suspected links to the notorious international gunrunner, known only as Le Sauvage. The Judiciaire was now working with Interpol on the possibility yakuza was in France to purchase weapons and that a potential deal had gone wrong. The reporters spoke of Marin as, "the man in custody from the first shooting," who was not cooperating.

At Václav Havel Airport in Prague, Koi watched the international news from under her hat. Her body shook as she took her first real deep breath since fleeing France to discover that the mysterious Japanese killer had yet to be unidentified but, "authorities are confident she will be located soon and taken into custody. The Judiciaire are asking anyone with information to call..."

They were also seeking the whereabouts of a possible hostage of the Japanese woman, whom social media had taken to calling the Ninja Destroyer, one Sacha Allain Trudeau of Nice, a bartender at the Stade Charles-Erhmann.

Feeling a little less obvious, Koi retreated to the furthest rear booth of a coffee shop and studied her ticket to Hong Kong, where she'd make a connecting flight to Osaka. She had to sleep soon or lose whatever clarity she still had. She'd bought Dramamine and would take two with a glass of wine to accelerate the process of forcing rest on herself. She could no longer make coherent plans without sleep and knew she could do nothing useful from inside a fuselage to help either her mother or her own cause, no matter what state she was in.

She needled herself with questions about her life and career choices and found herself resigning to defeat. *"Sokka shooganai na,"* she said aloud. "This is not what I expected life to be." How many bodies was she directly and indirectly responsible for on one trip? How many more before it was over and how many would that make in such a short life?

The way those men came to that apartment, she believed she was not meant to survive. The news media said the building's superintendent, who had worked there for more than twenty years, was found dead in her kitchen, stabbed through the heart. If they were willing to kill for information that would lead to her, Le Sauvage's people would have been prepared to kill her as well, and now with more members of their crew dead, she had to be a priority target. The only good Koi could see in this scenario was that Sauvage could be drawn out by the chase. So far, his men had failed him; he'd need to flex his dominance or risk his reputation in the underworld.

***

Toru Nakane watched the same reports on the international news. He knew sending Koi after Le Sauvage involved this risk.

The Japanese newspapers ran the story as well. Given Japan's strict anti-gun laws they began to wonder if perhaps a yakuza turf war was in the works as that would explain yakuza's possible interest in transacting with Le Sauvage, but exactly which clans might be battling they didn't know. The police declined to comment, mostly because they had no intel on a possible turf war and were caught unawares. Yakuza trafficked in weapons, but usually only as brokers. This smacked of desperation and impending violence.

If Koi were captured and identified, Nakane's rivals would also wonder if a turf grab were in play and possibly begin countermeasures, including a preemptive strike. They would know Koi was part of his organization. They would suspect he had a battle plan. The status quo could unravel with a speed Nakane couldn't rein in but he wasn't about to meet with rival bosses to discuss sharing the gold.

He'd not heard from Ino since he had arrived in France. He called him several times but got no response. His frustration grew into anger, but he was in a box. He couldn't send yet another member to France without raising a stir within the organization and questions from Hayato. Nakane had lost most of what could be termed affection for Hayato over the span of their relationship but Hayato was still his brother in yakuza, still well regarded and of substantial station within the organization. It would be imprudent to hint at any sense of discord in the higher ranks. That kind of sentiment is smelled like blood in the water and could bring in sharks looking to take over the top positions.

Rumors have a way of fulfilling their own destiny. Any suggestion of internal conflict along with suspicions of a new turf war had to be quelled. Nakane called his rivals and told them simply that Koi had gone rogue and he would take care of it. Whether they believed him or not didn't matter for the moment.

Hayato advised Nakane that Koi had contacted him from Europe and would be returning. Nakane would wait for her return to question what might have become of Ino. It occurred to Nakane that Ino had fallen into the hands of Le Sauvage. He began to consider plans for offering the lives of Koi and Ino in exchange for a split of the gold. Better to deal with Le Sauvage than begin a war that would bring in the police and his rivals. A war that would be *itachigokko*, impossible to win.

Chapter Sixteen

CHASTAIN TILTED HIS HEAD to speak to Ino, still bound behind his back and hanging naked by his chained feet in the old farm slop house. His Oni mask tattoo was streaked with blood. The full display of yakuza tattoos had the look of experimental art under the circumstances, though no one in that room felt like a gallery patron at the moment.

Orsu and his younger, half-wit brother had chopped off most of the toes on Ino's left foot with a hatchet and bound the foot with butcher paper and duct tape to stem the bleeding until Chastain arrived.

With the first message delivered, Ino's muscular arrogance waned even further as Orsu's brother pushed the dangling Ino over a gated corral occupied by two grey wolves captured by him and Orsu in the Haute Alpes and kept underfed. The animals had weakened but the taste of Ino's toes invigorated their appetites and they curled their lips and snapped at Ino when his body swung above their cage. They strained against the chains holding them to the back wall.

Chastain held up a hand for the brothers to stop. "What is your name?" asked Chastain.

"Ino."

"Good. Who are you?"

"Ino."

Chastain hit him in the ribs with a truncheon. "I know

your name, asshole. Who are you and why are you in France?"

"You don't know who you are dealing with. My organization is very powerful. We have people all ov—"

Chastain hit him again with the truncheon, this time in the balls. "Here is how it works. You answer my questions only. I don't need to hear any other bullshit."

Ino groaned and vomited, not much but enough to run down into his nose, making it difficult to breath. He gasped air and tried to clear his nose. Some of it ran into his eyes, burning them with stomach acids. His tomato-colored face had begun to swell from being upside down for so long.

Chastain didn't want to lose him without getting information about Koi. "Lower him down," Chastain said to Orsu. "Just on his back, leave his legs in the air."

Chastain gave him a few breaths, let his face return to a less roseate color then stood on his chest. Ino wheezed and struggled under the weight.

Orsu's brother peed in the corner into a waste drain, picked his nose and wiped it on his shirt, then shuffled back.

Before he passed out Chastain stepped off. Ino took in a gulp of air and Chastain kicked him in the ribs. Orsu slapped Ino's bloody toe stumps with the side of his hatchet. Hubert said, "Fuck your organization. You are here alone with us and the boss is just beginning to make your last day on earth very, very painful."

Ino tried to look stoic but Chastain saw the doubt in his eyes. He kneeled on his chest, squeezed Ino's throat and hammer-fisted him across the bridge of his nose, crunching the cartilage underneath. The blood trickled into Ino's ears. Orsu and his brother took turns kicking Ino up and down his legs. The overfed younger brother tired before Orsu stomped Ino's knee with his boot and hyper-extended it, tearing the ligaments. Ino screamed.

"Enough," Chastain said. The men backed off a step. The wolves growled louder at the display of alpha maleness and the smell of fresh blood. Chastain wiped his fist with a handkerchief. "Now, Monsieur Ino, as you can see we have an appetite for this sort of negotiation so spare yourself the inevitable and tell me why you are in France and why this skinny Japanese cunt keeps killing my men."

Ino found within himself a shred of warrior fortitude. He knew he would die this night, so he decided to die with dignity. No more screaming. What angered him more than the indignity of the beating was the idea that a woman had somehow been involved in his final night, so he decided to set these men loose on her by spilling what he knew. "I am a yakuza enforcer. I have been sent to shadow another enforcer named Koi. I was to report on her dealings here."

"Why was she sent here? Report to whom?"

"I only know she was to locate a man named Le Sauvage in Nice, but I was not told why. I assume you are him. You seem to be in charge."

Ino told Chastain all he knew about Koi. Out of pride, Ino told him his clan was based in Osaka but out of loyalty refused to divulge the names or ways to contact his oyabuns. Orsu's brother kicked him in the temple and knocked him out.

"Get this fat fucking moron out of my sight before I feed him to the wolves," Chastain said. Orsu flicked his hand and chased his brother out to watch the vehicles.

Ino came to but the damage had been done. His brain began to swell from internal bleeding. He sounded incoherent. Chastain tried to get one more answer from him. "Who is Koi? How do I find her? What is her real name? What's her name?"

Useless. Ino died on the slop house floor in a pool of body fluids. Chastain fired five rounds from Hubert's gun into the body and pointed the smoking muzzle at Orsu. "Burn his things and feed his body to the wolves and if I ever see your idiot brother anywhere near my organization again I'll kill you both."

Orsu nodded. He was tired of lugging his brother around anyway. He'd send him back to Corsica to work the family mule and feed the chickens, maybe send him money for wine and cigarettes.

In the car, Chastain told Hubert to have Mayko prepare to travel. He needed another body for the trip as well. He asked Hubert, "Do you trust Potente?"

"He's got combat experience and he's a good wheel-man," Hubert said.

"I didn't ask you that."

"I trust him, boss."

"Fine then. Tell Mayko to prep him. We're going to Osaka."

Chastain called Bouchet and advised him to arrange for access to cash and weapons. There would be other heavy equipment he would need but he would give him details later. "And, Bouchet, use your contacts and see what you can find out about a yakuza hit man named Ino, who he works for. I need to meet his boss."

Chastain noticed Hubert looking over at him. "Keep your eyes on the road," Chastain said.

"Heavy equipment? Are we going to war with five guys against yakuza?"

"That's not the heavy equipment we're going to need," Chastain said. "I'll tell you all about it on the flight. We're flying private, no prying ears."

"Private? Big investment in this job, eh?"

Chastain told him the payoff could be beyond anything they'd ever hauled in. Enough to retire.

Retire? "Boss, I have to ask you something. Please don't take offense."

"The girl," Chastain said. "You want to know why I want her alive?"

Hubert affirmed.

Chastain continued. "I'm fast running out of people to trust so listen and keep this conversation in this car for now. Almost thirty years ago when I was still a merchant seaman I met a woman in Osaka when we were laid up there for a month or so waiting on engine repairs. You know the story, young love makes us do impetuous things. She got pregnant and told her family I was the father and she wanted to marry me. Her father, a small-time yakuza member who tried to keep his family out of the business, was pissed off his daughter had gotten pregnant by an outsider, a gaijin they call it. He wanted her to get an abortion and she refused, so he cut her off. Meantime he wanted me dead for what I'd done to his family. She sent me away to save my life without ever telling me she was pregnant and I never returned. You know the rest."

123

"What has this got to do with this Koi girl? Is she...?" Hubert asked.

"The woman I was in love with is dying of cancer. She doesn't have much time left. I have a daughter by her. I've never seen her. But this Koi knows her. She protects her."

"So what, what's with the heavy equipment? You want to battle yakuza just to say hello to a girl you never met?"

"Of course not. The girl, my daughter, is also yakuza but she is in danger within her clan. I have promised her mother I will find her and get her out. It's her dying wish, I have to honor it."

"So, that's why you slipped out to Japan."

"Yes. I need Koi alive. Once I find my daughter I'll get rid of the little bitch for killing my men, but first things first. Oh, one more important thing I should mention. My daughter has tattoos like all the yakuza do. Hidden in her tattoos is a code to unlock a secret to a stash of gold, a lot of gold."

"This sounds, I mean, boss, no disrespect but tattoo clues and hidden gold? This isn't, I mean it doesn't sound, realistic."

"I have reason to believe it is," Chastain said, then proceeded to tell him the story of the Shōgun, his relation to Cazeneuve and the military cache.

"Holy shit," Hubert said. "Do you really want to retire if we find it? I mean, what you said on Spanky's boat about cleaner ways."

"I do, Hubert. I do."

"Okay, I'm in, all the way. We find Koi, get the information, find your daughter, kill Koi, of course, then— who knows? Maybe I retire as well."

Chastain half smiled. He couldn't imagine Hubert retiring but then, he never thought he'd be having this conversation. "The most important thing of all, and I will kill anyone who disobeys me—no one kills Koi but me and not until I am completely satisfied that we can find my daughter. I already have money. Gold won't make me feel any better about fucking up the last wish of this woman."

"Understood, boss."

"I need a drink," Chastain said.

"In the satchel, behind you on the floor. There is the bourbon you like."

"*Merci.*"

"Boss, what about the Filipinos?"

"Bouchet can make the arrangements. If we have to, Spanky can deliver the crates and they will make a deposit. If there is a problem, we hunt them down. They've been warned not to fuck around. If we can get back to Vietnam before the swap, we'll do it ourselves."

"They'll be back for more anyway," Hubert said. "These guys don't care if they die."

"Religion is good for our business. I understand that. What I don't understand is why this woman is after me? I know why I want her but what does this Koi want with us? That fucking moron Corsican—I should have shot him."

"That Ino guy said she was looking for you. Do you believe also that he didn't know why?"

"I can't be sure, but I think he didn't know. It can't be they just want our business. They would have tried to make a deal first. The yakuza are businessmen."

"Something personal?"

"Like what?" Chastain asked. "I haven't been near

Osaka in almost thirty years. What could she want with me? It doesn't make sense. Perhaps she wants to be sure my daughter is safe if we make a move on the gold, but she could have just sent a message somehow. I wish I knew."

"Did you tell anyone else about the gold?"

"Bouchet knows, but he owes me his life. He wouldn't speak of it. I just don't know, but we're going to find out. Thanks for the bourbon."

***

Back in downtown Nice, the Police Judiciaire were putting the last details on a raid they'd be conducting at a local residence in the hills near Château Bresson, at the home of the last family member Trudeau had called, his aunt Lara. They were advised to use extreme caution; the Japanese woman was considered armed and very dangerous and she might have two hostages.

Aunt Lara met the *"porcs capitalistes"* of the entry team with a twin blast from her bird gun. They returned fire, killing her. They found no one else in the home, no Peugeot. She died wearing her red beret.

Chapter Seventeen

SACHA DIDN'T FOLLOW his aunt's orders to go straight to the police. He couldn't muster the nerve to walk in and lie to them. He drove the outskirts of Nice in the early morning, afraid to get close to home but not knowing what else to do. He wouldn't involve his friends and he didn't want to call work and hear that he'd been fired.

Sacha had not been to his parents' home in five years since his father forbade it. Sacha told them he was gay over a lovely Christmas dinner, believing, though he feared otherwise, that his father would be in the Christmas spirit and give him the gift of acceptance. He gave him instead the gift of getting polluted on vodka, cursing his wife for raising his boy to be a *pédé* and throwing Sacha out of the house.

That night Sacha slept at a friend's and never returned. He still called his mother twice a month at her job as a billing clerk at an air-freight insurance company. She was the only person he could call right now. He told her he was in trouble.

She told him Tante Lara had been killed in a police raid. He said it was his fault. She said he needed to go to the police. He was too scared. She didn't understand.

He was at a public telephone when two police officers spotted the Peugeot and called for backup. They surrounded the car, pushed Sacha to the ground and turned in every direction, guns searching, looking wide-eyed for a killer within range of their pistols.

The phone dangled from the receiver. Sacha's mother called out to him, raising a commotion in her office. She fainted. Her boss hung up the receiver as an officer picked up the public phone. "*Allô? Bonjour?*" Silence.

"Where is she? You're safe with us, where is she?"

"She's not here, she's gone," Sacha cried out from under an officer. While pinned to the sidewalk, he thought of the aunt he'd put in danger, and the mess he was in, but none of it would have happened if Koi hadn't come into his life. He had started to like her but he would tell the police everything he knew.

The supervisor called for additional police to set up a perimeter and search for the Japanese killer hiding in a nearby store, perhaps with a new hostage. It took some time before Sacha could convince them she really had already left and that he had helped her escape.

"I know I'm going to jail for helping her, but I don't care anymore. I don't care." He tucked his face down into his knees in the back of a detective's car, put his arms over the back of his head and cried.

Sacha was brought to an interview room at the Judiciaire, where he was given a cheese sandwich, coffee and a window of opportunity to tell his side of the story. He told all he could remember, often going off on tangents about guitar players and Koi's confrontational sense of humor. He told them about his socialist aunt and her instant affection for Koi.

The detective who interviewed him saw Sacha as more of an accomplice than a hostage. He knew, or had reasonably established, that there was no way Sacha could have known Koi before the shootings yet he seemed reluctant to see Sacha purely as a victim. "Why did you bring her to your aunt's house? Did you not think this was dangerous for your aunt? You had seen this woman kill people."

"I thought it would be safe."

"Why would you want her to be safe?"

"I wanted us both to be safe. I thought if she felt secure then maybe I could befriend her and she wouldn't kill me."

"That makes sense, psychologically," the investigator from Interpol intervened. She saw her role as a sympathizer, to find that moment after an outlay of empathy where Sacha would see her as a helping hand, one whose help merely required the opening of one's heart. "It seems Monsieur Trudeau was in survival mode, no? On the exterior, it would appear he was aiding or abetting this, what did you say her name was, Koi? But Monsieur had to buy time. Time meant survival. Isn't that right, Monsieur Trudeau?"

"Yes. Now that you put it that way. Yes, there is something likable about her but at the same time, she is scary."

The Judiciaire detective felt outnumbered. He threw his pen on the desk and folded his arms.

"Tell me again about the tram. Why were you on it? Where were you going? What did you see? When did she come into your apartment? Did you let her in?"

After a half hour of this coaxing, she helped Sacha remember details he might have forgotten or let go because he presumed they weren't important: her phone calls from the bathroom, Osaka, her strange missing father, her emphasis on "the mission" and most critical, her insistence that she was running out of time.

"Why was there a timetable?"

Sacha offered nothing else that helped but began to feel relief. He tried to believe his cooperation would keep him out of prison. It might. He'd felt a tinge of guilt for not obeying Aunt Lara's admonition to tell the police Koi had gone to Canada. His fears of being caught in a lie overrode his familial ties.

The prosecutor was angry and a little embarrassed about his charges having killed the aunt and needed a scapegoat to deflect criticism from the press. He thought he might fault Sacha for not calling the authorities sooner, which would have avoided the unfortunate incident. No use. A mediocre defense attorney would eat it up. Sacha was a hostage, desperate and frazzled beyond logical thinking. Who could hold him accountable for the death of his favorite aunt? Hadn't he suffered enough?

The various law enforcement agencies convened and decided not to release Koi's name to the public. They feared if she thought her identity was known she would go into hiding. They wanted her to feel secure in her anonymity, perhaps make a casual mistake. They let it be known to their informants that the men who sent the shooters to Trudeau's apartment wanted a meet to clear the air, knowing, or hoping, she would take it as a challenge. She'd never get the word, but Chastain did. He could to use this information to trap her in Osaka.

***

Koi landed in Kansai Airport, tired but rejuvenated at

being on home turf, despite the looming threat from her own clan. She'd taken as much cash as she could off her bank card while in Prague, so her transactions wouldn't appear in Japan. She changed her Euros back into Yen, ate a quick meal of rice and *nimono* vegetables and caught a taxi. She booked a cheap hotel in the Sin-Imamiya district rather than go to her apartment, fearing her bosses had it under surveillance; fearing more that her fingerprints or DNA had turned up a link to her. She knew the television dramas exaggerated the abilities of law enforcement to catch criminals but she suspected they knew more about her than she could hope and they'd track her down before she finished her mission.

She did some dynamic stretches, showered and took a ninety-minute nap. She fell asleep sure of one thing, she'd lit a fire in camp Sauvage, now she just needed to figure out which man would lead the return assault.

Koi woke with her internal clock, then dressed to visit her mother. She thought about Hayato telling her that they were watching her. She had the taxi driver circle the hospital but didn't see any familiar faces or vehicles. As underworld figures go, yakuza tended toward the obvious, a reminder to everyone around them that they were to be feared and respected. Undercover surveillance wasn't their thing. Still, she wore her socialist scarf and hat with a light raincoat she'd bought at a thrift store by the hotel. She tried to walk with a wider, western gait as a final touch but looked more like a kung fu cowboy than an American millennial. She gave up in the elevator, which she rode two floors above her mother's room before taking the stairs down.

Koi's mother had weakened.

Cancer tavern. She lived on IV shots and morphine chasers. Her body looked like a tea stain on white sheets. Koi stood at the door and waited for someone who wasn't there to invite her in, someone who understood Koi's life and loved her anyway, someone like her mom used to be or one day, thirty years ago, had hoped to be.

She looked for permission from the revenant of the very best friend her mom never had, standing over her near-dead body, a polite smile and nod. "It's okay, come in. We've been waiting for you. She can hear you. Just talk, Emiko—say what's in your heart." But the mirage wouldn't take form, an inconvenient truth of reality.

She stepped in—the hallway behind her not as busy as she had remembered. The monitors beeped but in slow motion, quieter, deferential. She took her mother's hand and held back her tears. Her throat hurt.

"I knew you would come back to see me. The days go so quickly," her mother said. "They have given me so much pain medication I sleep the time away. I've asked them to cut it back but then I don't remember. I don't remember if I asked them. Have you eaten? I can get you something."

"Okaasan, I am fine. I ate before, *ookini*. How are you feeling? Can I get you some water?"

"I feel good, I think. I don't want to be here but it's peaceful. I miss my Chi-Chi so take care of her for me, promise?"

Chi-Chi. Her mother's cat had died five or six years earlier. Koi's mother slipped in and out of lucidity. The morphine and her body's degradation shared blame. Her mother would sing to the cat when she came home from work and they would fall asleep on the couch. She never lost her charm, even as she suffered the indignities of being a single mother and the looks of fear and disdain when she'd shop for food with her tattooed daughter. A prostitute or yakuza or both, it didn't matter. She always felt like an outcast but shielded her Emiko as best she knew how.

The nurse backed off the morphine but warned Koi she might see her mother in some pain. Talking would be easier in a short while. "Give her time."

Koi got tea from the family waiting room and checked the halls again for anyone who seemed out of place. No one did. She read some literature that talked of death and the celebration of life. Koi threw it on the table and went back in her mother's room.

"*Okaasan. Okaasan*, can you hear me?"

"I can hear you."

"Do you want something to eat? You're so thin. Do you want another blanket? Some tea?"

"I don't want anything else but for you to be safe and happy. I want you to live a long time. No more yakuza. You have to try."

"I have to ask you. Did a man come to visit you in the last few days, a *gaijin*?"

"Hmm, a *gaijin* by reputation but his heart is in Osaka."

"I don't understand."

"I sent him to look for you. It is important for you to meet him. He can help you. He wants to help you, Emiko, but you hide behind Koi."

"Help me with what?"

"A new life. He knows about the tattoos. His name is Tiago Chastain and he once loved a hopeful Osaka girl. He can find the gold and help you with your tattoos." She began to cough. Her body had just enough strength to expel air but she groaned in pain and her heartrate rose. The nurses came in.

"*Okaasan*, you're not making any sense. Why do I need help with my tattoos? Who is this man? Why was he here?"

"Perhaps you should let her rest," a nurse said, more sternly than Koi appreciated.

"Perhaps you should get away from my mother while you can still walk."

The nurses were accustomed to grieving relatives becoming emotional but the venom in Koi's voice sent them out at a quick step.

"Please speak to me. I don't understand."

"Let him find you, Emiko. Yakuza is a life of misery and suffering." She yelled at a lash of pain across her back. The monitors rallied. The nurses took over. Koi backed out of the room.

Her time would end soon.

She had to fix this thing and get back to say goodbye, to give her something hopeful to take with her.

The rain had kicked up as she left the hospital. She heard a familiar voice call to her from behind a pillar. He wore a dark trench, his face obscured by cigarette smoke.

"Oyabun," she said. "It is you who watches my mother?"

"Always impertinent. No, Koi. I am watching you."

"I don't need watching."

"Perhaps you should listen before you put up walls. The rain is cold, why don't we sit in my car?"

"I rather enjoy the rain, and this jacket is warm." She wrapped her arms at the waist and grabbed the handle of her tanto knife, letting her senses tell her if someone else was near. Hayato would not strike but he might give a signal.

"Leave your tanto where it is, Koi. If I wanted you dead I'd have had it done already. Now listen."

She didn't move. *An old trick, stay alert.*

He went on. "You know I am loyal to the clan and yakuza, but I am also a man of my word. When I sponsored you, I brought you in under my wingspan. That included my protection. I cannot reveal private conversations, but I can ask you questions as a test of your yakuza knowledge, to make sure you have been studying."

Her chest rose and fell with her breathing. Her ears attuned to the near space within striking distance. She listened with her heart and expended little energy responding, only a nod before he asked, "Do you know what is *itachigokko*?"

"A game impossible to win," she said.

"*Hai.* Do you know the term, *mizushobai*?"

"Our business. Our profession has a high risk of failure."

"Hai." He nodded. "Some things are not only high risk by nature, but by design."

"I understand," she said. *Suicide mission.*

"Perhaps you should cut and run while you still have your life. *Akirameruna.*"

"I never give up." She could see he knew it to be true.

He hunched his shoulders to the rain and walked toward the waiting Mercedes, as the man holding his door open looked at Koi, looked right through her.

"*Chotto*," she said.

Hayato looked back towards her.

"I thought the Chinese were the inscrutable ones."

Hayato said, "They got it from us."

Hayato confirmed what she had suspected; she was set up to fail. This was a shit sandwich and she was the filling. She had Le Sauvage's guns after her from one side and Nakane waiting to drop the hammer from the other. *Watch the shadows.*

Yakuza was betraying her; she would beat them to it. She had to find a way to get a message to Le Sauvage that could save his life and perhaps they could share the gold. She thought he probably wanted her dead more than anything else, but he was also a gangster like her. Gangsters make deals if they can save face and make money. It's always about the money.

The only way she could think to reach Le Sauvage was the marina manager. He'd sent her into a buzz saw before. He knew the right people. If she got lucky he would be at the marina though dawn hadn't quite broken. She called.

"You missed me, *geretsuna otoko*. I'm still alive." She spat the words after recognizing his voice. She couldn't remember the French word for cocksucker.

"What? Who is this?"

"You sent me to get killed at the condominiums. I

survived. Now, coming for you. But first, business."

"Hey, I didn't mean for— I was just looking out for my friend. Leave me out of this," he said.

"Too late, you're in it. Want to live? Listen carefully. Get a message to your friends. I have information they need that will save their asses and make them rich, but to get it, they must find me in the motherland. Got it, asshole?"

"I got it."

"Wait, one more thing. What size blade do you take?"

"Huh?"

"In your throat." She clicked off.

Chapter Eighteen

CHASTAIN BROODED over several bourbons on the private jet. While Hubert read, the others ate and slept. He knew he could only keep these men from exacting revenge against Koi for so long. Their own pride demanded it along with the reputation of the group. There was one tack that might ensure her safety; he could have her arrested, but then he feared an attack from yakuza. If they were any good, they'd have a man on the inside. It would be easy. Unless...

Chastain stepped into the small kitchen and called the Osaka police, the Taisho Station nearest the apartments where Mikie had said Koi lived. He routed the call through a mobile operator in the Philippines so the number would appear restricted. He claimed to be Inspector Sacha from Interpol and demanded to speak to an English or French-speaking supervisor immediately, Priority Zenith—a meaningless term. He gave them information from a resource intercept that a twenty-eight-year-old Japanese female, commonly known as Koi, had recently entered their jurisdiction from France, via surreptitious conduits. This woman was wanted for questioning in a series of murders connected to a high-level international espionage and illicit weapons operation. Her testimony would be critical in breaking a ruthless band of gunrunners and terrorists led by the infamous Le Sauvage. They had intel that this Sauvage would be en route to meet with Koi in

Thailand. Local authorities were being asked to cooperate in this delicate investigation by finding and detaining said Koi for possible extradition, pending negotiations through diplomatic channels. She was to be considered armed and extremely dangerous but was to be taken alive. If she were to be killed or incapacitated to such a degree that her testimony became inaccessible, serious implications could arise.

"The appropriate paperwork is in my hands. I will deliver it personally to your supervisors. Any questions? No? *Au revoir.*" *That should shake a few trees.*

***

The supervisor called his commanding officer who authorized him to form a team to develop a profile of possible suspects and effect an apprehension. It didn't take long. The alias file for yakuza members is extensive, if not comical: Pelican, Mister Sunday, Algebra and Ancient Mother; they ran an eclectic gamut. The police had her address, a small apartment near the brothels on Tobita-Shinchi, where she could keep an eye on business and visit her mother who lived just a kilometer north.

Koi's black Hayabusa sat in the garage as if being patient for her return. She'd had it finished in a monochromatic matte black, black wheels and no chrome, adding only a twisting orange koi fish, custom painted on the tank and the *hiragana* character for strength stitched in orange onto the leather seat. The men told her she couldn't handle a bike with so much power. Everything she did proved them wrong about her and they both respected and hated her for it. When she prowled the streets, checking on the business in the brothels and occasionally softening up a client who got rough with one of the girls, she rode as slowly as possible, to demonstrate her control of the machine. Once in a while, she would open it up just to make an exit.

The police knew her but were never able to arrest her for anything serious. No one dared rat on her. When the police stopped her she never had any weapons on her but always an arsenal of alibis. They rarely pressed her. Like so many they thought, as a woman, she didn't know as much as the men. Cops and gangsters always underestimated her. Many feared her and most misunderstood her, but one thing they agreed upon; she could strike you before you knew it was coming. An enforcer in her prime with relentless training habits and a gut full of anger all made her a formidable foe. A woman like Koi was destined to sprout legends. It was rumored she could see a flea on the ass of a *kishu ken* at fifty meters and tell you if it was coming or going. Her skill with a Beretta required only a double-tap to solve her most sticky problems.

She walked home from the subway. She knew she couldn't stay the night but needed some clothes, cash and an inventory of whatever weapons and resources she might have available. The rain stopped and the evening cooled. *Thirteen days left in the morning.* Her senses alerted as she got closer. She got that cold feeling in her belly. The streets seemed different, a little quieter. The people of the streets knew—they always know when something is about to go down. Someone either had a beating coming or the *marubo* were going to make an arrest of a clan member. Tension.

141

Countdown to Osaka

Koi cinched her backpack and jumped a fence behind a closed restaurant under renovation, then climbed onto the roof. She made her way through the two-story neighborhood from the backside of the rooftops, quietly loping low, trying not to silhouette herself against the brothel lights from the streets. She jumped to a utility pole and across an alley to a small iron foundry that had an overhead front sign she could hide behind to scan her apartment building and surrounding area. The cops had posted a car on each end of the street, no doubt there would be more cops on the front side. A light flicked off in her place where they had searched for her then moved to the exterior perimeter to lie in wait. She couldn't make her way around to the front without being seen but one officer stood by the rear entry at the garages where her Hayabusa waited inside. He shifted his position and looked up and down the street, double-checked his equipment and watch several times.

He's nervous.

She slid down the clay leader of the old building and stood in the shadow until the right moment. He looked at his watch again, turned to once again make certain her garage door lock hadn't been touched since the last time he checked. She darted across the street with the sound of a passing truck on the next block. Before he could reach for his radio she had her tanto at his throat and her fingernails under his eyeballs. He'd just earned this assignment after three years of downtown foot patrol in the mall, but he knew enough not to flinch or call out. She asked why they wanted her.

He told her they were there to arrest her.

"On what charge?"

"No charges, a warrant, for Interpol."

"Interpol? You're lying," she said.

"No, no I'm not. At the briefing, they told us an Inspector Sacha would be arriving from Nice in France and we were to take you alive for him. That's all I know."

"No, it isn't." She pressed the edge of the blade through a few layers of skin.

"Okay stop, look, they said you were involved or connected to an international ring, maybe guns and espionage. And murders, wanted for murders. That's all I know, I swear but they said most important we were to keep you alive."

It hit her. *Inspector Sacha. He'd sent a message. He wanted a meeting and he was going to do it right in the fucking police station. He's got huge balls.*

Koi figured he wanted to know two things: why she hunted him and what she knew about the gold. It was her chance to cut a deal with him. He'd probably laugh at her, but she had no options.

"Listen closely, *marubo*. I need some time but because you have a nice face I'm going to let you live."

He nodded, waited for his instructions.

"You see that alley across the street behind me? Get on your radio and tell them you saw me and you are chasing me down the alley. Run into one of the brothels and up the stairs. They'll follow you and you say you lost me. Got it? I give you my word I will turn myself in. I'll even say you scared me when you chased me because you looked so brave." She looked into his eyes. "My word of honor. Go now."

"Unit four, I see her. She is running east through the alley toward the brothels. Cut her off, she is still running..."

She flew up the fire escape and into her apartment. The officer guarding her door ran down the stairs to the front. She pulled a go-bag from under her bed, a large brown duffel. She grabbed some cash from behind her toilet and the keys to the motorcycle. She took a quick look around but whatever she thought she might do there escaped her. It'd have to wait anyway. She climbed out the window and down to the garage. She fishtailed the Hayabusa with the tires smoking and cranked the throttle, shifting gears as it screamed into the night.

Within three hours she would walk in the front door of the Taisho Station wearing biker boots, urban-camo pants and a black tank top, announce her presence to the room and "any motherfuckers" looking for her, spread her stance and put her hands behind her head.

Fifteen minutes after that, Nakane picked up his phone and received a message that Koi had put herself in police custody. Hayato and Nakane had discussed her desire to leave yakuza and that sometimes those in her state might go to the police to inform on the clan activities in exchange for police protection, not to mention immunity. Turning herself in to the police confirmed his suspicion. He now believed her to be an informant. He called Hayato. "The timetable just ended. I want her dead. I want her dead, now."

Hayato began to let go of the idea that he could help her. She had become a rat.

Koi had thought this through. Criminal groups fear

subversion from within. She knew serving herself up to the law would bring the wrath of Nakane. She hoped his anger would spawn a competition with Le Sauvage to see who killed her first. She might slip out during the inevitable macho mêlée or be shredded between them. The *kiken* hit an extreme level, but the rewards and revenge outweighed the peril.

***

Chastain's jet landed at Kansai Airport in Osaka Bay. Hubert assigned two men, Ayoub the Tunisian Beard and Picard, another wayward Legionnaire with a quick wit and a faster draw with a throwing-knife, to oversee the refueling, double-check their equipment and secure the immediate area. Both men had combat and prison experience, occupational imperatives in Chastain's world.

Mayko stayed on board to protect Fournier so he could focus on double-checking the readiness of the aircraft. Mayko had spent some time with loyalist militias fighting the Russians in the east, but most of his street smarts he developed selling meth and collecting debts for the Ukrainian mafia. The coal mines offered him no hope, but he had become very good at breaking things. Mayko tried to make small talk, grumbling to Fournier about Koi, but the pilot said nothing. Mayko gave up and drank coffee.

Hubert and Bouchet had changed into dark suits along with Chastain. Potente, in a black turtleneck and tactical pants, would drive. They'd hired a boat to take them along a water route to the police station. They all strapped on the same Glock-19 pistols, 9mm with fifteen-round magazines, 'a good suit gun' Hubert had said in the past. Two extra magazines in rear pouches. Bouchet carried a leather

145

envelope with the bogus arrest papers prepared on the fly from their best document forger. They contained errors but nothing that would be discovered until they were long gone with Koi.

The local police commander could lose some face when the deception was finally understood. He could possibly endure a suspension, but the worst outlook was that the prefecture was rid of another yakuza enforcer, one fewer thug in their midst. His bosses would not divulge to Interpol that she had ever been in their custody. The commander would assign detectives to look for Koi. Another show.

Merci beaucoup.

In the bay, the tankers and cargo vessels floated over the Sauvage crew like steel Godzillas. The harbor water pelted the windshield of the hired boat. Chastain looked at the skyline and thought about how many ways it had changed since he docked there long ago.

"This port reminds me a little of Rotterdam, uh, boss? Smaller but..." Bouchet said.

Chastain pointed around without commenting aloud, looking preoccupied or not really sure. Hubert asked what they were talking about.

"On the jet," Bouchet said. "You asked why I was so loyal to the boss when I could sit behind a desk and steal with my computer. It was at the port in Rotterdam almost twenty-five years ago, making a deal for some rocket parts we had procured to sell to a Chinese extra-military group. Apparently, they didn't want to pay our rate and thought they could take the parts along with our lives. Our crew

Joe Hefferon

lost two men and almost a third, me. I caught a round in the shoulder and fell into the bay. Tiago could have saved his own ass and fled but he jumped into the water and pulled me to safety. They were shooting at us from the starboard rails. I'm not much of a swimmer. They don't teach that in accounting." He laughed.

"The boss risked his own life to save mine that night. Since then we make a good team. He has *des billes* for ten men and I can count cash with my eyes closed in a hurricane."

Hubert scoffed at the boast, but Bouchet's story had colored in another layer in the mental picture of his leader.

Chastain didn't hear them talking. Osaka Bay evoked an ebb of memories that time and survival had pushed into forbidden stores, where a young and cocky seafarer, named Tiago after his uncle, would walk hand in hand with Mikie along the pier at the Nanko Fishing Gardens and eat a fried lunch from paper sacks in the salt air of the bay, and sometimes the wind picked up from the Kiisuido Strait tossing her hair across her face and he would move it behind her ear so she could eat. Someone else's life now, watching a movie he couldn't quite remember, starring faces he no longer recognized. The once and happy Chastain, a man himself once saved by a young woman, now dying, who for a flash of time pulled him with shy smiles from a life in the black mist of the underworld.

The men climbed the wharf ladder and got into a waiting black Range Rover, rented at a premium, the keys set on the driver's-side front tire as instructed, retrieved by Potente. He waited outside Taisho Station while Chastain and Bouchet presented the papers to the commander.

147

Hubert watched the officers and the door, his hands crossed at his waist. He neither returned bows nor smiled at anyone, same as his partners—all business.

Bouchet signed for the body while Chastain was led down the hall to Koi's holding cell. Two guards armed with machine pistols watched wide-eyed at the drama acting out before them. Chastain stood at her cell door with his hands behind his back and stared at her, expressionless.

She stood and came to him, folded her arms and whispered in French. "I got your message. So let's talk."

Chastain didn't respond. He couldn't believe this woman-child had not only found him but taken out half his crew. He wanted to reach through the bars and choke her purple, to feel the life squeeze from under the crush of his hand and into the ethers, out to sea.

She sensed it but stayed firm. He saw milliseconds of fear in her expression. A staring contest between two people who either killed out of obligation or necessity but never for thrill—a defendant's mitigation.

Chastain, by gesture, asked the guards to leave them be. Koi stepped back out of reach.

"I'm not going to kill you here," he said.

"You're not going to kill me at all."

"Oh, and why is that?"

"Because," she said. "I have information that will help you find this gold you seek and keep you alive in the process. But you have to do a favor for me."

"I'm not inclined to do you any favors."

"The yakuza want you dead. They have people everywhere in this country. They know you want to steal the gold but they don't know how you plan to do it. They don't even know where it is."

"Why are you so disloyal?"

"They used me to get to you. They held something very personal over my head as leverage. They don't respect me in their hearts because I am a woman. Screw them all."

"Well, I am certainly not going to tell you any of my plans, unless it's right before I end your short life."

As they looked at one another, neither noticed she had inherited his nose. Perhaps it was what made Trudeau remark about her not looking, "as Japanese." The higher bridge stood out among her cohorts, giving her, by Japanese perspective, an exotic look, something else to marvel about her.

"I am no fool," she said, "although I have acted foolish in the past. I have a letter ready to go to Interpol. It is with a trusted friend. If I turn up dead in the near future the letter will be sent identifying you as the notorious Le Sauvage." Koi needed to buy time to find a way out. She didn't know how she could help Chastain, but she intended to stick around long enough to figure it out.

"Your threat is not only improbable but insulting. I don't need any more reasons to want you dead."

"Think what you want but we can help each other."

He said they would not talk there any longer. Walls listened. He called the officers back and offered them his handcuffs; 'remove her from the cell', the nod said.

The commander offered to take the inspector's team back to their boat with a marked police escort. "For extra security."

"That won't be necessary. We are professionals, we don't need a parade. But thank you and a job well done.

We will inform you when the prosecution is completed and appropriate letters of commendation will be sent from our offices in Paris."

The commander swelled.

***

Chastain had said yakuza would have a man on the inside. They did, sort of. Her name was Chisato, the commander's secretary. She followed in the shadow of an ancient tradition of ninja women, the *kunoichi*, acting as career undercover spies within the enemy castle. No tattoos for this yakuza sister. She notified Nakane of the inspector's transport of Koi and the location of their boat. Nakane called and had Hayato rally men. "She will not leave this island alive."

Chapter Nineteen

KOI SAID, "Before you stuff me in the back of this truck, there's a duffel bag behind that dumpster. I stashed it earlier. You will need it, trust me."

"We don't trust you, whore," Hubert said. "What do you think, boss?"

Chastain wondered if information about Emiko might be in the bag. "Grab it before we stand here too long. It isn't a bomb, that's not how she is going to kill herself."

Chastain rode shotgun while Koi sat in the back between Bouchet and Hubert, both staring her down, still disbelieving. She looked forward at nothing.

Potente tried to sneak a peek at her in the mirror but had to focus on driving. He pulled into the roadway and spurted through traffic toward the waterfront.

Koi spoke to Chastain. "You told the commander where you were going. Do you know what that means?"

Chastain ignored her. Bouchet suggested she didn't aggravate his boss any further. Koi ignored him. "It means they will tell my people where I am going. They have someone on the inside, the secretary is from my clan. She'll call my kumichō. He will order a hit."

Chastain sighed. "Do you really think they will try to break you out of custody? You aren't that important to them."

Hubert smirked at her. She could feel the look.

"No, I don't think that. They want me dead. I've

already told them I want out of yakuza, not that it's any of your business why. Once I turned myself into the police station I signed my own death warrant. They will think I am a weasel."

"So what?" Hubert asked.

"So, this is what. They think I'm about to leave the country with fucking Interpol. They don't know it's a trick. They will send men to the port to take me out. They won't care who gets in their way. This is personal and I know too much about them. Their survival as a group depends on stopping me."

Bouchet commented on her plea. "She might be right."

Chastain agreed, but said they had no choice. They didn't have the time to dick around in unfamiliar Osaka turf. The police would eventually figure out the warrants were forged. They had time but not much. He told Potente to drive faster and get them to the port. Once they boarded the boat they could get to the airport before the local gorillas. "Call ahead to Mayko. Alert The Beard and Picard. Let them know to get the jet started. We're coming in hot."

"Maybe you will beat them there, but they are coming."

"Shut up, whore, no one is asking you."

"You will need me. I'm the best fighter they have. Uncuff me and let me at my bag."

Hubert's face reddened. "Are you out of your mind? You are our prisoner. I'm not letting you free and giving you weapons. Shut the fuck up now. Enough."

"You will see. Fools," she said.

Chastain reached back and slapped her across the face. "Drive, Potente. Let's see some driving, now."

As they pulled into the broad container yard, Koi spotted a familiar vehicle. "Uncuff me now. They are here already. There, to the left, the black Audi."

As she said it, two shots hit the right front fender on Chastain's side. "Crossfire," he said. "Fucking amateurs."

A third vehicle launched through the yard gates and at their back end. Koi struggled with the cuffs. Potente dropped the windows. Bouchet fired out the window at the chase car. It swerved and resumed the chase.

"To the right, Potente, pull behind that container. We'll bail and you draw their fire after we get set up. Conserve ammo." He turned to Koi. "You get your ass down. I need you alive."

The men bailed. As soon as Koi got room in the back seat she slipped the cuffs under her rump and pulled her feet through. Potente yelled for her to get down as he raced for further cover. Bullets sang past the Range Rover but just one round hit the rear bumper. Potente pulled behind another steel container and before he set up Koi was out of the vehicle dragging her duffel with her. As she ran she managed to rip one hand free of the cuffs, tearing off strips of skin with it. Potente ran after her but caught a round in the knee. He dropped and crawled back to cover, cursing her and his doomed career more than his wound.

Chastain's men felt safer with the water behind them, an unlikely angle for an attack. Hubert had climbed up Bouchet's back and lay prone on top of the container. From a higher vantage, he killed the two yakuza to his left.

Potente yelled into his handheld radio. "She slipped the cuffs, she's running east. She's getting away."

Chastain bellowed and punched the steel.

Hubert tracked her. "No, boss, she's not running away, she's flanking them. God fucking damn, she's fast."

Koi slid onto her hip behind a forklift and opened her bag. She reached under a sweatshirt and belted on her katana. She pulled out a Beretta M9 and flicked off the safety, dropping two extra mags in her cargo pockets as she ran behind the chase car. Hubert could see her in the yard lights. "Hold your fire," he said. "Hold for my signal, she's at the chase car."

Her former comrades had stopped the car and opened the doors, firing through the open windows using the doors as cover. Koi drew her katana, ran up the back of the car in two steps and came down on the driver, decapitating him. She squatted and pulled a custom *shuriken* from her belt, threw it across the inside of the cabin into the other gangster's carotid. He stood up in shock and Hubert took him out with a shot to the temple.

Koi was already moving to the next car. They spotted her and turned their attention from Chastain's men. "Fire now," Hubert said. "Cover her, she's moving." The yakuza fired at both targets in a frenzy. Koi charged harder.

"Hold your fire, hold your fire." Chastain had moved left to a better angle. He watched her drop to a knee and place two double-tapped nine-millimeter rounds into their chests. She scanned the area, listened, waited.

As she waited, Nakane stepped from Hayato's Mercedes where they'd been watching the action from the shadow of a container crane. He drew his Korriphila 45 and took a shaky aim at Koi. She turned and spotted him, saw he had the drop on her. She closed her eyes.

One shot popped. She felt no pain. *I'm not hit.* Koi thought Nakane had missed and rolled to her right to return fire from her knees. She looked for her target. Nakane lay still on his face, blood pooling under his head. The tires smoked and Hayato's Mercedes raced off the pier and into the night. *Dōmo arigatōgo, Hayato san. Dōmo arigatōgo.*

Hubert and Chastain gave an all clear together. Potente limped back to the vehicle and drove to his team. He stayed in the truck to wrap his wound. Koi scooped her duffel. She was about to put the katana in the bag when Chastain yanked her to the ground and grabbed her throat.

"We no longer have time to play games with you."

"I told you that you needed me."

"I need no one."

"Let me up and let's get out of here. You can thank me later."

"You fucking cocky bitch. You don't get it. I need only one thing from you and I want it now. Whether I kill you quickly or slowly will depend on your answer."

"Fuck you."

He squeezed. She lurched.

Hubert thought about pulling him off her, blaming this on the adrenalin rush of battle. "Boss, maybe you sh—"

Chastain shook her. "Tell me now. Tell me where Emiko is." He eased off, just enough so she could speak.

"Are you drunk? I thought I smelled booze on you at the station. I am Emiko, you *baka chaun.*"

"What do you mean?"

"My name is Emiko. Koi is my yakuza name."

He let go and rose to his feet. His anger dropped off his face, his jaw slackened.

"What?" she asked. "What's with that look?" She stood up and rubbed her neck. The men looked back and forth from Koi to the boss.

"Your mother," he said gently.

"Leave my mother out of this." She grabbed at her katana. Hubert and Bouchet pointed their weapons.

"It's too late, I am afraid, to leave her out of this. Maybe too late for many things."

"Never." She drew her katana and set her stance. The men teased at their triggers.

"Your mother—her name is Aiko, but…" he bounced his head back and forth, "I used to call her Mikie."

"Oh no, don't say it." She dropped her guard.

"Yes, Emiko. I am Tiago Chastain. I am your father."

She dropped her katana to her side. "You motherfucker." She drew the words out.

Hubert and Bouchet looked at one another, knowing their plan to avenge their crew members had just vaporized before them.

"I was hoping for a friendlier greeting."

"Friendly? Now I have to kill you." Raising it up again.

"I disagree." He held up his palms. "Allow me to explain."

"Explain nothing. You are already dead to me, at least I can finally close this myself."

"I'm here to protect you from yakuza, to gain your freedom, for your mother."

"Lies. You abandoned my mother. Your own people tried to kill me. You brought the police to my door. You

156

brought me here where I could have died."

"It's a complicated plan, not without risks."

She screamed in frustration and slowly regained composure as she slid the blade into its scabbard. "You have three minutes before I attack you and your boys kill me."

"Guys, go help Potente, who by the way is lucky I don't shoot him in his other leg. I'll be right there."

"Sure, boss, but one thing—the local police will have heard about all this shooting. They'll be..."

"Go."

Chastain tried to explain to Koi why he ended up in Osaka again after so long. He didn't know how to begin. "It started with a letter. She wrote to me about you. I went to see her. I made a promise. I must keep it." He told her she held the secret to the gold written in the tattoos on her back.

She looked at him in disbelief and confusion, emotions ripping around inside her like hornets.

He didn't care about the gold, only keeping one promise to Mikie.

The Osaka police sirens wailed.

"Boss, we must go, now," Bouchet said.

Chastain grabbed her by the shoulder and said, "We'll talk on the jet. Let's go. Now. If we beat them to the airport we're good. Move."

Hubert launched the hobbled Potente into the rear bed and drove them to the dock. Once everyone jumped out he detonated a small incendiary device in the truck. The fire would destroy the prints and DNA residue. With such strict gun laws in Japan, a shootout at a commercial port would rate a higher priority than a burning car.

The men clambered down the gangway. Koi jumped onto the railing and slid past them on the balls of her feet.

"Where did you learn that move?" asked Chastain.

"Used to skateboard as a kid. Let's go."

Hubert gave the hired boat captain a fistful of cash and sent him packing as Chastain and the others boarded.

Five police vehicles arrived seconds later, surveyed the scene, saw the carnage and split off looking for the surviving combatants. One spotted the boat and called to the others, too late to get shots off. They hollered into their radios for more units to head to the airport and get harbor cops in the water. Only one fast-boat made it in but the harbor cops had no idea who they were chasing, or why.

An Osaka lieutenant tried to direct them from the pier but their radios were on different frequencies. Bouchet spotted the tail. "Boss, we have one harbor police unit on us."

"Do you like cops?" Chastain asked Koi.

"What do you think?"

"Dump 'em, Hubert."

Hubert swung the boat round towards the oncoming police. They pulled their weapons but didn't shoot when they saw a woman. They veered as Hubert cut the throttle and swung the boat's tail at the cops, heaving water on them and knocking one into the bay. As the cops struggled to pull in their officer, Hubert opened it up to the airport.

The Tunisian Beard signaled from the tarmac with his light. Picard took a rear-guard spot behind the jet. The boat smashed into the dock, almost flipping over. Potente held the boat against the bulkhead while they jumped off, then The Beard helped him up and ran with him to the jet. Picard was the last to board as Fournier whined the engines. The airport cops surrounded the wrong private plane. Chastain's crew took off.

When Mayko saw her, he lunged at her. "You fucking bitch, I'll kill you."

Chastain intercepted him and swept him back against a seat. He said, "Do not ever touch her. Ever. You understand? You go near her and I'll cut your heart out."

"Boss, I..." Mayko let it go. He went for the bar.

Her eyes followed Mayko, then back to the others, who said nothing. "Well, Dad. You sure know how to show a girl a good time."

Chastain froze. The men laughed at the release of tension. Drinks were agreed upon and a Chastain toast followed. Chastain bowed for a moment then told them he took responsibility for the deaths of the men in Nice. He said if he'd been more forthright sooner the confrontations might never have happened. He regretted it and they shouldn't hold on to anger at Koi. She was being a good soldier and trying to help her mother. "I'd call that honorable if it didn't happen to be against us."

They mumbled in agreement.

"Gentlemen, in case you haven't quite let this sink in, may I present to you, Miss Emiko Konno, my uh, my daughter." He took a swig of bourbon.

Hubert topped off his glass.

"She looks a little like me, no?"

"Well," Bouchet said. "She has your balls, so to speak."

"Enough of this back-slapping. Where are we going?" she asked.

He said, "We are going to refuel in Taiwan, grab some food and then off to Vietnam. We have a place there we can discuss getting out of the arms business. Gentlemen— we are going to embark on a final mission as a team, one that will make all our troubles worth it, one that will allow us all to retire into luxury, or whatever ill-conceived plans you may be hiding. We are going to steal us a lot of gold, a shit fucking big pile of Japanese gold."

They all raised their glasses for the idea, but not the specifics. What was Chastain referring to?

Hubert said they might be marked now. No doubt the Japanese had their pictures from the CCTV. They would notify Interpol. They could all be finished.

"I don't think so," said Koi. "They will be embarrassed that they let a bourbon-swilling gunrunner and a yakuza woman outsmart them."

Chastain looked at his glass.

She said, "They'll handle it internally and not reveal the incident to Interpol. They would not want the Kinki Regional Police Bureau to find out. It would be a scandal."

Picard asked, "The kinky police?"

She turned to him. "Not kinky. Kin-ki. They are a higher authority than the local police. The Osaka police will tell the press the shooting was another yakuza turf war that will be investigated with the utmost priority. Actually, one is about to start so..." She looked back at Chastain. "Oh and thanks for the slap in the face."

Potente said nothing the whole time. He just stared at Koi.

Chastain shrugged and said, "Let's hope you're right. Meantime we have people in Saigon who will alert us if those types of inquiries make it across the desks of the Saigon police."

Koi said, "Your people? I had a run-in with a few of them. If a guy with a stump shows up with a guy holding his nuts, I won't say I'm impressed with your people."

He set his drink down and turned to Koi. "Speaking of 'your people', you know a guy named Ino?"

"An enforcer. Call him Snow Leopard. Why?"

"He met a rather abrupt end on a farm outside Nice. He said he was shadowing you."

"Not surprising. Didn't trust me, that's all. Fine with me. Nobody will miss him and the man who sent him just got killed at the port."

Chastain looked at Koi. She stared back at him. It was her turn to gulp her drink. Chastain led her back by the kitchen. The men busied themselves with reliving the firefight and attending to Potente's gunshot wound, more superficial than originally thought. Ayoub The Beard handled it.

Chastain handed her a wet towel to wrap her scraped hand. "Emiko. I know you are concerned for your mother right now. I am too. We can call her. Let her know you are not hurt and that we are together. But you can't go back there just now."

Koi's eyes watered.

"We can hope she will stabilize for a time. Hearing that we are together might give her hope."

"No, it won't. It will allow her to die."

Her wisdom stunned him. "Perhaps. I can't know. Why don't you call the hospital? This phone here is secure."

"Thank you," she said. "I will in a minute."

"Then I'll leave you alone. Tell her I miss her, would you?"

"I will." And for the first time in a dozen years, Koi allowed Emiko to cry. She pulled the wet towel off her hand and covered her eyes as she closed herself in the bathroom. She let out a deep sob. She pulled in a deep breath and called her mother, who said she'd never felt more at peace.

"Tell Tiago I miss him too. I will see him again."

Koi needed to compose herself, get back to business, to not appear fragile in front of her new crew. She called Hayato and thanked him for her life. He told her he would support her. He ran the clan now. Her honor would be protected.

Hayato expected his life-saving gesture to Koi would be rewarded with a substantial split of the gold, perhaps half. It was, after all, the least she could do for her fellow yakuza. Now that Koi and the French seemed to be together she could find out what Le Sauvage knew about the treasure. The fact that Hayato went along with sending her on a suicide mission in the first place was lost in his delirium over his share of the gold and what that kind of money would do for his clan. He could congratulate himself for saving Koi's life while seizing the opportunity to execute Nakane in a *coup de foudre* that struck him as he drove to the docks. Gold has a way of bringing out the opportunist in a man. He would claim Nakane died because his attack on Koi was emotional, poorly planned and not well executed, resulting in the deaths of many fine brothers. Best he was gone. He would take the reins and look to strike a deal with Chastain. He'd show them how to run an organization. If other members suspected he had killed Nakane, they would fear him even more.

Koi assured him she would do what she could, gratitude-wise, but Koi had no intention of helping Hayato or the organization she'd grown to hate. His efforts to save her were as self-serving as they were honorable. They only deepened the disgust she felt at a lifestyle that had brought heartache to her mother and no pleasure to her as Emiko, only as Koi.

Chapter Twenty

My mother asked me to tell you that. What does that mean?"

Chastain smiled. "It means she has my hat."

Koi gave up. "When are we landing? I need a shower."

"Twenty minutes. There will be two cars waiting for us. You and me and Bouchet will stay in one hotel. The others will stay in a private house belonging to a woman we call Miss Elizabeth. She is a party member and not to be trusted, but her eyes are easily averted by the sight of cash. She is well paid."

"What's the plan?"

Chastain told her the biggest obstacle would be finding someone who could decipher the poems on the art hanging in the museum.

"I can try."

"It's not the literal translation that is significant. We need to understand its meaning through the message on your back and other encrypted writings I have from a distant relative who fought with the Shōgun. I think separately they mean nothing but together we will have our answer. When we arrive, we will, I will, take pictures of your tattoos."

"No, Potente the gimp can do it."

"Why him?"

"Because you, Dad, or do you prefer, Poppa, are not seeing me half naked."

"Why don't you call me Chastain for now? And Potente it is, but watch him. He's young and well, he can be aggressive."

She laughed. "So paternal. I can handle myself." She thought a moment. "Clues to gold? I always wondered why the tattoo artist smiled the way he did after working on me. I thought it was because he liked my ass."

"Fine, just drop it. We are trying to find a Japanese historical scholar who can make sense of, or at least suggest some possible meanings for the poems and how they relate to your tattoos and the map. Right now, we don't know if the tattoos are part of the coded poems or hidden messages for what I have from the French military. When we land, we will get settled, meet to eat a relaxed dinner and begin this mission first thing in the morning."

"*Nan demo.*" She waved her hand. "Meantime I'll work on a literal translation of the poems and then try to make sense of it. Do you have the painting?"

"I have these picture, here, on my phone. The actual painting is like an architectural drawing, all in black except for pink trees."

"Probably cherry blossoms."

"Perhaps yes, your mother said so. It is on display in the National Museum of Art, in Osaka. Let's hope we don't have to steal it. We don't want to push our luck."

"That's understandable. Let me have the phone."

Hubert let out a laugh.

"What is so funny?" asked Chastain.

"Irony."

"Irony? Koi?"

"Yes, boss. The yakuza sent her to locate you and find

out information from you but they sent the information they needed, *to you*. Irony." He seemed happy with himself.

"Like I said, keep reading Flaubert."

***

Potente took the photos standing at the half-open bathroom door with Koi inside the small toilet.

She turned her back to him and lifted her shirt. "Don't stare at my ass too long."

"I'm not staring, oh *mein Gott*, I've never seen a woman with so many tattoos."

"Well I have to take my pants off so you can see the ones on my legs. Don't be nervous, I'll leave my underwear on."

"I'm not nervous. Stop saying it."

"I only said it once."

"Okay, well. What about, you know, in the front?"

She pulled up her pants, turned, took off her shirt, then turned to him with her hands over her breasts. "Do the best you can, German, I'm not moving my hands."

Potente began to sweat. "Okay, I'm done." He closed the door and handed the phone back to Chastain without looking him in the eye, then went straight for the bar.

The team spent the next hour making small talk and explaining their military backgrounds to Koi, how they met and why they worked so well together.

Koi explained what she could about yakuza culture and why this gold was so important to their pride as well as their business interests.

The dinner conversation remained loose and focused more on the tasty food and crappy drinks than the

167

mission. They enjoyed it for a while.

Potente asked why they sent just one woman to find a man like his boss.

"I am expendable."

***

The team met the following morning in Chastain's room. The events of Osaka Bay and for that matter, Nice, were behind them. A new mission had to be planned. Emotions had no seat at this table.

Chastain said, "From what I could gather from the diary and other writings of my ancestor, the gold probably did not move far from Osaka Castle, if it moved at all. The conflict was still ongoing at the time and the movement of that amount of gold would have been very difficult to do secretly. The gold was likely buried in or around the castle grounds, which has a considerably large footprint, some fifteen acres."

"Much of the original castle was destroyed and rebuilt," Koi said.

"It may be in private property?" Hubert asked.

"No," said Chastain. "Just the castle burned, but the grounds are still part of the castle complex, complete with high ramparts and moats. Before we go off on too many side roads—Bouchet, how much do you estimate the gold to be worth?"

"Depends on exchange rates. Intrinsic value versus historical and other factors, but I'd say well over one hundred million US. So, the usual twenty percent for the organization and eighty split between the operators. That's ninety million split twelve ways? Nice haul. I could retire on that."

"Wow," Potente said. His mind wandered to what he might buy with it all. Mayko lost himself in similar thoughts.

"Well if this is our last job as a team," Chastain said. "There is no reason for the organization to take a cut. Even split all around."

That roused them even more.

Chastain reminded them that the intrinsic value, the historical value and what they could actually unload it for, were often quite different. Better to consider the value in the weight of the gold and not bother trying to imagine what sentimental premium to add. Bouchet agreed. He estimated each operator clearing well over seven million, enough to think about getting out while they were still alive.

Hubert suggested they might be better off finding it and selling the location for a substantial price, but no one could agree on who would be most interested. Their contacts could always use the funds and would love to have a treasure at a substantial discount, but most didn't have the wherewithal to retrieve the gold themselves. Their clients were warlords and rebels, not master thieves. Picard thought maybe they could hire someone to retrieve it for them. Chastain dismissed that as foolhardy.

Mayko asked, "How can they be certain the gold is all there?"

"That would be their problem, no?" asked Picard.

"Yes," Bouchet said. "But the cost and risk of retrieving it would be factored into what they would be willing to pay for it."

"We would have to prove it was there first," Bouchet

said. "No one is going to pay so many millions for a fairy tale."

"You guys are operators," said Koi. "Let's not sell what we don't even have yet. I don't give up that easily. There may be a way to have it all."

Chastain told her it was just business talk. All ideas were welcome. It had to be done.

Koi's mind raced from Hong Kong to Saigon, to France, her dopey Sacha and finally to California. With the kind of money she and Chastain would pocket from this job, anything was possible.

Chastain didn't need the money. He needed to feel better about setting her up so she wouldn't have to look over her shoulder. Chastain broke her reverie. "Did you translate the poems?"

"Yes. It's not one poem but two separate ones. They seem unrelated to one another but of course that may be part of the riddle. Maybe my tattoos can help. The Japanese characters on my back are written in both *katagana* and *hiragana*."

"What does that mean?" asked Hubert.

"It's just different types of Japanese writing characters. Mine are randomly placed and traditional. They speak of courage, mercy, honor, loyalty and similar ideals from Bushido, the Samurai code. Nothing that matches up to the poems on the map."

Chastain raised a finger. "I should say, we only need to concern ourselves with your most recent tattoos, not your whole body."

"That would be the phoenix on my upper back. I had colors and details added over a year ago, but why?"

"I forgot. Your mother mentioned it."

"So, I didn't have to..." She looked over at Potente, who looked at his feet.

Chastain apologized.

The others laughed, then looked at the boss, who wasn't smiling.

Bouchet broke the awkward silence. "Well, what do the poems say?"

She recovered. "They are written in an old style. Probably goes back many centuries." She looked around at the men. "Don't laugh. I read poetry and old verses before bed. I sometimes have trouble relaxing so I can sleep. *Nan demo.* It's impossible for me to tell if they are original for the painting or from older verses written who knows when.

The first one says...
Fuyu sugite
Haru ki ni kerashi
shirotae no
i hosu tefu
ama no Tenpō zan"

Bouchet said, "Sounds nice, but what does it mean?"

"I will translate.
So winter ends and spring comes
Now white robes hang to dry
On Mount Tenpō

"I'm still working on the second one. It is old language so I must be careful."

Potente sat rapt in Koi's reading, then had a thought. He said, "Has anyone else wondered how much this amount of gold would weigh? I mean, looking around it seems I'd be doing a lot of the carrying."

"Bouchet?" asked Chastain. "Good question."

"The short answer is, it depends. But if it's anything close to what the history says about the amount, we're talking a metric tonne, possibly more, too much for even our German friend. Transport will be a problem, depending on where we find it and how it's stored."

"Unless we can move it in stages," the Tunisian said.

"Maybe. Stages take time. It also means that at the time of the war it would have been impossible to move from the castle, if that's where it was stored, without someone noticing. They'd have had to move it on wagons to a train. They would have been discovered. If it was there at the time the castle fell, it still is, unless it was moved some time after, perhaps during the transition of power."

"What if it was discovered by the emperor's people?" asked Hubert.

Chastain said that likely wasn't the case. "If the Emperor's people found it, there would be a record of the discovery, or a celebration. We're wasting time speculating."

"We need *der Sachkenner*," said Potente.

"What is that?"

"An expert."

Chapter Twenty-One

HUBERT HAD SPENT SOME TIME in Thailand running underground lottery operations for mostly European customers and a few Aussie expats. Business was crack until he had to escape Bangkok after breaking the neck of the leader of a prostitution ring who favored underage girls. Hubert caught him having sex with one in the men's room of a nightclub.

As Hubert told it, he was sitting at the bar, enjoying a beer, collecting vigs and taking numbers when he spotted the pimp walk the girl into the men's room. She didn't look too keen on tagging along. Hubert let the image sink in of what might be transpiring then followed in behind them. The pimp hadn't even closed the stall door, just bent her over the toilet. The girl had blood dripping down her legs and she cried for him to stop. The pimp slapped her across the head to be quiet or else to make her cry more—it didn't matter. Hubert flew into a rage at the sight.

Hubert beat him with a leaded-leather police slapper he carried in his waistband. The girl stumbled to the sink and tried to wash herself, crying and choking on her own snot. Hubert lifted the scrawny pimp over his shoulder and slammed him like a Mexican wrestler, snapping his neck on the glazed brick floor. He gave the girl a wad of cash and had a friend take her home.

The killing of a pimp might not have generally caused much of a stir among the authorities, but this one was connected to a well-placed army officer, who ordered a hunt for Hubert's arrest. A murder conviction would have gotten Hubert propped up before a firing squad, perhaps one last Gauloises before the salvo. Prior to fleeing the country, he arranged to get the girl to a convent. He never heard from her again.

What Hubert also remembered about Bangkok was a plump rummy named Boris Nethercote who taught Asian language history at Chulalongkorn University but may have been fired for coming to class drunk on local Sang Som, his overnight drink of choice. The afternoons he mostly washed away with Tiger Beer. He knew the professor to wade through degenerate waters, but what Hubert didn't know was how to get in touch with him.

"Tell me about him," said Bouchet.

Hubert told him he remembered the man always smelled of cigars and booze and that he sweated a lot. "He could raise the humidity of an air-conditioned room." He said Boris was from north London and told various stories of unrequited love that drove him to both Thailand and drink.

"But," Hubert said. "He was very sharp. The booze made him go off on sidebar conversations all the time, going on about rugby, Immanuel Kant, the Americans—a guy named William Buckley—and the unique blackness of a Thai-woman's eyes. 'They're like liquid coal', he would say, 'a carbon in an undiscovered state'. He gambled often, but for a drunk was pretty lucky with the lottery. He claimed to have a system. We made most of our money off guys with systems."

"But you don't know how to get in touch with him?"

"Maybe." Hubert made a short list of possible hangouts and fellow degenerates, then made a few calls that didn't pan out.

Bouchet came through for Hubert. He called his contacts, the sheer number of which repeatedly astonished his legion of gunrunners. Soon they located a bar owner who gave them an address where Boris could be found sleeping off the night-before with his regular squeeze, a grade-school teacher and part-time hostess named Phueng who lived on Charoen Krung Road by the hospital in Chinatown.

Hubert's standing arrest warrant asserted the need for Chastain to send anyone but Hubert to Thailand. He chose Bouchet and Picard to make the man an offer.

Meantime, the crew worked on the poems and Koi's tattoos, trying to make some sense of them. Mayko put himself in charge of food, in part because it afforded him time out of the way of Koi, who he still saw as the enemy. His penchant for vengeance could put him in a bad way with the boss if he didn't control himself.

Koi called her mother but could only speak to her for a few seconds before a nurse said she was too weak to talk. Frustration began to overwhelm her thoughts. She thought about calling Hayato but decided to let him wait.

***

Thailand hung on the receding edge of its rainy season, when the air is still as hot and sticky as a taffy on the chew or the inside of a bee's ass. Bangkok offered choices. You can't dress for the weather; you can only endure it. Bouchet and Picard sat on plastic chairs outside a café drinking Singha beer under a Pinky Go Go sign. Guy behind them holding a poster in a wooden frame advertising a fish massage. A young Thai chick in a nearly sheer yellow dress hemmed halfway up her thighs, stood leaning on one red heel and holding an oversize red umbrella for shade, her thighs in silhouette against the afternoon sun.

"Ketchup and eggs," Picard said.

Bouchet asked if he was hungry.

Picard poked his lips toward her and said, "No. The girl in red and yellow. Makes me think of ketchup and eggs. You think she's wearing underwear?"

"Would you?"

"I wouldn't wear that dress."

"Thank you. Let's drink these and find that apartment of his before dark. I want to see the layout."

"You expecting trouble from a drunk professor?" Picard asked.

"No. Habit. Some habits are good to keep, my robust friend."

"Yes, especially in this heat." Neither man spoke for several minutes. Picard picked at the wet label of the beer bottle. "The beer tastes good, no?"

"What's on your mind?" Bouchet asked.

"This thing. The gold. Do you think it's really there?"

"I try not to get hopeful about much. However, from what I've read it makes sense, maybe not in the huge amount that is estimated but if it's there, it will be a nice job. Very nice."

Picard continued to pick at the label. "Nice."

"But," Bouchet said. "That is not what is on your mind,

no?"

"No. It's the boss, this girl. The boss is acting..."

"*Différent?*"

"*Oui, différent.* He is very protective of this girl. He watches her every move."

"It is his daughter."

"Ahh, he doesn't know her."

"Maybe he wants to," Bouchet said. The girl in the yellow dress had moved on. A woman offered to change money for them. A policeman walked by, trying to look tough. Picard stared him off. Bouchet said, "Sometimes a man comes to a reckoning. He doesn't know when it will come or if it will ever come. He may never think of such things. But I think, for Chastain, it has come. He owes something to her, but he is not sure what. He loved that woman in Osaka. She never left his heart, all these years. Perhaps he sees her again in Koi. He needs to make it better."

"Make what better?"

"The accounting of his life. He'll do what he can for this *fougueuse assassin* and maybe he can feel better about something. Anything."

"He has money and influence. He is feared."

"Such things are fleeting. They have no standing with a man looking back at his life from a regretful future."

"Let's go find a professor."

"*Oui, allons-y.*"

***

It had been a tiring day. Everything Bouchet learned about Boris had been accurate except for the address, a dead end. The information Hubert provided had aged. The men couldn't find any of Hubert's old contacts. They were a transient bunch. They moved in and out of sunlight and dark bars; strip joints and sidewalk eateries. They found a store that sold Gauloises. Picard thought that was a good sign.

After nearly three hours of walking in the heat—eating, drinking, buying drinks for locals and slipping cash to dancers, they found one of Boris's colleagues in the Bookshop Bar, drinking only a seltzer water with a lime. He had liked Boris, and sent along his good wishes which the men later neglected to pass on.

Bouchet and Picard found Boris Nethercote at home in an unexpected state of sobriety, though his plans for the evening would soon change that condition. He lived on the second floor of a fifteen-story high-rise. His apartment afforded him some afternoon comfort in the shade of a Bodhi tree that reached for the third floor.

Bouchet affected the accent of a Parisian anglophile which put Boris at ease upon introduction, during which Bouchet expressed their affiliation with the French Consulate.

"We understand you used to deal with a man named Hubert. Some years ago in the lottery trade."

"I remember him, forbidding chap. If this is about money I assure you I owe him nothing. He may, in fact, owe me. Where is he?"

"That is immaterial, but he sends a message. He needs your expertise and he is willing to pay for it."

"Expertise in what?"

"Not gambling or drinking," said Picard.

Boris said, "Well if volume determines expertise then I

am guilty as charged but, as you say, immaterial. He wants me? Why?"

"Monsieur Hubert and his associates, us included, are in need of your sundry skills in Asian languages, poetry and history, particularly the Japanese Shōgunate."

"Interesting. I'm listening. I'm also rather surprised to learn Hubert is back in Thailand."

"He isn't. He is in Vietnam," Picard said.

"Vietnam? Surely you can find an Asian scholar in, where, Hanoi, Saigon? Why go through the trouble of locating me?"

"Monsieur Hubert is working on a project that certain authorities would deem inappropriate—perhaps feeling that it might be better suited for government officials to oversee."

Boris nodded as though he were playing an adagio in his head. He said, "I am beginning to understand why he chose me. But in terms of vigor, I'll admit to an unrestrained drinking style and I've been a bit player in the numbers. Been out of sorts lately. I hardly think I'm up to the task of international intrigue. I have my teaching, I ha—"

"He'll pay you twenty-five thousand, US," Picard said. "For a few days' work."

The offer struck Boris into a trance. Bouchet noticed. "If you've encountered any recent financial setbacks I'd not be surprised if a sudden influx of hard cash would get you out of a squeeze, eh, my dear fellow?"

"It would indeed," Boris said. "When does he need me? I have a few things to get in order first."

Picard had run out of politeness. He gave Boris the

same look he'd just given the tough-guy Thai cop. "We leave at oh-seven-hundred. Be ready and be sober." Picard told Bouchet he would wait outside. He popped a Gauloises from the pack.

Bouchet said, "My friend is a good man, a solid soldier. He does have a short stock of patience though, so I recommend when you're around him that you make faster decisions, *comprenez vous*?"

Boris cleared his throat. "Yes, *oui*. I'll be ready and likely sober, but I can't promise I'll stay that way. I work better when I'm, relaxed."

"So it is. I'll assume your passport is current. We'll be downstairs at seven. Pack light. *Au revoir, Monsieur.*"

"Goodbye, sir."

And within just a few unexpected minutes, Boris saw through the haze of his lifestyle. In a moment of retrospective clarity, he was a boy at Eton again, about to play in a rugby match at that distant school, an away game with unknown rules.

The idea that he would fly to another country with strange men to meet a known criminal and further to involve himself in an extra-governmental affair would be harder to explain to his girlfriend than he had anticipated. She said she hoped he got himself killed, so she didn't have to smell his malted perspiration any more. "You sweat too much for one man. It's not natural."

It pleased him that she got angry about his leaving. He smiled, knowing he would return bearing a lovely gift.

***

At 08:15 the next morning, Boris and Chastain's men

Joe Hefferon

flew a charter to Saigon, bribed enough familiar people to bypass customs and took a taxi to the hotel.

Picard made a quick introduction around the crew and showed Boris to his room where he could set down his bag.

Koi hated him on sight. "Ech, he looks like a big diaper."

"He is a bit rumpled," Bouchet said. "But in his defense, we didn't give him much notice."

"Or choice," Picard said.

"I hope he's smarter than he looks. Why is he wet?"

"He sweats some."

"It's the equator," Hubert said. "Let's give him a shot. This is the best we have right now."

Boris returned from his room. Hubert shook his hand and said, "How are you, you old scholar?"

"I am well, Hubert. You look fit as ever."

Chastain greeted him after being introduced as Jacob. but one said, "We just call him boss."

Chastain had Mayko arrange for trays of food to be delivered, along with a large pot of coffee and a plastic bin filled with ice over cans of Tiger beer.

Boris wiped his brow.

"Help yourself to food," Chastain said.

Boris grabbed a beer, looked at everyone staring at him and picked up a spring roll. He toasted the room with the appetizer and opened his beer. "So, gentlemen, and Miss, how can I be of service to you?"

Chastain said they needed him for a specific purpose, which he would explain later. He said, "We have most of the information we need to execute a plan except for a couple of small but critical elements. To proceed, we must

181

unravel a riddle hidden in two poems which are part of a large painting."

"I see."

"And their relationship to symbols in tattoos which are on Koi's back." They'd planned to tell Boris the minimum he needed to help. "However, once translated and further understood, the information they reveal could possibly help us decode an encrypted message written in French over a century ago. But don't concern yourself with that for now."

Boris's face showed his surprise at the odd task ahead but he didn't remark about it. He asked how the riddle affected their interests.

Bouchet said, "We are under contract to find some relatively valuable relics. It's possible they could sell in the open market at a higher price than the officials who would claim them would be willing to pay. We believe the poems are linked to images in the tattoos. Together with the coded message, they reveal the location of these rare items."

"French consulate and antiquities dealers?" Boris let out a proper English belly laugh, punctuated by a belch, for which he apologized. Koi liked him a little less. "Well I was intrigued before but now I'm captivated. Always loved a good mystery. Perhaps there's a succession, in which one clue helps to unravel the next. Where is the painting."

"We don't have it," Chastain said. "It's in a museum in Osaka. It is too large to move, practically, without possibly damaging it. We have only these photographs. Koi translated them but the literal translations don't seem to help."

"Well let's have a look." Boris sat, swigged his beer and stared at them, switched eyeglasses and stared some more. Took notes. Switched between the photos and Koi's translations. Grunted. Drank more beer.

The crew milled about, picking at the food and going out on the balcony to smoke.

Chastain pulled Bouchet into the kitchen. He wondered if Boris was playing them for fools. "He says nothing. He just stares and moves papers around. He's putting on a show."

Bouchet said, "He's an Englishman with a Russian name and an Irish sense of caprice. Probably studied theater. He has a flair for the dramatic." Chastain said nothing. Bouchet said, "Look, he's a smart man in a foreign country surrounded by men who can't hide their jagged edges. He knows if he screws with us we'll cut him into pieces. I think he's actually having fun. Let's be patient. When do we show him the diary and other papers?"

"Not yet. And I don't like being exposed like this. We are all clumped together. One hand grenade could get us all. Have Picard, Potente and The Beard go back to their hotel and relax. Especially Mayko, he needs to let go of being pissed off and get on with this business before us now. And where is Fournier?"

"Where he always is, checking over the plane."

"Tell him to join the others. We'll call them when we need them."

"As you wish."

"And tell them to surveil the area first and report back if they see anything, anything at all that's suspicious."

"*Oui.*"

Chastain stayed in the kitchen and plotted out the tying-off of loose ends, the Abu Sayyaf transfer, small arms for FLEC in Angola, RPGs for Aguilas Negras in Colombia, the Chechen money issue and what to do about Marin, still undoubtedly in police custody unless his lawyer had gotten him out. His girlfriend had gotten word to Picard that his wounds were all recoverable.

Although they'd mishandled the pick-up of Koi in Nice, Marin had just taken bullets and endured an interrogation for the organization and Chastain would not leave him out of the payoff. Marin wouldn't make the trip east, but could be useful in Nice. He'd get a piece.

Hours passed—Bouchet on the balcony speaking with contacts about particular equipment, Hubert nodding off on an armchair.

Chastain came into the living room to find Koi and Boris poring over the images. She'd gotten over the aroma of fresh sweat. She liked the way he used his unlit cigar as a prop. She admired the alacrity with which he moved from English to Japanese and back, how he drew her into the history of the poetry. Chastain watched her listen to Boris, listened to her questions. *She would have been a good student at university*, he thought.

Boris said, "If you don't mind my saying, you have many tattoos. Why are we looking at just these?"

"The last ones I had done. The information we have is that the clues were placed during these last works."

"I see, but I don't see. I don't see anything in these tattoos that you haven't already discussed. Let's focus on the poems for now."

Koi said, "They sound a little like poems I have read before, old ones, I think may have been changed."

"That's a strong possibility, girded by the historical perspective, but it's also possible the writer was even more clever than we realize and they are indeed not only true but an homage. Perhaps they are merely old poems with minor adjustments to fit the needs of those who were trying to hide, whatever it is."

"This one," she said. *"Fuyu sugite. Haru ki ni kerashi.* Winter ends and spring comes."

"Spring represents many things, such as fertility and rebirth, change of some kind perhaps, but it's too vague. There's context I'm missing here."

Chastain admitted to himself that too much secrecy was hurting the cause. Boris couldn't help him without the context. He said, "This painting was given to the emperor after he regained power from the Shōgun following the fall of Osaka Castle. The treasure belonged to the Shōgun and was hidden away after the defeat. We are trying to determine where the relics might be. Does that help?"

"Of course, it helps a great deal." Boris filled in the historical details. "Osaka Castle fell in the winter of 1868. The poem is about a turn of events taking place as spring arrives. This would seem to be the clarion call to marshal the troops loyal to the Shōgun, the arrival of spring, but why?"

Koi continued, *"Haru ki ni kerashi, shirotae no, i hosu tefu.* Now white robes hang to dry. Japanese is a beautiful language but doesn't sound so pretty in English."

"What does your Japanese gut tell you, Koi? Trust

yourself," said Boris.

"The Shōgun's warriors traveled under white banners."

"Ahh, good, so yes, a clarion to the warriors. 'Spring is our time,' no?"

"And Mount Tenpō is close to Osaka Castle."

"An attack from the mountain?"

Chastain asked, "How do we know it was a call for that particular spring and not one some years further down the road?"

"Doubtful. It's unlikely they thought this would carry on more than a hundred days, let alone years. They only wanted a chance to regroup. They were optimistic, only thinking a few months out. They could have been making battle plans in the mountains."

Chastain said, "I think not. The relics, according to what I've read, were to be sold *after* the Shōgun was back in power to raise money to rebuild his power base. I think this is more metaphorical, coming down from the mountain in white says it is the will of something greater, a deity perhaps. The French are Catholics so they could have influenced this thinking."

Bouchet and Hubert nodded in agreement.

Boris added a thought. "This painting is large, yes? Perhaps by its sheer size it was intended as a statement, a fuck-you, to put it bluntly."

"Perhaps a gesture of conciliation?" asked Hubert.

"That's the other extreme," Boris said. "My experience is that the truth is in the middle, or in this case, the muddle." He tended to laugh at his own jokes. "I think we can do a broad database search of pieces of each poem, line by line, or narrow it to individual words if we have to. This way we may stumble on lines of an old poem that will help us know if we're singing in the right church."

Koi mumbled that she should have done it sooner and quickly scrolled through her phone and laptop. She slapped the table.

"Got it?"

"Found this poem written by Empress Jito, centuries before. She died in the year 702. Almost identical poem, must be where they got it."

"Excellent but at this point I think, irrelevant. Probably just referencing the Empress as a poke in the eye. It's a distraction, but what it means is that a timetable may be relevant, perhaps for the last assault or—"

Chastain cut him off. "Celestial coordinates, the mark of spring, the equinox. If it's a clue to a location then the only reason to mention seasonal changes would be because of the location of the sun, moon, etcetera for navigational coordinates. We can back-test it against almanac data so we would know which constellations and planets would have been visible in the spring/summer changeover of 1869."

"Agreed," Bouchet said, "I think it's simply saying, the time to track the coordinates is in the spring and we can do that now with computer models. Would you agree, Boris?"

"Yes, indeed."

Hubert asked if the Japanese had this type of knowledge back then.

"They did," said Chastain. "There was a naval training school and the French navy had been using the ports in

Countdown to Osaka

Tokyo for decades. They knew."

Boris said, "As the castle fell, the story goes that the Shōgun escaped by boat at night. He'd have gotten nowhere without celestial navigation."

Chastain said, "The sun is over the equator twice a year, at the autumn and spring equinox, it is vertically above it. Knowing this angle helps to find the latitude." Chastain sketched it on the white board for the group. "The meridian must be established first, but once it is, the height of the sun above the horizon as it crosses your meridian, when subtracted from 90 degrees, is our latitude. But what is the meridian?"

"Maybe in the second poem," said Koi.

太陽の光線
Taiyou no kousen

奪取され、黙殺される
Hakudatsusare mokusatsusareru

そして沢山の背嚢で運ばれる
Soshite takusan no hainou de hakobareru

そこで私は
Sokode watashi wa

親愛なる貴方を
Shinainaru anata wo

もう一度

Joe Hefferon

Mouichido

賞賛することができるのか
Shousansurukotoga dekirunoka

Taiyou no kousen
Hakudatsusare mokusatsusareru
Soshite takusan no hainou de hakobareru
Sokode watashi wa
Shinainaru anata wo
Mouichido

"It translates, 'Even flaming fire can be snatched up, smothered and carried in a case,' but here is used the word, *hainou* which is a kind of backpack. It finishes, 'Why then can't I meet my dead lord again?'"

"What could the flaming fire refer to?" asked Hubert.

Boris said, "Maybe the relics you seek are, in the vernacular of thieves and cops, hot or stolen. Perhaps the bags refer to what we might call black bags, for thieves."

"No," said Koi. "This word, *hainou*, it means a backpack but it's the kind carried by soldiers in those times." She looked at her mobile. "Reading here—would have only been carried by military."

Hubert suggested that the flaming fire was not hot but golden, like the sun. "The Flaubert is working."

"Ahh, brilliant."

"Why are you smiling like that, Boris?" asked Bouchet.

"A few things are coming back to me, no doubt because of the passion with which this young lady reads

189

her poetry. This poem is rather well known."

"He is right, but with a small change."

"Yes. It's written about the death of the Emperor, uh, begins with a T?"

"Temmu."

"That's it. This would seem to corroborate what you said, boss, about this being after the battle. The poems would appear on the painting as nothing more than an homage to former emperors, but it is in fact a statement about the death of imperial rule and may not have anything at all to do with coordinates."

Hubert said, "Then we are back to square one."

"Not so fast," said Chastain. He looked at Boris. "Without getting into too much detail, we have an encrypted message that we'll be decoding at some point, perhaps with your help, but it doesn't appear that the poems will help us, so maybe the tattoos. Any ideas?"

Boris said, "The second poem is a call to action, establishing a vision of the troops carrying the treasure, your relics, on their backs to the Shōgun. What's missing is the link from the exhortation on the parchment to the relics, not only the exact location of the relics, but the fact that the knowledge of that location exists. What I mean is, certain people must know that the treasure is buried and they must relay that information to the troops. That link is missing. I don't see anything on these tattoos that helps."

Chastain said, "Unless the tattoos are just more symbolism like the poems, they won't help us on their own, but they could help with this." He lifted his leather bag and took his time setting it on the table as he gathered his thoughts. He didn't want to reveal his identity to Boris by telling him he was related to Cazeneuve. "How I came into possession of these documents is irrelevant, but here they are. Boris, among the French soldiers who were at the castle when it fell was a corporal named Cazeneuve. He not only kept a diary of his time fighting with the Shōgun but eventually, after the Shōgunate fell, was contracted by the Imperial army to train their horses. It kept him fed and gained him access to the enemy camp. He kept notes and wrote poems. Among his papers is an encoded message. Perhaps the tattoos can help us break that code."

"As they say, only one way to find out."

Bouchet said it had bothered him that whatever message was held or communicated among Cazeneuve's Japanese counterparts would not likely be in pictures. "Cazeneuve would have been working with Japanese soldiers who spoke French. How did their part in this get reduced to tattoos?"

"It could simply be that it was orally communicated," said Hubert. "Among a carefully selected group of confidants, the message might have been that Cazeneuve had the precise location memorialized in his private papers. Let's hope the tattoos aren't also useless. We've wasted a lot of time on this already."

"Oral messaging is risky. Mistakes are made too easily, especially dealing with a force comprising two very different languages. Lost in translation would mean a fortune is lost," said Bouchet.

Koi said, "Maybe he was going to hide them within the castle or put them on another work of art inside the castle walls. Maybe the tattoo matches something inside. We'd have to get in there and look around."

"An excellent point, young lady, but for now we have only your skin to work with, so let's have a look at this coded message."

Chastain slipped it out from the bag and placed it on the table. Everyone just stared at it. Boris asked if there was something stronger to drink besides beer.

***

Back at Interpol, investigators completed their interviews with Sacha Trudeau and every witness the local police had. They had located the hotel where she'd stayed, dusted it for prints and found nothing tying her to anyone in France.

Interpol investigators checked all new information and the weapons recovered at the scenes of the shootings against their illicit arms management system, known as iARMS, along with cross-referencing weapons and recovered cartridges and bullets against ballistics and firearms databases, the Ballistic Information Network and Firearms Reference Table.

They located the manufacturers and dates of shipment, but Chastain's complex digital spider trails and shell companies made it almost impossible to determine the final destinations of either the weapons or the ammunition. They'd keep working, but Le Sauvage remained several steps ahead.

They replicated her grainy CCTV image from the marina and took to doing old-fashioned gumshoe work, looking for any witnesses who had seen her there or knew why she was in the area before going to the condos. The marina manager said he didn't remember seeing anyone who looked like her.

"We've found another CCTV image that appears to show you talking to her. Are you certain you don't remember anything?"

"I talk to people all day long. Unless they are boat owners or their guests, they are usually just tourists looking for directions. I can't remember all of them. I am sorry."

He had already moved Tanguy's catamaran to another marina.

Chapter Twenty-Two

"A CODED MESSAGE requires a code book to decipher," said Boris. "This is just meaningless numbers without it."

"True," said Bouchet.

Hubert said, "Another thing missing here would be some way to alert the right people that they would receive a message when the time is right, say, after the big battle to take back the castle. It would have to be in both French and Japanese."

"I think I have that," Chastain said. "Yes. I have what I think is a draft of such a letter. There is much crossed out and rewritten. He must have sent the edited version on. It's sort of a 'stay well and keep your powder dry' note to the loyalists. In his diary, he mentions he needs to tell the men to look for a gift to the emperor."

Bouchet asked an obvious question. "If Cazeneuve had a message for his comrades, he would have written it down in both languages or sent two letters. Maybe that missing letter to the Japanese eventually got translated down to tattoos." Boris looked up at Chastain. "Do you have it?"

"I do." Chastain produced it from his leather satchel. "I dismissed this when I first read it. I thought he was just a bad poet, but now I see there may be significance."

Chastain read the French poem.

"Quand je vois votre chrysanthème doux
Écrasé par l'oiseau flamboyant
Je deviens chaud, comme au début de la saison

Countdown to Osaka

Et priez pour que vous ne reveniez jamais
Dans les murs
Le soleil, le soleil doré
Va débloquer un destin une fois enterré
Par étoiles nos chiffres
À venir bientôt

Bouchet said he could understand why the boss was unimpressed. Boris asked for a translation.
Chastain said, "It means...
When I see your sweet chrysanthemum flower
Crushed in the grip of the flaming bird
I become warm, as in the early season
And pray for you never to return
Within the walls
The sun, the golden sun,
Will unlock a destiny once buried.
By stars our numbers
Arriving soon."

Boris asked if there was a picture of her entire back, particularly the image of the phoenix.
"But there are no characters on the phoenix," she said.
"But there may be clues. Is this the best photograph you have of the phoenix? The wings are a bit blurred."
Chastain said they were the only photos and glanced over at Koi.
"Hang on a minute," Koi said. She went into the bathroom and returned shirtless with a towel held over her chest, her yoga pants pushed low on her hips. Boris popped the tab on

196

a beer. Chastain's lips tightened. She turned and flipped her hair off her back onto her shoulder. Even under the intricate tattoos, her muscles were evident.

She said, "The chrysanthemum flower is an imperial symbol. I never thought of it as crushed before but saved from the fire around the phoenix. There, in the claw, you see? I'm shocked I've been walking around with this."

"But it does indeed look quite crushed." Boris focused in on the phoenix, stepped closer, adjusting his glasses. He pointed at it with his cigar. "What do you make of these?" he said to Chastain and the others. "Look closer. These small discs about the wings..."

"They are stars," Koi said.

Bouchet provided help from a small flashlight.

"They are, generally, in this type of art, but although they appear randomly placed... Hmm, what if they were put here in this order on purpose? They may represent numbers; you see? Six, seven, six, five."

"I see," said Bouchet. "This is interesting. What could they represent?"

Hubert sat upright. "Maybe the combination to a safe."

Chastain suggested an address, the numbers on her back and the street name in the coded message. He dismissed it as soon as he heard it out loud, then he said, "A sequence, yes? Put them together, what do we have? Six-seven-six-five ."

Boris raised a finger in agreement. "My thoughts exactly, perhaps related to your code matrices or one matrix in particular. Let's take a few pictures here and let the young lady get dressed."

Koi went into the bathroom and as soon as she reemerged

went straight for the food. She asked what they should do now and why no one else was hungry. She piled food on a plate and took a beer from the ice.

Bouchet sat, thinking about a conversation he'd need to have with Chastain. Both men could probably determine they'd make the best use of Boris's talents if he knew the truth. He'd have to buttonhole Chastain as soon as practical. "This number is familiar," he said, as he scribbled numbers on paper. Yes, for sure. Six-seven-six-five is a part of the Fibonacci sequence."

Collective questions arose.

Boris said, "Yes, I've read about it but mathematics wasn't my strongest suit. What do you make of this?"

Bouchet explained the sequence of numbers discovered by the mathematician more than eight hundred years earlier. "Each number in the sequence is the sum of the two that came before it. Their difference, approximately 1.61 times the preceding number, is referred to as the Golden Ratio, which is found in many instances in nature and is a composition pleasing to the human eye. It has been used by artists and architects for hundreds of years to establish relationships in form. But let's not get too far afield here. Boss, do you have the code matrix handy?"

"*Oui*, it's here in this bag. What are we looking for?"

Bouchet said, "Look here. There are missing boxes above the alpha characters, twenty-six across, no doubt representing the western alphabet."

"So the Fibonacci number is a clue to the letters?" asked Boris.

"Yes, or it could be a clue to a starting point. If the numbers in this message each represent a letter of the alphabet, then one simply has to determine where to begin to find the missing letters. That's always been the big hurdle for breaking old codes like this."

"The number 6756 is the twenty-first number in the Fibonacci sequence, so that puts us here on the matrix." Bouchet placed an X in the box above the number 21. "This gives us a jumping-off point in the horizontal or X axis. What we now need is something for the Y axis, that's these Japanese symbols running vertically. Koi?"

Koi said, "Those are, how would you say, kind of place numbers, like first, second, third, down to twentieth."

"Yes," said Bouchet. "Do you have anything in that bag that might help us here?"

Koi said, "The other clue must be in the tattoos if the first one is here, right? What if the artist put the symbol in a different tattoo? We have to look again."

Chastain brought out the original pictures. Koi went into the bathroom. She spotted it while looking in the mirror. "I have it, I think." She yelled from the bathroom, then came out pointing at her chest. "Here, see this pattern around the koi? I had some shading done here about a year ago. Looks geometric but this part is shaded different. If you look at it sideways, like I was lying down. You see? This is character for fifteenth."

"Outstanding," said Bouchet.

Chastain squeezed her shoulder.

Bouchet drew a line from the fifteenth symbol across to the letter in the column under where he'd placed the X. "That means our starting letter is K."

Chastain said, "Starting letter. Explain."

Bouchet said, "this is actually a rudimentary type of code.

Each number or set of numbers represents a letter in the alphabet. They probably deployed several systems to create coded messages based on this matrix. Each one would provide a different starting point. That's why the numbers in the tattoo. It tells the recipient to use the Fibonacci code and not one of the others. Now that I know how this coded message is deciphered, it's relatively easy to figure out."

"Why would he use such a code?"

Boris said it was probably just a stall tactic, to prevent a courier from knowing what was in the message or to slow down the enemy if he was captured. "It wasn't meant to detail a major military operation like the bombing of Dresden. In these times, few people had the type of training in these codes. It would have been almost impossible to decipher."

Bouchet interjected, "He's right, I believe. It would have been delivered by a trusted agent within the ranks."

Koi asked if the French were keeping it a secret from the Japanese.

"No," said Boris. "It's why the imagery is on your tattoos and why the Y axis is in Japanese. That tells me they were cooperating and needed one another to decode the message. Yes, we are missing the nexus between the French and Japanese interaction to decipher it, but if you had it, you wouldn't have hired me in the first place, yes? I say good show all around."

While they talked, Bouchet worked over the message against the code matrix. "Done."

Chastain took the paper from him, looked at it and smiled. "Bouchet, you've done it again." He read it aloud. "*Coordonnées géographiques des fonds de guerre, trente-*

quatre, trente et un, cent quatorze." He pointed at Boris and Koi. "Thirty-four, forty-one, one-fourteen. They sound an awful lot like coordinates—degrees, minutes and seconds."

Chastain asked Boris if the person responsible for hiding the relics would have the wherewithal and tools to mark the coordinates.

"Yes, yes they would," said Boris. "As I said, the Shōgun Tokugawa is said to have fled the castle by sea at night, so they would have had to possess navigation tools. These were noblemen, educated. The use of the star symbols suggests they were guided by constellations and the moon, a lunar schema, but given some time we could get pretty close."

Bouchet said, "I'll work on the coordinates. With readily available technology we can translate them into GPS coordinates."

"Hang on," said Boris. "Obvious question—these poems were written more than a hundred years before Koi was born. The tattoos?"

Chastain told Boris how the clues had been secretly passed down and preserved in the tattoos before the artist died.

"Shakespeare couldn't have written it better."

"Let's all just keep working, huh?"

"What do I do?" asked Koi.

"Eat," said Chastain. "Eat and then close your eyes. We're going to be here a while."

Chapter Twenty-Three

HAYATO PACED IN HIS OFFICE.

He'd lost count of the number of days that had passed since he had heard from Koi. Convinced she had turned on him, he grew increasingly paranoid. He began to devise a strategy to have her executed, but then he thought about the expense and fruitlessness of sending crews out around the globe looking for her so he trashed it. He cursed himself for losing his legendary patience. If he was wrong, he'd lose any possibility of ever finding that gold and might be seen as nothing more than a renegade who'd stolen power for power's sake. He could not afford that kind of reputation.

He dialed her number but disconnected before it went through. He needed a distraction.

He called downstairs to have a bottle of Uozumi single-malt whiskey brought from his reserves to his booth along with the two prettiest girls on duty in the lounge. He would sit between them and tell tales, watch them giggle, feel the push of their pert breasts against his arms as they leaned in to be entertained.

***

The team in Vietnam kept at it. His alcohol intake didn't slow Boris's determination. He studied the poems again and compared them against his text books and notes. He took a short break to eat and laugh with Hubert about their brief history together. The team worked with

Chastain to review the GPS coordinates and Boris worked well into the night before finally crashing on the couch. He sweated in his sleep.

Chastain, as usual, beat the sunrise to the day.

The door opened, surprising him. He reached for a pistol on the table. He set it down when Koi came in, soaked from an early run to the river and back, pull-ups at a construction site followed by handstand presses. She smiled at Chastain. "Just me."

He said, "You ought to be more careful going out alone. Not everyone in this country sells trinkets on the street."

Koi laughed and let out her ponytail. "The people who might mean me harm are still sleeping and if you haven't noticed, I can take care of myself."

"That's not the point. You are part of a team. Understood?"

She decided against saying something sarcastic. The run and the prospects of finding this gold had invigorated her and helped her tamp down the anxiety she felt for not being at her mother's bedside. She nodded and said she needed a shower. "I'll make coffee when I get out."

"Good."

Something stirred on the couch. "Did someone say coffee or was I dreaming?"

"Someone said it. Not ready yet. After Koi gets out you can wash up. Breakfast and coffee will be ready by then."

Boris rubbed his eyes, tossed his hair and scratched at his chins. "Interesting name, Koi. Symbolic, no?"

"Yes, I suppose it is." Chastain didn't yet trust Boris with her real name, it being inconsequential in the scheme of things. "What do you think about the coordinates?"

"I thought a lot more about them. We've gone through every scrap of paper in your satchel. The technology of the sextant existed, and those chaps were probably enamored with lunar-based celestial plot points." He reached for his notes, blinking his eyes in the growing morning light. "All this talk of poetry and celestial markers. They only need be slightly different than modern GPS coordinates and we'll be off target."

"I was a seafarer. The moon tracks differently depending on the time of year. There are almanacs."

"Yes, true. I think we're on the right track with this though. It feels right. It makes sense the relics are still on the castle grounds."

"I don't move a team on feelings."

"Understood, but you are an educated man, *Monsieur*. Surely you know Napoleon spoke of the *coup d'oeil*, a stroke of the eye."

"Intuition."

"Precisely. Based on the facts and circumstances presented here thus far, my instinct tells me we are onto something."

"I will concede that much. Now the question remains. Is it still there?"

"Ahh, the rub. Yes, well after breakfast I'll give it all one last go. It may be easier to find something now that I know what I'm looking for. My only fear is we have to wait until the right season to match the coordinates to the lunar orbit."

"I think not. With our shipping experience, Bouchet's gift for mathematics and your knowledge of history, we can construct it, or deconstruct it if we are, as you say, on the right track."

There was something menacing in the way he said it. Le Sauvage was never far beneath the surface, no matter how gentlemanly Chastain could appear. Boris sensed it; he decided to drink less and think more that day.

Koi came out in athletic wear, drying her hair in a towel with a lithe exuberance. Men around her usually pretended they hadn't noticed her. They had.

"So what's up?" she asked. "Where are we, what can I do? Breakfast. I said I'd make coffee. Let's get that started. We can talk while I work. What do you have for us, professor? We're not paying you just to drink all our beer."

Chastain looked toward Boris, who said he'd take a rinse and be out to answer all their questions.

Koi and her father stood alone in the room, alone really for the very first time. Each of them sensed both the awkwardness and elegance of the moment, one of those flashes of time you know in that instant that you'll remember forever, an *epimoment*, or so it's been described, a feeling that you are in the epicenter of a uniquely timeless point of time, a recognition of quantum energy within your body, parallels, when your heart races with fear and exalts with understanding, a personal epiphany of self.

Neither spoke for a long, slow pull of time. Koi said, "Would you like me to make breakfast?"

"I would like you to know that I see my face in you. I see your mother. I see where I have failed as a man."

Joe Hefferon

"Wow, that's deep, Dad. I mean... It feels stupid to call you boss or Monsieur Chastain. I don't like to pretend reality doesn't exist, you know?" He didn't answer. She looked only at his eyes. "I don't see a failure when I look at you. I just see a man I wish I knew better."

"I am not a failure. I have failed your mother."

"Thanks."

"And, you too, of course."

"It's like you love her but owe me."

"That's not what I meant."

"It's what *I* meant."

"Is it all right with you that I love her? I can't change what I feel. I will find a way to see it all work out."

"That's fucking vague, I don't mind telling you. What does work out mean?"

"Before this is all over, this thing...before I—"

"I? You mean, before *she* dies."

"Yes. Yes, that's what I mean. Before she dies, I will make her happy."

"It's too late for her to know anything, Chastain. Just call her. Get my mother on the phone now while she can still hear your fucking French voice. Tell her that I love you and we're fucking happy and let her die in peace, okay? Can you do that for me...Father?"

Koi turned and left the apartment, nearly breaking the door off its hinges when she flung it open.

"Emi."

Chastain walked out to the balcony.

Boris came out of the bathroom looking for breakfast, finding only an empty room.

207

Chapter Twenty-Four

BORIS MADE BREAKFAST. He surprised Chastain with the quality of the coffee and eggs. Koi did not return for most of the morning.

Chastain had a sense she would be fine, that she could have returned sooner but her stubborn side wouldn't allow it. He understood.

She walked the streets of Saigon in search of a temple. She didn't know it at the time but when she found it, understood what she had been looking for. She needed serenity but couldn't create it; she needed to be in the kind of space where it belonged, and attach to it.

She walked into the gray-blue smoke of the Thien Hau Temple. The incense reminded her of something from her childhood but she couldn't remember what, only that she felt small in the memory. Dozens of smoking incense spirals hung from the ceiling, incense sticks burned from the sand in bronze pots, prayers on scores of red ribbons suspended from the ceiling; red candles and limes in dishes.

Even in the still burgeoning morning, tourists took photographs as if the offerings were freak shows. *Look at what they do here, these savages, they haven't been saved, the poor dears.*

A spirit intolerant, begged for quiet among those deaf to the call for reverence.

Koi sat and offered her thoughts to the nomadic

smoke, the soft candlelight, the veneration that arose after the tourists left, *finally*. She measured her breaths, meditated, found herself on a street in Osaka, an almost woman but still Emiko, the girl from the apartments.

Her first kill came her way by chance. She hadn't planned it, but owned the opportunity. She had walked home from school to find her only friend crying, curbside. Some boys stood nearby, the future yakuza teen roughnecks who'd given up on school and ran small errands and did shit work for the initiated gangsters—just some boys swimming in testosterone; they laughed at Emiko's friend, laughed at her for crying because she had touched them when they asked, made them hard and didn't know what to do after. They pushed her face in their teen crotches and made her gag, then they knocked her down and called her an untrained whore. "One day you will learn and then I will fuck you," the tall one said. The others cheered his words.

Koi called them out, glaring at the tall one. "You want to fuck, big boy? Fuck me. Come here now, boy. Come here."

He walked toward her, looking back over his shoulder at his friends huddled together and waving him on. "Go get her."

When he got within range she spun like a coiled cable, smacking the side of her foot across his chin. He stumbled. She went after him, grabbed his face with both hands and drove her knee into his solar plexus. He lost his breath and fell onto his side, straining to inhale. She stood over him and stared the other boys down. They ran. Koi looked back at her friend who was crying and looking away, at a life with no joy, destined to be used up by yakuza. Koi stomped the kid's neck, severing his carotid artery internally. He gagged and she left him.

The other boys were too scared to go to the police. No arrests were made.

But word spread in the right circles. Within weeks she was recruited by Hayato. He paid for her to master meditation and upgrade her street fighting skills via private lessons from a Shitō-ryū Karate sensei.

She thought about Hayato and how in the end they would turn against one another to survive. She thought about her mother and the police. They had her picture now and her fingerprints. Even if they decided against telling Interpol about her arrest and jailbreak, they still knew her. She had killed men in Osaka. She could never go back. Koi leaned back, her face lifted toward the slatted ceiling, and held her hands over her eyes.

***

While she meditated, Chastain acted. For the first time in nearly thirty years, Chastain followed orders, those of his daughter. He called Mikie from outside by the hotel garden. He spoke in reassuring tones. He went back upstairs to conduct business.

***

Koi returned to the war room. The whole team had regrouped and milled about. Something had changed about the atmosphere. The men encircled a white board on the dining table. Bouchet and Boris argued over plot points. Picard and The Beard took sides and bet money they hadn't yet earned. Fournier watched from his perch on the high counter stool from the kitchen. Chastain trusted Bouchet's math, but his gut told him Boris had the right idea.

Bouchet took time to explain their findings to the rest of the team. He said, "Each piece links to the next. The preparation for hiding the relics would have been part of the exit plan or else they would have stayed and fought to the death. This large map coming from France would have stood out among the gifts. Why would someone give them a map of something they already owned, you see?"

"Because people loyal to the Shōgun would have seen it as well," said Picard. He liked that he caught on.

"Yes. I think the poems are meant as encouragement as well as pointing toward a place to locate the relics, using the coordinates. It's as though Cazeneuve was saying, 'fear not, we will survive this and we will revive the Shōgunate with the buried treasure', am I right, Boris?"

"I believe you are, sir."

"How does it tell us to look for the tattoos?" asked Potente.

Bouchet said it didn't but deferred to Boris to explain.

Boris said, "Let's remember the tattoos are just the last place the final clues were set down. It was never the intention of Cazeneuve to have these coordinates be on the young lady's back, only that they be held in secret. My guess is since the people who commissioned this painting of the castle knew about the relics, they would have entrusted the coordinates to someone who would be in a position to retrieve them when the time came, always believing that the time would arrive, sooner or later. The poems are merely a call to stay strong and know that the coordinates will provide them with the precise location of the items, somewhere within the confines of the castle grounds, as alluded to in the poems."

Chastain said they'd settled the argument over the final coordinates but would only have one shot at it. They had to get in and either take it or confirm it for a sale to the highest bidder.

"I get it, the poems, I mean, but I don't understand how the other part of the clue ended up on my back." Koi had been listening from the door.

Chastain smiled.

Boris conceded it was an excellent question. The Beard said he was just going to ask that. Boris said, "What I think and what I fear is the original second part of the mystery was written down as sort of a treasure map, but guarded so jealously that the person who had it, perhaps our Frenchman, Cazeneuve, lost it or destroyed it and it passed on verbally. Eventually it found its final stance for revelation tattooed on your back."

"So it could be all wrong?" Koi asked. "Like, lost in translation?"

"Not lost," her father said. "Lost its way, and here it is."

"Well done, old man."

Bouchet said, "We are trying to work past this hump. If the coordinates we agreed upon put us in a reasonable place, we take the shot. If they had put us in the middle of Osaka Bay? Well…"

"We are screwed," said Picard.

"Who invited him?" asked Koi.

Potente said, "The French had the coordinates and the Japanese had the timing. Work together, just like today.

This is like time travel."

She laughed, "Stop watching movies with subtitles."

Boris suggested everyone take a break for a couple of hours. Too many hours compressed into a pressure-filled situation and maybe they needed a break to allow a distraction so they might free their collective subconscious minds and arrive at a reasonable conclusion. Once Boris made the suggestion, the room quickly agreed to it. They settled on a time to be back in the room to make final plans.

Chastain knew they were right. He'd put extra pressure on the team because of Mikie, a fact he didn't share with anyone, not even Koi. For any other mission, he would have demonstrated more patience in the critical planning phase.

Boris said he would be going to the Brodard for lunch if anyone cared to join him. Potente liked the sound of it, "German, *ja*?"

Koi said she might find them in a while.

As they walked toward the central city of Saigon, Boris considered the idea that he liked the place, liked the undercurrent of excitement of a people enjoying a tenuous taste of capitalist freedom. He could see it in their fashion, in the western fast-food restaurants, in the wake of the European *parfumer* thrown off the young women thumbing mobile phones. *Maybe Phueng doesn't miss me.*

What he saw was not Ho Chi Minh's Saigon. Maybe he'd just stick around a while, perhaps find someone to love among the eager populace, or write a book about finding sobriety on the equator when it's too late to go back home to the fading bouquet of a woman who drove him to suicidal ideation, but settled instead on the notion of Thai-rum-actuated liver damage—self-inflicted.

Boris. A man with a morning-after voice and a Celtic sense of wearing tragedy as a battle ribbon. It didn't matter if he'd earned that ribbon or simply absorbed it with the gin while commiserating with his drinking mates.

He sat at the Brodard bar with Potente and talked over Saigon "33" beers about Thai women, whom Potente said he had never thought about before. Boris explained the country's unnatural allure for western males. "As long as there are Thai women who still lived in Thailand, a Thai clerk in a dry cleaner's shop in Surrey won't have the same appeal. Perhaps it is the distance from what is familiar."

"I like this Saigon beer better than the Tiger," said Potente.

Boris silently toasted his agreement with Potente's critique.

Potente told Boris that he liked Koi. It took him three beers to admit it. Boris laughed and said he'd noticed, along with everyone else, including Jacob.

"Who?" asked Potente.

"The boss. Didn't they introduce him as Jacob?"

Potente the soldier kicked in. "Yes, that's his name. Sorry, I'm a little dizzy from beer and lack of sleep."

"He's a man who commands respect."

"Or fear. There's a way about him. We've all been in combat in one theater or another. But something about the boss is different. He's a killer of killers. A great white shark."

"In zoology, he'd be classified as an apex predator."

"You are a smart man, Boris."

"I am an educated man, but smart enough to use my education to its fullest. And what about you, what education have you enjoyed?"

Before he could answer the door swung open and Koi's presence captured the room.

"Well here she is, young man," Boris said. "The girl you've been staring at for thirty-six hours."

"Shut up."

Boris waved her over.

Koi sat beside Potente and drank from his glass of beer. He blushed at the closeness of her action, as though she knew he wouldn't protest.

Boris paid for the other two to have a round and left them, "to wander the city," he said. "Don't drink all their beer, and come back sober enough to work."

"How did you know I would still be here?" asked Potente.

"What makes you think I came here for you?"

"My instincts about such things."

"Don't make me start disliking you."

"Are you hungry?"

"A little bit."

"We can split something."

Chapter Twenty-Five

KOI DIALED HER NUMBER.

She answered, "I am still alive and still a whore."

"How is your family, your brother?"

"I have not seen him in three years. He lives on Kyushu somewhere, I think. He won't speak to me."

"*Gomen'nasai*," said Koi.

"No need. It's not your fault."

Despite Koi's having saved her from the junior rapists years before, the girl remained on the bottom of the yakuza food chain; a prostitute, hooked on speed and never finding the strength to climb out of her own grave. Koi said, "I need to know—is there any talk of me in family circles?"

"They say you are a traitor and some want you dead, that you went to the police and talked about yakuza. I don't believe them."

"*Arigato*. I did no such thing. I went to the police for reasons I can't explain now. What about Hayato? Have you heard anything?"

"They say he protects you for some reason, something more than just being your sponsor. Perhaps you owe him money. He is growing impatient and people are starting to look at him as weak. You may be in danger."

"I probably am. Thank you for the warning."

"You saved me once, a long time ago."

"I am sorry for that as well, I'm afraid."

"No need to be. I did this to myself. I have to go."

"I wish you well. *Odaijini.*"

"Koi—one more thing."

"What is it?"

"Your mother is not well."

And the line went dead.

Koi shut her phone and resisted the urge to smash it. She looked over at Potente who waited in front of a souvenir shop, far enough away to be respectful but close enough to watch her. They stared at one another and then she walked back toward the war room. He caught up with her, elbows touching. They didn't speak.

***

Lyon, France: North on the A7 from Marseille, in the office of the Interpol General Secretariat, the detective superintendent issued Blue Notices for the arms merchant known as Le Sauvage and anyone in his company at the time of his detention, to hold for questioning and possible arrest. "A Red Notice will be imminent upon receipt of certain information."

The office dispatched a team of inspectors and detective sergeants to work with the Japanese authorities in developing a strategy for the arrest of an unidentified gunrunner, in an unspecified location, conducting unknown and possibly criminal activity in conjunction with probable accomplices, all based upon information received from confidential informants. No more vague law enforcement operation had ever been undertaken in Osaka.

Back in Lyon, the lead detective stared at two boards,

representing two criminal organizations, one with Le Sauvage on top, written on an index card, and the other with Koi, both unidentified. Chastain's board had photos of Marin from his booking, as well as Tanguy, Beatto and Chuinard, all post mortem. It held news clippings, sketches of possible associates, maps, images and more index cards packed with notes.

The other board had two pictures of Koi: a still taken from a grainy surveillance camera on the street near the condo construction site, the other at the marina in Nice, taken from the rear. Tanguy's catamaran could be seen in the background but Marceau never noticed it.

The arresting officer had questioned Marin both in hospital and at the police station. Interpol questioned him after the second shooting incident. In each instance, Marin provided no useful information to the investigators. He was simply walking down the street when a crazy Asian girl shot him. He didn't know who the gun on the street belonged to nor did he know the men in the Peugeot. He wore gloves because he has poor circulation and his hands got cold. "Why is a crime victim under arrest? Are the French police mad?"

His attorney secured him bail. He slipped the police tail with ten minutes though he still walked with a limp. He had not been seen since.

By training and Chastain's protocol, Marin would maintain radio silence for several weeks, barring any information immediately threatening to the boss or the crew. Marin would spend time recuperating at his villa in Côte d'Ivoire, near Tabou, flying under a Swiss passport.

"Sergeant," said his aide. "We have received an email

from a woman named Chisato at the police headquarters in Osaka. She says the pictures and description we sent her do not match anyone in their database of known yakuza associates, but is diligently searching local files for this possible suspect. She regrets not being more helpful at this time."

The detective sergeant snatched the printed copy of the email and crumpled it. He turned back to the boards. "*Putain. Nous avons seulement la merde.*"

"I suppose this is a bad time to tell you they lost Marin."

"Get out."

***

The walk served Boris well. He returned to the war room with an idea, knowing his odds of getting it past a group of what appeared to him to be seasoned outlaws, lay in single digits. He had been told he'd been brought here for one task and then he'd be sent on his way. He offered his suggestion as a question to Hubert, spoken loudly enough to be heard by the group.

"You treasure hunters, as it were, are you self-employed or are you working for a government organization?"

No one answered at first, but clearly the question turned on their serious side.

Bouchet stepped in and said, "You are paid well, well enough to understand you operate within the confines of the poems and tattoos. Why we have formed this team is of little consequence and certainly not something with which we would burden you."

The room grew cold. Boris got the message, polite and

clear. Don't ask questions. Do your job. Go back to Bangkok. He couldn't help himself. Boris said he understood. "It's just that I thought I might be of further assistance."

Hubert put down his coffee and walked towards him.

Chastain cut him off. "We are under contract with an agency within the Japanese government, sort of like the American NSA. We need to find these items to avoid a national outcry. It's simple."

Boris took Chastain's tone as an opening. "Then why are you in Ho Chi Minh City?" he asked.

"We are sworn to secrecy. We signed NDAs."

"Good plan. Careful, those Japanese. Good planners they are and savers by the way, almost obsessive about it."

Chastain sneered at the knowing smile Boris wore. "What is it, Boris?"

"My walk helped to clarify a few points that had been mucked up. All this talk of poetry and bands of soldiers bearing weighty backpacks." He hesitated. "You aren't looking for relics, are you?"

Chastain said, "It's none of your business. Trying to make it your business could prove inconvenient for you."

"I'm trying to do nothing of the kind, sir. I assure you. But as long as I'm here and I've figured out this much, it might be helpful if we were forthright with one another. Perhaps if I knew the complete story I might see something in the data I hadn't before."

Bouchet stepped in. "Perspective, boss. He may be right."

Chastain stared at Boris, thinking it through.

"For what it's worth," said Boris. "I'm not much of a

fighter and although I don't have the physique of many on your team, I don't wish to see my pudgy body cut into chunks and fed to the sharks in the Sea of Japan. This is, well, up until the last few moments, the most fun I've had in a long while. If this works and you see fit to pay me more than the original amount we agreed upon, then I'll be elated. If not, so be it. In either case, I'd like to see this through."

"Boss?" asked Bouchet. The other men looked at each other.

"Agreed," said Chastain. "But now you are on a shorter leash. No more trips downtown without an escort. You are on a very narrow ledge, *Monsieur*, and it wouldn't take much for me to push you off."

Boris understood, smiled and shook hands all around. Chastain decided to give him the rundown about the war funds and a cold beer as a temporary sign of good will. "Truth is we aren't concerned with any relics that may or may not be buried under this castle."

"Do tell."

"When I do, you will be deeper into this than you might have anticipated."

"Meaning if I repeat it, I won't enjoy the consequences."

"Exactly."

"Full throttle, mate, let's have it."

"We have reason to believe there is a large cache of gold buried somewhere on those castle grounds or very close to it. How much is irrelevant right now but suffice to say it is substantial. We need you to understand the gravity of this investigation. I'm sure you understand that both time and secrecy are critical."

"I do indeed. So, shall we continue?"

Bouchet said, "That went well. Yes, proceed."

Boris Nethercote, still suitably oiled up from his trip to the Brodard, jumped back into character and began his summation. "Chaps. After reviewing the spectrum of possibilities, the coordinates, the possibility that the coordinates are precisely imprecise, I believe Monsieur Bouchet can agree on the following: the gold probably exists, much of it in its original state. Given the estimated amount, it's unlikely the gold traveled with the Shōgun, who at the time was more interested in saving his arse than his fortune. The most plausible scenario is Samurai loyal to the Shōgun, along with a contingent of Cazeneuve's troops, hid the gold with hopes of getting back to it one day, which of course, never happened."

"What if they stole it themselves?" asked Hubert.

"Good question. They could have taken some to support their short-term efforts but the bulk of it would have stayed on the grounds. They were loyalists, willing to die for an ideal; they wouldn't steal from themselves. I'll bet wherever they stashed it is where it remains today."

Chastain remembered aloud that Boris had a reputation for winning more bets than he lost, a small accomplishment among a few unmentionable failures. Boris concurred and after several minutes of silence, reflection and looking around the room for a cue, Bouchet spoke first.

He said, "We have a very good idea where the gold is at this point." Bouchet showed everyone the map. "And I agree we should use the lunar plot points. It makes sense from a historical perspective."

"Wait," Chastain said. "Where are Koi and Potente?"

Boris said, "They may be delayed. I can always fill them in."

As he spoke the door opened. "I'm right here, Boris," she said. "Fill me in now."

Potente looked toward Chastain, then spent the rest of the meeting staring at the white board.

"Our only problem, and it's a big one, is this—how do we confirm the location, which will require some digging, without drawing attention from the law, or at the very least, the people responsible for the castle grounds?" asked Hubert.

The Beard said, "We can't just announce ourselves and plant a flag."

"Leave that to us Brits. We've a bit of history with that technique."

Chastain almost smiled, but at the same time thought about Boris becoming too friendly with his crew and too involved. He looked toward Bouchet who read his mind.

"Boss, can I speak to you on the balcony? I need some air, one of these guys needs a shower," Bouchet said.

Koi offered to make coffee.

Chapter Twenty-Six

THE NEXT FEW HOURS produced little but agitation about how to confirm the location of the cache and its likelihood of there being gold in this unknown void. The problem was the heat from Interpol which, coupled with the embarrassment of the local cops exacerbated by the yakuza who would want revenge, made an exploratory mission too risky. A one-off strike might be plausible but if they were wrong, there would be no second chance.

"Unless," Boris said, "we operate in plain sight."

"You mean just show up with our passports and shovels?" asked Picard. "Maybe you should lighten up on the beer."

Boris shrugged off the sarcasm. "Lads, I've got an idea. My father was a geologist. He spent a good deal of my youth in Chile, Peru and Colorado in the states, working with molybdenum miners."

Potente interrupted. "What miners?"

"Molybdenum is a metallic element used in the production of steel and iron to make it hard, helps to resist corrosion and so forth but that's unimportant. What is important is I speak the lingo of men in this field. I have some knowledge of the equipment."

"You want to pretend to search for this moly stuff on the castle grounds?"

"No," Bouchet said. "He wants to develop a ruse to use his geological survey equipment on the grounds."

"Precisely."

"And I bet you have access to the types of documentation one would need to be given entrée to the property," Chastain said.

"Yes. It would be old but we could manufacture new bills and enough confusing issuance that we might get a few hours on the property before being tossed."

"No heavy equipment for digging?"

"No, only ground-penetrating radar. Just a look-see."

Chastain said, "We wouldn't be doing any digging, so maybe they would have an easier time accepting you or us. We could only use the team members who weren't on the job when we released Koi from the police station."

"Right again, sir. I would need a few people with me, a driver, rental van and equipment operators."

"We can't afford to hire experts like that. There would be too many questions."

"We wouldn't need experts. I'm your expert. I'll operate a remote geophysical survey instrument that uses GPR, the ground-penetrating radar we spoke of. The other team members merely have to give the appearance of assisting me. It would be a preliminary or exploratory survey and we'd say we would compile a report and get back to them in a few weeks. I speak enough of the language that I could represent the team. What we must determine is what we will say we are looking for. It should be reasonable but not so commonplace that they couldn't do it themselves. Ideas? Anyone?"

Koi spoke up. "Flooding. It's mostly surrounded by water so we could say we are looking for ways the place might flood, say, if there was an earthquake or something."

"Ahh, yes, major or growing fault lines in the walls."

Chastain asked Bouchet what he thought. Bouchet said, "No, it's good. We could say we are an international team of aquatic degradation experts hired by the national historical society, or whatever they have in Tokyo. It's about preserving a national treasure."

"I like it."

"I know someone in Venice who can get us enough documentation about work done there to cover us for a few days."

Chastain said, "Monsieur Bouchet, you are the most well-known unknown man in the world."

"I do what I can."

Chastain said it sounded like a feasible plan. "You'll say your team is working the property in segments, with a report to follow each day. Of course, on day one you'll only work the portion we've identified and never return and all your contact information would be false."

"Except for a disposable cell. He'd have to give them at least one way of contacting him to make it seem legitimate," said Hubert. "They might want to call and offer him lunch or something to be polite. Normal business stuff."

The team latched on to the idea and worked through the details over the next hour. Koi suggested using local expat students to help overcome the obstacle of forming the exploration team. She said they were always looking for day work to pay for extra expenses while they attended school. They would know nothing except to drive a van and help unload equipment.

"Plausible deniability, very good."

"We'll pay them in cash. Good idea. That's your responsibility. Your English is good so you can handle setting that up," said Chastain. Koi smiled at him. Their eyes locked for a moment until he turned away.

Boris said, "One last detail, the matter of the coordinates. I've considered everyone's input, Monsieur Bouchet's calculations and the perspective of the seafarers. All told I'd say it puts us roughly here." Boris pointed at the map with a fresh cigar. "In the area formerly known as the Sengan Turret, on the opposite side of what was the Treasure House."

"Now called Nishinomaru Gardens, not far from the ticket office," said Koi.

Boris continued. "East of the location is a dry moat. It's possible at one time there was egress to the moat from underground. I could see on such large grounds there would be several hidden passages and escape routes."

"So, we agree on the location as guided by the coordinates but if we look at this logically, this seems like a reasonable spot," said Chastain. "How large an area should we attempt to cordon off?"

Bouchet said, "Roughly fifty meters by another fifty, about twenty-five in each direction from where we think the center point is. If nothing is found and there is time, Boris can extend it."

Hubert offered that they could cover more ground with two units. Boris agreed. Bouchet said there wouldn't be time to train a student to read the equipment. Boris agreed with that also but said, "The kid would not need to read it immediately. I can review the data after and

228

triangulate it against mine. I'll start him in an area further out and have him work a grid pattern to me." He turned to Chastain. "Is there time and funding for the rental of two machines?"

"Get whatever you need."

Bouchet said they could rent the equipment on relatively short notice. All agreed to the plan. Chastain directed Bouchet and Boris to work on developing the paperwork they would need. Koi would work with Hubert on logistics. They would move in five days. They would show up at the castle with little or no notice so there wouldn't be time to question the validity of the survey.

Meantime, Chastain had business to attend to with Filipino terrorists. He brought the rest of the team to a storage facility on the Mekong where the weapons for the transfer were stashed. The most dangerous aspect of their profession would take place the following morning, pre-dawn. Abu Sayyaf might want revenge but what they wanted more were those weapons and judging from the looks on their faces at the last meet, to be as far from Le Sauvage as possible, as soon as possible.

Nevertheless, in the early morning, the small team rechecked their weapons at the hotel, out of sight of Boris. They dressed like tourists in guayaberas or floral print shirts to cover their weapons. They took separate routes to the vehicles.

Chastain had hired two local drivers to bring them to a location where they would pick up a different set of vehicles to drive to the meet. He organized everything in cells so no peripheral hires had too much information that could be sold or interrogated out of them.

The crew took separate stairs and elevators downstairs to meet them at opposite ends of the block. Upstairs, Koi spotted Chastain's watch on the counter and ran down to give it to him. Her impetuous act both annoyed and pleased him. The driver of the lead car had one arm wrapped in a dirty bandage at the wrist. That arm looked to be shorter than the other. Koi recognized him and said, "Hey, Lefty, how's your friend's balls?" He got in the car and slammed the door.

As he stepped into the car Chastain asked Koi what that was about. She laughed and said she'd explain later. "Get back upstairs and don't ever meet me like this again when it's not planned."

Koi pouted a little but knew he was right. She ran back in.

Inside the car Mayko said to Chastain, "Does it bother you that she killed our men?"

"Of course it bothers me that our men died. They were working for me."

"Our men. She killed them."

"I fucking know who killed them. She was working as well, for someone else who expected her to do what she was trained to do and survive. Did you forget where you came from?"

"I remember. I am wondering about you."

"Shut your fucking mouth right now, Mayko. We have a job to do today and we don't need this bullshit distracting us. She is my daughter and if she wasn't I would have killed her myself. Now are you ready to work today or do I need to cut you loose right here?"

"I am always ready."

"Good."

***

Back at the hotel camp, Boris slept. Potente looked on as Hubert and Koi worked in the kitchen on logistical matters: boats, transport, equipment rental, supply lines. He showed her how to sketch out a contingency plan to present to the boss, in case Boris were to be compromised.

"Would my, would the boss leave Boris there if he is, like you said, compromised?"

"What do you think?"

"I guess not."

"Good guess. We would do what we could to extract him but I think this character Boris might like being arrested. Another adventure."

"Only if they have beer in Japanese jails," said Potente.

Hubert said there was an issue yet unresolved. "The boss has not discussed with all of us if he thinks it is better to try and take as much gold as possible or sell the coordinates to the yakuza. If he decides it is too risky, and I think too cumbersome to attempt, then how can we be sure this yakuza boss will believe what we tell him about the coordinates?"

"Hayato. Yakuza boss is Hayato. Difficult to say. If you were yakuza he would take your word for it based on respect and honor among the clan. But you are a gaijin."

"What's that?" asked Potente.

"It means an outsider and not just outside the clan but a foreigner. And you are committing a crime in yakuza territory. Much about this would lead them to not trust you. They would need proof."

Bouchet walked in. "Proof of what? Who needs proof?"

231

Hubert explained the dilemma of Hayato possibly not believing they had located the gold. He might suspect the team would take his money and leave them empty-handed. Bouchet rubbed his chin on the back of his hand. He needed a shave.

Koi said, "Hayato believes in that gold. He believes it is somewhere, he just doesn't know where. He also thinks Chastain has the secret to finding it. He's already in a position to want to believe us."

"We talked about this," said Bouchet. "The boss and I think the best or safest plan, given the location of so much gold, would be to sell the coordinates to Hayato for fifty percent of the approximate worth. Still a nice score. But we can't show our plan to him or he'll use his connections with the police to direct Interpol's investigation toward us. He'd steal the gold and we'd be lucky to escape with our lives."

Koi said they needed a sample, something she could take to Hayato.

"Take to Hayato? You?" Bouchet laughed and just as quickly got serious. "The boss would never go for that plan. Too dangerous for you. It defeats the purpose here, for him anyway. No way."

"I could talk to him," she said.

"You won't. It is not happening. End of discussion. We will figure something out about this yakuza boss or else we'll just take it all for us and screw him. We owe him nothing."

Hubert said, "It's just conversation now anyway. We don't even know what we will find. There could be nothing, in which case we go home and move on to the next job. It wouldn't be the first time a job got cancelled."

"You are correct, Hubert. Let's keep working on this."

As he left the room Koi began to think of her mother, how in the excitement of the hunt she hadn't had time to be sad. *If the gold is not there, what will become of me, of my mother and her grave?*

On her way out the door, Koi said she would be downstairs at the bar to think.

Potente looked at Hubert and flicked his head toward the door.

"Yes," Hubert said. "Give her a few minutes then go check on her."

Potente waited as long as he could without seeming anxious, though everyone noticed he was. Hubert gave him a nod and he left.

He found her at the bar, staring at a glass of beer. She hadn't drunk any. She saw him come in and took a sip. He sidled next to her and ordered a beer. He didn't speak.

"So, what's your first name, or is it just Potente, like a rock star?"

"It's Helmut."

"Helmet? Like a helmet?" She tapped his head.

"No. Helmut, like, Hel-mut."

"Oh, that explains it. It's an unpleasant name."

"I was named after my mother's father. They called me Bärchen when I was a kid because I was stocky and had a belly. I looked like a little bear."

She smiled and said, "Like a Teddy bear?"

"Yes. It means, little bear, in German."

"How about I just call you Ted? Rhymes with head. You have kind of a big head."

He pushed his hand through his hair. "I knew telling you my nickname was a mistake as it left my mouth."

"Settled. Like to make decisions quickly. You should know that about me, Ted."

"What else should I know about you?"

"Nothing."

"Nothing? Is that because you refuse to tell me or there really is nothing else?"

"That's a stupid question. No one is that simple and if I wanted to tell you more, I would, so don't ask it anymore."

He sat in the muting shadow of her reproach, or what he saw as one—*don't get too close, I'll cut you.* He drank more beer and listened for her breath over the din of the café. He found it hard to track. He said, "So you like poems though, right? I heard you say. You read them to relax."

"So?"

"So, nothing. It's good. My mother tried to get me to like them but I just couldn't."

"Maybe she gave up on you too soon."

He drank. "You don't know how true that statement is. Anyway...who is your favorite? Do you have a favorite poet?"

"I have some types of poems I like more than others. Don't care who writes them."

"If you cared you could find other things the poet wrote and like them as well."

"Don't tell me how to think and we can get along better."

"I'm not telling you, I'm just talking, okay? *Scheisse*."

"I know we're talking. Just stop and drink. I need to think about how we can get this gold. Okay?"

"Yeah sure, whatever."

The silence squared, exponential quiet. It weighed on Koi, and her back had grown too tired for more pressure. "Hey. Give me a break. Not accustomed to having conversation with German teddy bears. Are you hungry?"

"I'm always hungry. Let's get something."

"We should split a sandwich. You know?"

"Yes. I mean, what? Know what?"

"They shouldn't have named you helmet if you had a big head."

"You take getting used to."

"*Boke, tsukkomi.* You just don't have a sense of humor."

"And you do?"

"All the funny people in Japan come from Osaka."

"That doesn't mean all the people from Osaka are funny."

"Hey, maybe there's a brain in that big skull."

"Let's eat, okay?"

"Ted."

***

Back in Nice, the detective sergeant finished a long evening of reviewing current Interpol investigations of yakuza factions who were operating internationally, a much longer list than he'd anticipated. He cross-referenced those files against the random files and suspicious activity reports sent to him from the police in Osaka. The yakuza had a broader international operation than he had known: pornography with the Italians in Chicago, heroin in Canada, gambling and narcotics in Hawaii, money laundering in Boston and Hong Kong, handguns in the Philippines, but nothing, not one file, hinted at a connection to any of the known or suspected players in the operations of Le Sauvage.

He threw the last of the files into a box and pushed it across the table to his aide. "Waste of fucking time. There must be a third party working these two groups, a broker or someone who made an introduction."

The aide offered little help. "It has to be the girl. She must know someone."

"No. She is a local player. There's no history of her operating outside her city, let alone her country. And she's an enforcer, not the type you send to establish a rapport. Something is missing. Let's get some coffee. We are missing something in Sauvage's crew."

The sergeant continued over coffee. "We know he has dealt with Asians before, both the Triads and warlords in Afghanistan. He has been linked or suspected to be involved with Abu Sayyaf, but they are in the Philippines and we don't know where they transact business. One of these groups has to be a nexus."

"Well, sergeant, it wouldn't be the Triads. They hate the Japanese. Not going to help them."

"They all have fragile loyalties as far as I'm concerned. If the money is right, they dispense with allegiance to principles. You take Abu Sayyaf. I'll work off the Afghans. Maybe one of them has dealt with this yakuza clan. We need a place to start."

"Do you watch movies with police?"

The sergeant ignored the question, pouring coffee and reading. "What did you say?"

"Movies. I asked you if you watch movies about police or television shows."

"Yes, I suppose, why?"

"They never show how tedious our jobs really are. They only show the car chases and shootouts."

"Would you watch a movie about a pair of assholes looking through boxes of files?"

"I guess not."

"Try not to distract yourself." He pointed at the files laid out before his aide. "Read."

After two hours of silent shuffling through papers, photos, maps and reports, the detective sergeant stood up, flipping his chair behind him. "Why?"

"Sir?"

"Why am I wasting so much time looking for a ghost, uh?" He looked at his aide as though the whole investigation had been the young man's idea. "Why am I looking for a connection to tell me why yakuza is working with Le Sauvage? Because I think if I find this connection, the whole picture will come crystal clear, like finding Jesus fucking Christ in my pantry. Oh, since you are here in my home, why don't you explain all these things that make no sense. I will have everything I need to shut down Sauvage, uh? All the pieces suddenly come into view. It's bullshit. Who cares why they are working together? Let's just focus on what we know."

"We know this yakuza woman came to Nice to meet with him, or so we can assume. Then she doesn't meet with him, we don't think, but kills a bunch of his people.

Why? Are we to believe yakuza sent one skinny woman to avenge a wrong by Le Sauvage? No. Is she a one-woman hit team sent after a group of ex-legionnaires, spec ops and seasoned criminals? No. Did she come to negotiate a deal and then suspect Sauvage was ripping her off? No, she wouldn't get out of the country with her ass intact. Is she a spree killer who happened to travel ten thousand kilometers and stumble upon this crew? Of course, not. That's preposterous. Then what in the holy fucking hell is going on here?"

"Sergeant, perhaps we should wait until we have all the warrants for the dragnet from the Japanese courts and the Tokubetsu Sousakan."

"No. Say nothing else. Go home. Go home to your wife or your mistress or your goddamned dog, I don't care. We'll have warrants soon, warrants to search for a fucking ghost. Take a break. Have some wine. Come back tomorrow. I'm going to get drunk and regret this assignment. Go."

The aide nodded and left. Marceau shoved his coffee mug across the table.

Chapter Twenty-Seven

CHASTAIN AND THE TEAM returned from the transaction without any patent wounds, but most of the crew walked in quietly—introspective in the way men are when they return from committing a dangerous crime. It's a survival mechanism, born of guilt, relief and the need to deconstruct those milliseconds where things could have gone violently wrong, but on that day, inexplicably, did not.

Chastain said hello to no one and poured a bourbon over ice and went out on the balcony. Boris looked up from his notes and nodded. Bouchet and Hubert took a walk downstairs and stayed outside long enough for Hubert to smoke two cigarettes. The rest of the team left Chastain alone. After conversation began to return to a normal decibel, Koi went out to the balcony. He seemed to know it was her though he looked out toward the evening purple haze to the east.

She said nothing at first. She stepped closer and gave him a fresh drink.

Chastain said, "Your mother always liked sunsets. I liked sunrises. Together we embraced the best parts of the day, no?"

She smiled. "How did you meet her?"

"I was a merchant seaman on a refrigerated gas carrier, a tanker vessel. We had mechanical difficulties with the coolers which meant we couldn't keep the gas in a liquid state. Repairs needed to be completed and we had to dock the ship for a long stay. Some of us were offered work on other vessels but I stayed to perform maintenance and security work. I had nowhere else to go and I got paid."

"What did you do with your down time? Or, shouldn't I ask?"

"You can ask. I used to read on the deck. When I ran out of books I began to wander, first just close to port and then into the city in larger and larger half-circles away from the ship. I visited businesses, tried to communicate with the locals. I ate from roadside vendors."

Koi enjoyed the way he told his story, the way he changed from Le Sauvage to a man who could have raised her. He talked about the day he met Mikie.

He came into the lacquer-ware store where she worked selling goods, mostly to tourists. He found the shop on a congested canal-side strip; a rattle of fishmongers, souvenir doll shops, dumpling stands, kitchen utensils, fried octopus, and t-shirts for the cruise-line shoppers. Molecules of stale, brackish backwater hung over the street, but inside her shop, the smell of sandalwood added an air of tranquility to an otherwise hurried atmosphere. "She had the most—her smile..." He choked a little. "She had the brightest smile. Her whole face smiled with her. I had never seen anything like it. She had a perfectly happy face and the whitest teeth in Osaka."

"You saw a lot of teeth in Osaka?"

He smiled and poked her shoulder. "Shush. It is a conclusion I drew based on people I saw at the harbor. Most of the men on my ship didn't have all theirs. I noticed, okay?"

"Okay. What else did you notice."

"She had a wonderful complexion, so clean and untouched, yet she didn't seem put off by my grimy, rough hands. I bought something small at her shop every day for a week. I finally got up the nerve to ask her to come with me outside. We held hands a lot when we would go for walks. People would give us looks but she pretended not to notice. Sometimes I think she did."

"Culture can be cruel to love."

"You like the poets, don't you?"

"Yes, but I have made my own conclusions."

"I see that is how you are."

They watched the lights of the city begin to glow in the rising darkness. Koi asked him why he chose his life. "You are an intelligent man. Bouchet is brilliant and even Hubert could be something other than what he is."

"You are a member of a criminal organization and yet you are asking me why I would choose such a life?"

"I am curious about such things. I didn't have the same options as you. You didn't just wake up one day as a black-market arms dealer. You had to... I don't know."

"It started small. I met Bouchet in Hong Kong. We became fast friends. I took his side in a fight that got a little out of control. We escaped the situation without involvement of the police. Bouchet had access to people who wanted to make more exciting investments than their brokers offered them. I knew people like Hubert, who knew others, who led us to men of a certain caliber, ex-military looking for adventure. One job led to another. We acquired access to a weapons depot in Lebanon that had been abandoned by the US Marines. It was a lucrative deal and we had developed a knack for anonymity. *Pour vivre heureux, vivons caché.*"

"That means what?"

"It means, to live well, live discreetly."

"Yakuza clan leaders think this way, not the soldiers."

"It is best. We have since developed extremely secure communications protocols to avoid being set up. We are good at what we do. *Que puis-je dire?* It is a logical life for men without roots."

"What about your reputation? May I ask? You don't earn the name Le Sauvage by accident."

Chastain stiffened. He had no desire to relive the moments that earned him his name. A reticence took over him. He tried to smile through it. "Sometimes in the heat of the moment, things have to be done for the sake of prowess. It is a tenuous business conducted by dangerous men. Respect can give you an edge."

"You mean fear."

"It prevents people from testing you. I've seen you fight. You understand."

"I have more to prove in my world."

"We are all just trying to survive, Emi. Let's go inside."

"Someone is missing. Is that why you were so quiet when you got back? What happened to Mayko?"

"I offered him another assignment. He'll be conducting some preliminary negotiations on another job, something in Africa where he is strangely at home."

"Did he screw up today?"

"No. He doesn't want you around. He doesn't get our relationship. He thinks I'm being romantic, that perhaps I am losing an edge."

"He wants to kill me, right?"

"He would slit your throat, but not his own. He wants to eat and we are his best shot at staying employed and staying clear of the law."

"Can you trust him? What if he goes to Interpol?"

"He has a vengeful heart, not a vindictive one. He won't say anything. He's not an idiot. He knows he couldn't hide from all of us. It will be fine." Chastain pointed inside. "Shall we?"

Everyone gathered assumed Mayko had gone off to procure more food and drinks, except Hubert. "Wait, where is Mayko? I thought he was picking up food," he said.

"From now on that's Picard's assignment, Potente can help," said Chastain.

The room grew quiet. The oh-shit faces came upon them. Hubert asked, "Boss, did he make it? Did he get busted? What happened?"

"He's going back home."

Picard laughed. "Probably running some meth for his mafia friends in Odessa. Anything for money, eh?"

"He has an assignment. No more questions."

***

Chastain called Bouchet and Hubert to the balcony. He sipped his bourbon then swept the skyline with his glass. "A nice view, but we should be home in our gardens, drinking pinot noir and smoking cigars—enjoying the sun."

Bouchet said, "Something is on your mind, Tiago."

Chastain took a long breath. "Yesterday I was in

charge of the way things ought to be, within this group. Not so long ago, I was a younger man who had left his future to chance and lived for the thrill of survival.

"Today though, has come quickly—or it seems that way. Tomorrows always come to us quickly, we think, but in reality, they don't—they come slowly, season after season until decades have passed and you suddenly take notice. The realization is what comes at you quickly even if the days do not. The acceptance of it doesn't come easily but when you finally do accept it, you have to acknowledge that life has begun to run past you and suddenly you can't catch up. You try to slow it down but you can't. The days outpace the living.

"As we get older, the days are difficult to enjoy because tomorrows come upon you too soon. The days keep coming at you, relentlessly. When clarity finally comes, it stands before you and demands you make a decision about where you are and what, if anything at all, you will do with the few good seasons that remain. You feel desire begin to drain from you, the desires of young men: love, conquest, riches and notoriety, until they all, on that day, no longer exist. They are neither desirable nor achievable.

"I feel I...I have to say that day may be upon me. I look at Emiko. I think...I know, I have to give something to her I never could give anyone before. But I fear the life I have chosen will intercede in my...beckonings, and I will die a disappointment to her and myself. But there is one problem."

The men waited for it.

Chastain swirled the ice in his drink. "I like what I do. It has become who I am. I don't know how to set it aside

244

gracefully. As much as I want to take what fortune I've made for myself and find a rare place in the world where I can set her up for a happy life, there is a big piece of me that wants to take all that gold, divide it amongst the team and shove it right up Hayato's ass. The very idea is exhilarating. It drives me in spite of the imperatives of an aging desperado who wants to be a father. I worry that these things that pull on me, the things that come to all men as youth withers—I worry they will be a distraction and I might not perform as I should. People could die, or worse, they could spend their lives in prison. It is a difficult time for me."

"We will always support you, boss," said Hubert. "We all struggle sometimes, with things we don't understand. And it is easy to get caught up in the emotion of such a potentially large score."

Bouchet said, "Hubert is right. We support you and trust you will make the right decisions when critical seconds count. Besides, those yakuza pricks have skimmed my profits more than a few times in my career. I would not object to getting the last laugh. Let's stop talking and rejoin our team."

"Agreed."

As they re-entered the room Chastain said he'd love to know, before they progressed, exactly how much gold was buried.

"Gold we haven't established is actually there, I'm afraid," said Boris.

Chastain told the crew to just listen, to try and push emotion aside and think pragmatically about what they might undertake. He said, "Whether the gold is there or not will only determine how quickly we move out of the area and regroup. I think we must make this decision before we go forward. I must decide if I want to go on at all. I have to be in the game one hundred percent before we put a plan in motion. If I decide to go along, then whatever happens, happens. If the gold is there we make a practical decision about whether or not we can move it. If we can't, then we sell it to yakuza. If there is no gold we sell them an idea, perhaps we can give them a discount." He laughed so the men could laugh.

Bouchet agreed. He said the decision must come now so that any future choices within the plan were made with a clear head and based on the objective, with training and experience, not grandeur. "We must, as always, be nimble. We must move quickly and decisively, with no tolerance for hesitation. That's how people get hurt." He spoke to Chastain. "Boss, I think I know how you feel but obviously not exactly. I am the closest to your age and I have questioned how much money I need myself. It may sound strange to newer members but when you are in it for just the thrill it's easy to make thrilling mistakes. When you are in it for the money, you can make pragmatic decisions because it's just money and there will always be other jobs, you see?"

"Very interesting." Boris added another. "Very interesting."

"So, team, what do you think?" Chastain said team but he looked at Koi. The look on her face would help him make a decision. He knew they had found themselves here because of her and because of her desire to bury her mother peacefully and have a normal life. She had no use for gold. She had been caught up in the excitement of the last few weeks in part to prevent herself from thinking about her mother. This talk of finality had gotten to her. Chastain could see it.

Koi hadn't expected the speech. She also hadn't expected to want to do something right by him with almost as much fervor as she wanted to do it for her mother. She began to feel that if she made them both happy, it would mean she had fulfilled some unsolicited obligation and arrived at the time for her to quit everything, to go in peace to her new life, likely never seeing either one of them again, for her own safety. By going along with this plan, she was going against the decision she'd made that had gotten her to this point, to leave the life. She had put her life and her mother's life at risk to approach Hayato in the first place. But now she had become a part of planning one more job, one that had attractive elements despite its contradictions to her goal. It confused her.

"Going for a run." She looked at Chastain. "I know it's getting dark but I'm going for a run. When I return I expect you all will have made a decision. I will go along with whatever you decide." She changed in her room and left without saying anything else.

"She did that for you, boss," said Hubert. "I have a daughter. I know how they are."

"Your daughter is no more than ten," said Bouchet.

"They start young."

Chastain told Potente to go out after her, not to stop her, just to keep an eye on her.

Potente said, "Boss, I couldn't catch her with two good legs."

"I didn't say catch her, I said watch her. Just be out there. Take a taxi out front and head toward the river. Go."

"Right away."

The crew began to discuss their options. None of them wanted to go against Chastain but they had their own self-interests to consider. The consensus leaned toward completing one more job, one great adventure that would give them enough money to retire on.

***

Koi took the Dinh Tiên Hoàng toward the water. She ran full out for a thousand meters before slowing it to a moderate pace. Her pores opened up. She tried to concentrate on the running and her breathing but could only see her mother's face. The traffic held her up at a light.

As she took a step off into the intersection a scooter buzzed her. She hollered after it. She flipped him off and took a step but another cut her off. She turned back toward it, cursing the nonexistent traffic laws and the...

"*Xem ra, xem ra,*" the rider yelled as he ran his 200cc motorbike up behind her, pushing the wheel between her legs. He pushed his hand into her back and yelled again. "*Xem ra.*"

"Watch where the fuck you're going, you little shit!" Koi pulled away from his bike when the first scooter clipped her arm. Within seconds four or five scooters and small motorcycles were buzzing her and hollering. Koi took a stance at one coming at her from the front. She spun in the air and kicked him in the face, knocking him off his ride. She wheeled to face the other when one threw a chain at her that hit her in the neck. The traffic grew

248

more congested around what looked like a display of callow machismo. People yelled from the sidewalks. They pulled back, then lined up side by side in front of her, one still on the ground nursing his swollen skull. They revved their engines louder. She tried to scare them off by stomping the one on the ground. She smashed her heel through his teeth.

They didn't move, continued to rev their engines and taunted her.

She called them out. "Come on, you motherfuckers. Get off and fight."

From the back seat of the taxi, Potente looked out through the congested street at the commotion ahead. He knew it had to be her. He jumped out and fought the crowds to reach her as a panel van pulled up beside her. The side door opened and two men jumped out. They kidney-punched her and dragged her inside onto her belly. Within seconds, three men were on top of her. They blindfolded her and held her down. The driver jerked into traffic as Potente reached the back door. He grabbed at the rear door handle but the van sped away. The motorbike riders split off in different directions.

"*Scheisse, scheisse, verdammt, scheisse.*" He took up the bleeding man's bike and tried to chase the van. He swerved to avoid a woman carrying two young children. He lost the van within three blocks. He pulled over to puke.

Oh God, I let her down. His breathing tore at his throat. *Chastain will kill me.*

Inside the van she tried to fight. The men held her down and tied her wrists and knees, one spoke in

Japanese. *"Anata no rokkotsu ni jū ga arimasu."* She felt the muzzle of a pistol jammed into her ribs.

***

Potente called Hubert, screaming into the phone that she'd been taken. He could identify the van, had a partial plate. He couldn't see the men who grabbed her. They wore Halloween masks. It all happened so quickly.

"Get back here immediately. Don't waste any more time, just get here."

"I tried, I didn't know which street she went running on. I caught up to her too late. I'm so sorry. I can't believe this is happening."

"Now, Potente, hang up and get here now."

***

Hubert had told the boss. When Potente walked in Chastain slammed the heel of his palm into Potente's nose and bounced his head off the wall.

"You fucking idiot. How could you let this happen? I told you to watch her."

Boris tried to intervene. *"Monsieur,* the man is smitten with her. He would not want anything to happen to her."

Chastain grabbed Boris by the shirt. "Shut the fuck up. This is not your business." He shoved Boris who fell back over the coffee table. The others stepped in. Bouchet said, "Boss, you must stop and think. One man could not have prevented this. He had no way to stop it. He would have been shot and we would know nothing."

Chastain fumed. "If they have her they knew she was here. That means they know *we're* here. It must be those fucking yakuza monkeys. I'll kill them all." He looked down at Potente who held on to his broken nose.

"Someone attend to him. Boris, pack up your maps and books and get ready to move. Hubert, get this place wiped."

Bouchet told Picard and The Beard to go to their hotel and pack. "Be extremely careful. We don't know who is out there or how many men they have. Expect the worst."

Chastain called Fournier to alert him.

The crew stepped into gear, cleaning the rooms with silent precision. The garbage, food and glassware were packed in three large plastic bags and dropped into separate dumpsters off site. Three timed incendiary devices were dropped with the garbage. With the hour three dumpster fires would keep the locals busy and create distraction.

Boris stayed quiet and packed his things. Watching them work, he realized they'd been through these actions before. The atmosphere changed on a beat and he felt immediately like an outsider.

Everyone was to meet at a prearranged safe house across town in groups of two. No one was to move to the safe house unless they were certain they weren't being followed.

By 10pm they were assembled. The Beard was put on first perimeter watch.

Time for action. Not much time to think. Wait for the call they knew would come.

Chapter Twenty-Eight

THE KIDNAPPERS DREW OPEN the sliding door in the refrigerated storage facility at the pier. They threw her, still hooded, onto the floor. Her hands, still tied behind her back, couldn't break her fall. She arched her back but her chin struck the cold, damp floor.

The men taunted Koi, lifted her shirt and reached into her sports bra. "Nice, firm. Here, you see." Another. "Ahh, nice tits for a mongrel." They pulled her running pants down and remarked about the tattoos on her flank running down to her "nice ass".

"Nice, right? No fat."

"Yeah, nice enough to beat."

They told Koi she was no longer yakuza, nothing more than just another *baishunpu* and they would all have her before they sent her back to be killed by Hayato. They dumped cold water on her and chained her to a pallet of fruit, set to be loaded and shipped to Hong Kong by dawn. They cursed her as a weasel and left her there half stripped to contemplate her fate

Though shivering, she promised to escape and disembowel them.

A third man kicked her in the back. She let out a grunt.

An hour passed as Koi breathed to relax, focused on warming her body. She worked herself to her knees, got her running pants up and felt behind her for a lock or a way to break the chain free of the pallet.

Judging from where they'd stashed her, she knew they would move her soon. It seemed to be a place of business, open-air in which voices echoed, a warehouse perhaps—not small. She worked what links she could reach, up and down as far as she could strain. The kick bruised her back, making the twisting even more difficult. She determined that if she had time, she could tear off a corner of a box of mangos, then work at the nails holding the corner of the pallet.

She heard the men coming and lay on her belly. *Will they move me now or rape me? The grandmother-fucking cowards; I wish I was on my period.*

They came in, quieter for reasons she couldn't imagine. She could smell liquor. *This is it.*

One of them lifted the hood and held a phone to her ear. She recognized his face. He worked for Johnny Kubo's clan. *Is this part of a turf war or did Hayato sell me for vengeance?*

"She is listening," he said.

The voice brought her chills back.

"Emiko. You have failed me."

"Hayato. I have only failed my mother."

"We will get to her in a minute. You were supposed to let me know what was going on. You haven't called. You killed members of our clan without approval. You are working with Le Sauvage. You have failed in your duties and I must end this embarrassment to my reign."

"You won't kill me. I have information you need."

"I no longer need it. I will get it from your father, in exchange for your life, but I won't promise it will be a life worth saving."

My father? She lost all the control she had trained so hard to maintain; always in control, a good yakuza warrior. "*Shinjimai.* You son of a bitch. Your mother sucks dick. You *hine daikon* old man, I'll cut your head off. You got to my mother? I will haunt your children's children."

"Your mother was not hurt, although I prepared myself to. The poor sick thing. She was easy to manipulate. She told me about Chastain. Now in exchange for the gold, and your life, I will not go to Interpol. For that I give my word."

"Your word? The only words I will hear from you is a plea for your own death."

The thug pulled the phone away and kicked her in the crotch. She screamed in pain, anguish and hatred.

***

Hayato had gone through her phone back at his hotel. The numbers appeared coded except for Potente's. From somewhere in the warehouse, he dialed the number.

"It's her," said Potente. "She's calling me."

Chastain said, "Give me that phone. It's not her." He took in a long breath and pressed the green dot. "Yes. Speak."

"Ahh, Monsieur Chastain. So interesting to speak with you under these circumstances. I'll not waste any of our valuable time. We are professionals. I have something you want. You have something I want. But I'm afraid, for you, I also have leverage."

"You have nothing. You have a girl. I have more gold than you monkeys can count. You want the gold? Come and take it from me." He hung up.

255

Chapter Twenty-Nine

CHISATO TELEPHONED the Interpol headquarters who transferred her to the commander of the Sauvage investigation. The lead detective told his boss he had a call waiting from Japan.

"*Sergent-Détective* Marceau."

"*Bonjour, Monsieur.* This is Miss Chisato Hara from the Osaka police. I am calling you unofficially, but there is something you should know about a man they call Le Sauvage. I believe your organization is hunting him."

"I'm listening." He said it with a controlled voice, but silenced the squad room with a frantic wave.

"I have reason to believe he and a crew of men were recently in Osaka and I have further reason to believe he will be returning soon."

"Where is he now?" asked Marceau.

"I can't be sure. He was in a gunfight with members of a yakuza clan. It occurred just before he left by private plane."

"Have any of the yakuza been arrested or interviewed in hospital?"

"They are all dead."

"How many?"

"Seven, including a clan leader."

"How can I know this information is credible?"

"I will send you documentation when I can obtain it."

"Very well. Take my personal number as well."

"Yes, sergeant, oh one more thing."

"*Oui*?"

"One of the dead was decapitated with a katana, we believe it was done by a woman known as Koi, a yakuza enforcer."

"*Bordel de merde*...it must be her. *Merci, Mademoiselle*."

The detective sergeant hung up and called an emergency meeting of all personnel assigned to the case. The focus of the investigation would shift to Osaka.

Detectives wondered why this Koi person would kill her own. They concluded she must be a turncoat working with Le Sauvage.

But on what? Why?

What could she have to offer Le Sauvage that would necessitate her actions against her own people? Who was she that she could kill Le Sauvage's people as well as her own?

From a florist shop outside Lyon, Marin called Hubert. "Get word to the boss. Interpol has been active. Headed your way. Don't know what they have. They have something."

Hubert relayed the message to Chastain, who accepted it as though he'd been expecting it.

Chastain had been squeezed before, but had always seen it coming and reacted by aborting and dissolving. The team would vanish, leaving no trace. And why not? There would always be another deal. But this time he didn't know Interpol had received the tip. This time the squeeze was on and he didn't know it. Not yet.

***

At the safe house, Chastain and Bouchet told Boris to proceed with the plan to search the castle grounds, knowing yakuza would not be looking for him; he'd operate undetected. They'd need to figure out a quick, secure way for Boris to report his findings to Chastain, who may be on the move. If he was compromised, an extraction would expose the team.

Hubert said he would work with locals to get Boris out, if necessary.

"No." Bouchet and Chastain said it together. Chastain said, "No locals. We don't know who we can trust. Any local talent would likely be affiliated with yakuza anyway. We need you back here as quickly as possible. Get Boris to some place where he can take a taxi to the airport."

"*Oui.*"

"Boris, when you get to the airport, buy a prepaid phone then call Hubert with the number. After that you'll have to destroy your phone. Take it apart in the toilet and flush the inner components."

"Sounds all rather MI6. I'm on board."

Chastain was in no mood for Boris's wit. They rehearsed Boris's movements, his channels for contacting the team and local contacts for picking up his GPR equipment. The fake work orders would be awaiting him at his hotel, in English and Japanese. After the job, assuming all went as planned, Boris was to relocate north to Ishikawa on the coast to await contact. Boris sweat through the first twenty-four of seventy-two hours without booze. Standard spin-dry stuff. Lay off the sauce for three days. Get it out.

He'd make it. He needed clarity.

Hayato had expected Chastain to be a tough negotiator, but didn't expect him to imply that Koi's life meant nothing to him. Perhaps he really was a savage. Perhaps he'd overplayed his hand.

Hayato called back. It was his second mistake. It gave Chastain a sense of the upper hand, a familiar feeling to an experienced black-market *revendeur*.

Hayato tested Chastain's resolve. "Our conversation seems to have been cut off. Perhaps it is the international connection. You must understand, *Monsieur*, I have no compunction about ending this young woman's life."

"Nor have I for taking yours. What do you want?"

"You have information I want. I have someone you want. It's simple enough."

"Not really. There are complications."

"Such as?"

"I have a different perspective. If I kill you, which I will, and keep the gold, I will then run your organization, without all the self-aggrandizing body art. So how about this offer? I don't kill you and you give me the girl. I keep the gold and I give you a stake as a consolation for losing this war. I really have no desire to run your organization. I like things the way they are."

"Your bravado is admirable if not misplaced. You would never survive in our culture. But such is the way of negotiation."

"With every word you speak, Monsieur Hayato, you step closer to death. I want proof of life. I want to speak to her, now."

"I also want proof of life. I have reason to believe you have an associate of ours. His name is Ino."

"Was, Ino. He is dead. He cried like a little girl on his way out. He no longer exists so he is not a part of this discussion. Now let me speak to Koi."

Hayato hesitated. He knew Ino might be dead and had no reason to think Chastain was bluffing. He walked to the cooler where they held Koi. He motioned for them to open the door. Two men dragged her out to the boss. Hayato whispered to her that she should be cautious. "Just speak and let him hear your voice."

Hayato said, "*Monsieur*, I will let her speak to you. She doesn't know where she is, so don't play games. Just accept your proof and we will continue our conversation."

Koi had listened when her guards weren't nearby. She surmised she sat in a walk-in cooler by the pallets and smell of fruit. She'd heard the sounds of the river, and knew she hadn't traveled far from where they snatched her.

"Koi, are you okay? Have they hurt you?" Chastain asked.

She spoke in the best French she could muster. "I certainly wouldn't come here for peace of mind. Frozen Kobi not my thing."

Hayato pulled the phone back and signaled for the men to put her back inside. Chastain smiled on the other end.

"You see she is quite alive. Now let us discuss the manner in which we can conduct this transfer of information."

"Ben Tanh Street Food Market, inside by the café

sellers and the *ngoc linh*. Eleven o'clock tomorrow morning. Bring her. I will bring information you need. If it is a trap, I will kill her first, then you."

"Eleven it is."

Chastain hung up and set the team into action. "She is in a refrigerated storage facility by the river. There can't be too many of them. Let's find out which ones are closed overnight. We move before dawn."

Bouchet and the others asked how he could be sure.

"She mentioned being at peace there. She is only at peace around water. That means the river. She referred to herself as frozen Kobi. That tells me she is somewhere cold. The only place cold in the industrial area by the river is a refrigerated warehouse. This was not an elaborate plan. They had to stash her away quickly. It's Sunday night. The place is closed for now. They have to move her early in the morning. We have to get there first."

Bouchet said, "So the market is a back-up plan. If we miss her at the warehouse we have an alternative. That won't be an easy switch. They'll be expecting something in return."

"We are only taking, not giving. Let's see. Let's just see which organization can operate more swiftly in this country. Everyone here is looked at suspiciously by the party people. Those tattooed *malfrats* can't blend in. We have the advantage, so let's stop talking and fix a plan."

Potente studied the area and found a warehouse situated at the end of a route the van could have taken from where they grabbed her to where he had lost them. "Bien Dong Trading." The three-story facility had refrigerated units available on the third floor, according to online advertising for their services. "It says the place has twenty-four-hour security."

The Beard said not to worry about security. It was likely just security cameras or else the yakuza wouldn't be operating inside.

"Unless they killed the guards," said Picard.

The Beard, doing pushups, laughed. "Well then we don't have to worry about security either way. If there are alarms they are already tripped or shut down. If they are inside, we can get there as well."

***

Chastain had predicted correctly that yakuza would be understaffed at the location. Hayato had brought a bodyguard, unarmed. The three who pulled off the kidnapping had managed to sneak into the terminal area unnoticed and broken into an employee entrance to the facility. Security cameras recorded their activity on internal hard drives but had no notification system for local police.

Just three yakuza soldiers ran the kidnap and hold operation, taking turns watching the exterior, their boss and the prisoner. Fatigue had begun to set in. Hayato waited back at his hotel with his bodyguard with orders to his men to move Koi in the morning and wait in the van until he notified them to bring her to the market for the swap.

Three tired combatants versus a half-dozen trained, experienced soldiers of fortune, led by one very angry commander. The odds of a yakuza victory were in the toilet, unless one of the yakuza panicked and killed Koi. Chastain's team needed to move quickly, quietly and with deadly precision.

The Beard, freshly jacked up from his push-ups, volunteered to stand watch. Picard and The Beard went to the roof and scoped the area with night vision, ensuring they weren't under surveillance. The other members rested for three hours. Chastain set a wake-and-ready for 03:30. They would hit the facility at 04:30.

The men conducted final preparations, reviewed the layout and call signals, double-checked their weapons then loaded into two vehicles. Potente drove Hubert and Picard, who would disable any perimeter security. The Beard drove Chastain and Hubert, who would leapfrog the first team and make the primary entry. Fournier would stay back to help route an alternate evac plan.

They parked their vehicles northwest of the target, fifty meters out by a bus terminal. They ran the final fifty through the cover of containers and standing vehicles. The river breathed slowly to the east under a new moon.

Picard carried a medical bag and a blanket for Koi.

They used only hand signals once they were within striking distance. Potente's quick survey of the perimeter showed one kidnapper outside, smoking and kicking stones at rats feeding near a dumpster. Picard hugged the wall, came in behind him and in one motion, covered the yakuza's mouth and rammed a Swedish field knife past his spine and through his heart. He twisted it and yanked it out. The man died on the spot. Picard signaled the next move.

The teams drew their weapons, all small arms except for Potente who carried a tactical rifle and Picard with a sawed-off pump-action shotgun, loaded with 12-gauge buckshot. The Beard led Chastain and Hubert through the door while Bouchet and the others waited for ten seconds. Potente would remain outside to watch the escape route back to the vehicles.

The first trio took the ascension without a sound, then waited at the top of the stairs for the next two soldiers. To conserve electricity, the warehouse set in minimal night lighting, leaving just enough to pick up ill-defined shadows on the CCTVs. Down a row to the left, one man stood outside a sliding door, partially open. Spill from the light inside put him in silhouette. Chastain sent Picard and Hubert across the floor to the far right to flank him. He would give them just thirty seconds to get into position.

The man outside the cooler guarded nothing. He concerned himself with his partner inside the cooler, taunting Koi and preparing to drag her into the warmer aisle to rape her. His senior status gave him first whack at her. As he untied her knees, Hubert popped up from behind a crate of rattan furniture and shot the yakuza guard in the chest and head. The gunfire caused the rapist to slide the door shut from the inside. Koi tried to stand but her muscles cramped. She said, "They're here, you pig. You lose tonight. Did you shit yourself already?" He didn't answer her.

The team ran to the cooler door. Chastain tried it but the yakuza enforcer had blocked the groove for the wheels with a piece of timber. Bouchet looked up and said, "Boss, the wheels."

"Do it," said Chastain.

Picard and The Beard set charges to blow off the top wheels. Ten seconds later the men pulled the door forward and it slammed to the floor. The yakuza held Koi in front of him with a knife to her throat.

The others drew down on him. Chastain walked up to him, looked him in the eye and said, "I am here, Emi. You are safe now."

"It's about time. This guy was just about to stick his puny prick in me."

The yakuza froze with fear and hopelessness. Chastain grabbed him by the throat. He let Koi loose. Bouchet untied her arms and blindfold while Picard stood ready to wrap her in the blanket. The yakuza, hands shaking, raised the knife. Chastain pushed him against the wall and shot him in each leg, then the gut, then in his balls. The man's knees buckled as he screamed in pain. Chastain stared into his eyes for a moment, then shot him in the heart. "Let's get her out of here."

She shivered. "You almost missed me here."

"They were going to move you?"

"No, I was just about to escape."

"Yes, you looked ready for action. You have an odd sense of humor."

"Hey, I'm from Osaka."

Bouchet had signaled to Potente that they were on their way back down. Despite his wounded leg he ran ahead to start the vehicles. Twenty minutes later, they were all in the safe house.

Once Koi had eaten and had coffee to warm her bones, she told Chastain about her conversation with Hayato. "That fucking animal got to my mother. He may have hurt her. He said she was easily manipulated. He knows about you. He knows about us. I want him dead but I need to kill him myself. I need to see my mother, Chastain. I need to see her. Why the fuck did you wait so long to come back to her?"

Her words gut-punched him. "Emiko. You will have your way with Hayato. I know you want to see your mother but Hayato has probably alerted the police. They may have a guard on her in case you return. It will be impossible for you to get close to her while she is in that hospital."

Koi yelled and raised a fist toward him, then whirled and kicked over a lamp. She sat on the couch holding back tears.

Chastain tried to comfort her by putting his hand on her shoulder. She shrugged it off. He said he would let her alone for a while. They still had a plan to intercept Hayato in Vietnam, but it would be a long shot. The team would be spread thin. "Vengeance is never a good prerequisite for an operation. Emotions cloud judgement. There is a practical reason, though. We have to stop him from going to Interpol. Once we take him out, I don't think anyone in your clan would have access to the level of detail Hayato had about the gold. By the time they figure it out, we'll be drunk on a beach in the Mediterranean."

"I'll be fine. I want in on this part of the plan. I just need an hour to lie here and rest my legs. I'm still chilled from that place with those fucking rapist animals."

"Did they..."

"No, no they never did. They came close, but no."

He let out a deep breath. "Rest. I'll wake you in one hour."

"Wait. What happened to Potente's nose?"

"He fell."

Chapter Thirty

IN THE MAIN ROOM of the safe house, Chastain and the team reviewed the rescue of Koi over drinks. Normally these men would be in a ball-breaking mood with the rush of booze and adrenalin, but they had begun to feel the squeeze. They couldn't be sure what the Osaka police had told Interpol, if anything. But all agreed the possibility existed. Yakuza would not simply go away. They had no plan for Koi and found themselves counting on Boris, who had no field experience. Chastain wanted to capture and kill Hayato for Koi but even he knew that wouldn't help the big picture. Killing another clan leader would put the whole of yakuza, not to mention the Japanese authorities, on high alert. It would bring them no closer to the gold but it would virtually eliminate any obstructions to obtaining it.

Chastain said, "And to make things worse, we can't trust the locals to help us. Someone told them she was here. It's the only way they could have known she was in this part of the city and that she went out for runs. They had to be watching her."

"It's time to cross this country off the list of places we will operate in," said Hubert.

"And we need to get out soon," said Bouchet. "If they know about her, they know about us or at least suspect who we might be. We would attract a handsome reward."

"We leave tomorrow night, whether we get Hayato or

not. Hubert and Picard—I want you to work on several routes we can take to get to a plane and move quickly. Fournier must have a second with him whenever possible."

"*Oui*, very important," Bouchet said, "We can't fly commercial. We can't trust the authorities. Miss Elizabeth might know something. I'll set up a meeting, offer her some cash."

"No," said Chastain. "It's too risky. She may have already sold us out, the bitch."

"How long have you known me?" Bouchet raised his glass to Chastain then took a swig. "I'll set it up for twelve hours after we're out of the country. She can fuck herself."

"I should have known. *Je suis désolé, mon ami.*" He toasted Bouchet.

Picard cut in. "Boss, one problem. You told Hayato we would meet him at eleven. His stupid crew would have to move Koi long before that, so they don't get caught when the place opens in the morning. Whatever they have planned to secure her in the meantime will go to shit once he doesn't hear from them and he can't make contact."

"Yes, yes, I know. And the local police will be called to the scene. Hayato will know early and try to move."

Bouchet suggested they call him and make the switch early, but all agreed that either way, Hayato would know early on that his men had been killed and Koi released.

"We may be screwed."

Koi had been listening from the doorway. She stepped in. "I'll call him."

"Ahh, you are up already? No, I can't have you call him. What for?"

"I can tell him. Just tell him you rescued me and his idiots are dead. Now what? He'll get nervous and run? Maybe. But what if I tell him I don't wish to run any longer. Just want to see my mother before she dies. I can tell him I've spent my life being loyal to yakuza and I'm feeling badly about what happened. Tell him I'll go back with him, and tell him everything I know. Let me see her and then I don't care what he does with me. There is truth to it. I will sound sincere."

The men didn't speak. Chastain said, "Are you sincere? I have to ask."

"No, you don't have to ask, you fool. Of course, I want to see my mother but I am an adult. I understand the way things are. I hate that fucker for using my mother to get to me and using me in the first place to get to you. I'll turn it on him. I will...be sincere. Give me a damn drink and a few minutes to get my thoughts together. I will call him and arrange a meeting for just after dawn. You can watch me slit his throat."

"Okay but wait. Let's run this around. Why would Hayato believe we are willing to give you up to him?"

"Access to the gold," said Bouchet. "We tell him in exchange for Koi, we have unfettered access to dig up the gold. We admit we will have great difficulty moving it out of the country and offer him half as payment for egress from his lovely country."

Chastain didn't need long to agree. He gave Koi her a drink. "Here. Emiko. Before, what I meant was, are you sincere in that you would put yourself out there as bait and...I don't know what I'm saying. Never mind." He poured another bourbon.

Bouchet said, "He may not answer the phone if the call is not from his people. He may be suspicious."

"No worries," said The Beard. He reached into his bag. "I scooped up one of their phones on the way out for intel. I left it on but so far, no incoming calls. It looks like a prepaid phone."

"Nice work. Yes, it is prepaid." Chastain handed it to Koi. "Get yourself together and call him. Say that you'll tell us you will go for a run and meet him at the same market at 06:00 instead. You will have the information he seeks."

"He will respond faster if I've killed you. It was my original mission."

"Fuck him. Just tell him I am well protected but trusted you enough to tell you where the gold is. You know what? Tell him we're already moving on it, leaving today. He hasn't much time. What's a city by Osaka that we can tell him we are going to?"

"Kyoto. It's north of Osaka and a logical place along a route the original Shōgun loyalists would have taken if they had moved the gold there."

"Fine. Tell him we are going to Kyoto and you will provide him the details on your trip back to Japan, but he is to leave us alone or we cut him out. Then hang up, don't wait for him to change anything. If he calls back, don't answer. He has no say in this."

The Beard asked, "What if he doesn't believe her and thinks it's a set-up?"

"Then we lose him. He doesn't make the meet." He turned to Koi. "I'm sorry. We have one shot at this. Win or lose, we have to get out of Vietnam."

"Understood."

"Good. Let's go over the plan."

They reviewed the operational plan three times, including the flight out of country. The Beard would ghost Koi in proximity to where she would contact Hayato. He looked less European than the others with his full beard and dark complexion, so he could stand closest without being made. Chastain, Bouchet and the rest split into two teams in taxis nearby, out of sight of a potential yakuza scout. Koi would cover her head with a scarf and work her way through the fishermen, shopkeepers and delivery men preparing the market for the day's crowds. Chastain held her shoulders and looked directly at her; his voice held a tenor she hadn't heard from him before. "If you spot Hayato before you get to the spot, call me from the prepaid phone. Tell me if he has any men with him and give me clothing descriptions, then ditch the phone. If you see a gun when you approach them, raise your hands at your shoulders, like this. What will be in your backpack?"

"Just clothes and my identification—some cash, Japanese. He can check my bag, nothing to find."

"Okay, Emiko. You are prepared."

"I can't wait to end his life."

"Emi."

"What, Father?"

"You don't have to do this. We can get to him another time. Killing him has to be about free access to money, not emotions. I understand they exist but this is very dangerous."

"Has to be this way. If I don't get to him first he may have my mother killed. I can't let that happen."

"If this goes wrong, you could die. I can't allow it."

She closed her eyes and turned away from him. "I'm going to try and rest."

The team got no more than a few hours of sleep. Koi got none. She thought about her mother, tried to remember a time in her life when things were good. She only remembered moments, pieces of days when they'd had a laugh or a great meal or when, for the blessing of the weather and crowds and her mother's big smile, she could forget about their difficult lives and live for a day captured from someone else's, a friend's home or an invitation to the lake.

She thought about the day she took out Johnny Kubo and the young couple on the subway stairs enjoying their little boy. She thought about how many people she'd beaten for Hayato and her street family. Her mother's sinless life punished by custom. She cried just a little.

The Beard had taken second watch and woke the team at 05:00. They drank coffee and ate sandwiches in silence. They drove to downtown Saigon after setting devices to torch the rural safe house beside the ardent green of the rice fields.

Potente dropped Koi off in the opposite side of the market from the meet spot. He turned to her as if to say goodbye but couldn't bring himself.

"What is it, Potente? Just say it."

"I was scared. I can't remember ever feeling that way."

"Scared when? What are you talking about?

"When they grabbed you off the street. I... I thought

they might be killing you. I'm so sorry I let them get to you. I should have been faster, followed you more closely. I was thinking you'd see me and get mad, so I hung back. Your father sent me to watch you."

"You were scared of what my father would do to you?"

"No. Don't you? Ahh, Emiko."

"Koi."

"Emiko. That is your—"

"Whatever."

"Emiko, I was scared I wasn't going to see you again. I don't know if that's the right way to describe it, but that's what I'm thinking now, you know, about how I felt."

She grabbed his shirt as if she were about to shake him out of his apology—then she kissed him full on his mouth. Pressed her palm against his whiskers and closed her eyes, smelled his skin.

He touched her arm. His hand shook.

She had never felt whatever was swirling around inside her at that moment. She didn't understand why she did it. She just kissed him for a long, soft moment. It felt right, felt natural. And just as quickly, felt like a mistake. She pushed away from him as though he had made a drunken pass at her.

"What?" he asked.

"*Tokiniha sekai ga watashini totte haya sugiru.*"

"That means?"

"Sometime the world spins too fast for me."

"I'll slow it down for you."

"You're full of shit but your lies are sweet."

He blew out a breath and grabbed the steering wheel with both hands. He looked at her and looked at his watch.

275

"You'd better get going. I don't have to tell you to be careful, I guess."

"Hey, German. Look at me. Get your head in the game. I need you. I will make it. I have to. And hey, helmet head, don't be checking out the Saigon girls while I'm gone and forget about me."

He laughed and looked down at his lap. "I won't. Now get out before I drive you to Thailand."

She shut the door behind her, tucked the scarf inside her collar and tapped the car. All clear, so far.

Potente watched her. If there were a more perfect time for a blues soundtrack to play over his thoughts at that instant, he'd never imagine it. He drove off.

Game on.

Koi spied the crowd. She looked for a familiar Japanese face among the tourists. One couple. Honeymooners—no threat. Time slowed. The morning rush of shoppers and workers like players in a slurred drama, extras in the movie of her last days, voiceless.

She walked into the market, already swarming, into the sweet smell from the first stand, the prime spot, selling dried fruits, candies, the *nho mỹ* and *hong loan*. She became distracted for a moment passing the incense stand; the smells reminded her of the temple. Each stand loaded to bursting with cone hats, trinkets, Buddha statues, teapots, flowers and local art. She saw no familiar faces, noticed no one scanning the crowds for her or the dangerous Sauvage.

The Beard waited outside the main entrance, under the clock as if he were waiting for a ride. From the front archway, he had a line of sight to the café stand, but the morning sun had the market in shadows and he couldn't see well to the inside. He had to make a move closer, get inside as a tourist and buy a belt or a lacquer box. Look like a frustrated haggler, struggling with the culture but needing a gift.

Chastain looked through his binoculars from the across the circular park and the Quach Thi Trang roundabout, standing under a billboard praising the communist workers. He could see The Beard. A green city bus passed through his view. When it moved on, Chastain lost sight of The Beard. He grabbed his walkie-talkie. "*Putain*, where is he? Did he go inside? Anyone see him?"

Potente had been driving back and forth from the filling station through the roundabout. "I don't see him, boss. Should I go inside?"

"Wait. Bouchet, what do you see?" Bouchet saw two men exit a taxi on the south side of the market, one older, walking with a younger man who looked anxious but in good physical condition.

Bouchet said, "I see them. Not The Beard, the target. It must be them, they are wearing suits. One is much older."

"Where did the other guy come from?"

"Back-up plan. Probably had him waiting as a last resort. They're walking east now toward the main entrance. Beard, can you hear me?"

The Beard had managed to find a noisy spot near a woman pan-frying shrimp and goat brains, and spoke into his sleeve. "I copy you. I have eyes on her. She is okay, walking toward the café."

Chastain cut in. "Stay put, Beard. Yakuza is here. I don't see any back-up. Unless there are more men inside I think it's just the two of them. Picard, move in from the rear. When they get to the door we are moving closer."

Potente said, "My car is in position, facing south. I can see the entrance. Hubert?"

"I'm going round the traffic circle to drop off the boss. I'm good."

Bouchet made his way to the entrance just after Chastain. They squinted inside as they adjusted to the change in the lighting. He fell in behind Hayato and his bodyguard. He planned to tackle the bodyguard so that Bouchet could finish him off. They didn't want to shoot from behind and risk hitting Koi. Guns would bring the police and they didn't have the best escape plan.

She gulped in air. He hadn't seen her yet but she saw them. Tanaka the Bull came around a food stall first. *Hayato will be right behind him.* He turned the corner by the café and stopped. She thought he looked tired. She removed her sunglasses and scarf, walked into his view. He didn't react, not that she could see. Tanaka smiled, and not because he felt happy to see her. He had been ordered to kill her once they got back to Japan. He planned to enjoy it.

She didn't bow, a sign of disrespect. "Oyabun. I see you brought your pet gorilla."

Tanaka smiled again, a little louder this time.

Hayato said, "You are feeling pretty good about yourself I see. Considering everything that has gone wrong for you lately, I would think you might be humbled. Perhaps you are too stupid to realize the mess you've made. I supported you, made concessions for you, excuses really. You have let me down."

"Is my mother alive?"

"Yes, for now. But, she is quite ill. It could turn badly for her quickly. Where are your new friends, Koi?"

"They don't bother with me on my morning runs. They are back at the hotel, probably with hangovers."

"I would like to meet Le Sauvage. I've heard so much about him. Does he speak well of your mother?"

Hayato could see that she was breathing heavier. He thought his remarks angered her. He backed off. "Let's stop this foolishness. We are here for business. Come, we have arranged transportation. You can tell me your story on the plane. We will confirm it of course."

Koi stood close enough to strike. Tanaka sensed it and stepped between them. As he did, the woman frying brains banged a pan and yelled at The Beard for hanging around and not buying anything. Koi slipped up. Her eyes widened when she saw The Beard. Tanaka spotted her reaction and attacked. He shoved her into a stall.

Go.

Chastain moved on Tanaka but slipped on fish oil that had dripped onto the glazed brick floor and slammed onto his back. Koi threw a roundhouse kick at Tanaka but he caught it and threw her backwards. The market erupted. The patrons and shopkeepers began screaming. Hayato had gone to his knees and crawled under shops and into the maze of people, aisles and wares. Bouchet called for everyone to converge except the drivers.

Chastain regained his footing and dove on Tanaka's back as he sparred with Koi. "Let me have him," she said.

"Get the old man," Chastain said. "I've got this."

Tanaka the Bull had an appropriate nickname and had

trained as a Sumo. He had legs like pile drivers and stood with Chastain on his back, swinging him in a circle as Bouchet and Hubert tried to go low on him. The Beard crawled through the stands after Koi looking for Hayato but became entangled in the mosh and gave up. Police sirens and security whistles whipped through the whooping crowd. Chastain got two fingers into Tanaka's eye and he dug it out. Hubert managed to get a knife into The Bull's groin. Like a pack of wolves on an elk, they eventually got him down. Tanaka broke Bouchet's nose and Hubert's rib before Hubert struck the final blow into Tanaka's neck and he slumped.

Chastain yelled to move out. Bouchet hollered into his walkie-talkie. "Mobile teams, Potente, Picard, pick us all up out front."

"Where is Koi? Where is The Beard?"

The Beard made his way out a side entrance, into an alley where they sold flowers and live poultry under tents. It all looked quiet. If Hayato had come this way, he did so with a soft step. No one seemed aroused except for the look of wonder at all the sirens in the air. The Beard ran out of time and ran to the front of the market. He jumped into the back window of Potente's car as the team pulled off and split up, police in pursuit of Chastain in the lead car.

Potente hollered at the team. "Where the fuck is Koi? Is she alive? What the fuck happened in there?"

"I don't know where she is. She is after Hayato. I knew we shouldn't have tried this. Just fucking drive. Lose these cops and let me think."

Potente lost the cops in short order. The team had

arranged to dump the vehicles and meet at a friendly hotel, hoping the owner had remained loyal to Chastain's money and not turned like the others. Chastain tried calling Koi's phone. She didn't answer. He pounded his fist into the door. "Fuck, fuck, fuck."

***

The Interpol investigative team boarded the Dassault Falcon in a late-evening downpour. The interior set up for a command post, not comfortable for long travel. On board were the lead investigator, Detective Sergeant Marceau, two Parisian detectives, de Trévise and a female named Perrin. They rounded out the international team with a Japanese gang expert named Aoki and an Aussie with money-laundering experience, name of Palmer. They would have a refueling stop in Oman, then hug the Indian lower peninsula across the Bay of Bengal, the Gulf of Thailand and finally, Vietnam air space, where they would contact national authorities for priority landing. The local Saigon police, along with the Vietnamese People's Security, had contacted Interpol for a conference call to discuss the murder of three yakuza gang members discovered by a warehouse supervisor on his opening rounds. Within the hour, the investigators said their goodbyes to family, gathered files and shuttled to the airport.

The idea that the yakuza would be operating within Vietnam's borders caused "grave concern" for the controlling authorities. It was not good for public perception. In addition, another body that turned up several weeks earlier floating in the Mekong was identified as a Philippine national with ties to Abu Sayyaf. The man

281

had suffered a fatal gunshot wound to the head. The bullet struck just above his nose. Nothing indicated the crimes were related but under the circumstances of the triple murder, authorities quietly enlisted international assistance.

Interpol started to tie events together: the dead terrorist—likely a Sauvage client, three dead at a warehouse, a kidnapping on a street in Saigon in daylight, the Nice shootings and now a crazy story out of a police station in Osaka. How deeply was yakuza tied to them?

After many years of chasing the shadows of Le Sauvage, Marceau privately believed they'd finally caught a break. Le Sauvage had gotten sloppy. Was he desperate, old, on the run? He pushed his team to rework every piece of intel they'd gathered. They hadn't treed the bear yet, but the hounds were barking.

Chapter Thirty-One

THE DIN GREW BY LEAPS in decibels as police tried to quell the yammering crowd. The market squabble centered around the dead yakuza operative on the floor. Police had lost control of the crowd early on. The locals trampled the crime scene trying to get their stalls back in order. Witnesses gave varying accounts of European or Australian men who had come to the aid of a woman being attacked by the dead man. "Maybe she was the older man's lover. The one that got away, yes. There was a man with a beard. He could be an Arab. Everyone ran out the main door. The girl ran away in shame. Nobody knew in which direction she had run. She ran very fast. Shame, that's it. The dead man must be her husband. She had tattoos."

Koi had snatched a woman's jacket off the back of a chair in the mêlée, removed her cash and papers from her backpack and ditched it. She carried only a small commando dagger Potente had given her. Koi's hunter instincts told her to run hard for the rear exit; Hayato would need a quick retreat. She hit the white morning sun and looked in both direction, sirens in the air around her, no sign of him. Left or right—the correct choice or lose her chance. *He'll need to get lost in the crowds.*

She chose to go right, toward the busy thoroughfare, rather than the alleys. If she saw him, she could run him down.

Hayato turned as he passed a street vendor and saw

Koi round the corner of the building, her eyes scanning, looking for an anomaly in the movement and sway of the proletariat.

She saw the black suit parting the women in bamboo *nón lás*, the teens in western T's and young girls in *ao dais*, the heads turned toward the stranger among them. He ran as best as his aging muscles could carry him toward his car. Koi ran over and through everything in her path but he had a hundred-meter lead.

He started the car and pushed into traffic, running against the flow of the roundabout. She cut right to head him off, jumping over scooters, across car hoods. The street people began to notice.

She closed the gap.

He punched the gas, striking a motorbike carrying live ducks. Several hit the windshield and blocked his view. He swerved left just as an oncoming lorry made the same move. They hit head-on. His engine stalled. As he tried to start it, Koi kicked in the driver's window. She grabbed his throat and pulled him toward her.

"You trained me well, Oyabun. Now comes the time for the student to deliver a lesson and a message. All I asked was one small favor and you used me like toilet paper." She had the dagger at his throat. Blood trickled over the tip of the bade. The people surrounded the scene as the lorry driver called for help. She heard none of it.

He didn't resist. For the first time since she'd met him, she saw fear in his eyes, fear and resignation. Her rage dissipated. She tried to collect it—clenched her teeth and squeezed the knife handle but couldn't push it through. She saw the same fear of death she had seen on her mother's face. She let go, pulled away, dropped the knife in his lap and walked into the crowd.

In that moment, Hayato knew she had grown stronger than him. She had become the ultimate warrior, who would no longer kill for revenge. She would not kill out of vindictiveness or yearning. She only wanted her mother well again but killing Hayato would not, could not, accomplish it.

The crowd closed in on his rental car, curious and angry and confused. Hayato saw no way out except arrest. He would be turned over to Japanese authorities if a rival clan didn't get him first.

He took the honorable route, as honorable as one can be ending a life of crime. Hayato saw it as a final act of shame for a failed coup and for letting a female protégée show him pity, to see him as pathetic. He took off his jacket and sat in his white shirt, sweat stinging his eyes. Police pushed through the onlookers. A woman leaned into the car to check his welfare as he skewered himself on Potente's dagger. She screamed and fell backward onto the black pavement.

***

Chastain called Koi as his vehicle paralleled Bouchet's west of the market. She didn't answer. He pounded the dashboard. *"Putain, merde. Je savais que c'était stupide."*

Potente drove. He said, "She knows the meet spot, right? If she gets separated she knows where to meet us. She'll be okay, I know it."

"Watch the road." Then to Hubert behind him, "You reminded her of how to get here, *n'est-ce pas?*"

"Oui, she has instructions. Hayato can't go after her.

He has to get out of here as well. She should survive this unless..."

"Unless what?"

"Unless she is hunting him down. She could get arrested and then she is done for." Into the hand-held radio he said, "Did anyone see her? Which direction?"

"I know what the fucking consequences are, Hubert. I don't need you to remind me."

Chastain began asking the same questions of the crew in the other car. No one had seen her once the mêlée started. Potente began to slow the vehicle.

"What are you doing?" asked Chastain. "Keep moving."

"Boss, no one has been behind us for a while and no helicopters. We should take it slower. Maybe we can all think better if we slow down, uh?"

Chastain took a deep breath and agreed, then advised the other car to slow down if no one followed. They would meet where planned and try to wait for Koi. Chastain knew he couldn't leave her. He'd have to let the others go on ahead. The local authorities whom Chastain had bribed wouldn't stay loyal very long. The prospect of life imprisonment would supersede a layout of cash from a fugitive. They weren't above playing both ends.

Chastain's sources in Europe had heard rumors that Interpol could have a lead in the case and it involved yakuza gangsters. As he thought about that intel, his gunrunner experience screamed at him to get away from the situation but his loyalty to the wishes of Mikie pulled him in another direction.

If Interpol was indeed moving their way, that put every member, including Koi, in jeopardy. They had to move quickly, decide within a small window of time how this would play out or they wouldn't get airborne.

They'd leave plans in the vehicles, accidentally on purpose for the police to find wedged between the seats. The plans, written in an elementary code, sketched flight plans along a route following the Cambodian coastline into Trat in Thailand where they could take a boat to Singapore that would get them out of the area. They included what appeared to be a contingency plan to stay in country, north of Hanoi, but didn't say which scenario would trigger the contingency. The diversion would confuse investigators and buy them time.

Meanwhile, Chastain could move. His men would fly into Taiwan where they could regroup and find out what Boris concluded in Osaka. That conversation, if he hadn't been arrested, would determine whether they would move on the gold or split up back to France.

***

Koi walked away from Hayato's car as though she were going to Sunday brunch. The screaming woman behind her told her what Hayato had done. The police activity had the ant-farm traffic slowed to a grind. Many of the curious teens had set their motorbikes down to wade in for a closer look. Koi checked the fuel gauges on two nearby bikes—close enough. She chose the one with a bigger engine, put on the flimsy helmet and rode out through the crowd, west to the rendezvous point.

A vendor who had been inside saw her tattooed arms and ran over to speak to an officer. The officer hollered into his police radio and the chase commenced.

Two motorized units from the Saigon police picked her up coming out of the roundabout. They had the advantage of knowing the streets. She had the advantage of balls and desperation. She swerved around a cart, down-shifted and squirted between two cars. Her bike leaned in and out of bicycles and scooters; her eyes focused forward like a sea hawk, peripherals activated. In milliseconds, she judged the speed and direction of objects moving into view, the sounds of the sirens behind her.

She exited the roundabout nearing top speed then spun the bike into a stop, shifted down into first gear and smoked the tires, racing headlong at the chasing officers, who split off as she rode between them. Koi headed back toward the market, up on the sidewalk and directly into the wash of police and spectators, scattering them. She cut right and drove the bike through the center park, gaining a fifty-meter lead on the two bike officers who had followed her onto the sidewalk. One hit a pedestrian and dumped his bike, snapping off the clutch. Done. The second bike took her bait and went after her in the park. As he jumped the curb into the roundabout, a police sedan sideswiped him. Bike cop number two, down.

Koi maneuvered through traffic, separating lovers and schoolgirls from their handholds. The police couldn't keep up with her violations of personal space and the laws of inertia. They ran into one another trying to both follow her and cut her off. She took them on another tour of the roundabout then shot off into the cityscape.

Ten blocks later she ditched the bike, bought a long-sleeved Pokémon t-shirt and paid a rider to take her to the fringes of Saigon, where she called Chastain.

A member of the team thought they saw his eyes well up when he got her call, but no one would confirm it. Potente made a fist and punched the air.

One hour later, after reuniting the team, checking wounds and paying off two skinny miscreants to take them to a private air strip, they managed a collective breath, but not before Chastain threatened to come back and kill both the men's families if they ever spoke of seeing them. The fear in their eyes said they would abide.

Bouchet held an ice bag to his nose. Potente helped Hubert wrap his ribs.

"We almost left you here," Chastain said.

"Thanks for the confidence." She looked over at Potente who pretended not to hold her eyes.

Chastain said, "You know that is not what I..."

"Dead. Your next question," she said. "Hayato is dead. Dead or dying, it doesn't matter. He is out of the picture. There will be a fight for his spot. I have some ideas who will take over his clan. There are two people most likely to be in the best position. Have to deal with one of them."

"With Hayato dead we no longer have to deal with anyone."

Hubert and Bouchet agreed, though nothing was yet certain. They survived for the moment, but Interpol had eyes on their operation and they still had not contacted Boris. Hubert tried his number.

"Well how are you, old man? I'd almost given up. You caught me at lunch. You really must try this Sapporo beer, delicious and shall we say, more bounce to the ounce. So how are things in Vietnam?"

Hubert looked at the others as though they had heard Boris's ebullient greeting. "We're okay for now but things got a bit hairy. We will talk. Let's not fool around. What have you found?"

"Let me change locations here. Navigating. It's a bit crowded, *gomen'nasai*, my lovely."

"Boris."

"Almost there, ahh, here we are, the world's tiniest veranda. So. Gold. It's there. At least I believe it is. The problem is, it is confined to a hole in the ground some ten meters deep and out in the open under a garden. It would be impossible to excavate without an elaborate ruse."

"How can you be sure it is gold and not just munitions or other useless junk?"

"Density. The equipment we rented was top notch. I'm able to discern a pocket in the earth but then look at anomalies within that pocket and measure the varying and relative densities in comparison with surrounding strata."

"Speak a language I understand."

"What lies beneath matches a signature of a metal with similar properties to gold. Clear enough?"

Hubert gave a thumbs-up to the crew who smiled for the first time in many miles. The liquor flowed with the questions. "Ask him how much is there. Can we retrieve it? Is it well protected?"

Hubert waved them off and continued with Boris. "Is it in a big hole?"

"No. It appears to be in some kind of tunnel not more than two meters wide and not much taller, more of an escape tunnel than something used for any long storage. I could only go so far. I was attracting too much attention so I decided to cut it short. The tunnel begins somewhere in the middle of the compound under a side building adjacent to the main castle, perhaps an old officers' quarters, and then continues out toward the water. I'm going to presume it was an escape route of some kind but I have no way of knowing the ingress and egress points or how well they are sealed. There's been reconstruction at the site so no telling without a more extensive survey, which we obviously don't have the resources for."

"So there could be access from one end or the other?"

"Yes, that's correct, but from which direction and what equipment we'd need to breach it is just too difficult to determine right now. Since it's safe or rather, obvious, to presume the folks who carried out the reconstruction and repaving over the years didn't know about the gold, there's nothing to show that they didn't build right over the tunnel entrances."

"All right. I understand. I'm giving the phone to Picard. Give him your location and anything else he asks you. Stay put and, Boris..."

"*Oui*, Hubert?"

"Try not to fall in love. We need you sober and available."

"*Certainement, mon capitaine.*"

"Goodbye, Boris."

Chapter Thirty-Two

THE INTERPOL TEAM landed in Saigon, greeted by a stoic police captain, a less pleasant army lieutenant and a febrile afternoon sun. Detective-Sergeant Marceau descended the stairs first. His hosts filled him in on recent events, the mêlée in the market, the dead yakuzas, the missing Europeans. Marceau's team filed behind him, sweating before they hit the tarmac, looking at one another as if to ask, *do you feel this heat—is it just me?*

Marceau wrote notes as he spoke to those who greeted him. "Saturate the airports and get personnel to the seaports and train stations. They can't hide here, they must have a plan to leave the country."

The military man addressed Marceau in wooden French. "You have studied history in university, I presume?"

Marceau looked at him. "Yes, of course. Why do you ask?"

"Then perhaps you are sensitive to the idea of a Vietnamese military officer's hesitance to take orders from a French authority upon that officer's arrival in his country."

Marceau looked down at the man's dull boots, half in deference, half in frustration. He took a breath and looked back at the lieutenant. "Look. I am sorry to be abrupt but time is something we cannot spare here on formalities. These men are professionals. They will have had a plan.

They aren't going to wait for us to find them. Why don't you and the captain here step onto our air-conditioned plane and we can devise a quick strategy."

"We have arranged a meeting table and coffee for our guests in the pilot's lounge. It is private and swept for bugging devices. Follow me please."

"Fine."

Beneath a green tent on the tarmac, Marceau sweated through what would be, under other circumstances, a delicious cup of coffee, as the lieutenant reviewed the events as they understood them, complete with visual aids in the form of poster-sized photographs stacked on an easel. An aide removed them, one at a time, as the lieutenant first reviewed the scene at the cold storage facility, then the location of the dead gangsters and spent shells collected at the scene. Fingerprints lifted from the scene were still being classified to help in identifying possible suspects. "We also have a report from the prior day of a young woman apparently kidnapped off the street in downtown Ho Chi Minh City. A van matching the description of the one used in the kidnapping was found outside the storage facility."

Marceau said, "So this could have been a ransom deal that ended violently, no?"

"It is a possibility. We are still gathering evidence and looking for witnesses."

Aoki said, "It's not like yakuza to be involved in street kidnappings for ransom in foreign countries. Doesn't fit. They don't even do it in Japan."

The Vietnamese lieutenant moved on to the next photograph, the market. "This is the location of the murder of the yakuza member by the Europeans."

"How do you know they are Europeans?"

"My apologies. Caucasians. The closed-circuit cameras captured images of their vehicles here and here. It looks as though they had planned this hit, because the Caucasians moved in upon the arrival of the victim and another older man. They met with a Japanese-looking female just before the incident. That same female later caused injuries to our officers who had chased her on a stolen motorbike. This was after she ran down the vehicle of the old man, also yakuza, who witnesses said killed himself in his rental car in the middle of a traffic circle, as the young woman walked away. That's when she stole the motorcycle used in the chase."

"Wait. Ran down? You mean on a different motorcycle?"

"No. She ran after the vehicle. She is a fast runner, well-conditioned, I might suggest."

"I'm inclined to agree." Marceau made a note.

"A jilted lover?" asked de Trévise.

Perrin asked him, "You mean the dead guy was her lover and the old guy her husband?"

"Something like that."

Marceau instructed his people to let the lieutenant finish.

"We don't think so," he said to the detectives.

"Where are the bodies?" asked Marceau. "We will need Monsieur Aoki to view them and take photographs of their tattoos."

"They are in a mortuary under guard at Cho Ray Hospital. We will have a car take your investigator."

"Have you contacted authorities in Japan?"

"Yes. We will be sending along photographs, fingerprints and DNA samples before the day is complete."

"Excellent presentation, lieutenant. Now if we could move on getting people to your airports and railways...do we have photographs of the uh, Caucasians?"

"We have some stills from CCTV, but some are distant, not the best quality, I am afraid."

"Well they will do for now. These people will be in a hurry. We'll have to stop everyone."

Marceau ordered his people back to the plane to cool off and divide up into surveillance teams. Ten minutes later, the Interpol group had their assignments which they hoped to coordinate with the locals. Perrin and the Aussie would ride together. They were about to step outside when Perrin said, "There's a soldier running toward us. He's carrying a piece of paper."

They waved him up the stairway and led him inside to Marceau. The young sergeant looked around as he caught his breath, trying not to look impressed at his surroundings. He saluted. In rehearsed French he said, "Sir, we have received this message from an investigator who discovered one of the vehicles used in the Ben Thanh Market killing. They found what looks to be travel plans stuffed between the cushions in the back seat. It is written in code."

"Well done. Let's have a look."

They offered the sergeant a bottle of water. He accepted with a nod.

Marceau and de Trévise examined the find while the others reviewed the CCTV footage provided by the local authorities.

"It's a lousy code, easy enough to decipher," said Marceau. "It looks like they left themselves two options, one out of the country, probably determined by how the meet in the market went."

Perrin asked an obvious question. "Does it say which exit strategy goes with which result?"

"No, no, nothing like that. *Merde.* We'll have to split up. There's no time to call in a second team. Get the Vietnamese lieutenant on the phone. See if he can spare us a couple of men who speak English or French. And if I'm right, a helicopter to Hanoi. We'll never catch them on the ground."

The Interpol jet streaked off the tarmac with the army lieutenant aboard, Marceau reviewing the schematics of the shipping lanes and the possible pinch points where the local authorities could assist in choking down the exit of Le Sauvage. Marceau took a brandy to calm his nerves. The lieutenant declined, then participated. The party didn't last long.

The teams and their local law enforcement guides conducted surveillances at the critical locations. Not one person who remotely resembled anyone from Chastain's crew appeared. Everyone needed a hot meal and a shower.

Less than seventy-two hours after they had landed in Saigon, the Interpol team admitted the prescient intellect of Sauvage had bested them once again. He had vanished.

Le Sauvage's ruse had worked, and now the gunrunners had a three-day head start. They could be anywhere in the world.

Chapter Thirty-Three

The Ukraine.

THE CITY OF ODESSA hunched under a rain that formed off the Black Sea and lashed the area for three days. In the Moldavanka district, the weather only added to the dolor. In an urban ghetto like this, the amount of graffiti is inversely proportional to signs of hope. The cars on the gray streets are older than the memories of youthful aspiration. In the courtyard near Pushkinskaya, the broken hypodermic needles lie underfoot as the old women sell cherry jam on the corner while the boys, those still boys, roast the chestnuts they've collected during the summer malaise. It hasn't yet sunk in they have no future.

Meth, prostitution, guns. Name the country, name the city. Misery is a bird that shits on every people.

There's a level of comfort in familiar surroundings; even if all you know is a slum, at least you know what kind of crap to expect in your own streets.

Mayko felt at home in Moldavanka, where he could hold some level of sway over the transactions that occupied his time. He'd earned a bestial reputation among people who weren't generally impressed by notoriety. Everyone has the capacity for viciousness if put in the right situation, but Mayko seemed to find himself in more of them than the average bloke. Life in Odessa can be hard, but not as hard as the people who survive it. Mayko enjoyed being one of the people who made it tough to sleep there. He didn't like cherry jam.

Home.

Mayko put his phone in his pocket, pulled the hood of his sweatshirt over his head and ran across the street to the alley, down a side basement entrance to a condemned Greek church.

He met them a hundred or so meters into the catacombs where they had a makeshift bar set up on a ledge, a bottle of vodka cooling in a damp hole in the wall, candles burning and a battery-powered lantern, a propane heater. Damp barrels for seats and a permanent sense of underworld in the cold air. Spray-painted epithets recounted the courageous expletives of drunken teens and anarchists, demonic symbolism and other 'fuck the world' stuff. All of them smoking except Mayko, who was met at the church entrance by Artem and led to the meet spot through the dark tunnels by the light of Artem's headlamp.

Mayko noticed the leg bones on the bar and the small skull guarding the vodka. He asked why they chose such a dramatic place to meet.

Artem said, "The police are reluctant to come down here without reason. They might find another dead girl. Who needs the trouble?"

"What dead girl?"

"It was in the newspapers, forget it. You don't like Odessa no more. You moved on," said Zelay. "What you want with us now?"

"I like Odessa just fine. I have business elsewhere. You coal miners need to open your eyes. Who is this one?"

Zelay pushed a thumb toward the one with bad skin. "Is Oleks. He is good man. Worked in the mines with us since fifteen years but the money is shit so he comes with us to make deliveries. He's good with Kalashnikov. Killed many Russians, eh, Oleks?" Zelay pushed the wiry Oleks who just laughed.

Mayko looked hard at Oleks. "He looks like he uses as much meth as he delivers."

"Hey who is this fucking guy. Fuck him." Oleks said it without making so much as a lean in the direction of Mayko.

Zelay told Oleks to shut up, turned to Mayko. "Enough with the bullshit. Why did you need to see me?"

Mayko lit a cigarette. "Is that vodka cold? I need a drink, c'mon, let's open it. I have a proposition for you. Can this junkie keep his mouth shut?"

Oleks feigned another protest but Zelay cut him off.

"He's a good one, I tell you. I told you already. He's good, right, Artem?"

"Good." Artem opened the vodka.

"You need us to deliver guns for you?"

Mayko said, "No. This is much better but you may have to travel. Your passports are valid?"

"Of course, we make trips to Russia every week. What do you think?"

"Okay, okay, good. I have information that some people will be moving a fucking huge stash of gold, but I don't yet know when or where. You have to be available to move on short notice. I will have weapons for you at the location. Who is good with a rifle?"

"I told you, Oleks is goo—"

"No, not him. I mean a sniper rifle. You have a man for a long-range shot if we need it?"

Artem said they had one, a veteran of loyalist opposition surges. "Crack shot, no worry."

"Good. Here's the thing. We can't just sneak the gold away from them. They are pros, we have to take them out."

Zelay laughed. "Pros? You mean your crew? You are double-crossing them?"

"No, asshole, they did *me* dirty. They don't like Ukranians. Le Sauvage thinks we have no class. He says we're all a bunch of alcohol babies or something."

"Well, fuck him. We will show him what we can do. How much for us?"

"Even split. Whatever we get we bring it here and split it. Every man for himself to sell it on the black market."

"The fucking Russians will buy anything," Oleks said.

"I thought he told you to shut up." Mayko worked his former cohort over with vodka and stories of gun running in South America. He played on their nationalist pride to convince them to work for him with no up-front money. Avenge Ukraine. Revolution. Money and bitches. They drank to their new partnership.

The plan would be simple. Mayko would determine the Osaka exit strategy for his former crew. Choke them off and move in. Exit plans for the Odessa cluster would be forthcoming. First a commitment and a pledge to secrecy. Details to follow in a week or so.

Before Artem led him out of the catacombs. Mayko turned back over his shoulder. "Hey, junkie. If this fucks up I'm blaming you. You won't like the way you die."

Oleks turned to Zelay who only shrugged.

Chapter Thirty-Four

CHASTAIN'S CREW FLEW to Taipei for refueling, then north over the East China Sea to the Gimhae International Airport in Busan, South Korea. From here, there remained only a three-hundred-sixty-five-mile flight into Osaka. Regroup and plan.

Chastain directed everyone but The Beard and Koi to walk the airport terminal, to eat and notice. See if there appeared to be police activity or chatter related to unusual events on international television.

They met on the plane ninety minutes later. Bouchet brought breakfast for The Beard and Koi, extra coffees.

No man reported anything to raise concern.

"I was thinking," Hubert said. "I wonder how many yakuza really know about the gold, I mean, specifically. Hayato killed his boss and then himself, so who knows?"

Koi said, "Hayato told me they had people looking into the value of it and so of course, they knew about the history, or perhaps thought they knew about it. They no doubt spoke of the idea that someone named Le Sauvage had information. People know. Someone brought this to Nakane's attention in the first place."

"That is who we need to meet. Do you know who it is?"

"No, not immediately. But I've been thinking about this too. Something bothers me."

"What is it?" Chastain asked.

"My mother knew about the tattoos, so did other

303

people—people from my past. My mother's father was a low-level soldier, but not from Nakane's clan. He was from the same clan as Johnny Kubo."

Potente asked, "Who the hell is Johnny Kubo? I can't keep track of all the players here."

"Let her speak."

"He was the last contract I got. After I got rid of him is when I asked Hayato to let me out of yakuza. Eliminating him bothered me more than other things I've done. I thought it was just because I had finally had enough, and I have, but now I think it also bothered me because Johnny wasn't really much of a threat to our clan. I think they wanted him executed for other reasons."

"Like maybe he knew about the gold?" asked Bouchet.

"Maybe, but more than that, Johnny was not very disciplined, kind of a wild guy who drank too much and gambled even more. Perhaps he knew something and they were afraid he would sell the information, I don't know. Something never felt right about it."

"All this really means is that someone above Hayato and the guy he killed—"

"Nakane."

"Nakane, right. It just means the guy above these two knows about the gold. Who is his boss?"

"Yukinaga, full name, Kinjoh Yukinaga. Sometimes called The Stick. Very feared, but old. Still has power over the whole island of Honshu. You won't be able to speak with him. You will never get close enough. He lives in a walled compound under constant guard with cameras everywhere. He would never discuss business face to face with a gaijin."

"Then we will have to bring him out to us," Hubert said.

"Doesn't work that way. His people maybe, but far removed from him. Never him."

Hubert said, "All men have a price or pride or something you can either tempt them with or insult."

"That may be true but how men react to such things in the west is different. He will not let you see it. You have to accept this about him."

Chastain said, "It doesn't matter. None of it matters. They only know some things in general but we have the critical details. We are forgetting that only we know the most likely place the gold is waiting. That is our advantage. They also do not know when we would move on it. We could get in and out quickly before any police or yakuza know what hit them. Who knows? They might even guess we would wait a year and come back after everything dies down and Interpol goes back to France. They can't know. But whatever the case, we have to keep Koi out of it."

She stood up. "Why?"

"Relax, not completely out, just off the streets. You are too well known. If someone sees you, the whole operation is blown. They will know we are here. You must stay back and help from here."

"Fuck. Just, fuck."

"What is it, Emiko?"

"You know what it is."

"I will figure out a way for you to get there. This is separate. One cannot interfere with the other. Please trust me."

"Right, but it will be too late."

"Being seen will not help you or her, irrespective of what it will do to this heist. You will either be killed or arrested, or both. It helps no one. I'm sorry, but this is the way it has to be for now. Get your head in this. We need you alert."

The others waited for her response. She offered none. Then she did. "They still want you more. What if you expose yourself?"

"They don't know who I am. I could walk down the middle of—"

"Boris knows who you are. Do you trust him?"

The room got so quiet it hummed.

Chastain sensed she spoke with a daughter's heart and not as a team member. Perhaps.

"Listen to me," Chastain said. "All of you, listen to me. Boris is a part of this crew, maybe not a permanent asset but for now, and unless I have reason to believe otherwise, he's a part of it. That's the end of it."

Koi looked around the room but caught no one's eyes. Potente watched her.

Bouchet said, "It's true that if we act quickly, we could be in and out before yakuza finds out, assuming we can evade the law. We all took a liking to Boris but who knows if he's been drinking and bragging. Stupidity may have more to do with his loose tongue than disloyalty. They could have the castle under surveillance."

"True," said Hubert. "Except he's the kind of guy who likes to see things through. He will brag one day, but not before he can do it in a luxury suite at the Ritz surrounded by admiring eyes and perky breasts. I don't think we need to worry about him." Hubert looked around. "Anyone else we should consider?"

Koi's voice was steady. "Just the curators. This is Japan. Things have to be done properly for such an honored place."

Chastain said, "Koi is right. Get Boris on speaker phone and let's see if we can do this thing in plain sight."

***

"No." Boris thought that type of excavation impossible. "These people were very suspicious of my testing. I caused the disruption of not a blade of grass and yet they appeared unhappy. To come in there with a backhoe without the heads of the castle and the curators knowing ahead of time is pure fantasy. Our work would be immediately halted."

"It's the damn Japanese in us. We don't like or trust foreigners meddling in our strictly Japanese stuff. He's right, I'm sure they didn't like him or what he was doing there. They were probably turned off by his sweat."

Chastain said it would appear their only hope of salvaging anything from the trip was to sell the location to yakuza. His tone belied his reluctance. Everyone knew he didn't want to expose Koi but might have to in order to get through to the secretive boss to propose a deal.

Chastain would have to at least appear as though he were offering Koi as a sacrifice to show his sincerity. By now Yukinaga probably knew the Frenchman was Koi's natural father, but Yukinaga's general disdain for the gaijin could prove to be an advantage. It wouldn't be a stretch to think Le Sauvage cared more about a deal than a distant progeny. He might even expect it. Chastain could exploit that sentiment.

Koi perked up. "The castle grounds are closed on Mondays," she said. "What if we moved the equipment in on a Monday and told security we would be back in the morning to review the proper documents with the curators?"

307

Bouchet said, "Sounds good but too risky. They would undoubtedly call their superiors. We wouldn't get near the place again."

"Unless we went back at night," said Hubert.

"Exactly. Potente and I could secure the guards while you all did your work. We could get most of it out within a few hours."

"I already said, I don't want—"

She cut him off. "I would only go in at night and I'd be covered. By the time anyone recognized me, we would all be gone."

"She might be right, boss."

"Why are you so eager to be a part of a heist? Do you crave adrenalin rushes?"

"I can't explain it now."

"Try."

"I won't."

Chastain realized he was airing a personal conversation among a group of increasingly uncomfortable soldiers who wanted nothing more than orders to fight or move on. Chastain let it go. "Everyone stand down for a short while. I'm going to take a walk with Bouchet and Hubert. Stay put. Talk about other things. Close your eyes. Eat. Just stand down."

Bouchet was already at the door. Hubert took a rear position as they walked out. Everyone looked at each other, then they all looked at Koi.

"What the fuck are you all looking at?"

Chapter Thirty-Five

MARCEAU LEFT HIS DIRECTOR'S OFFICE that evening with his ass in his hands. His superiors gave him, out of respect for his past accomplishments, thirty days to have Le Sauvage in handcuffs or he'd be reassigned to conducting background checks of Legionnaire applicants.

In retrospect, he decided he should have recognized the escape plans left behind by Le Sauvage as a hoax. The outlaw hadn't evaded identification and capture for decades by leaving written clues to his whereabouts.

"Enculer, Sauvage. Brûle en l'enfer." The afterthought that Le Sauvage or the revealed Chastain might burn in hell was of little consequence to the agnostic Marceau. He just wanted the opportunity to say, "fuck you" to the man's face after his arrest. Was it too much to ask?

Marceau left the director's office as darkness fell on Nice. He stopped off on the way home to buy two bottles of Grenache. One bottle for his wife and her mother and the other for him. He ate while mostly ignoring their questions about shootings in the quiet suburb, their fears and her mother's wishes that he transfer to a safer assignment in the administration. Her daughter shouldn't be a widow.

He smiled and ate his soup. He drank a glass of wine with dinner and finished the rest on the balcony with his cigarettes, watching the smoke hang on the moonlight in the breezeless evening. He comforted himself with thoughts of the demise of Le Sauvage. He knew that men such as him thrived on mystique as much as actual deeds. If it was becoming known that his organization was in tatters and he was on the run from Interpol, his options for both escape and trust grew thinner with each passing rumor. Thirty days may not be much time, but it might just be enough.

"I am walking *Maman* home," his wife said. "Wait up for me."

Marceau waved his hand to acknowledge her request.

***

"Try him again. What could that sweaty fuck be doing? Is he answering?"

"Boss, I called five times in the last hour. Maybe he's sleeping one off. Let's give him a little time. It's early."

"I know what time it is, *putain*. The fucking English have no sense of time. It's why they can't build a decent watch."

"This is a true fact," said Bouchet.

Chastain and his confidants had decided the time was right to move on the gold. There would be no negotiations with the yakuza kingpin until after they had something definitive, either gold or an empty chamber, but they wouldn't bargain unless it was from a position of strength.

One problem.

No one could get a hold of Boris.

Potente quietly wondered to Koi if Boris had become a rat or gotten scared and gone back to Thailand. Neither option sat well with her.

Koi began to lose faith. "I'll never see my mother and

we'll have nothing to show for this. If he sold us out, I'll cut him in fifty pieces."

"You'll have to fight me for him," said Potente.

"Your bravado reminds me of a poem I used to like, a story really, about a wounded ninja. He had only one good leg but always tried to prove himself by limping to the front of the battle. The others laughed at him."

"Do you think the others laugh at me now?"

"Didn't say that. Just a reminder. Don't be sensitive."

"I've never talked about poetry before."

"Me neither, I guess, except with my mother. Never a man."

"Why do you like it so much?'

She shrugged. "Don't always have a lot of time to read and you can learn a lot about life in the short words of a poem."

"Why are you in such a hurry?"

"My mother is dying. I am marked for death."

"That's now, you weren't always in this spot. Things weren't always this, you know, the way they are now."

"Maybe I always knew my life would be short."

"Maybe you set it up that way."

"That's bullshit psychology."

"Oh, so my psychology is bullshit but you knowing the future is legitimate?"

"Are you trying to get me to kiss you again?"

"No, I was—"

"Why not?"

"C'mon, Emiko, not in front of the men."

"They can't hear us talking."

"They aren't stupid, just wait. Your father is right

here."

Three hours later and the tension had ripened. No sign of Boris.

Hubert apologized to Chastain for bringing Boris in.

"We don't know where he is right now. He could be dead. No apologies necessary."

"I know. It's just—"

Chastain cut him off. "*Mettre fin.*" He stood up and ordered the crew to move on to Osaka. "We'll go in without him. We know where it's supposed to be. We'll blow the fucking walls out if we have to. Koi, come here, please, I have to speak with you."

They stepped outside while the crew readied for a long-awaited overt act.

"Emi. We are going to see your mother. We'll figure out how on the way. I can't have you wait any longer. I'm going to take a chance that they aren't expecting us to do this right now, especially with Boris missing. At this point, either he is a rat or they have him. If they have him, they would expect us to be working on getting him back or trying to get out of the country. Either way, they are probably expecting us to focus on that problem and not be visiting hospitals. The Boris situation would need to be our priority, but we have something to do for you and me that takes first place. Whatever happens going forward, I want to know that I at least got this far for you and Mikie."

She thanked him and bowed to him, half out of respect and half out of not knowing how to show affection for him. It was hard enough to work out a personal-fondness dance with Potente. There just wasn't enough to go around.

He put a hand on her shoulder and squeezed. She lifted her eyes to him, wet eyes. He smiled a paternal smile. *We'll be all right.*

She ran back inside to tell Potente.

Chapter Thirty-Six

THE CREW LANDED in Yao Airport, eight kilometers east of Osaka Bay and seven kilometers southeast of the Osaka Castle. They rented a private hangar to plan their next move.

During the trip, Bouchet reviewed the castle maps and the coded messages to gain confidence about the coordinates. Koi helped as best she could while Potente, Picard and the others cleaned weapons and made an inventory of what tools they had and what they might need. The operation had escalated to a pitch that pumped out the stress hormones. It was what they lived for.

No response yet from Boris.

Everyone surrounded Bouchet, who had said he was open to any and all ideas about not only the location of the gold but a method for retrieving it.

Hubert asked, "What if Boris lied to us about where the gold is buried or figured out something he didn't tell us? He could be in the real location right now, taking it all for himself or dealing with those tattooed pimps."

"He could very well be," said Bouchet. "But our professor, even if he did lie, isn't likely to have access to the resources he'd need to get the gold out of its location and to dispose of it on the international market. He would be discovered in a matter of days trying to sell it."

"Then where the hell is he? He must be up to

something."

"Again, possibly, but unless he's with an Interpol sketch artist putting together a composite of everyone on this plane, I say we focus on what's before us."

Potente sat with Koi, who read the poems to him, explaining their significance to her tattoos and the Shōgun.

Picard asked Bouchet if he was certain of the coordinates.

"Relatively so. There could be errors, not only in our own reading of them but in their original translation into whatever documents came into possession of the tattoo artist. I'm sure that, out of pride in his work and perhaps nationalism, he would have been as accurate as possible, but we don't know what he was looking at yet."

Koi jumped up, knocking Potente's coffee on his lap. "Look at this. There are characters written into the border of the castle painting. They are part of the decorative scroll work. It has bothered me since I first saw it. Look here." She turned the pictures clockwise as she read. "This says...

With the evening to guide you
Leave behind the golden afternoon."

Bouchet waited for her to explain.

She stared back at him, waiting for him to understand. She grew impatient and said, "Not the sun. I thought maybe it meant the golden sun setting in the west." Bouchet shook his head. She said, "Ach, thought you knew. In the main tower of the castle there is a golden tea room. It was built by a Shōgun, Toyotomi, in the sixteenth century. Same guy built the temple. He was fascinated with gold. The whole room is covered in it, floor to ceiling

316

and even furniture."

"This proves the coordinates are correct to the extent they put us on the castle grounds."

"Exactly," she said. "The gold is reference to afternoon tea in the golden room."

Potente finished toweling off his pants. "I'd be happier if I didn't have burnt balls right now, but nice job, Koi. Nice."

The Beard said, "Your balls have been hot since you met her."

Picard laughed. No one else seemed to notice or care.

Bouchet said, "Hang on here. The wind. I have nautical charts here, yes. The wind tends to blow westerly in the area of the castle, off the bay." He spread out the diagram of the grounds and drew a line west from the main tower. "Koi, do you know exactly where in the tower is this tea room? Which side of the building?"

She thought for a moment. "Not sure, but maybe here."

That's fine," said Bouchet. "West of that area is the same broad section near the turret as Boris said."

"They would have afternoon tea in the golden room."

"That's civilized. Then of course the night sky would guide them to the right location, beginning west of the tower, perhaps looking back at it for the right star pattern."

Hubert said, "They would only have to be close. If at that point they had taken back control of the castle they would have crews of soldiers to dig in that section until they found it, probably in one of the escape tunnels."

"Yes, Boris said wait, here it is, a dry moat. Perhaps—"

"Perhaps, perhaps," said Chastain, who had been watching the unfolding clues. "But let's not forget this place has been destroyed and rebuilt many times after fires and wars. There could be many chambers and tunnels, escape routes and who knows, the gold could be buried under rock. We need Boris's readings from the GPR."

"It would help."

"What about the internet?" asked Potente.

Everyone looked at him and said nothing. Koi asked him what he meant.

"I mean if the equipment Boris rented was so sophisticated, maybe the people he rented it from store the data in the cloud or the machine itself sends data to a server as a back-up. We can hack into it. Everything is in the cloud today, yes?"

Picard and The Beard turned to one another and shrugged.

Koi smiled at Potente. "Good thinking, Bärchen."

"Bärchen?"

"It's nothing, boss, a childhood nickname."

"Well, whatever the case, Koi is right. It is good thinking but we don't know where Boris got the equipment."

Koi said, "There can't be too many in the area. Probably only one. I will check it out with, Bärchen." She whispered the nickname.

"Shhh. Okay, boss, then if we find it, I'll see if I can't hack into their system and download the data."

"You can do that?" She seemed impressed.

"You forget I was an amateur fighter. I had a lot of

down time when I trained. Couldn't go out to bars. I used to play a lot of video games. I met some people online who taught me how to hack. Everybody does it."

Chastain said, "Enough talk. We are running out of time. We're counting on you, Potente. Get moving."

"Yes, boss."

Koi looked at Chastain and nodded her head in approval of Potente's potential. She winked at Chastain. He poured a bourbon.

***

After a tense hour, as the plane made its final approach to Yao Airport, Chastain walked over and stood in front of Potente, who looked up at him smiling. "I have it. I have it, boss."

"Good job. Print it and bring it to Bouchet."

"Well done, young man," Bouchet said. "Now let's see what we have."

"You can read this stuff?"

"I'm not worried about reading rock densities, just looking to triangulate the most likely location. Let me think. Go get ready to land, please."

Picard and The Beard slapped his back. Picard said, "If we get this gold I'll buy you your very own gym."

The Beard said he'd buy him a lap-dance.

Koi didn't hear him. She went over to Chastain. "We are very close now. We have to decide whether we take a chance to get this gold or try to sell it to yakuza. Boris could be anywhere. Hope he just got drunk and arrested. Maybe he got scared and left the country."

"We are tracking the debit card I gave him. No unusual activity. He's probably still in the area.

Countdown to Osaka

Somewhere."

***

Before he left with Koi for the hospital, Chastain ordered Hubert to try Boris's phone every fifteen minutes.

They walked the four hundred meters to the customs office to get off the airport grounds. Chastain traveled on his Belgian passport. Koi's hadn't been tested. Bouchet had purchased a Malaysian passport for her from an associate in Korea who trafficked illegal laborers across Southeast Asia.

"This is crazy. What if they ask me a question in Malaysian? I don't speak it. I'll be arrested."

"We're here on business. Speak English. Don't say much, just yes, no and here for business. I will go first. Watch, it will be easy."

They passed through customs with no consequence. The woman who checked their passports seemed more interested in catching Chastain's eye than noticing Koi.

Chastain and Koi took separate car services to the hospital. She was to ping him when she arrived and he would ping back when he was within a hundred meters. She would go to the floor below her mother and wait for his arrival. They would ascend to her floor together. Father and daughter, arm in arm, hands on ready.

They walked up the back stairwell in the silent echo of footfalls laid in trepidation. Their heart rates increased in sync.

"We're too late," Koi said. "I know it. I can feel it's over. We're too late."

"Shhh, little one. Don't race to conclusions. You will have your peace."

Chastain had the same feeling, but couldn't say it to her.

They opened the door to her floor and Koi's knees buckled. He held her.

There's something about that moment of death in a hospital. The experienced workers move in. They know who to work on and who to let go. The new ones look scared to be around it all but they try to pretend it's routine. They try to act as though they've been trained for it.

But you can see it. It's in the way they move, the way they look at one another, that, 'another person just died where I work' look. Most professions don't deal with it. Customers don't die in insurance offices or Chinese restaurants. But in hospitals, on cancer wards—people die. Friends and lovers, the forgotten and the mothers. They die. Koi and Chastain could see it in the flow of the living, walking among a fresh expiration. Everyone in a place like this, for a whiff of time, thinks about their own mortality, even if they don't acknowledge it. They display it on their faces no matter how much they think they don't.

Koi pulled away and ran to her mother's room.

Chastain walked behind her, his legs heavy as beam timber.

Koi slid as she made the turn into her room just as the nurses pulled the last of the IVs from her mother's arms. "I think she is dead now," one of them said to her.

Koi couldn't muster a retort. She looked around for her father.

Chastain came in behind his daughter, looking past Koi's shoulder to the half-open mouth he used to kiss, a moment that would be forever in his memory. He didn't notice the activity around him or the young woman who bent over her mother's still form, talking to her lingering spirit through a body not yet dead enough for her to accept.

Chastain knelt beside her and put his arm around Koi without taking his eyes off the woman he let down. "Goodbye, Mikie."

Koi said, "She died alone. No one held her hand. No one told her not to be scared."

The doctor assured Koi her mother had been given extra pain medication and slipped off quietly, with no suffering.

Koi ignored him, angry with herself. After ten minutes of silence, she stood up and turned to leave. "You coming?"

"Yes. Yes, just one moment."

"I'll be in the hall."

Koi held her emotions in check long enough to sign some papers about the arrangements for her mother's body. She'd made them with Chastain's help as a precaution, never believing she'd need them so soon.

As Chastain headed out a nurse called after him. "*Sumimasen?*" She held out Chastain's watch cap. "She holding this when she died."

"Then she must want it. Give it back to her. *Merci.*"

In the hallway on the way to the elevators, Chastain reached for her arm.

She didn't pull away but didn't return his grip. *It's over now. Nothing left but to fight.*

They took a taxi together. Half a kilometer into the ride and neither had spoken, neither did they let go, he to her arm and she to her scarf, twisting it and turning it round her hands like the hurting she wished to rip apart and make go far away. She cried some. She sniffled and Chastain passed her a napkin from his pocket. "Here."

"Thank you." She reached for it, wiped her nose and tossed her head, shaking off sorrow. She was about to say something but did a double-take and spun in her seat looking out the side window, past Chastain who hadn't quite caught on that something had caught her eye. "It's him! It's that sweaty blonde pork roll."

"What? Who, Boris?" Chastain turned over his shoulder.

Koi said, "Back there, the black Audi, A8. I know that car and the two ugly apes in the front seat. The driver works for Yukinaga. Saw Boris getting into the back seat."

"Are you sure it was Boris?"

"Fat, blonde liar. I can smell his sweat from here."

"Maybe it was not. I don't know how they could—"

"Then they're kidnapping the Swedish ambassador, otherwise, no blonde gaijin getting in that car with those two assholes, unless they putting him in the trunk."

Chastain accepted what Koi already knew. Boris had fucked them. He leaned into Koi to whisper. "This explains it. He's been telling us we can't get at that gold to buy time for a deal with yakuza. I'll cut him open and feed him to the wharf rats. We need to move quickly. Can you still see the car?"

"No. It turned around and went opposite direction. Kuso!"

Chastain spoke in French into his phone. "Bouchet, we may be compromised. Boris is working with the local enemy. I'll explain. Put everyone on high alert and be prepared to move out without me. Text me if it comes to that before I get there. I'm on the way. Fifteen minutes."

Chastain offered the driver extra cash to push it, but traffic slowed them down. They paid the fare and got out to walk and talk away from prying ears.

"Why are we walking?"

"We need to sort this out. I don't know that driver or what he really understands. We'll get another car after we sort this out."

Koi took in a long, slow breath as Chastain paid the driver. As they walked, Koi said Boris might be trying to save his life and get paid for his efforts.

Chastain asked, "What do you mean, save his life? He is in no danger from us, well he wasn't, but he is now."

"Hey, you're a scary guy to most people. Maybe he thought you weren't going to pay him and were just going to eliminate him once you had what you needed."

"I have more honor than that."

"It doesn't matter what you think of yourself, only what he thinks. He'll take a piece of the gold for himself and go back to England where he feels safe. Makes sense to me."

"You might well be right, but that doesn't help us. We have to assume yakuza knows everything. Who knows, they might even tip off Interpol. We need a plan, now."

Bouchet called and said the plane was ready to go at short notice but there were no signs of yakuza or police activity nearby.

"*Très bon,*" said Chastain.

"Tiago, the woman, any news?"

Chastain coughed. "*Non. Elle est partie.*"

"*Mes condoléances.*"

"*Merci.*" Chastain hung up.

Koi surmised what transpired between Chastain and Bouchet but didn't acknowledge it. She said, "He doesn't know, right? Boris, I mean. He doesn't know where we are right now?"

"Right. And he doesn't know where the plane is, so we have some time. No more airport runs for coffee or food. Everyone will need to stay on board. Assume the worst."

"The worst already happened."

"I am sorry, Emiko. I am very sorry."

"Should have known it would be this way. There is nothing left for me now."

"You are alive. There is hope. I will get us out of this." He tried to lighten the mood. "Besides, I think that Potente is enamored with you."

"Shut up." She called another taxi.

Chapter Thirty-Seven

DETECTIVE SERGEANT MARCEAU poured a second cup of coffee and sat at his desk. He took in a breath then pulled off the fat rubber band holding together the file on Le Sauvage. He opened up to a fresh sheet of note paper and began to sort through the file. His intercom alerted. "Sir, you have a call on line two."

"Take a message."

"Caller says it's urgent and pertains to Le Sauvage."

"*Putain.*" He pulled his notepad closer and picked up the receiver. "If this is a prank I swear I'll have your ass in jail."

"No prank here, girlie, and I don't give a fuck who you want in a cell but it won't be me."

"Who is this?"

"A recently claimed enemy of one of your enemies. That makes us friends in some parts of the continent."

"Which continent?"

"Africa, ya stooge. I'm callin' from South Africa."

"What can I do for you, friend? Do you have a name?"

"The name is not as important as the 411 I'm about to spoon ya."

"What is this about?" Marceau hated this part of the game. "Just tell me what you know and what you want for the information, okay?"

"Point. I've been contracting with a ruffian known about the world as Le Sauvage. He fucked me good recently and I'm givin' him up to ya."

"How did he screw you? How recently?"

"Just in the last two weeks. I'm talkin' fast here, ya see? Don't want you *boeres* tracin' the line. I am friendly competitor of Le Sauvage."

"Friendly?"

"Friendly—meanin' I travel in the same circles. Often as we work for the same client is we compete for that client's business. It's the way it is. I had contracted with your Sauvage for a shipment goin' north to a large and now angry troop of Sudanese guerrillas. The client gave me a substantial down payment only Sauvage never showed with the weapons. Now I'm on the run as these sand lizards think I've scaled their deposit."

"You what? What the deposit?"

"Fuck, man, they think I've stolen their money."

"I understand. So where is he now?"

"I don't know or I'd have a knife at his throat instead of callin' you. He pulled a *jabupule*."

"A what?"

"A disappearing act, for fuck's sake and fuck Le Sauvage. He's going to get me killed with a delay like this. I have two hundred thousand US in a fucking leather satchel and no weapons."

"Where are you? We need to meet."

"Not possible. I'm layin' low. I was supposed to meet him in Libya but he's probably on the other side of the world now."

"Why do you say that?" Marceau took notes but struggled with the man's South African accent.

"For one he's leavin' me hangin' so he's probably workin' on a better deal, maybe in the Philippines. I can't say for sure but he told me he'd do business when he got back from Osaka. He said, what was it? 'Osaka won't wait,' that's what he said."

"What does he look like?"

"He's fucking French with a big nose and short gray hair. He has a bunch of French and European goons with him, all mercenaries. Shouldn't be too hard to find a crew like that in Osaka."

"I'm on my way there with a team. Call me if you hear anything else. I'll get you off the hook with the Sudanese. I'll try."

"Yeah, try. Fuck you too."

"You want to live, don't you, friend?"

"Yeah, sure I do. Oh, he's doing a big job there, some kind of theft to fund something big. I don't know for sure but must be a fair haul if he's workin' out of his usual line of business. I'm sure he's linked up with the yakuza. You can't take a shit in that country without their say-so."

"I'll remember that."

"I can't think of anything else right now, but I'll call you. Give me a cell number you'll answer."

Marceau called his wife and told her to have her mother come over for a few days. "I'll be home in twenty minutes. Start packing a bag for me, *s'il vous plaît*."

"How long will you be gone this time?"

"Three or four days. Japan. I may finally have a break. I'll be right there, *au revoir*."

Marceau ordered his team packed and ready for travel within the hour. "No delays."

***

Twenty hours later, as Marceau and his hand-picked Interpol team arrived in Osaka, they received another call from the South African.

"I hope you've made the right decision to go to Osaka. There's something afoot and it's happenin' sooner 'en I thought."

"What are you talking about?"

"Gold, your Frenchness, lots of it. There's about fifty million Euros in gold buried in a sub-basement of the National Museum of Art and Le Sauvage is going to steal it tomorrow night."

"How can you be so sure of the timing?"

"I've got a yakuza on the payroll, a fuckin' rat, but he is an inside man with the clan who is teaming up with these gunrunners to move on the gold."

"That explains the connection to the girl."

"What girl?"

"Nothing. Never mind about that. What time will they be inside the museum?"

"I'm workin' on that. I'll get back to you as soon as I know, so be ready." The South African disconnected.

Marceau turned to Detective Perrin. "Get me on a secure line with the head of the Osaka Prefecture police. I hate to risk a local talking about this but it's too big to do alone. We'll need their assistance."

"Yes, sir."

Chapter Thirty-Eight

Tokyo, just south of the Samurai Museum.

AFTER A QUICK RAMEN DINNER, Boris walked into
the first club on the list, let his eyes adjust to the light,
then looked the place over. He ignored the man who
greeted him at the door and went straight for the bar,
choosing a stool with a view of the door and the back
hallway, which he could see in the mirror. The young
manager sneered at Boris's rebuff, *stupid gaijin.*

Several hostesses gathered on a long, padded bench.
One in a purple satin dress stood up and glided to the bar.
She oozed into the moist aura of Boris, who immediately
ordered her a glass of champagne. She said, "Hi, I am Umi.
This your first time here?"

"I've passed through a time or two, dear, but I don't
recall seeing anyone as lovely as you."

"*Arigato.* I like your accent, sir. Where are you from?"

"I'm from a place where the ivy is a fertile green and
the fog is like pudding on the skyline."

"Sounds tasty, but I don't understand." She giggled.

"You aren't expected to, love."

"Do you like to talk about movies?"

"I love movies, especially gangster movies. Do you like
them?"

"Yes, of course I do. I like funny movies as well."

"Ahh, laughter is good for the soul. Do they have
gangsters in Tokyo?"

"You mean movies abou—"

"No, actual gangsters, like yakuza. I'm looking to meet one."

"I don't know what you mean." Boris thought she seemed confused. She likely didn't want to discuss the people who could make her life miserable if they chose to.

"I'd like to have a chat with a fellow they call Nogi." Boris waited for her reaction. It came as dismay.

She looked about the bar for a lifeline. One came in quickly. "Perhaps you need another hostess," he said. He nudged Umi away and waved over another girl. Before the replacement made it over Boris stepped up the inquiry with the bar manager.

"I was merely asking the young lady if she knew any gangsters."

"No gangsters here. You shouldn't talk like that in here. I will have to ask you to leave."

"Oh, I'll be happy to leave, as soon as you tell me where I can find Nogi. I have something for him."

The manager didn't respond. He called for Boris's bar tab and asked him to pay and leave.

Boris threw more than enough yen on the bar and wrote a short message on a napkin then looked at the man, tapped on the napkin and said, "Nogi. Tell him I need to speak with him about this. I'm going down the block to the Pink Zero. He can find me there."

The manager only pointed toward the door.

Boris gave the man a slight bow and left.

Boris never made it to the second bar. He found himself in a nearby alley, walled off by five men wearing well-tailored black suits, no ties, open collars and menacing looks.

Boris smiled as he sized them up with a glance. "Hello, boys. I see I've touched a nerve. Now which one of you is in charge?"

The one in the middle of the pack, Chizu, spoke a clipped pulp-novel English. He pointed at a black metal door behind him and said, "Give you one minute inside to tell story, fat man, then we jump you ugly." He nodded, to show he felt pretty sure his message was accurate.

Boris pointed for them to head to the door first. "*Sendō suru.*" He bowed.

Chizu grunted and two of the gangsters opened the door and stepped to the side. A third went in ahead of Boris, who was pushed in from behind by Chizu and the fifth man, a wiry sort, with vicious eyes, one Boris thought looked the most unappreciative of having a foreign guest disrupt their afternoon. They closed the door behind them and left two posted outside. The pulsing base from the adjoining bar vibrated the plasterboard walls. They led Boris down the dark hallway to another door where an overhead light on a motion sensor lit up as they approached. Boris could make out a camera above the doorway in the shadow. Chizu's soldier pressed the buzzer. The door opened after a twenty-second delay.

Chizu motioned for Boris to sit on the wooden chair. "*Arigato gozaimasu,*" said Boris.

A moment later a man emerged from the bar. The din announced his presence then quieted as he closed the door behind him. His bodyguard followed, making the same entrance. Nogi looked Boris over as he smoked—a man accustomed to making people wait. Under his shirt, unseen by Boris, Nogi's *Tengu* tattoo stared Boris down.

Boris thought he looked portlier than he would have expected, but behind his horn-rimmed glasses were serious eyes, eyes that knew what a dying man looked like at the end of his knife, eyes that expected his wishes to be carried out. Smart eyes. He placed his burning cigarette in the crystal ashtray and walked around the desk, spinning a jeweled ring on what remained of his left ring finger. He sat against the front of his desk, within striking distance of Boris. No one spoke.

Boris cocked his head off to one side as if to show he enjoyed the ritual. He waited for Nogi to make the first move.

"Speak," said Nogi. "And don't waste my time."

Boris answered him in perfect Kansai dialect, which had the others looking at one another. "I have been in the company of men who have a knack for getting what they want, at various prices from honor to blood. These men have information you want, but they aren't in a negotiating mood. They plan to remove a large amount of precious metal from your shores and they'll be moving soon."

Nogi listened. He sucked air in between his teeth and tongue and pointed for his bodyguard to open a cabinet to his left. "Do you drink fine whiskey, sweaty man?"

"Indeed, I do. Feel free to pour a round."

Nogi held up two fingers and the bodyguard poured the drinks, neat, a Yakazaki twelve-year-old single malt.

Boris tried to raise a toast but Nogi ignored him. Boris sipped anyway. *Delicious.*

Nogi asked why these men were in such a hurry to

move on the gold. Boris explained their Interpol problem.

"Why are you turning on your employer? I don't appreciate infidelity."

"Ahh, bollocks. It was those greasy French who turned on me. They promised me a larger share if I helped them with some translations, but I recently overheard a conversation that leads me to believe they are not only cutting back on what was promised, but have a plan to leave me hanging around for the local police to interrogate while they make their escape." Boris sat back in his chair, feigning discontent. "After all we did for them during the war. Sorry, mate, but your folks didn't fight in Western Europe."

"I have no use for the French, or the British for that matter. You're all the same rapacious swine in my eyes. What do you want from me?"

"What I want is a guarantee of safe passage out of your country, and a case of cold Sapporo beer for the trip." Boris laughed. Nogi didn't. "I know where the—can I speak freely in front of these men?"

Nogi cleared the room of all but his bodyguard and Chizu. He moved back to his seat behind his desk. Chizu helped himself to a Yamazaki.

Boris continued, but leaned in towards Nogi for effect. "I know where the gold is hidden, but I don't yet know when they are going to move on it. I'll need the help of some of your foot soldiers for a bit of surveillance. Do you have men who can handle it?"

Nogi nodded. "This gold belongs to Japan, the Japanese people and of course, my people. We will do what is necessary to keep it from getting in the hands of the French. But tell me, Mister..."

"The name is Stonehouse, John Stonehouse of Southampton."

"Well, Mister Stonehouse. Why shouldn't we just persuade you to tell us where the gold is and then give you safe passage out of Japan in the hull of an oil tanker?"

"That's a good question. And the reason is you are a businessman. If you allow me to complete this phase of the operation you will not only get the gold but a bit of good favor with the law, who will swoop in and arrest the Frenchman, commonly known as Le Sauvage, for attempting to pilfer a national treasure. I get a payday and revenge against those brutes. You get two things. First, you get a substantial fortune and dare I say, a virtual free pass from the law to operate without interference. And second, I imagine you would like a face-to-face with a former enforcer for your clan, goes by Koi? She'll be with Chastain. Consider it a bonus. You're welcome."

"The police will take the gold and the girl is already dead to us. How does this help my people?"

"The police will take the gold we allow them to take. Once we know when Le Sauvage is making his move, we will remove half of it. What might actually be there is based on legend and verbal history, so who is to say how much is really there, and how much we allow the law to find, eh?" Boris raised his glass. Nogi poured.

"What do you want?"

"I want a flight back to Thailand and ten percent of whatever we remove from the cache."

Nogi stated the final terms. "You'll get no trouble from the customs people leaving Japan and you'll be happy with five percent and your life."

***

Agent Phillip Arterton sipped from his paper cup of coffee in the rear of the black taxi and watched the Thames through the dirty side window.

"Ever clean them?" he asked the driver.

"Clean what, sir?"

"These bloody windows. I can hardly make out the river."

"It's the same river it's always been, just the water is different. I'll clean them when we've taken our country back from Europe. Call it a celebration."

"For now, we'll just call it regular maintenance."

"As you wish, mate."

The buzz from his private cell surprised Arterton. *Too early for a coup, what's this then?* "Yes?"

"Artie, old man. Good to hear you are still in service. How's Gemma?"

The voice stunned him for a long moment. He pulled back and looked at the phone again. "She's just fine. In the garden early these days, tomatoes this year, I suppose, if the weather looks favorable."

"Lovely woman, Gemma. Would have made a fine meteorologist."

"Indeed. This isn't a social call, is it?"

"Call it a reckoning if you will. It's time to heal old wounds and pay it forward, as the Yanks say. Give some now and hope for a quiet return, free of the rancor these old bones can no longer fret over."

"It's been a long time. Why bother now?"

"I'm not well, Artie. I suppose it's time to let some

337

things go."

"How can I be of service?"

"How formal of you. Ever cautious. Can't say I fault you on that account. Thing is, I have been involved in a few, let's call them, interesting exchanges of men and property in the past few years. I've made a fair bit of money in the process. But something has come to light recently that has my patriotic nerves on alert. Some things just won't let go, eh?"

"I understand. What is it you have?"

"Interpol has been looking for a very dangerous man, a gunrunner. He's never been identified but is known as Le Sauvage."

"I've heard of him. He's earned the moniker."

"Yes, he has. Turns out he's about to pull a major caper in Japan and plans on using the proceeds to negotiate a grand arms deal with some folks who'd like to see Gemma in a burka."

"I see. Well, listen, I'm just getting out of a taxi at Babylon, so can I call you from a secure line in say, fifteen minutes?"

"I'll call you in ten. This is serious business, Artie. We've no time for formalities or personal vitriol. Ten minutes." He hung up.

***

Eight hours later, at approximately 01:00, on a misty Japan morning, a panicked woman telephoned the security desk at Osaka Castle. The night supervisor took the call.

"A man has been shot," she said. "He is in the back of a taxi in front of the main entrance to the castle. You'd

338

better hurry and get out there. I have called the police as well. Someone hurry, please."

"What man? Who is this? I will call the police."

"He's dying. Just go, now. Save him."

The supervisor left a man on the cameras and took the two remaining guards toward the main gate. A taxi idled at the curb twenty meters ahead.

"Use caution. You, go around this way."

As they approached the taxi, they heard a loud hiss followed by a hot, purple light from inside the car. The taxi burst into flames.

The supervisor spoke into his handheld radio. "Call the fire department. The taxi is here. It caught fire. You, go inside and turn up the front emergency lights."

As the guard stepped into the security office, the security cameras went dark. The lights flickered. The emergency generator kicked in. The base station squawked. The monitors for all the exterior cameras remained dark.

"What's going on here?"

***

"That should keep them busy for a while. Where is he?"

"Easy, mate. He's fast but it's a long run round this set. Here he comes now."

"Right. Det-cord in place?"

"Ready to blow a nice fat hole for you. I'll meet you below the berm. Go."

Unnoticed among the chaos of the taxi fire, the sirens and the second incendiary device set in the parking lot on the east side, the team detonated a charge at the water line under a ballistic blanket.

"Let's get in there and see what we have before it floods."

They found sixteen crates, each weighing roughly fifty kilos, wrapped in oil cloth to protect them from the salt air.

"Let's move, we have just a few minutes before we'll need fuckin' scuba gear to get out of here."

The team hoisted the crates, bucket-brigade style, and loaded them onto two large rubber boats with quiet outboard motors.

Two more men waited in a stolen rental truck near the wooded park-side along the southwest border before the city proper.

One looked through his night-vision glasses. "Here they are, right on time. Let's go."

Four and a half minutes later, the rafts sank into the moat and the truck rolled off into the night.

***

Two hours after the Osaka Castle heist, as his men and Koi rehearsed one last time their own plan to extricate the gold from the castle, Chastain stared at the local news on the satellite screen. He drank a large swallow of bourbon. "Stand down. It's done."

Bouchet joined him at the screen. "What do you mean, it's done?"

Chastain pointed at the news coverage of an attack on Osaka Castle.

"They are talking about terrorism. The whole place is swarming with cops and media."

340

The rest of the crew began to gather around, asking what had happened.

"Look," Bouchet said, pointing at the screen. "Helicopters from the news stations are pointing their search lights at the wall."

"There's a hole in it."

"Koi, what are they saying? Everyone shut up."

"They say there were three explosions. One blew up a taxi in front and another not far from that spot in a parking lot. The third one went unnoticed until the helicopter spotted it. Police are moving in. They say officials don't know why that part of the wall was blown. There is nothing there, just some old tunnels, long considered empty and unstable."

"Now what?"

"Wait. They are saying police scuba teams will investigate in the morning with officials from the castle. No suspects and no one was hurt."

"It has to be that fucking Boris." Chastain smashed his glass on the table.

Hubert said. "Of course, it's Boris. He's the only one who knew, but how did he pull it off? Koi, can yakuza pull a job like this? Drugs and porn but this? This is a professional-level heist."

"Yakuza has their fingers in everything, even the government," she said. "They could have members in the military they teamed up with thieves. Yes. Possible."

Chastain said it didn't matter. "What's done is done."

A collective disappointment and worry spread across the room.

Picard said, "If he is such a shithead rat he may have

told them about us. It's going to be hard to get off this island and disappear. He may have given us up to Interpol."

Bouchet offered another perspective. "Not so fast. In order for him to involve Interpol he would have to risk this operation at the castle. We may have time but we'll have to move quickly. Our last-resort contingency plans to go our separate ways will have to be put in place. Unless."

"Unless, what?"

"Boris either sold the gold to yakuza and walked away or he's sitting on it, waiting to make a transfer."

Chastain said, "They didn't walk away with hundreds of kilos of gold on their backs either."

"Precisely, boss. Potente, use your hacking skills and see if you can tap into anything transmitting out of the castle, like emails or alert notices to authorities. Koi will translate. Let's see what they say. Koi, keep watching the news and update us if necessary."

"We have to find him before he leaves the country," said Chastain. "I want his ass."

Hubert said, "If he did this job with yakuza, they probably paid him in cash or wired the money to his account in Thailand. He's going home."

"Or back home, back to the UK." Bouchet offered the alternative but said he hoped it wasn't true. "He loves those Thai women."

Chastain didn't want to consider hunting him around the world. "Gold, cash, Thailand or fucking England, I don't care. I want him before he leaves the country. He's not going to screw us like this and get away with it. He'll know where the gold is. We'll get our share."

Hubert looked at Bouchet. Both men sensed the boss's temper was overriding his usual sense of reason. He'd flown into rages before, but in the heat of battle. This time he was different, dangerously different.

Potente sounded off from behind his laptop. "Bouchet, I may have something. Looks like a bunch of short emails going in and out of the castle. Koi, come read these."

Koi kept an ear tuned to the satellite television and knelt beside Potente, looking over his find. "The emails are to the director. He is on the bullet train coming in from Tokyo."

"Why don't they just call him?"

"Probably official protocol to document it," said Bouchet.

"Also, he wants his phone open," said Koi. "He been speaking with the governor of the prefecture. Wants to leave line open."

"Fine, fine," said Chastain. "What do the emails say?"

"Hang on, I'm reading. First couple just tell him something happened, some kind of attack or explosions. 'Better return, quickly,' it says. This one says a hole was blown in a western wall but they can't find any records of anything on the other side to steal. Suggesting a random attack."

"Random."

"Wait, one more says surveillance cameras picked up a truck idling in woods near southwest border. Short-handed tonight. No men to send. Called local police then taxi blew up. Truck gone."

"That's probably it," said Potente.

"Did they get a license plate?"

"They have an image but it's dark. Hard to see. Says they will give to police to be enhanced."

"Shit. Doesn't help us now."

Koi pricked her ears toward the television. "Listen. This is big news. Reports coming in from all over the prefecture. Say a truck was stolen from a rental yard that evening. What you think, Bärchen, you can hack the rental facility and get license?"

Chastain said, "We don't need a license, we need to know what it looks like and where it's going. This will all take too long. We don't have the time or the resources to do slow detective work."

The team sat in mostly silent anger, trying to put aside the emotions and think like soldiers. Koi watched the television and filled them in on details that offered no clues.

"Call him."

"Call who, boss?"

"Fucking Boris. See if he still has our phone. Call him. If he answers, I'll talk to him. Maybe he's still in a negotiating mood after dealing with his new Japanese friends."

"There's no way he—"

Chastain's phone rang in his pocket. "Shit. It's fucking Boris." He pressed the button with his thumb like he was squeezing Boris's temple. "You fat, slimy cocksucker, where are you and where is my gold?"

A female coughed then spoke English with a Japanese accent as though she were reading from a missal. "We have your friend and the product you desire. Come to

Kobe Port at 05:30. Pier eleven, Onomichi storehouse, second floor. Bring the woman. No police or no deal." She hung up.

Chastain called the number back but it went to a default voicemail. "This doesn't feel right."

"What did he say, boss?"

"It wasn't him. A woman gave me an address to meet them, whoever they are, at 05:30 and we get Boris and 'the product' she said, 'the product you desire,' which can only be gold. There is nothing else here for us."

Hubert said, "Except a confrontation with whoever wants us out of the picture."

"Or Interpol," said Bouchet. "Boris knows why we're here. He could be baiting us."

"It's too dangerous for all of us to go and I'm certainly not bringing Koi. I got us into this. I'll go alone and take the chance for all of us."

The crew balked. Koi said she should go because she knew the streets.

Chastain waved them off. "It's done. I will take one with me." He looked at Hubert.

"Of course, boss. I'm with you. It's 04:40. We'd better get ready."

"Bouchet, if you don't hear from me by 05:45, assume the worst and get everyone out. Pay them and wish them bon voyage. Bring Koi to my home alone." He grabbed Koi by the shoulder. "If I live through this, I'll get word to you."

"Sure, whatever, Chastain, but—"

"But what? It's safe there and Bouchet will—"

She punched his chest. "Ahh, kuso! I want Potente

with me, okay? I have nothing. I have no one. I have no master plan like you guys. What about me?"

"It's okay, Koi. I'll find you," said Potente.

"No it's not okay and you won't find her," said Chastain. "If you try you'll both get killed or captured. No. You go with her. Look after her, please."

"*Hai*, finally." Koi spun and walked away.

"No more bullshit talk. Everyone be ready for a quick getaway. Fournier, is there enough fuel to get to Taipei?"

"*Oui.*"

"*Très bon*. They'll have Vietnam and Philippines covered. Taipei buys us time. Hubert and I will leave in fifteen minutes. Potente, get me an aerial view of that port and the Onomichi building."

"Yes, boss."

"Don't bother, Potente," said Fournier. "I have it already. Pilots need to multitask."

"Everyone, *en garde*, high gear. Let's go."

Chapter Thirty-Nine

CHASTAIN AND HUBERT came in from the rear of the Onomichi building and saw no vehicles close by. Hubert searched the rooftops with night vision and saw no movement. They ascended the metal stairs offset from one another with Chastain in the lead. Chastain carried a 9mm in his hand and another in his waist. Hubert carried a French Saint-Étienne combat rifle, 5.56 caliber. They heard a low voice, perhaps someone giving orders or speaking into a phone. They reached the top. The door to the second floor had been propped open with a mop. Their hearts pounded as they scanned the room.

"*Prenez-garde*," Chastain said with a look.

In the meager morning light, they could make out the silhouette of a man, leaning back against a box. Chastain signaled to Hubert to stay alert and to move in from the right. Chastain cocked his weapon.

Hubert lit up the man with the light on the rifle rail. "Are you alone?"

"Quite." Boris sat on a wooden crate, smiling as though he'd scored the winning try in the Rugby World Cup. He took a pull of beer and spotted the pair of guns trained on him. "Monsieur Chastain. What took you so long? I almost flew back to London with all this beautiful gold."

Chastain and Hubert put down their guns and looked back and forth at the crates stacked behind Boris. Chastain pointed at Boris. "What is going on here, asshole? And if I even suspect you're lying, you'll die before you finish the sentence."

Hubert looked over the crates and said, "Boss, I think this is it. It's all here, eh, Boris?"

"Indeed, it is, but first, you boys look thirsty. That smaller crate there has plenty of iced-down Japanese beer. I've developed a fondness for it, I must say. Help yourselves."

"You double-crossed yakuza?" Chastain asked. "How did you pull this off?"

"Wait," Hubert said. "Why did you have the woman call us? Why not just call us yourself?"

"I assumed you'd think it a ruse and come in shooting. I had to leave open the possibility I'd been kidnapped. It ensured your caution."

"You might be right about that. I had several ways I thought of killing you. Now, what happened?"

"Have a beer, mate, this will take a moment. Yes, I double-crossed yakuza, wasn't that difficult. That much gold makes men go blind to reason. But more importantly, I double-crossed my former colleagues at MI6, a good half-dozen of whom are desperately trying to explain themselves to the Chief of the Intelligence Service from the confines of the Osaka Detention House, something about a run-in with the chief of the Osaka Prefecture Police, along with a SWAT unit and a very pissed off detective sergeant from Interpol who flew a team to Japan based only on a story from an imaginary South African informant." He pointed his beer toward Chastain. "The Interpol sergeant is one of your compatriots, I'm afraid. Ugly diplomatic mess."

"Boris, you're drunk and rambling. What the hell are you talking about? What do you mean, former colleague, and how is MI6 involved?"

"Pass me another beer, would you, Hubert? Obliged. Turns out I'm not everything you once thought I was. My education and gift for languages kept me employed in the service of the Crown. I'm a former operative for MI6, and I had a grudge to settle."

Hubert said, "Wait, you mentioned MI6 before you left for Osaka."

"Yes. I had been thinking for several days that this sortie that you all so serendipitously dropped in my lap would be my opportunity to exact revenge on a few old mates who did me wrong. I seized on the chance to work MI6 and yakuza against one another and come out on the other end with the gold. It's kind of what I was trained to do."

"I'm not convinced," Chastain said. "Keep talking."

"This is just getting good." Hubert loved a good story.

"Thirteen years ago, I was involved in an operation in the Balkans. After a few minor scrapes with local intelligence operatives, every last one of them as corrupt as a Russian mobster, some information was leaked to the media, identifying some of our personnel. One chap was nearly killed before being shuttled back to London and millions of pounds that had been spent on an extensive operation were wasted with no forward progress. I was blamed for the leaks."

"Why you?"

"I entered the service through unconventional means,

which had the knickers of some of the old guard in a twist since my first day. In addition I had been, let's say, keeping the company of a young lady from Belgrade, who happened to be a reporter. They had undercover surveillance of our rendezvous but I assure you the only thing that passed between us was bodily fluids."

"Like sweat."

"Good show, Hubert. They kicked me out and made it difficult for me to get a good job in any of the larger cities. Eventually I gave up and traveled a bit on my inheritance, finally settling in Thailand." Boris grew sullen. "I'm a patriot, always have been. That really hurt me. I've been waiting a long time for this."

Chastain asked how he involved yakuza.

"Allow me to take you back some seventy-two hours to an evening I spent in the *mizu shōbai,* which means, water trade, that's where yakuza operates nearly all the hostess bars, boob bars and brothels in Tokyo's *Kubikichō* district. I used the last of my favors with a few sympathetic friends who helped me locate just the right two or three operations where I might get the attention I required. Working with you chaps had warmed me up but operating alone in the underworld, I really felt back in the game and must say, I was elated."

Boris told them the story of shopping for a yakuza boss in the hostess bars and their subsequent meetings to negotiate a deal for the gold. He left out no details.

"You called us greasy?" Hubert walked toward Boris with his fist cocked.

Boris hoped Hubert was joking. "Well, I had to seem authentic. Nothing like drinking scotch and cursing the

French while discussing a gold heist, eh? It had its intended bonding effect."

Chastain asked what he was doing when he and Koi saw him getting into the car.

"They were taking me to where they put me up in a safe-house of sorts, back in Osaka, away from whomever might have seen us meet in Tokyo after meeting with this Nogi fellow, quite an unpleasant demeanor on that one. They placed a woman at the safe-house who cooked and served me food and she was quite an engaging conversationalist, probably a hostess from one of their clubs. Sex was off limits but I could bathe with her if I chose. I never found the time. They had guards outside, and we had delicate telephone negotiations to complete. I only drank before bed."

"How did you pull it all together?" asked Chastain.

"I used what had already worked. I took the bullet train to Tokyo so anyone who had seen me at the castle in Osaka would not also see me meeting with yakuza. There are complicated intramural rivalries there but I managed to speak with the right people. I had the Chisato woman contact Interpol and say she had information from street informers about yakuza making a deal for gold with Le Sauvage. She told a Detective Sergeant Marceau that the criminal gangs planned to steal a great treasure of gold artifacts from the National Museum of Art in Osaka. Interpol took the bait. I told yakuza the gold was moved into a secret walled-off storeroom in a sub-basement directly under the exhibit that housed the map. I said it was kind of a joke by those who were responsible that it was almost in plain sight for all these years. I think the irony was lost on them."

"What about MI6? How did you explain what you'd been up to?" Hubert was so caught up in the story he almost forgot about the crew at the plane.

Chastain didn't. He called to explain, so they could breathe.

Boris continued. "I pled my case to the spies at MI6 and convinced them I was homesick and riddled with cancer. I wanted nothing more than to clear my name and die at peace in England and I'd be willing to risk my life to do it. I told them everything about working with you—the gold, the tattoos, secret messages in the poems. I told them everything except who you actually were and the real location of the gold."

"So you told them the same story you told Interpol?"

"Yes. I told yakuza they had to move that night because you chaps were planning on taking it the following night and of course, they were too greedy and eager to wait. They all converged on the museum in a cluster-fuck of cops, spies, gangsters and panic-stricken security guards. I hired a young lady to record the whole thing from across the street. It's quite hilarious."

Chastain said, "You'll be on the run your whole life. There will be a price on your head. How can you enjoy the money?"

"It's been the best time I've had in many years and for what it's worth, I plan on faking my death. I've got the resources, skills, passports and language skills to disappear. I'll be fine. I'd argue we're all in the soup at this point. Best to keep moving."

"What about all this gold?"

"I've got my two most loyal former Brit commandos ready to help me transport the crates to Kobe Port, where we'll load them onto what's called an offshore support vessel. They're watching us now through their rifle scopes."

"Figures. An OSV, uh? I'm aware of what it is."

Hubert said, "Well I am not."

"It's a specialized ship that provides repair and restocking to offshore oil rigs, an OSV in the trade," said Boris.

"You plan on staying on a rig?" asked Chastain. "It's hard to be inconspicuous on one of those."

"Haha, good question, *Monsieur*. I have an offshore helicopter set to pick us up with the crates and bring us right back to Osaka Airport, where we'll load the gold and the forged manifests on a cargo plane headed to Switzerland. My men will stay on the oil rig for twelve hours until other seaborne transportation arrives to extract them. They'll be paid handsomely for their efforts."

"And us?" Huber asked.

Chastain cut him off. "They'll be monitoring all air traffic. We need to get the crew and Koi together and make it across town from the airport to the seaport without getting picked off by yakuza or Interpol." He looked at Boris. "I assume MI6 won't be playing in this one."

"Fair assumption, that." Boris finished his beer. "Your team will join me on the helicopter back to Osaka. If the locals have any inkling we've left the country, no one will suspect we'd fly right back in. We'll take a private jet I've secured to Switzerland, where I'll meet the plane in Zurich and contact you when our fortunes are safely in the bank's vault. After that we'll have to convene to make individual plans to distribute the money, settle accounts and scatter."

Boris looked back and forth at the Frenchmen, who stared at one another. "I should mention I've already been in touch with a group of investors who will take the gold off our hands for eighty-five million US."

Chastain pursed his lips.

Hubert shrugged and said, "Let's do it."

Chapter Forty

ON THE WAY BACK to the plane, Chastain called Bouchet to let him know what had happened.

Bouchet laughed harder than Chastain had heard him in many years. "Bravo, *Monsieur* Sweaty Boris, bravo. He had every one of us fooled."

"Yes, he did. We haven't much time. Have everyone ready to move as soon as we get back. Do we have a motorcycle? I want to send Potente ahead to scout."

"We'll get one."

"Of course, you will. *Au revoir.*"

Chastain trusted Boris and his aging commandos to move the gold to the OSV. The flat, open deck allowed for easy loading of the type of crates they had. Chastain discussed the rapid exit from Japan with Hubert. "No one in Japan will be expecting Boris to be moving the gold this way and no one will be looking for his English commandos dressed as roughneck Norwegian deck hands."

"Yes, a brilliant but simple plan, uh? While the cops and spies are distracted and pointing fingers at each other over who is to blame, Boris leaves the country with the gold. We then, can move to the offshore vessel and leave the city, then circle back and leave the country. It could work but we need a place to land. Perhaps Taipei as we discussed before."

"I have to give him credit. He's a clever man. He seems

to have thought of every contingency."

"Except getting us to the boat."

"*Oui*. The way this plays out, we're the ones they are looking for. The police at a minimum will be searching and yakuza, no doubt, wants to serve Boris with a painful and permanent message. Maybe they'll cut him up for sushi."

"I'll never eat that stuff again," said Hubert.

"Fish should be cooked in butter anyway, eh?"

The men laughed, but not for long.

"This is the last move, then we will never return to Japan. Every police agency and spy in the country will be looking for western faces traveling with a Japanese woman. It's not going to be easy for us. A blind cop could find us."

"Yes but he can't shoot us. We have that at least. Boss, I've never seen you have doubts before. Don't let them win now. You finally have something to live for besides the next job. We will get through this. We have survived worse. When it's all over, I'll buy the champagne."

"Bollinger?"

"Is there another brand?"

***

In a fog as thick as chimney smoke, a crew of four rowed quietly to the starboard side of a fishing boat loaded with rock cod and horse mackerel, boarded it and slit the throat of the first mate and another hand. They held the captain at gunpoint and ordered him to move closer to Kobe port, towing the rubber assault boat.

They held their position one hundred meters offshore and awaited the signal.

***

Chastain and his crew cleared the plane of all weapons and identifying accoutrement. Fournier deleted what he could from the computer memories of the craft. He then added false coordinates for a future flight. Everyone wore latex gloves and wiped down every centimeter of the interior and ran gun oil along the exterior rails. From a distance, it would look as though they were merely cleaning but no prints could be lifted through the oil.

They packed everything in two vehicles and had Potente follow on an 850cc FZ street bike, perfect for maneuvering through traffic.

Koi walked over to him as he checked the bike. "Where did they find this?"

"I don't know. Picard is like a ghost. He moves in without being seen. It's from a nearby hangar, I guess."

"Bet I'm a better rider than you. They should have me on this thing."

"You probably are a good rider but—number one I used to compete and number two, your father wants you where he can keep an eye on you."

"Between Picard and The Beard?"

"Or Fournier and The Beard."

"He's ugly. I'd rather eat dog food than be close to that man."

"You'll never have to make that choice. Anyway, I guess Chastain figures if they take out his vehicle, you'll get away."

"Smart man, thinks of almost everything."

"Yes, he is. And I think he cares about you."

"Don't start with that right now, okay, Helmut?" She tapped his motorcycle helmet.

He shook his head. "Jokes, always jokes. One day you will be funny." He smiled at her.

She said, "Just stay close and don't do anything to show off for those Kobe women. They only want your money."

"I don't have any money."

"You will. What are your orders?"

"To jump ahead and scope out the route. If it's clear I will pass you in the vehicles and take up a rear guard. Then leapfrog. Simple."

"Simple and very dangerous." She looked at the rest of the crew then at the ground. "Bärchen, be careful, okay?"

"Sure, yeah, okay." He strapped his helmet.

She walked to the cars.

He called after her. "You too."

"What?"

"Careful. You too. Ahh, just go."

Chapter Forty-One

POTENTE TOOK SOME last-second instructions from Hubert and sped off toward the far side of the bay. The route was roughly thirty-two kilometers from the airport to the Kobe port where Boris's commandos loaded the gold onto the OSV. Potente could make it in forty minutes before signaling a clear route. He planned to get fuel then meet the crew en route for an extra gun in the fight, should one come their way. Chastain's team left fifteen minutes after he pulled off, driving nondescript rental vehicles.

Potente felt a sense of pride at being chosen to scout ahead but his fear at screwing up and getting Koi hurt overshadowed it. He crossed the Yodo River in some traffic. *The bridge will be a capture or kill zone if we get caught here. Have to move through quickly.*

Potente's senses buzzed with surging adrenalin. Everything around him seemed brighter, more detailed, moving slowly as he navigated the movements of vehicles and people around him, looking for an anomaly, someone watching, someone with a military bearing or a cop's face. All clear so far. His .40 caliber Sig Sauer dug into his hip, but he didn't dare touch it—a tell for an experienced detective looking for an armed man.

Twenty minutes later, as he passed the first sign for the Kobe Port. His heart rallied. A siren came up from behind him. He looked for an escape route, cars everywhere.

Countdown to Osaka

It was an ambulance. It veered north at the fork away from the port.

Potente breathed again. He stopped short of the access road and pulled off and pretended to check a loose cable on his bike. He could see the OSV docked where Boris had said it would be. He couldn't quite make out the ship's name in the heavy fog and dim morning light but there was only one OSV in port and he could make out the distinct orange and black colors. He called Hubert and headed back to meet the team, who by then were just eighteen kilometers out.

The sun hadn't burned off the morning fog. From the Kiisudo Strait, storm clouds rolled southeast of the port and blocked in the mist. Boris's men loaded the crates onto the OSV in silence. Boris slipped an envelope to the ship's captain. Boris's small team had big resumes, having served with the SAS in both Bosnia and Sierra Leone. Danger, cold morning air and rough-sea extractions were just breakfast for these two.

"And now we wait," said Boris.

***

As Potente pulled out of range of the port, the hijacked fishing boat landed with the captain tied and gagged in the pilot house. The four gunmen climbed into a white van that slipped into an alley next to a warehouse. The man in the passenger's seat slid open the side door and they all jumped out, as one ran to a vehicle that had been placed there earlier. Another man, carrying a black case, sprinted to the side of the next building and climbed the fire escape.

A security guard, half-asleep in the adjoining building, noticed the activity of the pale gaijin and called his boss, who told him to stay put. The boss called his contact in the clan.

06:25

Hubert drove Chastain in the lead vehicle. Picard drove The Beard, Fournier and Koi in the second. Potente had taken a long loop back to check for signs they were being followed. It all seemed clear.

Picard said he didn't like it. "Too dark. We can't see anyone around us."

"They can't see us either," said The Beard. "Just stay alert."

Koi asked where Bouchet was. "I haven't seen him since last night."

"He is working on an alternate plan. Insurance. He's either close by or across the globe. You never know with him."

"Shh," said Picard. "I can't concentrate."

Chastain gave orders. "Stay back some. You're too close. Make space between us."

Picard slowed down and cut the headlights. He left fifty meters between him and the boss. The morning sun had begun to give shape to the night shadows.

"One hundred fifty meters, on the left. That's our gangway. Let us start over then bring up the rear. Keep Koi between you."

"Shit. I'm fine." She spoke toward Picard's phone. "I can handle it."

06:28

Oleks discovered what it meant to be expendable. He'd

been tasked with leading the assault from the drop vehicle, cutting between the team and ramming Hubert's car from behind, shooting out the window with his left hand.

"Fuck, we're made!" The Beard leaned out the window and put a three-round burst through the rear windshield, killing Oleks.

"The alley," yelled Hubert.

"No, it's a trap," said Chastain. He keyed the mic on his hand-held radio. "It's a rip. Pull over to the right and split up. There will be more, we have to see where the rest are."

Chastain read the scene right. Artem and Zelay had to expose themselves to attack their vehicles. Chastain's crew pinned them down behind large rolls of steel cable.

Potente rode into the mix on the chaser bike, pulling his handgun, looking for Koi. Tunnel vision.

The sniper's first shot hit Potente in the knee, knocking him into Koi's car but he stayed upright. He looked about for the shooter.

Koi yelled his name when she saw him get hit. She scrambled out the door and took cover behind the car.

"Third floor, over there, sniper, nine o'clock," someone shouted. Potente yanked the throttle and spun the bike toward the building, dragging his mangled leg behind. The sniper fired at him but Potente zigzagged into the shooter's blind spot and slid his bike into a dumpster. He hopped off the bike on his good leg and checked his wound. The knee had taken every grain from the .30 caliber rifle slug. It pulverized his kneecap. His lower leg hung by some tissue and a few strips of tendon. His body pumped just enough adrenalin to overcome the blinding pain. After taking off his shirt and tying a tourniquet above his knee, he hoisted himself onto the dumpster and to the rungs of the fire escape ladder.

The sniper pinned Chastain down behind his car. Koi ran from her position toward her father, crossing through an open space at full speed.

Chastain saw her running. "No, stay put!"

A shot echoed off the walls of the port industrial complex. The bullet struck Koi in the forehead at a thirty-degree angle, just above her temple. Her feet kicked out from under her and she went airborne, landing on her hips. She lay supine in the runoff from the factory. Her tanto skidded across the wet pavement.

Chastain ran to her. His belly lurched. His eyes watered. He grew cold and weak in his limbs. He screamed, "Emi, no," and fell to his knees beside her. She lay still. Blood from the entry wound running back into her hair. One arm wedged under her hip. One leg turned outward.

His hands shook like leaves in a hurricane. He tilted her head to the side and tried to staunch the blood flow with a chunk of skull, afraid to touch the gray matter and not hearing the next shot, another round that skipped off the concrete near his legs. The last shot the sniper would fire. Chastain pressed his palm against the wound.

Potente had managed to climb the fire escape with one leg, leaned around the corner of the building while hanging on to the fire escape and with his off hand, shot the sniper in the heart. He fell forward on his weapon.

Down in the alley, bullets zinged back and forth from one team to the other.

Potente started to climb back down but saw the scene below and stopped. He dropped on his strong-side haunches and looked down at Koi and her father. The sobbing man told him what he needed to know. *She is gone.* Potente checked his mangled leg. He would have to lose it. Police sirens grew louder. He imagined a world in prison on one leg, without Emiko, without hope. His face contorted with pain and sadness, he put the muzzle of his .40 caliber in his ear. Police vehicles screeched into the scene below. His body slumped forward and slowly, as if caught in a glitch of the space-time continuum, rolled down the stairs to the next landing. His pistol bounced like a pinball against the steel to the pavement.

The yakuza boss had notified his contacts in the police who called Interpol. Everyone was coming. The gunfight continued. Picard managed to hit a running Odessa gangster with a glancing wound; he stumbled but kept firing.

At the OSV, Boris knew Chastain has been ambushed, but by whom he could only speculate. His commandos wanted in the fight, but they didn't know who the enemy was. They readied their weapons beneath their coats. "Steady, boys," Boris said. "The crew might pull through. If they head this way, I'll give you the go ahead to lay cover fire. I can't send you into that blind. Sorry."

With the firefight thumping around him, Chastain held Koi's head—his Emi, the daughter he never knew well enough to say he loved her. A few reeds of sun had found them. He looked her up and down as if one part of her might still be moving. He pulled her arm from under her hip.

He'd never felt that kind of pain before, a ripping, a tearing away of the ideals of mankind, the innate understanding of a need for blood relations, the love it requires to flourish, and the inchoate sentiment of yearning.

What sentimentality he may have ever harbored had been stomped with a dirty shoe by death incarnate, now standing over him like a drunken clown without his makeup, in the season of the failed rapture. Oblivious to the scene around him. Death stood over him. Death as critic—his tie loose, his suit wrinkled from sleeping in the alley behind a downtown bar, the suit he'd bought for a wedding that never happened, when his young bride left him for a braver man, in another traveling show. Sweaty Death. Booze-sweat Death. The cynical, foul-breathed, mocking bastard with a sagging stomach, cigarette ashes on his lapel and shit stains on his under-drawers.

Death pulled out his notepad, flipped it to a dog-eared page and ran a stubby finger across Emiko's name at the end of the list, then scratched his nuts with his pen. "Why do you weep, little boy?" Death asked. "Do you miss her already? Do you miss her mommy?"

Chastain straightened her clothes. He took off his jacket and covered her head, leaving her face exposed.

"That won't change a thing, Tiago. May I call you, Tiago? I feel so close to you now. Covering up her wounds won't make her fate less likely. It won't make her yours again. She is mine now, almost. You only own memories of things that never happened. Remembrance of future vision, if I might—how Proustian.

"Her leaving won't remove any burdens, just like leaving her mother didn't make your heartache go away. It only made you bitter, oh, and by the way, thanks for all the customers you sent me over the years. I suppose I owe you a favor, angry man." He laughed at his sarcasm. "I don't do favors. Hey, maybe you should check again. Is she dead?"

"Go fuck yourself."

"Clever. That the best you got? Huh? Le Sauvage, the fear-inspiring gun runner on his knees beside his daughter, staring at a consequence he could have prevented. She wouldn't be in this shit-storm if you had been a father instead of a coward. Not feeling so savage now, are you?"

Chastain looked up from Emiko into the milky eyes of a specter. Tears worked down his unshaven face, gray stubble. "Why are you torturing me?"

Death snorted and a bit of spittle lay on his bulbous lips. "I don't torture anyone, Frenchy. They do it to themselves. They create delusions in their heads of how life is supposed to be but they forget about me. *Ignis fatuus.* They ignore me. It pisses me off some but, then again, I always get my revenge. It feels good, I have to say, but it is fleeting nonetheless, never quite satisfying. I suppose that's why I keep at it."

"Fuck you. She didn't deserve this."

"That's rich coming from you, de Gaulle. How many people have you killed, or abandoned? Who deserved what you delivered?"

"I can't answer that. But I'll tell you this—"

"Oh, no, no, no. No, no, no." Death wagged a finger. "No, no. I will tell you and you will listen because right now, in this brief time we have together, I am in control. So, hear this, my confused weepy fellow. Everything you have ever done since you left home at seventeen has been for Tiago, the selfish prick.

"You joined the merchant seamen because your father tried to control you. It wasn't his hitting you that bothered you, no—it was that he did it to run your life. No one tells Tiago what to do. So you left. You wanted to be your own man—very admirable. Every morning your mother would look out at the new day and wonder if this would be the day you decided never to return. You came home only because you sailed away from Osaka.

"You pretended you left Aiko to honor her, or what was that dopey nickname you had for her, Mikie? Yeah, Mikie, hah. You only left her to save your own ass."

"She chased me away."

"And you never returned. Too busy running around the world playing with guns to ever call her and ask if her father had changed his ways or if you could return. You never tried because you were afraid. Tough-guy Tiago was afraid to hear she had been getting boned by another man. You couldn't handle that.

"You became a gangster and a fairly good one, they say, in my circles. You must have been proud of your protean organization, moving in and out of cultures and classes, shifting your personas to meet the demands of the clients or some unique peril presented by your counterparts. It was all so 007 for a while, wasn't it?

Finally, you aged. You grew tired of being you. You answered Mikie's letter and tried to right twenty-nine years of being a shit, a French turdy-merde remnant of a man. But oops, who is this? A daughter in my life. Now what? Oh, I know, I'll make everything right again through her. I'll be a good daddy and get her piles of gold and we'll move to Quebec and it will be wonderful. But you forgot about me.

"You forgot about who brings me, forgot about war, and the god-fearing men who perpetrate it. The very criminals you've been arming for thirty years are a relentless breed, always chasing war or running into it, giddy over fate. Did you think they would leave you alone? Did you think the world you helped to create would let you escape it? They don't know how to do anything else and they certainly don't give a rank shit about your little daddy plans."

Death lit a Pall Mall, offering one to Chastain. "The taste of death stings going down, doesn't it, boy?"

Chastain waved him away.

"Say goodbye, Frenchy, it looks as if she's coming with me. Oh and, see you real soon." Death faded.

The sirens grew closer. Three police units converged on father and daughter. The officers exited their vehicles and drew down on Chastain, ordering him to drop his weapon. Chastain turned toward the officers, the blue lights reflecting off his tears. He tried to raise the muzzle of his pistol at them, anticipating a fusillade of bullets, but officers pounced on him and cuffed him as they dragged him away from Koi.

Sitting back in his car, Hubert lit a cigarette and surveyed the scene. No Bouchet in sight. Three comrades dead or dying. The Beard and Picard getting arrested along with the only living member of the Odessa hit squad. Local police swarming like velociraptors and two Interpol unmarked units screeching up, doors flung open.

Cops everywhere pointing guns at them all and screaming over one another for the bad guys to raise their hands. In his peripheral Hubert noticed another vehicle, a polished black Mercedes with a fat gangster standing by the passenger side and his driver hanging over the driver's door, both watching the action.

Hubert measured the odds. He drew on his cigarette, set the last of his incendiary devices and threw it on the floor, rammed the car into gear and ripped headlong at the yakuza boss, screaming every Mediterranean curse word ever conjured. The boss tried to run but fell. The driver emptied his weapon at Hubert's car as it exploded in flames, taking the Mercedes and its occupants with it.

The storm clouds won the morning and began to pelt the port, the blood, the spent shells and players in the final act.

Fifty meters from the scene, in the shadow of a doorway, a thickset Ukranian sneered at the situation, feeling less satisfied than he thought he might at the carnage. He sensed the gun pointing at him. He turned to see that Bouchet had the drop on him. "Ahh, the money man. Come to give me my last accounting for your boss? I should say, former boss, from the looks of it."

Bouchet stared at him. "How did you know when to strike?"

"I'd like to brag but it was mostly luck. I had been shadowing Chastain. When I saw him clearing the plane I knew he would be taking another route out of the country. Had to be by sea. It's what he is."

"Why, Mayko? Tell me why."

"That little bitch killed my friends. She killed members of our crew and he did nothing. He showed weakness. Then he cut me out of the loop? Fuck him. After all I did for him."

"You acted in your own self-interest. You always did. She was his daughter, for God's sake."

"God? His daughter? Don't make me laugh. When did she ever mean anythi—"

Bouchet shot him twice before he finished his sentence. Mayko fell like a bag of meat. "She meant everything to him, asshole."

Bouchet tossed the pistol onto Mayko's body. He looked back toward Chastain one last time, pulled his hat over his eyes, turned his collar to the silver rain and walked off into the fog.

***

Boris looked back to the blur of emergency lights at the port as the last hatch drew closed on the ship. Deck hands worked the pulleys to draw in the lines as a tug pushed the ship from the dock. The captain blew the horn. The commandos sat down, backs against the crates, and closed their eyes. Boris raised his paper coffee cup to the scene. "Farewell, my friend. It was a helluva ride."

The End

About the Author

Joe Hefferon was born and raised in Newark, New Jersey, which is also where he worked for 25 years in law enforcement. He ended that epoch as a captain but still works with and trains cops in his home state.

Hefferon has published dozens of articles profiling successful women for About.com and equity research for Seeking Alpha.

Other books by Joe Hefferon include *The Last Meridian.*

He's is a fan of the classic crime writers, as well as, Dennis Lehane, James Lee Burke and Elmore Leonard, but his favorite author is Cormac McCarthy.

NewPulpPress.com